Praise for *Adam and Eve and Pinch M...*

'This is Ruth Rendell at her brilli... ...t
distinguishes *Adam and Eve and P...* ...ost
crime novels is its texture, th... ...ail with
which the characters are ... ...onderful to
see such a fine writer ... ...ding her range'
Simon Brett, *Daily M...*

'Here are the fears that haunt us, the nightmarish
urban myths of our time ... Rendell's books are
driven by character and location, but they retain the
powerful narrative and complex plotting developed
in the Wexford series ... I would say that Rendell
and Vine are now fused into a single writer, pos-
sessed of one of the most remarkable talents writing
today. Ruth Rendell is a Peer of the Realm, and she
deserves to be: she's a national treasure'
Jane Jakeman, *Independent*

'No-one recreates the minutiae of life better than
Ruth Rendell' T.J. Binyon, *Evening Standard*

'Rendell is a writing phenomenon. In the 35 years
since *Doon with Death*, her debut novel featuring
Chief Inspector Wexford, she has produced a body of
work unequalled by any other mystery writer for its
depth, scope and influence ... The way Rendell
draws the separate stories together is an abject lesson
in mystery plotting ... Utterly absorbing'
Peter Gutteridge, *Observer*

'Wonderfully readable, gripping ... The story moves
rapidly, with adroit cross-cutting. Rendell's eye for
the telling detail and her awareness of the revealing
social nuance are as keen as ever. It is all very
enjoyable' Allan Massie, *Scotsman*

'Rendell is nothing if not a page-turner' *Guardian*

'The apparently effortless writing, the recognisable but never stereotyped characters, and, above all, the portrayal of Minty's gradual mental decline are classic Rendell ... Rendell's psychological novels remain in a class of their own' Susanna Yager, *Sunday Telegraph*

'A tour de force of a crime novel' Mike Ripley, *Birmingham Evening Post*

'Her characters inhabit a surreal world of their own, appearing to lead normal lives in everyday circumstances, but seething with psychotic thoughts just below their calm exteriors ... No character in *Adam and Eve and Pinch Me* is undamaged. It is a fascinatingly scary universe that Rendell creates, riveting and disturbing' Marcel Berlins, *The Times*

'Ruth Rendell never tires of creating ingenious new situations to unsettle her readers ... An eerie tale; and a true page-turner' *Red*

Adam and Eve and Pinch Me

Since her first novel, *From Doon With Death*, published in 1964, Ruth Rendell has won many awards, including the Crime Writers' Association Gold Dagger for 1976's best crime novel with *A Demon in My View*, and the Arts Council National Book Award, genre fiction, for *Lake of Darkness* in 1980.

In 1985 Ruth Rendell received the Silver Dagger for *The Tree of Hands*, and in 1987, writing as Barbara Vine, won her third Edgar from the Mystery Writers of America for *A Dark-Adapted Eye*.

She won the Gold Dagger for *Live Flesh* in 1986, for *King Solomon's Carpet* in 1991 and, as Barbara Vine, a Gold Dagger in 1987 for *A Fatal Inversion*.

Ruth Rendell won the *Sunday Times* Literary Award in 1990, and in 1991 she was awarded the Crime Writers' Association Cartier Diamond Dagger for outstanding contribution to the genre. In 1996 she was awarded the CBE, and in 1997 was made a Life Peer.

Her books have been translated into twenty-five languages and are also published to great acclaim in the United States.

Ruth Rendell has a son and two grandsons, and lives in London.

RUTH RENDELL

ADAM AND EVE
AND PINCH ME

ARROW

Published by Arrow Books in 2002

1 3 5 7 9 10 8 6 4 2

Copyright © Kingsmarkham Enterprises Ltd 2001

First published in the United Kingdom in 2001 by Hutchinson

Arrow Books
The Random House Group Limited
20 Vauxhall Bridge Road, London SW1V 2SA

Random House Australia (Pty) Ltd
20 Alfred Street, Milsons Point,
Sydney, New South Wales 2061, Australia

Random House New Zealand Ltd
18 Poland Road, Glenfield, Auckland 10,
New Zealand

Random House (Pty) Ltd
Endulini, 5a Jubilee Road, Parktown 2193, South Africa

The Random House Group Limited Reg. No. 954009

www.randomhouse.co.uk

A CIP catalogue record for this book
is available from the British Library

Papers used by Random House are natural,
recyclable products made from wood grown in sustainable forests.
The manufacturing processes conform to the environmental
regulations of the country of origin.

Typeset by Deltatype Ltd, Birkenhead, Merseyside
Printed and bound in Germany by
Elsnerdruck, Berlin

ISBN 0 09 942619 6

Chapter 1

Minty knew it was a ghost sitting in the chair because she was frightened. If it were only something she'd imagined, she wouldn't have been afraid. You couldn't be when it was something that came out of your own mind.

It was early evening but, being wintertime, quite dark. She'd just come home from work, let herself in the front door and put the hall light on. The front-room door was open and the ghost was sitting on an upright chair in the middle of the room with its back to her. She'd put the chair there to stand on and change a light bulb before she went out in the morning and forgotten to put it back. Her mouth tightly covered up with both hands to keep the scream in, she took one step nearer. She thought, *What will I do if it turns round*? Ghosts in stories are grey like the people on black-and-white television or else see-through, but this one had short, dark-brown hair and a brown neck, and a black leather jacket. Minty didn't have to see its face to know it was her late fiancé, Jock.

Suppose it stayed there so that she couldn't use the room? It wasn't absolutely still. The head moved a bit and then the right leg. Both feet edged back as if it were going to get up. Minty squeezed her eyes tight shut. Everything was silent. A shriek out in the street from one of the kids that lived opposite made her jump and she opened her eyes. The ghost was gone.

She put the light on and felt the seat of the chair. It was warm and this surprised her. You think of ghosts as cold. She moved the chair back to where it belonged under the table. If it wasn't in the middle of the room, maybe he wouldn't come back.

She went upstairs, half expecting to see him there. He could have got past her and come up while she had her eyes shut. Ghosts didn't like lights, so she put them all on, all good hundred-watt bulbs, and he wasn't anywhere to be seen. She'd loved him, thought of herself as married to him though she wasn't, but she didn't want his ghost about. It was upsetting.

Still, he'd gone now and it was time for a good wash. One of the things Jock had liked about her, Minty was sure, was that she was always spotlessly clean. Of course, she'd had a bath this morning before going off to Immacue and she'd washed her hair; she wouldn't dream of leaving the house without, but that was eight hours ago, and she must have picked up all kinds of dirt from the Harrow Road and the people who came into the shops, not to mention the clothes they brought that needed dry-cleaning.

It was lovely having a bathroom entirely to herself. She said a little prayer of thanks to Auntie as if she were a saint (which was a way Minty had seldom thought of her when alive) every time she went in there, for making that possible. *Dear Auntie, thank you for dying and leaving me a bathroom. I'm ever so grateful, it's made a world of difference. Your loving niece for ever and ever, Araminta.* She took all her clothes off and dropped them in the Aladdin basket with the lid. It was expensive having more than one bath a day. She'd have a shower put in when she could afford it. One day, though not as soon as she'd hoped. Meanwhile, standing at the basin on the bath mat,

2

she used the big *natural* sponge Sonovia next door had given her for Christmas.

Like everything else in the bathroom, the nailbrush had been Auntie's. It was turquoise blue with a handle, which meant you could get a good grip on it. Minty scrubbed her nails. She had brought this hygienic measure to a fine art. It was no good just rubbing the brush across your fingertips, you had to insert the bristles on the outer edge right under your nails and move them rapidly back and forward. She washed her feet last, taking care to get plenty of soap between her toes, then using the nailbrush on her toenails. It was Auntie who had said soap was disappearing from the shops. Mark her words, the time was coming when you'd not be able to find a decent cake of soap. It was all this gel and essence in bottles these days, and powder stuff and cleansing bars, not to mention the soap that wasn't soap at all but a cake of something stuffed full of rosebuds and seeds and bits of grass. Minty wouldn't have given you a thank you for any of it. She used Wright's Coal Tar as she always had.

In the bathroom she felt safe. You couldn't imagine a ghost in a bathroom somehow, it would be all wrong. How about her hair? Should she wash it again? It looked clean enough, the fine, fly-away fair hair behaving in its usual way and flying away at all angles. Better put it under the tap and be on the safe side. She was going out with Sonovia and Laf later and she didn't want to give offence; there was nothing so unpleasant as greasy hair next to you. In the end she gave it a proper wash; it couldn't do any harm.

Minty dried herself and dropped the used towel into the basket. She never used a towel more than once and she never used body lotion or perfume. Deodorant, yes, and on the soles of her feet and palms of her hands as well as her underarms. Body lotion only dirtied clean skin as make-up did. Besides, she couldn't afford all that rubbish. She was quite proud of the fact that no lipstick had ever soiled her mouth nor mascara her pale eyelashes. Normally, since Auntie passed over, Minty would have walked naked across the narrow expanse of landing into her bedroom, as she might have if only the living Jock had been in the house. It was different altogether with a ghost, who was dead and shouldn't want to look at a nude woman from beyond the grave. She took a clean towel from the cupboard, wrapped it round her and opened the door cautiously. There was no one and nothing there. No ghost could have survived in that bright light.

Minty put on clean underclothes, a clean pair of cotton trousers and a clean jumper. No accessories, no jewellery. You never knew what germs were harboured by things like that. She was due to give them a knock next door at seven thirty. The cinema they were going to was the Odeon at Marble Arch and the film started at eight fifteen. Something to eat first and maybe a cup of tea.

Why had he come back like that? They said ghosts returned when they had unfinished business to attend to. Well, he had. An engagement isn't finished till it ends in marriage. She hadn't even seen his body or been asked to the funeral or had a pot of ashes like they gave her when Auntie was cremated. All she'd had was that letter telling her he'd been in the train that crashed and been burnt to a cinder. The fact was that she'd started to get over it, she'd stopped crying and got on with her life, the way they said you had to, and now his ghost appearing like that had brought it all back. Perhaps he'd only come to say a final goodbye. She hoped so.

The kitchen was spotless. It smelt powerfully of

bleach, a scent Minty liked. If she'd ever worn perfume it would have smelt like bleach. Although she'd just had her big wash she washed her hands again. She was very particular about what she ate. Food could be messy and make you dirty. Soup, for instance, or pasta or anything with gravy. She ate a lot of cold chicken and ham and salad and bread, the white kind, not the brown, which might have any filthy substance in it to make it that colour, and eggs and fresh unsalted butter. Her weekly expenditure on tissues and paper napkins and kitchen roll was ruinous but it couldn't be helped. She used the washing machine to capacity every day as it was without adding linen napkins to the load. When she'd eaten she washed up everything she'd used and put it away, and washed her hands under the running tap.

Was she going to leave all these lights on when she went out? Auntie would have called it a wicked waste. The upstairs ones would have to stay on. She wasn't going to go up there and turn the lights off and have to come down the stairs with all that *darkness behind her*. Out in the hall she took her coat off the peg and put it on. There was always a problem with coats because you couldn't really keep them clean. Minty had done the best she could by running up a couple of cotton linings on the Immacue machine. She could wash them and slip a clean one into the coat each time she wore it. The best thing if she was to have any peace of mind was not to think about the dirt on the outside of the coat, but it was a struggle not to do this and she didn't always succeed.

The light was blazing in the front room. Minty went a little way in there, retreated and, standing in the hall, put her hand round the door jamb and snapped off the light switch. Her eyes had closed of their own volition while she performed this action. Now she was afraid to open them in case Jock's ghost had taken advantage of her temporary blindness to seat himself in the chair once more. With the chair pushed up against the table, perhaps he wouldn't be able to. She opened her eyes. No ghost. Should she tell Sonovia about it? Minty couldn't make up her mind.

The street doors in Syringa Road opened on to tiny rectangular front gardens. Minty's garden was paved all over, Auntie had seen to that, but next door's had earth and flowers growing out of it, masses of them in summer. Sonovia saw Minty coming and waved from the window. She was wearing her new red trouser suit and a long scarf thing in powder blue she called a pashmina. Her lipstick matched her suit and her hair, newly done, was just like the shiny hat on the toby jug Auntie had brought back from a trip to Southend.

'We thought we'd go on the bus,' Sonovia said. 'Laf says there's no way he's parking the car down there and maybe getting clamped. He has to watch his step, being in the force.'

Sonovia always said 'being in the force', never 'being a policeman'. Minty was disappointed about the car but she didn't say so. She missed being taken about in Jock's car, though it was old and what he called a 'boneshaker'. Laf came out from the front room and gave her a kiss. His name was Lafcadio but that was a bit much of a name to go to bed with, as Sonovia put it, and everyone called him Laf. He and Sonovia were still only in their late forties but they had been married since they were eighteen and had four grown-up children, who'd all left home now and either had their own places or were still at university. Auntie used to say you'd think no one else had ever had a son a doctor and a daughter a lawyer, another daughter at university and the youngest at the Guildhall School of something or other, the way Sonovia went on about it. Minty thought it was something to be proud of but at the same time she couldn't really comprehend it; she couldn't imagine all the work and study and time that had gone into getting where they had.

'I've seen a ghost,' she said. 'When I got in from work. In the front room, sitting in a chair. It was Jock.'

They had never met Jock but they knew whom she meant. 'Now, Minty, don't be so daft,' said Laf.

'There's no such things as ghosts, my deah.' Sonovia always said 'my deah' like that when she liked to show she was older and wiser than you. 'Absolutely not.'

Minty had known Laf and Sonovia since they came to live next door when she was ten. Later on, when she was a bit older she'd babysat for them. 'It was Jock's ghost,' she said. 'And when he'd gone I felt the seat of the chair and it was warm. It was him all right.'

'I'm not hearing this,' said Sonovia.

Laf gave her a pat on the shoulder. 'You were hallucinating, right? On account of you being a bit under the weather of late.'

'Heed the wise words of Sergeant Lafcadio Wilson, my deah.' Sonovia glanced in the mirror, patted her hair and went on, 'Let's go. I don't want to miss the start of the picture.'

They walked along to the bus stop opposite the high wall of the cemetery. When she had anything worrying her Minty never trod on the joins in the pavement; she always stepped over them. 'Like a little kid,' said Sonovia. 'My Corinne used to do that.'

Minty didn't reply. She went on stepping over the

7

joins; nothing would have induced her to tread on them. On the other side of the wall were tombs and gravestones, big dark trees, the gasometer, the canal. She'd wanted Auntie buried in there but they wouldn't have it, there was no more room, and Auntie was cremated. The undertakers had written to her and said the ashes were ready for her to collect. No one asked what she was going to do with them. She'd taken the little box of ashes into the cemetery and found the most beautiful grave, the one she liked best with an angel on it holding a broken violin kind of thing and covering up her eyes with her other hand. Using an old tablespoon, she'd dug a hole in the earth and put the ashes in. Afterwards she'd felt better about Auntie, but she hadn't been able to do the same for Jock. His ex-wife or his old mother would have had Jock's ashes.

Sonovia was talking about her Corinne, the one who was a barrister, about what someone called for some reason the Head of Chambers had said to her. All compliments and praise, of course. No one ever said unpleasant things to Sonovia's children, just as unpleasant things never happened to them. Minty thought of Jock dying in that train, in the fire, a violent death which was a cause of a return from beyond the grave.

'You're very silent,' said Laf.

'I'm thinking about Jock's ghost.'

The 18 bus came.

'That was an unfortunate choice of film,' said Sonovia, 'under the circumstances.'

Minty thought so too. It was called *The Sixth Sense* and it was about a poor little mad boy who saw the ghosts of murdered people after they were murdered. Sonovia said that good it might be, but she worried about the effect on the boy actor playing the part. It couldn't be right for a child to see all that, even if it was only acting. They went into a pub in the Harrow Road and Laf bought Minty a glass of white wine. If it had been the pub where she'd first met Jock she couldn't have stayed, it would have been too much for her. She didn't know anyone in here.

'Now are you going to be OK going into the house on your own?'

'You go with her, Sonny. Put all the lights on.'

Minty was grateful. She wouldn't much care to have gone in there by herself. Of course, she'd have to tomorrow and the next day and the next. She'd got to live there. The house once more ablaze with light, Sonovia gave her a kiss, which she didn't often do, and left her to the bright emptiness. The trouble was she'd have to turn the lights out *behind* her before she went to bed. She went into the kitchen, washed her hands and Sonovia's lipstick off her face. The kitchen light out behind her, she walked down the passage, expecting to feel Jock's hand on her neck. He'd been in the habit of placing his hand on her neck and holding her head up to his before giving her one of his deep kisses. She shivered but there was nothing. Bravely, she switched off the front-room light, turned, walked to the stairs, the darkness very deep behind her. She ran up the stairs as fast as she could and into the bathroom, not closing the door, because she knew that if she did she wouldn't dare open it again.

She scrubbed her teeth, washed her face and neck and her hands again, her underarms, her feet, and the bit between her legs which was sacred to Jock. No other man would ever touch or enter it, that was a promise. Before she left the bathroom she touched every wooden surface, choosing three *different* coloured woods, the white of the panels that boxed in the bath, the pink picture rail, the pale yellow handle of the backbrush. She wasn't sure if something portable would do, perhaps it ought to be part of the fixtures. It had to be three surfaces or better still seven, but there weren't seven different colours in the bathroom. No one, no ghost, was outside the door. She'd forgotten her glass of water but never mind, it couldn't be helped, she'd have to do without. It wasn't as if she ever drank much of it.

Sitting on the bed she said a prayer to Saint Auntie. *Dear Auntie, please keep Jock's ghost away. Don't let him come back in the night. I haven't done anything to make him haunt me. For ever and ever, amen.* She put the light out and then she put it on again. In the darkness she saw Jock's face in front of her and though she knew that wasn't his ghost but a kind of dream or vision, it gave her a fright. She couldn't sleep very well with the light on but she wouldn't sleep at all with it off. She buried her face in the bedclothes so that it didn't make much difference whether it was dark or light in the room. Auntie used to hear voices, she called them 'my voices', and sometimes she saw things. Especially when she'd been in contact with one of those mediums. Minty couldn't understand, and no one had ever explained it to her, why a medium was called something that meant 'halfway between' and not 'best' or 'worst'. Edna, who was Auntie's sister, had been one of them, very much the worst in Minty's opinion, and when Edna was in the house or they were in hers she was frightened all the time.

Losing Jock had been a bad shock, especially coming less than a year after she lost Auntie. She hadn't been the same since, though she couldn't exactly have said how she'd been different. Something inside her head seemed to have lost its balance. He'd have said, but said it in a nice way, 'You never were all that balanced, Polo,' and maybe he was right.

She'd never get married now. Still, she had her house and work, and nice neighbours. Maybe she'd get over him one day the way she was getting over Auntie. She'd slept all right, the deep, dreamless sleep of someone whose dreams all come in her waking hours. The bath was filling with water as hot as she could stand it. Never leave a bath to run on its own, was Auntie's advice. Her sister Edna, the one who saw ghosts, did that; she went down to answer the door and when she'd taken the post in and a parcel she turned round to see water dripping through the ceiling. Auntie had a lot of tales to tell of her sister Edna and her sister Kathleen, especially the things they did when they were young. Sometimes her voices were their voices and sometimes they were God and the Duke of Windsor.

The water was hot and clear, unpolluted by bath essence. She lay back and dipped her head under, shampooed her hair first, soaped her body vigorously. Jock said she was too thin, needed to get some flesh on her bones, but it was natural, there was nothing to be done about it. It didn't matter now that she wasn't well-covered. She rinsed her hair, kneeling up and putting her head under the running tap. It could dry naturally. She didn't like hairdryers, blowing dusty air all over your head, not even the one he'd bought her that claimed to purify the air it puffed out. Her teeth well brushed, she rinsed mouth wash over her palate, under her tongue, round the back molars. Deodorant, clean underwear, clean cotton trousers and long-sleeved T-shirt. In the local Asda they called the ones they sold anti-perspirants, a name Minty didn't like at all; it made her shudder to think of perspiration.

Breakfast was toast and Marmite, clean and dry. A

11

cup of tea with plenty of milk and sugar. Minty put two bath towels, two hand towels, two sets of underwear, two pairs of trousers and two T-shirts and the coat lining into the washing machine, set and started it. She'd come back at lunchtime and put it in the dryer, and maybe make time to visit Auntie's grave. The morning was grey, misty, still. There was a queue for the 18 bus so she walked to the dry-cleaners past Fifth and Sixth Avenues, stepping over the joins. Minty had grown up with street names like that and couldn't see anything funny about it but it made Jock laugh. He'd only been in the area a few months and every time he saw the name he'd cast up his eyes, laugh that soundless laugh of his and say, 'Fifth Avenue! I don't believe it.'

Admitted, it wasn't a very nice part, but 'run-down' and 'a real slum', which were what Jock called it, were going a bit far. OTT, to use his own expression. To Minty it appeared grey and dreary but familiar, the background of her life for nearly thirty-eight years, for she'd been a baby when Agnes left her with Auntie 'for an hour at the maximum' and never came back. The row of shops ran from Second to First Avenue on the Harrow Road. Two of them had closed and been boarded up or they'd have been vandalised. The Balti takeaway was still there, a bathroom fittings shop, a builder's merchant, a unisex hairdresser and on the corner, Immacue. It was just as well Minty had brought her key, for Josephine wasn't there yet.

She let herself in, put up the blind on the door, slid back the bars on the window. Some very strange people roamed the Harrow Road by night. Nothing was safe. Minty stood still a moment, breathing in Immacue's smell, a mixture of soap, detergent, clean linen, dry-cleaning fluids and stain remover. She'd have liked 39 Syringa Road to smell like that but she

12

simply hadn't the wherewithal. It was a scent that developed over years of cleansing within a relatively small space. And inhaling it was the reverse of what Minty sometimes experienced when it was her lot to sort through the piles of clothes customers brought in and, as they were moved and lifted and turned over, there rose from them a nasty odour of stale sweat and food stains.

Exactly nine thirty. She turned the sign on the inside of the door to Open and went into the back room where the ironing awaited her. Immacue provided a shirt service and it was her job on weekdays, and Saturdays too, to iron fifty shirts before lunchtime. It was mostly women who brought them in and collected them, and Minty sometimes wondered who wore them. Most people were poor around here, single mothers and pensioners and out-of-work boys looking for trouble. But a lot of yuppies who worked in the city had bought houses nearby; they were cheap by present-day standards and near the West End, even if they were the kind of places their parents wouldn't have looked at twice. They must be the men who wore these snowy white and pink and blue striped shirts to go to their jobs in offices and banks, these two hundred immaculate shirts encased in cellophane and with a neat little cardboard collar and cardboard bow tie fixed to each one.

By the time Josephine came in Minty had ironed five. Always when she arrived in the morning she went up to Minty and gave her a kiss. Minty submitted to this salutation, even lifted up her cheek for it, but she didn't much care for being kissed by Josephine who wore thick, waxy, dark-red lipstick, some of which inevitably came off on Minty's clean, pale skin. After she'd gone to hang up her coat Minty went to the sink and washed her cheek and then she washed her hands. Fortunately, there were always plenty of cleaning materials, cloths, sponges and brushes at Immacue.

Customers started coming in but Josephine attended to them. Minty wouldn't go out there unless one of them asked for her specially or Josephine called her. There were still some who didn't know what had happened to Jock and who asked how her fiancé was or when was she getting married, and Minty had to say, 'He got killed in the Paddington train crash.' She didn't like having sympathy; it embarrassed her, especially now she'd seen his ghost last night. Saying he was dead and accepting the kind things they said seemed like cheating somehow.

They had coffee at eleven. Minty drank hers and washed her hands. Josephine said, 'How're you feeling, love? D'you reckon you're starting to get over it?'

Minty wondered if she should tell about the ghost but decided against. A woman customer had once said she'd seen her mother in a dream and in the morning got a phone call to say she was dead. She'd died at the precise time of the dream. Josephine had said, quite rudely, 'You can't be serious,' and laughed a scornful laugh. So better say nothing about it.

'Life has to go on, doesn't it?' she said.

Josephine agreed. 'You're right, it's no good dwelling on things.' A big, full-breasted woman with long legs, she had bright blonde hair as long as an eighteen-year-old girl's, but a kind heart. Or so everyone said. Minty lived in fear that a flake of the dark-red varnish she wore on her fingernails would chip off and fall in the coffee. Josephine had a Chinese boyfriend who couldn't speak a word of English and was a cook in a restaurant in Harlesden

14

called the Lotus Dragon. They'd both met Jock when he called for her after work.

'He was a lovely chap,' said Josephine. 'Life's a bitch, when you come to think of it.'

Minty would rather not have talked about it, especially now. She finished the fiftieth shirt at ten to one and went home for an hour. Lunch was free range eggs scrambled on white toast. She washed her hands before eating and again afterwards, and her face as well, and put the washing in the tumble-dryer. The flower-selling man had set up his stall outside the cemetery gates. It wasn't really spring yet, it was still February, but he'd got daffodils and tulips as well as the chrysanths and carnations that had been around all winter. Minty had filled an empty bleach bottle with water and brought it with her. She bought six pink tulips and six white narcissi with orange centres.

'In remembrance of your auntie, is it, love?'

Minty said it was and it was nice to see the spring flowers.

'You're right there,' said the flower-selling man, 'and what I say is it does your heart good to see a bit of a kid like yourself remembering the old folks. There's too much indifference in the world these days.'

Thirty-seven isn't a 'bit of a kid' but a lot of people thought Minty much younger than she was. They didn't look closely enough to see the lines coming out from the corners of her eyes and the little puckers round her mouth. There was that barman in the Queen's Head who wouldn't believe she was a day over seventeen. It was her white skin, shiny about the nose, and her wispy fair hair and being as thin as one of those models that did it. Minty paid the man and smiled at him because he'd called her a kid and

15

then she went into the cemetery, carrying her flowers.

If it weren't for the graves it would have been like the country in there, all trees and bushes and grass. But it was no good saying that, Jock said. The graves were the reason for the trees. A lot of famous people were buried here but she didn't know their names, she wasn't interested. Over there was the canal and beyond it the gasworks. The gasometer loomed over the cemetery like some huge old temple, commemorating the dead. Ivy was the plant that grew most plentifully in here, creeping over the stones and slabs, up the columns, twining round the statues and pushing its tendrils through the splits and cracks in tombs. Some of the trees had black, shiny, pointed leaves, like leather cut-outs, but most were leafless in winter, their bare branches sighing and shivering when the wind blew but hanging now limp in stillness. It was always quiet, as if there were an invisible barrier above the wall that kept out even the traffic noise.

Auntie's grave was at the end of the next path, on the corner where it met one of the main aisles. Of course, it wasn't really her grave, it was just the place where Minty had buried her ashes. The grave belonged to Maisie Julia Chepstow, beloved wife of John Chepstow, who departed this life 15 December, 1897, aged fifty-three, asleep in the arms of Jesus. When she'd brought Jock here she'd told him this was Auntie's grandmother and he'd been impressed. For all she knew, it might be true. Auntie must have had two grandmothers like everyone else, just as *she* must have. She was going to have Auntie's name put on the stone, she'd said. Jock said the grave was beautiful and moving, and the stone angel must have cost a fortune, even in those days.

Minty took the dead stalks out of the stone pot and

16

wrapped them in the paper that had been round the tulips and narcissi. She poured the water out of the bleach bottle into the vase. When she turned round for the flowers, she saw Jock's ghost coming down the main aisle towards her. He was wearing jeans and a dark-blue jumper and his leather jacket, but he wasn't solid like he'd been last night. She could see through him.

She said bravely, though she could hardly get the words out, 'What d'you want, Jock? What have you come back for?'

He didn't speak. When he was about two yards from her he faded away. Just vanished like a shadow does when the sun goes in. Minty would have liked some wood to touch or maybe to have crossed herself, but she didn't know which side to start from. She was shaking all over. She knelt on Auntie's grave and prayed. *Dear Auntie, keep him away. If you see him where you are tell him I don't want him coming here. Always and for ever your loving niece Araminta.*

Two people came along the path, the woman carrying a little bunch of carnations. They said, 'Good afternoon,' the way no one ever would if you met them outside in the street. Minty got up off her knees and returned the greeting. She took her parcel of stalks and her empty bleach bottle, and dropped them in one of the litter bins. It had begun to rain. Jock used to say, don't worry about it, it's only water. But was it? You didn't know what dirt it picked up on its way down out of the sky.

Chapter 2

Auntie's real name was Winifred Knox. She had two sisters and a brother, and they all lived at 39 Syringa Road with their parents. Arthur was the first to leave. He got married and then there were just the sisters at home. They were much older than Auntie who had been an afterthought, the baby of the family. Kathleen got married and then Edna did and their father died. Auntie was left alone with her mother and she cleaned offices for a living. Her engagement to Bert had been going on for years and years but she couldn't marry him while Mum was there dependent on her, in a wheelchair and needing everything done for her.

Mum died the day before Auntie's fortieth birthday. She and Bert waited a decent interval and then they got married. But it didn't work, it was a nightmare.

'I didn't know what to expect,' Auntie said. 'I suppose I'd led a sheltered life, I didn't know anything about men. It was a nightmare.'

'What did he do?' Minty asked.

'You don't want to know, a little innocent like you. I put an end to it after a fortnight. Good thing I'd kept this house on. If I'd any regrets it was not having any little ones of my own but then you came along like a bolt from the blue.'

Minty was the bolt and her mother was the blue. Her name was Agnes and she'd been Auntie's best friend at school, though they hadn't seen so much of each other since then. No one was surprised when Agnes appeared with a baby, she'd been asking for it, going with all and sundry. There was never any mention of the baby's father, it might have been a virgin birth for all the talk there was of him. It was the early sixties and people weren't anywhere like as strict as they'd been when Auntie was young, but they still looked down their noses at Agnes and said the baby was a liability. Agnes brought her to Syringa Road sometimes and the two of them pushed the pram round Queen's Park.

That afternoon in May when Minty was six months old there was no talk of park visiting. Agnes said could she leave Minty with Auntie just for an hour while she went to visit her mum in the hospital. She'd brought a supply of nappies and a bottle of milk and a tin of puréed prunes for babies. It was funny how, whenever she told Minty this story, Auntie never left out the puréed prunes.

The time Agnes came was just after two and when it got to four Auntie began to wonder what had happened to her. Of course, she knew very well that when people say they'll be back in an hour they don't actually return for two or three hours; they're just saying it to make you feel better, so she wasn't worried. But she was when it got to six and seven. Luckily, what few shops there were in the area stayed open round the clock, so she asked the lady next door – that was before Laf and Sonovia came – to keep a lookout for Agnes and she took Minty in the pram and bought baby porridge and more milk and a bunch of bananas. Auntie'd never had any children of her own but she was a great believer in bananas as nourishing, the easiest to eat of all fruits and liked by everyone.

'Personally,' she'd said, 'I'd regard anyone who

turned up their nose at bananas with the deepest suspicion.'

Agnes didn't come back that day or the next. She never came back. Auntie made a bit of an effort to find her. She went round to Agnes's parents' place and found her mum had never been in hospital, she was as fit as a fiddle. They didn't want the baby, no thanks, they'd been through all that when theirs were little and they weren't starting again. Agnes's dad said he reckoned she'd met someone who'd take her on but not the kid as well and this was her way of solving that problem.

'Why don't you hold on to her, Winnie? You've none of your own. She'd be company for you.'

And Auntie had. They gave her the baby's birth certificate and Agnes's dad put two ten-pound notes in the envelope with it. Sometimes, when she'd got fond of Minty and looked on her as her own, Auntie worried a bit that Agnes would come back for her and she wouldn't be able to do a thing about it. But Agnes never did and when Minty was twelve the mum who hadn't been in the hospital came round one day and said Agnes had been married and divorced and married again, and had gone to Australia with her second husband and her three kids and his four. It was quite a relief.

Auntie had never adopted Minty or fostered her or any of those things. 'I've no legal right to you,' she often said. 'It'd be hard to say who you belong to. Still, no one's showing any signs of wanting to take you away, are they? Poor little nobody's child you are.'

Minty left school when she was sixteen and got a job in the textile works in Craven Park. Auntie had brought her up to be very clean and though she'd been promoted to machinist, she didn't like the fluff and lint that got everywhere. In those days everyone smoked and Minty didn't like the smell and the ash either. Auntie knew the people who ran the dry-cleaners. It wasn't Immacue then but Harrow Road Dry-Cleaning and an old man called Mr Levy owned it. Minty stayed there for the next eighteen years, at first when Mr Levy's son took over, then when it became Quicksilver Cleaners, finally working for Josephine O'Sullivan. Her life was very simple and straightforward. She walked to work in the mornings, worked for eight hours, mostly ironing, and walked home or got the 18 bus. The evenings she spent with Auntie, watching TV, eating their meal. Once a week they went to the cinema.

Auntie was quite old when her voices began. Both her sisters had died by then but it was their voices she heard. Kathleen told her she ought to go to the pub after the cinema, take Minty, it was time Minty had a bit of life, and to make it the Queen's Head, it was the only one round there that was properly clean. She used to go in there with George when they were courting. Auntie was a bit doubtful but the sisters were insistent and after she and Minty had been to see *Heavenly Creatures* the two of them went shyly into the College Park pub, the Queen's Head. It *was* clean, or as clean as you could get. The barman was always wiping down the surfaces and with a clean cloth, not some old rag.

Edna didn't talk about pubs or having a good time. She kept telling Auntie to concentrate and she'd see her dead husband Wilfred. He was dying to 'get through', whatever that meant, though why Auntie should want to when she'd never been able to stand Wilfred Cutts she didn't know. Then God started talking to Auntie and the sisters took a back seat. Young Mr Levy said, 'When you talk to God it's praying but when God talks to you it's schizophrenia.'

21

Minty didn't laugh. She was frightened of having God in the house, always telling Auntie He was training her to be the Angel of the Lord and not to eat red meat. Auntie had always been a great one for the Royal Family and she could remember Edward the Eighth renouncing the throne for love of a woman, so it wasn't surprising when his voice joined God's. He told her he'd got a son, born in secret in Paris and *he'd* had a son and she was to tell the Queen she'd no business being where she was and this King Edward the Tenth ought to wear the crown. Auntie was arrested trying to get into Buckingham Palace and they wanted to put her away, but Minty wasn't having that. While she had her health and strength Auntie was staying put.

'She's been like a mother to me,' she said to young Mr Levy, who said she was a good girl and it was a shame there weren't more like her.

In the end Auntie had to go but she didn't live long in the geriatric ward. She'd made a will a long time ago and left Minty the house in Syringa Road, and all the furniture and her savings, which amounted to £1650. Minty didn't tell anyone the amount but let it be known Auntie had left her money. It proved Auntie'd loved her. When she added it to her own savings the total came to £2500. Any sum over a thousand pounds was real money, Minty thought, proud of what she'd amassed. It was after that that she collected Auntie's ashes from the undertakers and buried them in Maisie Chepstow's grave.

A long time passed before she went back to the pub. The following week Laf and Sonovia hadn't wanted to see the film so she'd gone alone; she didn't mind that, it wasn't as though she wanted to talk in cinemas. Wisely, she went to the six-ten showing when hardly anyone else did. There were only eight people in the seats besides herself. She liked being alone with no one to whisper to her or pass her chocolates. On the way back she dropped into the Queen's Head and bought an orange juice. Why, she couldn't have said. The pub was half empty; it seemed less smoky than usual and she found a table in the corner.

All her life Minty had never spoken to a man who wasn't someone's husband or her employer or the postman or bus conductor. Those sort of people. She'd never seriously thought of having a boyfriend, still less of getting married. When she was younger Sonovia used to tease her a bit and ask her when she was going to get a man of her own, and Minty always said she wasn't the marrying kind. Auntie's mysterious but horrific account of her marital experience had put her off. Besides, she didn't know any unattached men and none showed any signs of wanting to know her.

Until Jock. Not the first but the second time she went into the pub she saw him looking at her. She was sitting at that same corner table on her own, dressed as she always was in a clean pair of cotton trousers and a long-sleeved T-shirt, her hair newly washed and her nails scrubbed. The man she stole cautious glances at was tall and well-built, long-legged in blue jeans and a dark-blue padded jacket. He had a handsome face and a nice tan; he looked clean and his brown hair was short and trim. Minty had almost finished her orange juice. She stared into the golden grainy dregs of it, to avoid looking at the man.

He came over, said, 'Why so sad?'

Minty was too scared to look at him. 'I'm not sad.'

'You could have fooled me.'

He sat down at her table, then asked her if she

minded. Minty shook her head. 'I'd like to buy you a real drink.'

Auntie sometimes had a gin and tonic, so Minty said she'd have one of those. While he was getting her gin and a half of lager for himself, Minty felt near to despair. She thought of getting up and running away but she'd have had to pass him to get to the door. What would Sonovia and Josephine say? What would Auntie have said? Have nothing to do with him. Do not trust him, gentle maiden, though his voice be low and sweet. He came back with the drinks, sat down and said his name was Jock, Jock Lewis, and what was hers.

'Minty.'

'Yum, yum,' said Jock. 'Sounds like something that comes with a shoulder of lamb.' He laughed, but not unkindly. 'I can't call you that.'

'It's Araminta really.'

He raised his eyebrows. 'Minty, Minty, the rick-stick stinty, round tail, bobtail, well-done, Minty.' He laughed into her incredulous face. 'I shall call you Polo.'

She thought about it, understood. He didn't have to explain. 'I'm Jock. John, really, but everyone calls me Jock. Live round here, do you?'

'Syringa Road.'

He shook his head. 'I'm a stranger here myself but I soon won't be. I've got a place up in Queen's Park, I moved in on Saturday.' He glanced at her hands. 'You're not married, are you, Polo? You've got a boyfriend though, I'm sure you have, just my luck as usual.'

She thought of Auntie who was dead and of Agnes going off to Australia. 'I haven't got anybody.'

He didn't like that. She couldn't tell why but he didn't. She'd said it very seriously, of course she had, it was serious to her. To make it better she tried to smile. The gin had gone straight to her head, though she'd only sipped a few mouthfuls of it.

'Come on,' he said. 'I'll make you laugh. Now listen. Adam and Eve and Pinch Me went down to the river to bathe. Adam and Eve were drownded. Who was saved?'

It was easy. 'Pinch Me.'

He did so. Very gently on her upper arm. 'Caught you out, Polo.'

She didn't laugh. 'I ought to be going.'

She thought he'd try to stop her but he didn't. 'Here, have one for the road.' He offered her not a drink but a Polo mint. 'I'll walk you home. I've not got my car with me.'

She didn't believe in the car. Not then. Besides, if he'd had one and offered to drive her she'd have refused. She knew all about not taking lifts from strange men. Or sweets. They might be drugs. Wouldn't being walked home be just as dangerous? She couldn't refuse, she didn't know how. He held the pub door open for her. The streets round here were deserted at night except for groups of young men, wandering, filling the width of the pavement, silent but occasionally letting out bestial yells. Or you'd meet just one, loping along to the deafening beat of a ghetto blaster. If she'd been alone she wouldn't have risked it, she'd have got the bus. He asked her what was behind the high wall.

'That's the cemetery.' She didn't know why she had to add, 'My auntie's ashes are in there.'

'Is that a fact?' He said it as if she'd told him something wonderful, like she'd won the Lottery, and from that moment she started liking him. 'Your auntie was very important to you, right?'

'Oh, yes. She was like my mother. She left me her house.'

'You deserved it. You were devoted to her and did

all sorts of things for her, didn't you?' She nodded, speechless. 'You had a reward for your good services.'

Syringa Road didn't turn directly out of the Harrow Road but out of a turning off it. He read out the street name in the sort of tone you'd use to say Buckingham Palace or Millennium Dome. His voice was lovely, like something sweet and dark-brown and smooth, chocolate mousse maybe. But she was afraid he'd want to come in and she wouldn't know how to stop him. Suppose he tried to kiss her? Laf and Sonovia weren't in. No lights were on next door. Old Mr Kroot lived on the other side, but he was eighty-five and wouldn't be much use.

Jock dispelled her fears. 'I'll wait here and watch you in.'

She took three steps up the path and turned round. Five would have brought her to the door. 'Thank you,' she said.

'What for? It's been a pleasure. Are you in the phone book, Polo?'

'Auntie was. Miss W. Knox.'

If she hadn't wanted him to phone she should have said she wasn't in the book, which was true. *She* wasn't. But maybe she did want him to phone her. He went off whistling. The tune was 'Walk On By', the one about being strangers when we meet.

Jock wasted no time. He phoned her next day. It was in the early evening, she'd just got home from Immacue and was having a wash. No good thinking she could get to the phone when she was all wet and her hair dripping. She let it ring. It would only be Sonovia wanting to tell her something about what Corinne had done this time or the prize Julianna had won or where Florian had come in his exams. The phone rang again while she was arranging cold ham slices and cold boiled potatoes and cubes of cucumber on a plate for her supper, with a chocolate mousse she'd made herself to follow. The voice that was like the mousse said it was Jock and would she come to the cinema with him.

'I might,' Minty said, and then she said, 'All right.'

That was how it began.

Josephine said, had she found out if he was married? Sonovia said she knew nothing about him and would she like Laf to check on Jock's antecedents, which he could easily do on the police computer. When she told him, Laf said was she joking, a guy with a name like John Lewis? There'd be thousands of them. Not to mention the department store. Minty didn't much like any of this. It wasn't their business. How would they like it if she started checking up on their friends? Laf and Sonovia thought a lot too much of themselves, just because he was the first black policeman in the UK to have been made a sergeant. It made her keener on Jock than she might have been without their interference.

She and Jock met in the pub and went to the cinema. After that he came in what he called the 'boneshaker' to 39 Syringa Road to call for her. The car was about twenty years old but at least it was clean, he'd taken it into the car wash on the way. Sonovia was on the watch from behind her frilly lace curtains but had to go away two minutes before he arrived because Julianna was on the phone. One day he called for Minty at Immacue. Afterwards Josephine went on and on about how good-looking he was, as if she was surprised at Minty finding anyone like that. Next time Jock came in Josephine happened to be sitting on the counter where she could show off her legs in her Wolford Neon Glanz tights. If Jock was impressed he didn't show it. He took Minty to the dog races at Walthamstow and he took her bowling. She'd never been anywhere like that in her life before.

It was a long time before she plucked up her courage and asked him if he was married. At the time he was humming that song about walk on by, wait on the corner.

'Divorced,' he said. 'Don't mind, do you?'

She shook her head. 'Why would I?'

He was in the building trade. His hands would have been in a terrible state if he'd done rough work and they weren't, so she thought he must be a plumber or maybe an electrician. He never took her to his place in Queen's Park. She didn't know if it was a house or a flat or just a room, she knew only that it was in Harvist Road but not the number. He'd no brothers or sisters, no one except his old mother who lived in the West Country that he went to see every couple of weeks, travelling all the way down there by train. When he got divorced he had to let his ex-wife have his house. It was sad.

They'd been going out for six weeks before he kissed her. He put his hand on the back of her neck and pulled her face to his. She liked it, which she hadn't expected. She started washing herself even more. It was important to keep herself nice for Jock, especially now he'd started kissing her. He was clean himself, not so clean as she was, but no one could be. She was proud of that. On a Saturday evening, when they'd been to the Queen's Head, they brought back Balti takeaway for supper. Well, Jock did. She had a sandwich she made herself and a banana. Jock said he hated bananas, it was like eating sweet soap, and Minty couldn't help remembering what Auntie'd said about viewing someone who didn't like them with the deepest suspicion. But what happened next drove all that out of her head. He said he'd like to stay the night. She knew what that meant. He wasn't talking about dossing down on the front-room couch. He kissed her and she kissed him back but when they got upstairs she left him in the bedroom while she went to have a bath. It worried her that she couldn't wash her hair but it was no good going to bed with it wet. And she wished the sheets hadn't been on since Wednesday, she'd have changed them if she'd known what was coming.

What happened with Jock wasn't the way Auntie hinted it would be. It hurt but somehow she knew it wouldn't always. Jock was surprised she'd never done it before; he could hardly believe it just as he could hardly believe she was thirty-seven. He was younger but he never said how much.

'I'm yours now,' she said. 'I'll never do that with anyone else.'

'Good-oh,' he said.

She got up early in the morning because she'd had a bright idea before she went to sleep. She'd make a cup of tea and bring it up to him. And it would give her a chance to wash. When he woke up she was bathed and her hair washed, wearing clean trousers and T-shirt, standing meekly by the bed holding a mug of tea and the sugar basin.

'The first time,' he said. 'No woman's ever done that for me before.'

She wasn't as pleased as he expected her to be. Who were these other women who hadn't made him tea? Maybe only his mother and the one who'd been his wife. He drank the tea and got up, going off to work without having a proper wash, which shocked her. A week went by before she heard from him. She couldn't understand it. She went up to Harvist Road on the bus and walked up and down the street, going up to some of the front doors to read the names on the bells. His wasn't there. She looked along all the surrounding streets for the boneshaker but couldn't

29

find it. The phone rang twice that week. She touched three colours of wood before answering and prayed, *Dear Auntie, let it be him. Please.* But it was Corinne the first time, asking her to take a message to Sonovia because next door's phone was out of order, and a salesman the next, wanting to double-glaze her house. By the time Jock phoned she'd given up hope.

'I didn't know where you were,' she said. 'I thought you'd died' – her voice full of tears.

'I didn't die,' he said, 'I went to the West Country to see my old mum.'

He was coming round. He'd be with her in half an hour. She had a bath, washed her hair, put on clean clothes, all this for the second time in three hours. When the half-hour was up and he hadn't come, she prayed to Auntie and touched seven different colours of wood, the oak-stained living-room door, the cream front door, the pine table, the green-painted chair in the kitchen, upstairs for the white bath surround, the pink picture rail and the yellow back brush handle. Ten minutes afterwards he arrived. They went to bed, though it was the middle of Saturday afternoon. She liked it even more and wondered if there was something wrong with Auntie or was it with her? Jock took her to see *Sliding Doors* and then for a meal at the Café Uno in the Edgware Road. Next day, because it was Sunday, she said she wanted him to see something special, and they went into the cemetery and she showed him Auntie's grave.

'Who's this Maisie Chepstow?' he said. 'She's been dead a long time.'

'She was my auntie's grandma.' The fantasy seemed to come naturally. It might even be true. What did she know about Auntie's ancestors? 'I'm going to have a new gravestone done with her name on.'

'That'll be expensive.'

'I can afford it,' Minty said airily. 'She left me money. Quite a lot of money and the house.'

Jock didn't go off to see his mother again for a month and by the time he did they were engaged. They wouldn't get married until he'd got a better job and was earning real money, he said. Meanwhile, he borrowed £250 from her to buy a ring. It was her idea. He kept saying, no, no, I wouldn't dream of it, but when she insisted he gave in. He measured her finger and brought the ring round next day, three diamonds on a hoop of gold.

'I'll give him the benefit of the doubt,' Sonovia said to her husband, 'but they can make diamonds in the lab these days and it's no more costly than making glass. I read about it in the *Mail on Sunday*.'

Jock stayed the night of 30 June and in the morning he turned over in bed, gave Minty a little pinch on the shoulder and a little punch on the arm and said, 'Pinch, punch, first of the month. No returns.'

Another pinch joke. He said it brought you luck. But you had to be the first to do it. That was the point of the 'no returns'. On 1 April, he said, it would only be April Fools' Day till twelve noon and afterwards Tailpike Day. You had to manage to pin a tail on someone without them knowing.

'What sort of tail?'

'Paper, string, anything, you name it.'

'So they get to walk about without knowing they've got a tail?'

'That's the point, Polo. You've made a fool of them, right?'

It turned out that he was a general builder, he could do anything. She asked him to see if he could do something to stop the bathroom window rattling and he promised he would, but he never did it any

31

more than he mended the shaky leg on the kitchen table. If he had a bit of capital, he said, he could set up in business on his own and he knew he'd make a success of it. Five thousand in his pocket would make all the difference.

'I've only got two thousand and a half,' Minty said, 'not five.'

'It's our happiness at stake, Polo. You could take out a mortgage on the house.'

Minty didn't know how. She didn't understand business. Auntie had seen to all that, and since Auntie went she'd found it hard enough working out how to pay the council tax and the gas bill. She'd never had to do it, nobody'd shown her.

'Leave it to me,' Jock said. 'All you'll have to do is sign the forms.'

But first she handed over nearly all the money she had. She'd been going to give him a cheque, make it out the way she did the ones to the council but put 'J. Lewis' instead of 'London Borough of Brent', but he said cash would be easier for him because he was in the process of changing his bank. The money would buy a second-hand van, an improvement on the boneshaker and leave something over for advertising. She told no one, they wouldn't understand. When he talked about the mortgage again he was sitting up in her bed at 39 Syringa Road, drinking the tea she'd brought him. He wanted her to come back to bed for a cuddle but she wouldn't, she'd just had a bath. Her engagement ring had had a good clean, soaking in gin overnight. The house he reckoned was worth around eighty thousand. Laf had told her the same so she didn't need convincing. The obvious thing to do was take out a mortgage on it of ten thousand pounds, one eighth of its value.

Minty wasn't a very practical person but Auntie had taught her some of the principles of thrift and neither a borrower nor a lender be. She'd already done the lending and now she was going to start borrowing – but all that much? 'I'll have to see,' she said. 'I'll have to think about it.'

Jock had been spending every evening with her and most nights. When he hadn't come round or phoned for three days she phoned the number he'd finally given her in Harvist Road but no one ever answered. Perhaps it was just that he was with his mum again. If he never came back it would be because she'd hesitated over the mortgage. She imprisoned herself in rituals, praying, taking extra flowers to Auntie's grave, hardly moving about the house without touching wood, walking round the room like an old person who couldn't get about without holding on to the tables and chairs. The rituals brought him back, and the prayers and the flowers. She'd decided to let him have the ten thousand.

He wasn't as happy as she thought he'd be. He seemed a bit absent, as if his thoughts and his interests were elsewhere. She couldn't put her finger on it, but he was changed. When he explained she understood. His mum was ill, he said. She'd been on a hospital waiting list for months. He'd like to take her out of the National Health Service and pay for her op privately if he could afford it. The whole thing was a worry. He might have to go down and be with her for a bit. In the meantime he'd get the application forms from the building society.

Minty said she'd got about £250 left in the bank and he was to have that towards his mother's op. His bank still hadn't completed the changeover to the other branch, so she drew the cash out of the bank and emptied her account. He put the notes in the pocket of his black leather jacket and said she was an angel. The jacket looked new, it was so stiff and glossy, but he said, no, he'd had it for years, just never got around to wearing it. Next day he phoned her on his mobile – she didn't know he'd got a mobile – and said he was in the train going to the West Country. Thanks to her, his mother would be able to have her hip done next week.

Minty told Sonovia about the op, leaving out her personal involvement. They were in the cinema, waiting for the big picture to start and Laf to get back from the Gents. It was the first time Minty'd been out with them since Jock came on the scene.

'His mum's getting a hip replacement for £250? You have to be joking.'

'Ops cost a lot when they're private,' Minty said.

'I don't mean it's a lot, my deah, I mean it's nothing.'

Minty didn't like that. She'd always suspected Sonovia was jealous because her Corinne hadn't got a boyfriend. The lights went down and she accepted the pack of popcorn Laf handed her. She usually liked popcorn, it was dry and clean and not messy to eat, but this evening somehow it tasted stale. It'd be a shame if Sonovia and Laf were to turn against Jock when he'd soon be coming to live next door permanently.

Like the rest of the country, she saw about the Paddington train crash on television. She didn't connect it with anyone she knew. Jock had phoned her the day before from his mum's as he'd promised and he hadn't said anything about coming home soon. When he hadn't phoned or appeared for three days she looked so pale and ill that Josephine asked her what was wrong.

'Jock's gone missing,' she said. 'I don't know where he's got to.'

Josephine didn't say much to Minty but she said a

lot to Ken. He couldn't understand a word but she talked to him just the same. He liked the sound of her voice and as he listened, smiled with the tranquillity of the Buddhist at peace with himself and the world.

'Maybe that Jock's ma lives in Gloucester, Ken, or near it. What's the betting he was on that train, the one the local train smashed into? They haven't named all the casualties yet, there were horrific injuries. Minty'll be devastated, it'll about break her up.'

It did. She got the letter when Jock had been missing a week.

Chapter 3

The ghost came into Immacue. Minty was in the back, ironing shirts but keeping an eye on the shop while Josephine had popped down to Whiteley's. She heard the bell and came out. Jock's ghost was there in jeans and black leather jacket, reading the card on the counter that gave details of their special offer to pensioners. One free of charge if you bring in three items. She screwed up her courage to speak to it. 'You're dead,' she said. 'You stay where you came from.'

It raised its eyes to look at her. They had changed colour, its eyes, being no longer blue but a pale, washed-out grey. She thought its expression threatening and cruel.

'I'm not afraid of you.' She was but she was determined not to show it. 'If you come back I'll find ways of getting rid of you.'

The bell sounded as the door opened and Josephine came in. She was carrying a bag of food from Marks and Spencer and another one from the shop that sold cut-price make-up and perfumes. 'Who were you talking to?'

She could see through the ghost to Josephine on the other side. It was fading, blurring round the edges. 'Nobody,' she said.

'They say it's the first sign of madness, talking to yourself.'

Minty didn't say anything. The ghost was melting

away like the genie going back into the bottle in the pantomime Auntie took her to when she was little.

'But I see it this way. If you're nuts you don't know you're talking to yourself. You think you're talking to someone because you see things normal people don't see.'

Not liking that sort of talk, Minty went back to her ironing. It was five months since Jock had been killed. She'd been out of her mind with worry, though, funnily enough, she never thought he might have been in that train crash. It hadn't sunk in that the express was coming from the West Country, and even if it had she hadn't known where Gloucester was or that Jock's mum lived there. Besides, he'd said on the phone he wouldn't be coming back till the day after. Lists of casualties appeared in the papers but Minty didn't often read a paper. Laf brought round the *Evening Standard* when they'd finished with it but mostly she made do with the telly. You got a better idea from seeing pictures, Auntie always said, and there was always the newscaster to explain things.

She didn't get many letters either. Something coming in the post was an event and even then it was mostly a bill. The letter that came when she hadn't heard from Jock for a week had *Great Western* printed along its top in big sloping letters and it was done on a computer. Well, Laf said it was. It addressed her as *Dear Madam* and regretted to inform her that her fiancé Mr John Lewis had been among those travelling in the Gloucester express who were fatally injured. Minty read it standing in the hall at 39 Syringa Road. She went out just as she was, without a coat, letting the door slam behind her, and into next door. Sonovia's son Daniel, the doctor, who'd been out on a late night and had stopped over, was sitting at the kitchen table eating his breakfast.

Minty thrust the letter into Sonovia's face and burst into a storm of tears. Crying wasn't something she did much of, so when she did it was a violent explosion of long pent-up misery. It wasn't just Jock she was grieving for but Auntie and her lost mum and being alone and not having anyone. Sonovia read the letter and handed it to Daniel and he read it. Then he got up and fetched a drop of brandy in a glass which he personally administered to Minty.

'I have my doubts about this,' Sonovia said. 'I'm going to get your father to check up on it.'

'Don't let her go to work, Mum,' Daniel said. 'See she lies down and rests, and you could make her a warm drink. I'd better go or I'll be late for surgery.'

Minty lay down till the afternoon and Sonovia brought her several warm drinks, sweet tea and her own recipe cappuccino. Luckily, her neighbour had a key to 39 or Minty wouldn't have been able to get back in again. Whether Laf ever did check she never found out. She thought that maybe she'd dreamt Sonovia saying that. Jock was dead all right or the train people wouldn't have written. Josephine was very nice about her taking time off work. After all these years when she'd been as regular as clockwork, she said it was the least she could do. Minty got a lot of sympathy. Sonovia personally made an appointment for her with a counsellor and old Mr Kroot on the other side, who hadn't spoken for years, got his home help to put a card with a black border through her letter box. While Josephine sent flowers, Ken brought round a dish of lemon chicken with fried rice and Butterfly's Romance. He wasn't to know she never ate stuff from restaurant kitchens.

For five days she wept non-stop. Touching wood or praying should have stopped it but it didn't have any effect. All that time she only had one bath a day, she was so weak. It was remembering the money that stopped her crying. Ever since she had the letter she hadn't thought about it but she did now. It wasn't so much that it was her savings that were all gone but the money that Auntie had left her and which she'd seen as a sacred trust, something to be looked after and treasured. She might as well have thrown it down the drain. As soon as she felt able to go out again, she bathed and washed her hair, put on clean clothes and took her engagement ring to a jeweller in Queensway.

He looked at the ring, examined it through a magnifying glass and shrugged. It might be worth twenty-five pounds but he couldn't give her more than ten. Minty said, in that case she'd hold on to it, thank you very much. It took only a few more weeks for her love for Jock to turn sour and change into resentment.

Laf told Sonovia no Jock nor John Lewis was numbered among the rail crash victims, no one with a name even remotely like that. He got on to Great Western and found that sending letters of that kind wasn't their policy and, in any case, the woman who signed the letter didn't exist. Laf knew very well that news of a death in those circumstances would come via the police. A couple of police officers would have come to Minty's door. He'd very likely have been one of them himself. If, of course, they'd known of her existence. How would anyone have known? Minty wasn't married to Jock, she wasn't even living with him. The woman they'd have contacted was Jock's mother – if he had a mother, if any of what he'd told Minty was true.

'It's tipped her over the edge,' said Sonovia.

'What d'you mean, over the edge?'

'She's always been peculiar, hasn't she? Come on, Laf, face it, a normal person doesn't have two baths a day and wash her hands every ten minutes. And how about jumping over the joins in the paving stones like a kid? Have you seen her touching wood when she's scared of something?'

Laf looked troubled. When something upset him, his face, the same dark rich chestnut brown as his shoes and as glossy, fell into a mass of pouches, his underlip protruding. 'He made a fool of her and when he got himself a better proposition he was off. Or the idea of marriage scared him. One thing's for sure, he wasn't killed in any train crash, but we won't tell her that. We'll take her out with us a bit more. Get her out of herself.'

So Minty, who'd been shown the world by Jock and liked it, who'd late in life discovered sex and been going to get married, had her social life reduced to a once-a-fortnight cinema visit with her next-door neighbours. She never said another word to them about Jock until she saw his ghost sitting in the chair in the front room. Telling her not to be so daft and that she was hallucinating decided her against ever saying any more to those two about it. She'd have liked someone she could talk to and who'd believe her, someone who wouldn't say there's no such thing as ghosts. Not a counsellor, she didn't mean that. She'd kept the appointment Sonovia had made for her, but the counsellor had only told her not to bottle up the grief but let it all pour out and to talk to other people who'd been bereaved in that crash. How could she? She didn't know them. It hadn't occurred to her to bottle up her grief, she'd cried for a week. What would it look like, a bottleful of grief? A cloudy grey liquid, she thought, with no foam or bubbles in it. Anyway, it didn't work the way she'd been promised it would. She still felt terrible about Jock, wishing she'd never met him so that he couldn't come ruining her life. What she wanted most was someone who knew how to get rid of ghosts. There must be people, vicars or something like that, who'd tell her what to do or do it for her. The trouble was no one believed in her ghost. Sometimes it looked as if she'd have to get rid of it herself.

After the sighting in Immacue, she didn't see him again for a week. By now it wasn't so dark in the evenings and she was coming home from work in the light. She took care never to leave that chair in the middle of the room and she told Josephine she mustn't be alone in the shop, it made her nervous. Her nerves had got bad since she lost Jock. It was a funny position to be in, hating someone and missing them at the same time. Once she went up to Harvist Road to look at the house where he'd finally told her he'd lived. She thought the woman he rented the room from might have hung a black wreath in one of the windows or at least kept the curtains drawn but there was nothing like that. What would she do if the ghost came out of the front door and down the steps? Minty was so afraid she ran all the way back to the bus stop.

'It's best for her to think he's dead,' Sonovia said to her daughter Corinne. 'Your dad says he'd like to get his hands on him and if he shows his face round here after what he's done he won't answer for the consequences. What's the use of that sort of talk, is what I say. Let her get her mourning over with, that's the best way, and then she can get on with her life.'

'And what life would that be, Mum? I never knew she'd got one. Did he have any money off her?'

'She's never said, but I have my suspicions. Winnie left her a bit; I don't know how much and I wouldn't ask. Your dad says he can see the whole scenario. That Jock got talking in the pub and someone – Brenda, very likely, she can never keep her mouth shut – she pointed Minty out to him and said about Winnie Knox leaving her the house and a bit of money, multiplied it by ten, no doubt, and Jock saw the gravy train coming out of the tunnel.'

Corinne went to the window and looked out into the back garden, which was divided from next door's by only a chain-link fence. On the other side of it, standing on a black plastic bin liner which she had spread on the grass, Minty stood pegging out the washing. 'I'm being serious, Mum. How do you know if he ever existed? Did you ever see him?'

Sonovia stared at her. 'No, we never did. We keep ourselves to ourselves, as you know.' Her daughter looked as if she didn't know, as if it was a surprise to her, but she said nothing. 'Wait a minute, though. We did see his car, a real old banger. And your dad heard his voice through the wall. Laughing. He had a very deep, warm sort of laugh.'

'All right. Only people do fantasise. And now she's seeing his ghost, is she? D'you know if she's ever had psychiatric treatment?'

'Who? Minty?'

'No, Mum, Mr Kroot's cat. Who else but Minty?'

'Don't ask me.'

'I only ask because normal people don't act the way she does. Seeing ghosts and not knowing any men before Jock and always wearing the same sort of clothes, *exactly* the same. And all the compulsive things.'

'Now you mention it, that's just what I was saying to your dad.'

'I had a client like that. She was up on a charge of Actual Bodily Harm but she was doing most of the bodily harm to herself, cutting herself to relieve her tension, she said. She had so many compulsions she lost her job because she was too busy arranging things in the right order and going back ten or a dozen times to check, that she'd no time to do her work.'

'You'd have to be mad to go on like that.'

'Well, you said it, Mum,' said Corinne.

Auntie said Agnes meant to call her Arabella. Then her best friend apart from Auntie had a baby – she was properly married – and named *her* Arabella, so Agnes settled on Araminta, it being that bit different. They'd once talked about names, she and Jock, and he'd said that though his name was John his mother called him Jock because she came from Scotland. That was really all Minty knew about Mrs Lewis, that she was Scottish and must have lived somewhere in Gloucester.

Jock hadn't had time to buy a van or start a business, so he must still have had all her money when he died. Where would it be now? Minty asked Josephine, not mentioning names, of course, but just saying what would happen to someone's money if he died and hadn't made a will like Auntie had? She knew he hadn't made a will because he said so and said they must both make them after they were married.

'It'd go to his next of kin, I suppose,' said Josephine.

That wouldn't be his ex-wife because she was ex. It would be old Mrs Lewis. *She* ought to give Minty's money back. It wasn't rightfully hers, it'd only been a loan to Jock, not a gift, and not even a loan to Mrs Lewis. You wouldn't be far wrong if you said she'd stolen it. Minty often thought about Mrs Lewis having the enjoyment of it. Living in her nice house in Gloucester, using Minty's money at bingo and buying luxuries in the shops, Belgian chocolates and cherry brandy. She'd intended to use the money to have a shower installed. You didn't use so much water under a shower but you got cleaner. It would be easy having two showers a day and washing her hair at the same time. And it wasn't a hosepipe on the taps she had in mind but a real shower cabinet you walked into with a glass door and tiled walls. She'd never have it now, or not for years and years.

When Jock appeared again, sitting in the kitchen chair, she wasn't as frightened as she'd been the first time. Maybe that was because he was vague and misty, almost transparent. You could see the green-painted bars on the back of the chair through his chest. She stood in front of him and asked him why he'd let his mother have her money. He didn't answer, he never did, and he soon went away, doing his genie-vanishing-into-a-bottle act, disappearing like melting snow.

But in the night he spoke to her. Or he *spoke*. It might not have been to her or to anyone. His voice woke her out of deep sleep, saying, 'She's dead, she's dead . . .' That soft, sweet, brown voice. It didn't sound sad, but then it never did. Whom did he mean by 'she'? Not his ex-wife, she'd be too young. Minty lay in bed, thinking. The darkness was impenetrable when the curtains were drawn and the street lamps out. She looked for his ghost in vain, peering into the blind empty corners.

It must have been his mother he meant. And he wouldn't have been sad because old Mrs Lewis would be joining him wherever he was. Minty closed her eyes again but it was a long time before she went back to sleep.

Chapter 4

In Zillah's experience, men didn't propose except in old-time novels. They just talked about 'one day' when you and they got married or even 'making a commitment' or, more likely, as an unwelcome duty because you were pregnant. They never said, as Jims had just said, 'Will you marry me?' It made her hesitate about taking him seriously. Besides, there was another reason why he couldn't possibly be asking her to marry him. 'Did you really say what I think you did?' asked Zillah.

'Yes, I really did, darling. Let me explain. I want to marry you, I want to live with you and I want it to be for the rest of our lives. I like you. I think we'd get on.'

Zillah, who had been driven by poverty to stop smoking a week before, took a cigarette out of the packet he had put on the table. Jims lit it for her. 'But you're gay,' she said.

'That's the point. I am also the Conservative Member of Parliament for South Wessex and between you and me I think I shall be outed some time in the next six months if I don't do something to stop it.'

'Yes, OK, but everyone gets outed these days or comes out. I mean I know you haven't been but it was always only a matter of time.'

'No, it wasn't. What makes you say that? I take the greatest care to be seen about with women. I've been taking that ghastly model, Icon, about for weeks. Just think about my constituency. You live in it, you ought to know what it's like. Not only have they never returned anyone but a Conservative, they have never, until me, returned an unmarried man. They are the most right-wing bunch in the United Kingdom. They loathe queers. In his speech at the annual dinner last week the Chair of the North Wessex Conservative Association compared what he calls "inverts" to necrophiliacs, practitioners of bestiality, paedophiles and satanists. There'll be a General Election in less than a year. I don't want to lose my seat. Besides . . .' Jims put on that mysterious look his handsome face often wore when he made reference to the corridors of power. 'Besides, a little bird told me I have the weeniest chance of a post in the next reshuffle if I keep my tiny paws clean.'

Zillah, who had known James Isambard Melcombe-Smith since her parents moved into the tied cottage on his parents' estate as land agent and housekeeper twenty-five years before, sat back in her chair and looked at him with new eyes. He was probably the best-looking man she had ever seen; tall, dark, film star-ish in the way film stars were when beauty was a Hollywood prerequisite, slim, elegant, too handsome, she sometimes thought, to be hetero and far too handsome to sit in the House of Commons. It amazed her that those people like this Chairman and the Chief Whip hadn't rumbled him years ago. She'd even have fancied him herself if she hadn't known since she was sixteen that it was hopeless. 'What do I get out of it?' she asked. 'No sex, that's for sure.'

'Well, no. Best to call a spade a spade, darling. It would be, as you might say, a *marriage blanc* but also an *open* marriage, only that part would be our little secret. As to what you get out of it, that will not be

46

cat's meat, not in anyone's estimation. I have quite a lot of dosh, as you must know. And I'm not talking about the weeny pittance I get from the Mother of Parliaments. Plus my charming home in Fredington Crucis and my very up-market apartment within the sound of the division bell – valued, I may add, at one million smackers only last week. You get my name, freedom from care, lots of lovely clothes, the car of your choice, foreign trips, decent schools for the kids . . .'

'Yes, Jims, how about the kids?'

'I love children, you know that. Don't I love yours? I'll never have any of my own unless I set up home in a same-sex *stable* relationship and contrive to adopt one. Whereas I'd have yours ready made, lovely little pigeon pair with blond curls and Dorset accents.'

'They have *not* got Dorset accents.'

'Oh, yes, they have, darling. But we'll soon change that. So how about it?'

'I'll have to think it through, Jims,' said Zillah.

'Okey-dokey, only don't take too long over it. I'll give you a bell tomorrow.'

'Not tomorrow, Jims. Thursday. I'll have decided by Thursday.'

'You'll decide in my favour, won't you, sweet? I'll say I love you if you like, it's almost true. Oh, and about the open marriage aspect, you'd understand, wouldn't you, if I draw the line at that ex-husband of yours? I'm sure you know what I mean.'

After he'd gone, in the Range Rover, not the Ferrari, Zillah put on her duffel coat, a scarf that had been her mother's and a pair of over-large wellies some man had left behind after a one-night stand. She walked down the village street, thinking about herself and her situation, about Jerry and the future, about Jims and her relations with her parents, but

47

mostly about herself. She had been christened Sarah, as had six other girls in her class at primary school, but discovering by means of a blood test in her teens that her group was B, a fairly rare blood group in all but gypsies, and that Zillah was a favoured Romany name, she rechristened herself. Now she tested it out with a new double-barrelled surname. Zillah Mel-combe-Smith sounded a lot better than Zillah Leach. But then almost anything would.

Fancy Jims knowing about Jerry. That is, knowing about the sort of unwritten arrangement she had with Jerry. Or *had*. Of course, she didn't believe the letter she'd had, that was an insult to anyone's intelligence. He didn't own a computer. Some new woman must have written it. 'Ex-husband' was the term Jims had used. Naturally, he would, everyone did, though she and Jerry weren't actually divorced; they'd never got round to it. And now if Jerry wasn't dead, he wanted her to think he was, which amounted to the same thing. It meant he wouldn't come back; the 'arrangement' was over and the kids had lost their dad. Not that he'd ever been much of a father to them, more of a here-today-gone-tomorrow dropper-in. If she accepted Jims – how romantic and old-fashioned that sounded – would she be able to describe herself as a widow or would it be safer to call herself single? If she accepted him it would be one in the eye for her mother and might stop her being so insufferably patronising.

The village of Long Fredington was so called for the length of its main street, a full half-mile from Burton's Farm in the east to Thomas Hardy Close in the west. It was the largest of the Fredingtons, the others being Fredington St Michael, Fredington Epis-copi, Fredington Crucis and Little Fredington. All were picturesque, the stuff of postcards, every house, even the newest, every barn, the church, the mill, the pub (now a private house), the school and the shop (also now private houses) built of the same golden-grey stone. If you were well-off, especially if you were well-off and retired, it was a charming place to live. If you had a car or two and a job in Casterbridge or Markton, a husband and a nanny, it wasn't so bad. For someone in Zillah's position it was hell. Eugenie went to school on the bus, that was all right, but there was no nursery or pre-school for Jordan and he was at home with her all day. She had no car, she hadn't even got a bike. Once a week, if they hadn't anything better to do, Annie at the Old Mill House or Lynn at La Vieille Ecole drove her ten miles to the Tesco to pick up supplies. Much less often someone asked her round for a meal but these were rare outings. They had husbands and she was a very good-looking unattached female. Anyway, she couldn't get a babysitter.

At All Saints' Church, a handsome fourteenth-century building from whose interior all the priceless brass had been stolen and melted down and the unique mediaeval wall paintings defaced with graffiti, she turned left down Mill Lane. After two smartly refurbished cottages were passed, all occupied dwellings ceased. But for birdsong, it was silent. The lane narrowed and beech branches met over-head. Although late autumn, the day was sunny and almost warm. If this was global warming, thought Zillah, she couldn't get enough of it. Never mind the seas rising and the coastline disappearing, she didn't live near the coast. And maybe she wouldn't live down here at all much longer, not if she married Jims, her best friend, her childhood friend, really the nicest man she knew.

At the ford she trod carefully on the flat stones that formed a causeway across the brook. Ducks stared indifferently at her from the bank and a swan glided downstream. She had to admit it was pretty and it would be a whole heap prettier if she could venture out into it from Fredington Crucis House, wearing Armani jeans, a sheepskin jacket and Timberland boots, having left the Range Rover parked outside the church. But Jims was gay, a difficulty not to be underrated. And what about Jerry? He wouldn't have got whoever it was to send her that letter if he didn't want her to think he was dead, but he was brilliant at changing his mind. If there was one thing beyond his liking mints and hating bananas that – well – *defined* Jerry, it was his rapid mind changes. Suppose he had a re-think and wanted to be alive again?

A large duckpond dominated the front garden, if this it could be called, of the Old Mill House. Although no rain had fallen in Long Fredington for a week and the stream water was exceptionally low, the banks of the pond were a quagmire. Waterfowl had been slopping about in it, animals with hooves had churned it up, and now Annie's three children and her two were sitting in it, Annie's Rosalba instructing her sister Fabia, her brother Titus and Zillah's children in the art of face-painting with mud. When Zillah came up the drive she had just completed a rendering of a Union Jack in monochrome that extended from Jordan's chin and round cheeks to his high domed forehead.

'Jordan ate a slug, Mummy,' said Eugenie. 'Titus said there was this man ate a live goldfish and the cruelty to animals people made him pay a lot of money.'

'And Jordan wanted to eat one,' said Rosalba, 'because he's a naughty boy but there's no goldfishes in our pond. So he ate a slug. And that's cruel too and he'll have to pay a hundred pounds.'

'Not a naughty boy,' Jordan wailed. Tears gushed

out of his eyes and he rubbed them with his fists, ruining the Union Jack. 'Won't pay a hundred pounds. I want my daddy.'

Those words, frequently uttered, never failed to upset Zillah. She picked him up. He was wet through and covered with mud. Rather late in the day she wondered indignantly what Annie was thinking of, leaving five children, the eldest of whom was eight, alone beside a large pond that must be at least six feet deep in the middle.

'I only left them for two minutes,' Annie cried, running out from the front door. 'The phone was ringing. Oh, look at them! You three are going straight in the bath.'

Though she had no need to think of the cost of hot water as Zillah did, she didn't offer to put Eugenie and Jordan in the bath. She didn't ask Zillah in either. Jordan hung round Zillah's neck, wiping his hands on her hair and rubbing his muddy cheek against hers. The chances were she'd have to carry him all the way home. She waited for Annie to say something about picking her up in the morning and taking her shopping, but Annie only said she'd see her soon and if she'd excuse her she'd have to get this lot cleaned up as she and Charles were going out to dinner in Lyme and they'd have to leave by seven.

Zillah sat Jordan on her right hip with her right arm round him. He was a heavy boy, big for his age. Eugenie said it was getting dark, which it wasn't, not yet, and she'd be frightened if she didn't hold Zillah's hand.

'Why am I too big to be carried, Mummy?'

'You just are. Miles too big,' said Zillah. 'Four is the upper limit. No one over four gets carried.'

Jordan burst into loud wails. 'Don't want to be four! Want to be carried!'

'Oh, shut up,' said Zillah. 'I *am* carrying you, you halfwit.'

'Not a fwit, not a fwit! Put me down, Jordan walk.'

He trudged along, very slowly, trailing behind. Eugenie took Zillah's hand, smiling smugly over her shoulder at her brother. The sinking sun disappeared behind a dense wall of trees and it suddenly became viciously cold. Jordan, snuffling and whimpering, rubbing at his eyes with muddy fists, sat down in the road, then lay down on his back. It was at times like these that Zillah wondered how she had ever got into this mess in the first place. What had she been thinking of to get involved with a man like Jerry at the age of nineteen? What had induced her to *fall in love* with him and want his children?

She picked Jordan up and, in the absence of any handkerchief or tissue, wiped his face with a woollen glove she found in her pocket. A bitter wind had got up from nowhere. How could she hesitate about saying yes to Jims? She was suddenly visited by fear that maybe he wouldn't phone for his answer on Thursday, maybe he'd find some other woman who wouldn't keep him waiting. That Icon or Ivo Carew's sister Kate. If it weren't for Jerry . . . She was going to have to sit down when she'd got this lot to bed and seriously think about what Jerry was up to and what that letter meant.

It took three times as long to get back to Willow Cottage with the children as it had taken her to get to the Old Mill House on her own. Twilight was closing in. The front door opened directly into the living room where the bulb in the light had gone. She hadn't a replacement. The cottage wasn't centrally heated, of course it wasn't. It belonged to a local landowner and had been let at a low rent to various more or less indigent people for the past fifty years. No improvements had been made to it in that time, apart from perfunctory painting carried out by tenants and mostly left unfinished. Thus, the inside of the front door was painted pink, the cupboard door black and only an undercoat in uncompromising grey had been applied to the door to the kitchen. Electrical fittings consisted mostly of partly eroded cables passing, looped and knotted, from ten- and five-amp points, obsolete in the rest of the European Union and rare in the United Kingdom, to extension leads connected to a lamp, a fan heater and a very old 45 rpm record player. The furniture was rejects from the 'big house' where Sir Ronald Grasmere, the landlord, lived. It had been discarded forty years before, was old then and had come from the housekeeper's room.

The kitchen was worse. It contained a sink, a gas cooker from circa 1950 and a refrigerator that looked huge because its walls were nearly a foot thick, though its usable interior quite a small space. Originally it must have been a very good one, for it had lasted more than sixty years. There was no washing machine. Zillah stripped off the children's clothes and put jeans, T-shirts, sweaters and Jordan's anorak to soak in cold water in the sink. She switched on the fan heater and put a match to the fire she had laid earlier. It was strange how Jims never seemed to notice the state of the place or the inadequacy of the fittings or, come to that, the cold. At any rate, he never mentioned them. Did this augur well for a life companion or not? Of course, he was a pal of Sir Ronald. If she married him she and Jims would no doubt occasionally have Sir Ronald to dine. Perhaps in the Members' dining room . . .

As she began making scrambled eggs for the children's tea, Zillah decided that if she did marry Jims, no way was she going to do the cooking in future. Or any housework as long as she lived. Who was it said, 'I'll never be cold or hungry again'? Oh, yes, Scarlett O'Hara. If only she had a video in this bloody bloody place and the film of *Gone With the Wind* she'd play it tonight after the kids were in bed. If she married Jims she'd be able to watch videos every night. What an ambition! But she'd also be able to have unlimited babysitters and go to the cinema and the theatre and nightclubs, shop all day long, have facials and her hair done at Nicky Clarke and stay at health farms and be a lady who lunched at Harvey Nichols.

Was she going to marry him, then? Had she made up her mind?

The children would be able to play video games and have computers instead of watching whatever rubbish was currently on television: *Baywatch* or something of that ilk. Not great in black and white. She'd better bath them. Jordan had mud on his feet and in his hair. But Jims was *gay*. Besides, there was another pressing reason, not for just not marrying him but for not marrying anyone.

The letter had come in October of the previous year. For about five minutes, if that, she'd believed what it said and that it came from the people it said it did. Maybe that was because she'd wanted to believe it. But had she wanted to? Not entirely. Anyway, that hardly mattered, for she'd soon seen it was an obvious nonsense. Jerry hadn't been on a Great Western train going from Gloucester to London. He'd left her and the kids and Willow Cottage *ten minutes before* that train collided with the other one and driven himself off somewhere or other in his battered Ford Anglia, which was twenty years old if it was a day.

The letter purported to come from the Great Western. In fact, since she was his wife and still was on the day of the train crash, she'd have been the first to hear of his death and not ten days afterwards. Not in a phoney letter that cried out to be disbelieved, but from the police. They'd very likely have wanted her (or someone she named) to go and identify the remains. There'd have been a funeral. So after the first five minutes she hadn't believed the letter. But she'd wondered who'd written it and what Jerry was up to. Certain things seemed clear. He'd arranged for the letter to be sent to her and this must mean that he wanted her not necessarily to think he was dead, but to act as if he were dead. What he was really saying was: 'This is to show you I'm off, I won't be troubling you again. Just act as if I was dead. Shack up with someone, get married if you like. I won't interfere or put a spoke in your wheel.' Was he saying that? She couldn't think what he'd meant if he hadn't meant that.

Of course, he was always a joker. And his jokes weren't even clever or particularly funny. Zillah, Zillah, the rick-stick Stillah, round tail, bobtail, well done, Zillah. Pinch, punch, first of the month, no returns. If he happened to be sleeping with her on the night of the last of the month – it didn't happen that often – he'd always awakened her with those words and the corresponding gestures. 'No returns' meant the rules of the game stopped her pinching and punching him back. There was another one about going into the garden and meeting a great she-bear who said, 'What, no soap?' She couldn't remember the rest of it. Once, long ago, she must have found him funny. And his country singing and his mint-eating.

They'd not really lived together since Jordan was born and not much before that, and she'd never been such a fool as to think she was the only one. But she had thought she was the preferred one. 'All other

55

girls apart, first always in my heart,' as he'd once told her and she, being young, had taken it seriously. It was probably a line from Hank Williams or Boxcar Willie. Disillusionment set in when he was always somewhere else and about as bad a provider as could be. What was the good of setting the Child Support Agency on his track when he never earned anything?

Because they thought he and she were divorced, everyone believed that when Jerry came visiting it was to see his kids and that Jordan bunked in with Eugenie and he slept in Jordan's room or downstairs on the couch. The truth was, however, and there was never any question about it, that he shared Zillah's bed. Sex with Jerry was really the only thing about him she still liked as much as she ever had and there had been plenty of it that last weekend he'd spent at Willow Cottage. For a moment, running the children's bath, she wondered about that remark of Jims's. Something about he didn't mind what she did about sex but he drew the line at 'that ex-husband of yours'. She'd been too struck with surprise at his proposal to think much about it at the time, but did that mean he wasn't among those who believed Jerry had been visiting just as the children's father? Probably. It didn't matter. Jims, as she very well knew, was no fool.

It showed her something else as well. That Jims took it for granted she and Jerry were divorced. Did her parents? They no longer lived on Jims's father's estate but had retired to a bungalow in Bourne-mouth. Relations between her and them were strained and had been since she moved in with Jerry, got pregnant and dropped out of the art foundation course she was doing at a north London polytechnic. Strained but, since the original rift was mended, not broken off. It was her parents who'd persuaded Sir

56

Ronald to let her have this house. Still, when she spoke to her mother on the phone, she had the impression they considered her a divorced woman who had only got what she asked for.

The children had to share a bath. It cost too much to keep the immersion heater on for long. Eugenie stared searchingly at her brother until he said, 'Stop looking at me. Your eyes are making holes in my tummy.'

'Mummy,' said Eugenie, 'did you know his willy is called a penis? Some people call it that. Did you know?'

'Yes, I did.'

'Titus told me when Jordan got his out to do a wee. Are they all called a penis or is it just his?'

'All,' said Zillah.

'You should have told me. Annie said it's wrong to keep children in the dark. I thought she meant keep them in a dark bedroom but she said, no, she didn't mean that, she meant it's wrong to keep them in the Darkness of Ignorance.'

'It's a willy,' said Jordan.

'No, it isn't.'

'It is.'

'It isn't.'

'It is, it is, it's mine and it's called a willy.' He began to cry and beat the water with his hands so that splashes went all over the room and Zillah. She dabbed about her with a towel. Every towel had to be washed by hand and dried on the line, as she didn't need to remind herself.

'Do you have to provoke him, Eugenie? If he wants to call it a willy, why not let him?'

'Annie says it's wrong to teach children baby words for Parts of the Anatomy.'

Zillah got them to bed. When she had finished reading Harry Potter to them – though Eugenie could read perfectly well herself and had been able to for two years – she thought as she kissed them goodnight that they might not see their father again. It seemed, suddenly, intolerably sad. If he intended never to see her again he wouldn't see them either. In Jordan's rosy face on the pillow she could see Jerry's nose, the curve of his upper lip, in Eugenie's his dark-blue eyes and strongly marked eyebrows. Neither of them was much like her. Last time Jerry had been at Willow Cottage, when he was sitting at breakfast that final morning, Jordan had taken their two hands, hers and Jerry's, and laying his over hers on the table, said, 'Don't go, Daddy. Stay here with us.'

Eugenie hadn't said a word, just looked at her father with cool, penetrating reproach. Zillah had hated Jerry then, even though she hadn't wanted him to stay, hated him for not being a proper dad to his children. They could have a new one in Jims and everything a good father should provide.

Still, there was no getting away from the fact that she was married already. But Zillah knew it was hopeless to start thinking about divorce now. The children were involved, so it couldn't just be done by post. There would have to be a court hearing and custody decided. Jims wouldn't wait. He was notoriously impatient. He had to get married, or at least get himself engaged, before someone outed him and that might happen any day. If she hesitated he'd go after Kate Carew.

So if she married him, was she going to do it as a divorcee or a widow? If as a widow, wouldn't Jims find it odd that she'd said nothing about Jerry dying in the train crash when it happened? It would have to be as a divorcee. Or, better still, as a single woman. Then she wouldn't have to produce the decree absolute or whatever it was to show the registrar. Or the vicar. Jims might want to get married in church.

Zillah hadn't given a thought to religion since she was twelve, but so do old beliefs and habits resonate faintly throughout life that she baulked at marrying in church in a false character. Besides, she'd been married to Jerry in church and she knew enough about church weddings to know that the vicar would say something about declaring if you knew any impediment to the marriage. If Jerry being still alive wasn't an impediment she didn't know what would be. She was baulked but not put off the idea. Now she'd thought of these stumbling blocks she found she really wanted to marry Jims. There was no doubt. She'd say yes on Thursday.

Dragging all those sopping wet and still dirty clothes out of the now cold water in the sink was one of the things that decided her. To get away from that. And the crack behind the outfall pipe from the lavatory where water (or worse) dripped, and the clothes line that fell into the mud when overloaded and the life-threatening electric wiring. And when Annie didn't offer her a lift, having to walk two miles to Fredington Episcopi where there was a small, ill-stocked village shop, and two miles back, laden with junk food in plastic carriers. She'd say yes.

But somehow she'd have to get over the question of what, on forms you filled in, they called your marital status. And it was for Jims as well as the registrar or vicar. He was no fool. Why shouldn't she say she and Jerry had never actually been married at all?

Chapter 5

In the fruit and vegetable section of Waitrose at Swiss Cottage Michelle Jarvey was choosing food for her husband. Matthew was with her, pushing the trolley, for it would have been difficult attempting to buy anything if he were absent. Besides, they did everything together. They always had. He'd try kiwi fruit, he was saying, now the Coxes were over. He couldn't stomach any other sort of apple.

To the other shoppers Mr and Mrs Jarvey would have presented a sight almost comic. If to themselves they were a serious, and to some extent tragic, pair, Michelle knew quite well that the rest of the world saw them as a grossly fat, middle-aged woman and a man so thin, worn, wizened and cadaverous as to resemble someone freed after five years in a prison camp on a starvation diet. Matthew was too weak to walk far and when he pushed the trolley, which he insisted on doing, he was forced to double up as if in pain. Michelle's monstrous bosom rested on a stomach which, with her hips, resembled in shape the lower part of a spinning top, undulating as she walked. Today she wore a tent-like green coat with a fake fur collar in which her still pretty face nestled as if it were peeping out from a mound of clothes bundled up for the charity shop. The huge body balanced on surprisingly good legs with ankles so slender that you wondered why they didn't crack under the weight.

'I'll just get two kiwis, then, shall I?' said Michelle. 'You won't want too much. You may not fancy them.'

'I don't know, darling. I'll try.' Matthew shuddered a little, not at the kiwi fruit, which were just like bits of a tree, really, or even two small furry animals, but at an overripe banana among the rest, a banana with a brown bruise and squashy tip. He turned his eyes away, remembering to keep them lowered. 'I don't think I want any strawberries today.'

'I know you don't, darling, and no pears or peaches.'

Michelle didn't say because they bruise easily, they decay fast. She knew that he knew that she knew. They moved on past milk and cream and cheese, she helping herself surreptitiously while he looked the other way. She dared not buy meat or fish, she'd go to the local corner supermarket for that on her own. Once he'd actually vomited. It was the only time they'd ventured together into the meat section and she'd never risk it again. Among the cakes and biscuits she grabbed the things she knew she shouldn't eat but had to. To distract herself, to distance herself, to console herself.

'Those,' he said, pointing.

He wouldn't say 'butter puffs'. 'Butter' was among the words, along with 'cheese' and 'mayonnaise' and 'cream', he hadn't uttered for years. He'd be sick. She took two packets of the dry, flaky biscuits. His face had become even paler than usual. In a surge of love for him she wondered just how much torment being in a food store brought him. He insisted on coming. It was one of the courage-testing tasks he set himself. One of the challenges. Looking at a magazine was another, turning the pages and forcing himself not to skip the ones with the colour shots of soufflés and

61

pasta and roast beef. Talking to people who didn't know, watching them eat, watching *her* eat. They came to fruit juices. She took a carton of pineapple juice, looked at him, raising her eyebrows. He nodded, managed a death's-head smile, all skull and teeth. She laid her hand on his arm.

'What would I do without you, my darling?' he said.

'You don't have to do without me. I'm always here for you, you know that.'

There was no one near to hear them. 'My sweetheart,' he said. 'My love.'

She had fallen in love with him at first sight. Because it wasn't the first time she'd felt like that, though her love had never been returned, she expected, with anticipatory bitterness, that once again her feeling would be unrequited. But he had been the same and loved her back with a like ardour. He was a teacher and he had two degrees while she was just a nursery nurse, but he loved her, she didn't know why, couldn't account for it. They weren't very young, both of them were in their late twenties. Passion overtook them. They made love the second time they met, moved in together after a week, got married two months after their first meeting.

Michelle was – well – not thin then, but not plump either, just a normal size. 'A perfect figure,' Matthew said. If anyone had asked her the secret of their love and their successful marriage she'd have said it was because they were so kind to one another. He'd have said it was because no one else had ever mattered much to either of them once they'd met.

He was funny about his food even then (Michelle's way of putting it) but she'd always thought men quite different from women in their attitudes to eating. Really, it was just that, like most men, there were a lot of things he didn't like. Red meat was on his poison list and all kinds of offal, shellfish and any fish that wasn't white – in those days, when she could joke about it, she called him a 'fish racist' – sauces and mayonnaise and custards, anything 'sloppy'. He was faddy, that was all. But he began to get worse, though she never put it like that. Eating disorders as real illness were just beginning to be recognised, but everyone thought they only applied to young girls who wanted to stay thin. Because they talked about everything, they sometimes discussed, in depth, his problem. How he couldn't eat things that looked like other things. An example was rice, he'd just got it into his head that rice looked like maggots. Soon he couldn't eat anything that had once been alive, though – thank God, she said to herself – that didn't apply to fruit and vegetables, *some* fruit and vegetables. All pasta was like worms, all sauce – well, anything runny was so bad that he couldn't utter the words that described what they were like.

Gently she asked him if he knew why. He was such an intelligent man, intellectual, sensible, practical, an excellent science teacher. It frightened her to watch him grow thinner and thinner and see him prematurely ageing.

'I don't know,' he said. 'I wish I did. My mother used to encourage me to eat things I didn't want to but she never forced me. I was never made to sit at the table until I'd eaten something.'

'Darling,' she said, 'don't you ever feel *hungry*?' She did and so often.

'I don't think I ever have. Not that I can remember.'

At that time she had to stop herself envying him. Never to be hungry! What bliss! Only she knew it wasn't. It was a slow wasting away towards death.

Not if she could stop it, she thought then, not if she made it her life's work to help him. That was when she got him to start taking vitamins. He was quietly acquiescent, for capsules and tablets never look like anything else. They're hard and firm, and can be swallowed without choking. He stopped drinking milk and eating soft cheeses. Butter had gone long ago. She made him go to the doctor and went with him.

This was in the late eighties and the doctor, an elderly man, wasn't sympathetic. Afterwards Matthew called him a 'famine freak' because he'd told him to pull himself together and think of the starving millions in Africa. He prescribed a tonic, which he said was guaranteed to make the patient eat. The first and only time Matthew took it he vomited violently.

Michelle made it her business to discover all the foods he wasn't positively repelled by. Strawberries were one, provided she took the hulls out, every scrap of green. Oranges and grapefruit were all right. Fool that she was, she told herself, she'd tried him on a pomegranate and when he'd seen its interior he'd actually fainted. The fleshy red seeds looked to him like the inside of a wound. Bread he'd eat, dry plain cake and most biscuits. Eggs if they were hard-boiled. But all of it had to be in minute quantities. Meanwhile, she piled on the weight. He knew she gorged, though she tried not to eat too much in front of him. At mealtimes, while he sat miserably resigned, picking at half a lettuce leaf, a slice of hard-boiled egg and one plain-boiled new potato the size of a marble, she ate the same multiplied by five, plus a chicken wing and a bread roll. But when she went back to the kitchen and he returned thankfully to his computer, she filled herself up with the comfort food that consoled her for watching his sufferings: ciabatta with brie, fruit cake, Mars bars, crème brûlée and crystallised pineapple.

Their love never wavered. She'd have liked children but none came. Sometimes she thought it might be because he was so malnourished that his sperm count had sunk very low. It was no good going to a doctor, though the reactionary old GP had been replaced by a bright young woman who was always trying to put Michelle on a diet. No one really understood Matthew; only she could do that. She had to watch his body slacken and bend, his face wrinkle like an old man's, his joints protrude through the skin – you couldn't call it flesh – and that skin assume a greyish pallor. At thirty she had been plump, at thirty-five overweight. Now, at nearly forty-five, she was grossly fat. While she spoke often of his revulsion from food and they were always discussing what caused it and whether a cure would be discovered one day, he had never once mentioned her obesity. As far as he was concerned, she might still be the hour-glass girl of twenty-seven he'd fallen in love with.

She had a sister in Bedford and he a brother in Ireland and another in Hong Kong, but they had no friends. So geared is society to an eating and drinking together ethos, and eating was something they were obliged to avoid in public, that they were unable to keep friends or make new ones. One by one, people they knew drifted away when their invitations were refused and they were never themselves invited. Michelle's greatest dread had been that somehow they would be obliged to accept a summons to tea or supper and Matthew, confronted by butter or a jug of milk or pot of honey, would turn white and begin that dreadful dry retching. Better repulse people than risk it.

She had only one confidante. And that confidante

had become a friend. One day, nearing despair and terrified that he couldn't go on much longer, she had sat in her kitchen with Fiona, while Matthew worked slowly and feebly at his computer, and told her everything. And instead of laughing at a middle-aged man who couldn't eat and a middle-aged woman who couldn't stop eating, Fiona had sympathised, seemed to understand and even suggested remedies. She'd lived on such a varied diet, such novel and *sophisticated* food, she had all sorts of ideas for an anorexic who'd like to eat if only he could. A year later, which was last year, Michelle told her that she'd saved Matthew's life and they would both be eternally grateful.

When they got back from Waitrose to their house in Holmdale Road, West Hampstead, Michelle set about preparing Matthew's lunch. It was to include several of the foodstuffs Fiona had suggested and which Matthew found acceptable.

'Peanuts!' Fiona had said. 'Very nourishing, are peanuts.'

Matthew managed to utter the word, 'Greasy.'

'Not at all. Dry-roasted peanuts. Delicious. I love them.'

It would be an exaggeration to say that so did he. He loved no kind of food but he tolerated dry-roasted peanuts, as he tolerated her other suggestions, crispbread, things for children called Pop tarts, madeira cake, hard-boiled eggs chopped up with parsley, Parmesan cheese grated to a powder. Baby spinach leaves and roquette, Japanese rice crackers, muesli. Over that year his health improved a little, he was slightly less emaciated. Since then, though, the Pop tarts, which were the most calorific on the list, had fallen from favour. He couldn't help it. With all his heart he wanted to go on liking them but it was no good. Fiona recommended sponge fingers and shortbread instead.

Michelle put a lettuce leaf on his plate, twelve dry-roasted peanuts, a slice of hard-boiled egg with powdered Parmesan and a piece of Ryvita. She hoped, too, that he would drink the small wineglass-ful of pineapple juice but she wasn't banking on it. While she decorated his plate with these scraps, she ate peanuts herself and the rest of the egg and a hunk of olive bread with butter. Matthew smiled at her. It was his way of not looking at his plate, to turn his head away from it and smile at her as he thanked her.

'I just saw Jeff Leigh go by,' he said, picking up one peanut. 'Is he never going to get a job?'

Neither of them much cared for Fiona's boyfriend. 'I'd so much like to think he wasn't with her for her money,' said Michelle. 'I'd like to think he was disinterested, darling, but I don't. He expects her to keep him and that's the truth of it.'

'Fiona likes to be in control. I don't mean to criticise. To some it would be a compliment. She may want him to be dependent on her.'

'I hope you're right. I want her to be happy. They're getting married in June.'

Matthew ate another peanut and a fragment of Ryvita. Michelle had long ago mastered the art of not watching him. He sipped the juice. 'I'm afraid her friends won't think much of him if he does nothing and lets her keep him. He seems to have some skills. He's done a few useful jobs about the house for Fiona, putting in an electric point for one, and if you remember, he was something of a wizard on the computer when he came in here to write those letters or whatever it was he did.'

'Job applications, he said. That was in October,

nearly five months ago. I can't eat this lettuce, darling, or any more nuts. I've eaten the Ryvita.'

'You've done very well,' said Michelle, taking his plate away and bringing in a kiwi fruit, sliced, the core removed, and half a sponge finger.

Matthew ate two slices, then a third to please her, though he nearly choked on it. 'I'll do the dishes,' he said. 'You sit down. Put your feet up.'

So Michelle heaved her huge bulk on to one end of the sofa and put her slender legs and dainty feet, in which every delicate bone showed, up on the other end. She had the *Daily Telegraph* to read and Matthew's *Spectator*, but she felt more like just resting there and thinking. Six months ago Matthew wouldn't have had the strength to carry out the plates and glasses, stand at the sink and wash them. If he'd insisted on washing up he'd have had to sit on a stool to do it. The small improvement in his health and weight was due to Fiona. Michelle had come to care for Fiona, who was a real friend, almost like a daughter. Without envy and nearly without longing – for hadn't she her darling Matthew? – she could look at Fiona's slender figure, long, straight, blonde hair and sweet, if not classically good-looking face with nothing but admiration. Their houses were semi-detached but hers and Matthew's, though now considered a very valuable property more for where it was than for its design or convenience, was greatly inferior to Fiona's with its rear extension, large conservatory and loft conversion. Michelle had no envy about that either. She and Matthew had enough space for their wants and the value of their house had gone up by a dazzling five hundred per cent since they bought it seventeen years before. No, it was Fiona's future happiness that concerned her.

Jeff Leigh had first been seen in Holmdale Road in the previous August or September. Fiona introduced him to them as her boyfriend, but he didn't move in until October. He was handsome, Michelle had to acknowledge, healthy-looking, regular-featured, a little heavy for her taste. Thinking like that made her laugh. It seemed in the worst of taste to say she could only fancy *thin men*. Jeff had a sincere and almost earnest face. You could say that he looked as if he really cared about you, what you were saying and who you were; he was a truly concerned human being. This made Michelle think he didn't care a toss. And when he offered her one of his Polo mints, as he always did, he smiled to himself as she took it as if saying, aren't you fat enough? She loathed his jokes. Though he was out a great deal, he earned nothing, while Fiona, a successful banker, earned a lot and had inherited a sizeable sum when her father died last year.

Michelle wished she and Jeff would postpone their marriage for a while. After all, they were living together, it wasn't as if they were sexually frustrated – she recalled with tenderness how she and Matthew hadn't been able to wait more than twenty-four hours – so marriage surely wasn't imperative. Would she have the courage or the impertinence to suggest gently to Fiona that waiting a little might be a good idea?

It was comforting, Michelle thought before she drifted off into sleep, how the worst things that happen to one can sometimes lead to good. For instance, when Matthew had twice fainted in the classroom, when he had to sit down all the time in the science lab and could barely walk the distance to the Senior Staff Room, they had known he would have to resign. What would they live on? He was only thirty-eight. Apart from a little dabbling in journalism there was nothing he could do but teach.

She had long ago given up work to look after him, to occupy herself in the never-ending, nearly hopeless task of attending to his nourishment. Could she go back? After an absence of nine years? She'd never earned much.

Matthew had done some writing for *New Scientist* and an occasional piece for *The Times*. Now, because it was the most important thing in his life after her, he settled down to write, in his despair, what it meant to have his particular kind of anorexia. To hate food. To be made ill by that which was the staff of life. Eating disorders were becoming very fashionable at the time. His article was snapped up. It led to his being asked if he'd contribute to a prestigious weekly that came to be known as 'An Anorexic's Diary'. Matthew, the purist, objected at first and said the word should be "anorectic" but gave in because the money was so good. Michelle often thought how strange it was that though he could barely talk about certain foodstuffs he could write of them, describe his nausea and horror at particular kinds of fat and 'slop', define with a searching precision the items he could just bear to eat and why.

'An Anorexic's Diary' saved them selling the house and going on the benefit. It was immensely popular and inspired a lot of letter writing. Matthew got a huge postbag from middle-aged women who couldn't get off diets and starving teenagers and fat men who were addicted to beer and chips. It didn't make him famous – he and she wouldn't have liked that – but his name was once mentioned on a TV quiz show and was the answer to a crossword puzzle clue. All this afforded them a little quiet amusement. She hadn't liked it when Jeff Leigh clapped Matthew on the back and said insinuatingly, 'Wouldn't do for you to gain weight in your position, would it? Mind you keep the rations low, Michelle. I'm sure you can eat for two.'

That had hurt her because it was what you said to pregnant women. She thought of the child she'd never had, the daughter or son who would be sixteen or seventeen by now. Dream children she often dreamed of or saw before her closed eyes when she lay down. When Matthew came back into the room she was asleep.

Chapter 6

The knife wouldn't do. It was too big to carry about easily. Auntie had had quite a lot of knives, carvers and saws and choppers, which was funny because she'd never cooked much. Maybe they'd all been wedding presents. Minty went through them carefully and selected one which was eight inches long with a sharp point and a blade that was nearly two inches wide at the hilt.

She'd never really got rid of Auntie's stuff, apart from a few clothes she'd taken to the Geranium blind shop. They weren't as clean as they might have been and carrying them, even in a plastic sack, made her feel dirty all over. The rest she'd shut up in a cupboard and never opened again. She opened it now. It smelt awful. Just her luck when she was off to work, she'd have to have another bath before she went. The purse on a belt some people called a bum bag but Auntie wouldn't, it was too crude, hung by its strap over a hanger on which was a coat that smelt of mothballs. Minty resolved to have a real clean-up and clear-out that evening, take the stuff to Brent Council's old clothes bank and wash out the cupboard. The bum bag she brought delicately to her nose. One sniff was enough. She washed it in the bathroom basin, laid it to dry on the edge of the bath, then washed herself all over. When it was dry it would make a convenient holder for the knife.

As a result of all this she was a bit late for work,

very unusual for her. Josephine, all smiles, said nothing about her lateness but announced that she and Ken were getting married. He'd asked her over the wonton and prawn toast they'd had last night. Minty wondered what form the proposal had taken since Ken didn't speak any English.

'I'm starting my Cantonese conversation class next week,' said Josephine.

Minty accepted an invitation to the wedding. As she began the ironing she asked herself if she would ever meet another man who would want her as Jock had done. If it happened it mustn't be while Jock continued to haunt her. It wouldn't do to be out with a man in the pub or at the pictures and have Jock appear between them, or watching them. Besides, she'd promised him there would never be anyone else. She was his for ever and ever might be another fifty years. What did he want? Why had he returned? Because he was afraid she'd met a new man?

The shirts smelt of that indefinable clean scent she liked so much, newly washed linen. She savoured each one, bringing it to within an inch of her nose when she'd lifted it from the pile. Minty ironed the shirts not just as they happened to come, picking up the top one first, then the next one and so on, but choosing them according to colour. There were always more white ones than coloured, about twice as many, so she would do two white, then a pink, two more white, then a blue stripe. It upset her if the sequence went wrong and she found she had four or five white ones left at the end. This morning there were fewer whites than usual and she could see as she progressed that she was going to have the luck to make the ironing of a pink and yellow striped shirt her final task.

It was more than a week since she'd seen Jock and then, just when she thought he'd satisfied himself, found what he was looking for or simply got tired of the search, he'd appeared again. She'd gone to the pictures with Sonovia and Laf, one of the cinemas in Whiteley's, and seen *Sleepy Hollow*, a film people found frightening about a headless horseman, a ghost of course, that kept appearing in this town in America and chopping people's heads off.

'Never seen anything so ridiculous in all my life,' Sonovia said scornfully, passing her the popcorn. Laf had fallen asleep, snoring softly.

'It's scary,' Minty whispered, but more out of politeness than truth. Films weren't *real*.

But just as the tree split open again and the phantom horseman and his horse leapt out from its roots, Jock's ghost came into the cinema and sat down in the end seat of their row on the other side of the aisle. The way they were sitting, she two seats in from the end, Sonovia next to her and Laf next to Sonovia, meant she had an uninterrupted view of him. He'd sat down without looking at her but now, no doubt because he felt her eyes on him, he turned his head and fixed on her a dull expressionless gaze. She was wearing Auntie's silver cross on a ribbon round her neck and she put her hand up to it, clasping it tightly. This action, supposed to be a sure specific against visitants from another world, or so Auntie had said, had no effect on Jock. He stared at the screen. Minty touched Sonovia on the arm.

'D'you see that man at the end of the row?'

'What man?'

'On the other side, sitting at the end.'

'There's no one there, my deah. You're dreaming.'

It didn't altogether surprise her that he was invisible to others. Josephine hadn't been able to see him that time in the shop. What was he made of? Flesh and blood or shadows? She'd promised him that once she'd been with him she'd never go with anyone else. Was it possible he wanted to keep her to her vow and he'd come back to *take her away with him*? Minty began to tremble.

'Not cold, are you?' Sonovia whispered.

Minty shook her head.

'Must have been a cat walking over your grave.'

'Don't say that!' Minty spoke so loudly that a woman behind tapped her on the shoulder and told her to be quiet.

She was silent, shivering. Somewhere in this world was the place where her bones or her ashes would be buried. A cat, going about its nocturnal business, had trodden on that ground and passed on. Jock wanted to take her there, to that grave, and have her ghost with him wherever that was. She couldn't watch the film. Reality was more frightening. Jock had only been there ten minutes but he got up to leave. As he passed her he whispered, 'Polo,' and touched her on the shoulder.

She shrank back in her seat. His touch wasn't like a shadow or a breeze but real, a warm hand with a natural hand's pressure, heavy, possessive. 'Go away,' she said. 'Leave me alone.'

Sonovia turned and glared at her. Minty looked round, towards the exit, but Jock had gone.

After the film was over Laf and Sonovia took her for a drink in the Redan.

'What were you muttering about in the cinema?' Laf asked, grinning. 'Sitting there with your eyes shut, nattering away to yourself and making faces.'

'I was not.'

'Yes, you were, my deah. What's the point of going to the pictures if you keep your eyes shut?'

'I was scared. Everyone was scared.'

They denied it. But she couldn't talk about the film, neither able to agree with Laf who pretended to have enjoyed it nor with Sonovia who couldn't stop laughing over the frequency of the horseman's decapitations. Jock's ghost had distracted her entirely. It seemed that he had been threatening. She could still feel the pressure of his hand. He shouldn't take her with him, she didn't want to die, to be taken to some awful scary place inhabited by ghosts. She'd take steps to defend herself.

When she first saw him she wouldn't have believed a weapon would be effective against him, but the hard and heavy feel of his hand had convinced her that, ghost though he was, he was solid and unyielding. So she needed the knife and needed to carry it with her at all times. For who knew where he'd next turn up?

She finished the last shirt and slipped it into its cellophane bag, inserting a cardboard bow tie, spotted blue and white, under the collar. Josephine had popped down to the car hire place to make transport arrangements for her wedding and, when the doorbell rang, Minty thought it was Jock. It would be just like him to come today, the last time she'd ever be out without the knife. She picked up a pair of scissors from the shelf where they kept the stain remover and the spray starch. But it was only Ken, who pretended to be scared of the blades pointing at him and began clowning about with his hands up.

Josephine came back and the two of them started canoodling, kissing with their mouths open and all that. Funny, because Josephine had told her before she met Ken that the Chinese never kissed, they didn't know how to. Maybe she'd taught him. Minty quite liked them, but their going on like that made her want to stab them with the scissors. She felt left out, isolated, shut into a world of her own, inhabited only by herself and Jock's ghost. Like someone sleepwalking, she trailed into the back room and sat down on a stool, staring at the wall and turning the scissors over and over in her hands.

Jock had always had a pack of Polo mints in his pocket. That was why he'd called her Polo, she thought. He'd passed them to her when they were at the cinema and she'd liked them, they were a *clean* sort of sweet, they didn't come off on your hands. Pinch, punch, first of the month, she remembered, no returns. Just walk on by, wait on the corner . . .

She'd brought her lunch in with her, sandwiches of grated cheese and lettuce, a small plain yogurt. You never knew what went into the flavoured kind. When she'd eaten it she wrapped the remains in newspaper, then a plastic carrier and put the lot in Josephine's rubbish bin in the backyard. Even touching it made a more than usually thorough wash necessary. She scrubbed her nails with a brush, left her hands soaking in clean, soapless water for five minutes afterwards. When they came out and were dried the fingers were pallid and wrinkled, which Auntie had used to call washerwoman's hands. Minty rather liked them that way, it meant they were really clean.

It was one of those afternoons that passed uneventfully. A man came in with his seven shirts. He always did, once a week. Josephine asked him once if he hadn't a wife or a girlfriend to bring them in for him, not to mention washing or ironing them. Josephine hadn't put it that way but she *did* mention it and the man hadn't liked it one bit. Minty thought he might not come back but take his shirts to the place down Western Avenue. As it was, he took a fortnight before reappearing and Josephine was especially nice to him, remembering how tactless she'd been.

After that there was no one until a teenager came just as they were closing and wanted to know if she could pay by instalment for having her dress cleaned. It was a short red dress with bootlace shoulder straps and hardly any skirt, and Minty thought it would have washed. *She'd* have washed it. Josephine said, 'Certainly not,' and the poor kid had to take the dress away again.

Minty walked home. She had an uneasy feeling Jock would be on the bus. He'd never yet appeared in the open air. Old Mr Kroot was in his front garden, sweeping the path. He pretended not to see her. Maybe he hadn't been the one who had sent that condolence card but the home help without him knowing. She could tell he knew she was there. Something in the way he stiffened told her that, and the way his wrinkled old hands with tree-root veins tightened on the broom handle. When she was a child he'd been quite friendly and then, one day, while his sister was staying with him, she and Auntie had had a row. It was about the washing line or the fence between the gardens or maybe Mr Kroot's cat peeing up against the bushes, something like that but Minty couldn't remember what. Mr Kroot's sister and Mr Kroot had never spoken to Auntie again and Auntie had never spoken to them. So they'd never spoken to Minty again either.

The sister wasn't there at the moment. She lived somewhere else, a long way from London. Mr Kroot was all alone with his cat, which didn't have a name. He just called it Cat. He turned and looked through her as if she were a ghost like Jock. Then he went into the house with his broom, shutting the door much harder than he normally would have. The cat came up to the door just as he'd closed it. It was so old that Minty could hardly remember a time when it wasn't there, it must be at least twenty by now, and if you multiplied that by seven, which was what Auntie said you had to do if you wanted to work out a cat's real age, it must be a hundred and forty.

As Minty unlocked her front door and went into the house, the cat began a deep-throated senile yowling to be let in. She half thought Jock might be in the hall, waiting for her, but there was no one and nothing there.

Would a knife have any effect on a ghost? What were ghosts made of? Minty devoted quite a lot of thought to this. Before she saw one, before one *touched* her, she believed them composed of shadows and smoke, vapour and some cloud-like intangible substance. Jock's hand had been firm, exerting a strong pressure, and the seat of the chair he sat on had been warm to her touch. Was he the same person he'd been when he was on the earth? A thing of flesh and blood, not like a black-and-white photograph, a greyish moving image, but brown-haired, pink-skinned, his eyes that same dark blue? Blood – would he bleed?

She would try it. If it failed to work she'd have lost nothing. She'd just have to try some other way. Imagining it as she ran her second bath of the day, she saw the knife go into the ghost body and the ghost dissolve, disappear in a wisp of smoke or melt into a clear pool like water. There would be no sound, no cry or gasp, only a vanishing, an acknowledgement of being beaten, of her victory.

Thinking of it like this almost made her want to see him. She had her bath, using the big golden sponge that had once had a life of its own, attached to some rock in the sea. When she was done she washed it out in hot water, then cold. One day Jock had asked if they could have a bath together, the two of them get into the water at the same time. She'd said no, she'd been shocked at the suggestion. It wasn't what grown-up people did, it was for little kids. Besides, if she'd shared a bathful of water with him she'd only have had to take another bath on her own afterwards. He never seemed to think of that.

For a moment, naked, she half wanted to see him. She opened the bathroom door, stepped outside, crossed to her bedroom. He was nowhere. In the clean clothes she'd wear for the evening, an evening of a hygienic meal, an hour of television, two hours of cleaning up, she went downstairs into the dark hall. The ghost came in darkness or in light, nothing seemed to make a difference to that. She felt it with her, all around her, though she couldn't see it. As she was peeling her two potatoes and carving her home-cooked cold chicken, his voice came singing, like music heard from a long distance away: *Today I started loving you again* . . .

Chapter 7

Once she had said yes, Zillah thought she and the kids would move in with Jims and arrangements would be made for the wedding to take place later, say six months later. Jims had different ideas about that. The proprieties must be observed. The Chairman of the South Wessex Conservative Association had said only last week, apropos of some local pop singer, his girlfriend and their baby, that couples living together outside marriage should be banned from owning property and have their passports and driving licences withdrawn. Jims could think of no surer way of losing his seat at the next election than by letting Zillah move in with him. Besides, he'd engaged the services of a PR company and the woman acting for him was doing her best to get photographs of Zillah and himself into national newspapers. That slum in Long Fredington would be an unsuitable background and his duplex in Great College Street an improper one. He took a three-month lease on a flat in a purpose-built block in Battersea with a view of the river and the Houses of Parliament from the front windows. Jims, who knew about these things, said this struck just the right note. It was more *serious* than Knightsbridge and less raffish than Chelsea, it was dowdy but solid, besides having a suitably political air. As to her possessions and property in Willow Cottage, he recommended she set fire to the lot, then revised this advice, remembering the owner of the house, his old pal Sir Ronald Grasmere.

Much as she'd have liked to tell Jims she was now a widow, Zillah didn't quite dare do this. The first thing he'd have wanted to know was when did she hear of Jerry's death and why hadn't she told him before. So she plucked up the courage needed to tell him a lie he wouldn't much like but would mind less than the truth. 'I wasn't actually ever really married to Jerry.'

'What d'you mean, darling, "really" married? Did you have one of those funny affairs on the beach in Bali like Mick Jagger?'

'I mean we weren't married at all.'

He accepted it. The South Wessex Conservative Association Chairman would very likely never find out. Zillah had a few qualms when she remembered her wedding to Jerry in St Augustine's Church, Kilburn Park – but not many and not for long. The PR woman, Malina Daz, was told Zillah was single but had lived for several years in a 'stable relationship' with the children's father. Wisely, she decided to say nothing to the newspapers about Zillah's marital or non-marital status and not to mention the children, counting on Jims's relatively low notoriety quotient to make it unlikely questions would be asked. She was counting also on Zillah's beauty to solve everything. Zillah looked ravishing when the photographer arrived and she had dressed herself in her new Amanda Wakeley cream silk trouser suit with the Georgina von Etzdorf scarf knotted at her throat. Handsome Jims leant negligently over the back of her chair, his perfectly manicured hand lightly caressing her long black hair.

But when Malina changed her mind about Jims's fame and suggested they might describe Eugenie and Jordan as her niece and nephew, children of her sister tragically killed in a car crash, Zillah drew the line. So, rather surprisingly, did Jims. Malina must remember, he said, that he wasn't all that well known, he wasn't a *celebrity*.

'Temporarily,' said Malina briskly.

'If I get a post,' Jims said, dropping his voice, 'it will of course be rather different.'

All this was making Zillah nervous. 'My children won't go away.'

'No, darling, and we don't want them to.'

'It might be wise', said Malina, 'not to give any interviews to the print media for a year. Could we have your first husband tragically killed in a car crash?' Reluctantly she was forced to relinquish this favourite scenario. 'Well, no, maybe not. But by then', she added coyly, 'another wee one may be on the way.'

Zillah thought the chances of another wee one slender in the extreme. She had no experience of interviews or journalists but was already frightened of them. Still, she had long ago cultivated the art of banishing unpleasant thoughts from her mind. It was the only form of defence she knew. So every time a picture of Jims as Shadow Minister of State at the Home Office or Under-Secretary for Health came into her head and she had a vision of a reporter appearing on her doorstep, she thrust it away. And whenever a voice whispered in her mind's ear, 'Tell me something about your previous marriage, Mrs Melcombe-Smith,' she plugged it up. After all, she *knew* Jerry wouldn't reappear. What surer way could there be of making plain your intention to disappear than by announcing your death?

Jims bought her an engagement ring, three large emeralds mounted on a square cushion of diamonds. He'd already given her a Visa card in the name of Z. H. Leach and now gave her an American Express platinum card for Mrs J. I. Melcombe-Smith and told her to buy any clothes she liked. Wearing her new Caroline Charles green suit with the bead-encrusted bodice, she dined with Jims in the Churchill Room at the Palace of Westminster and was introduced to the Leader of the Conservative Party in the Commons. Seven years ago Zillah would have described herself as a Communist and she didn't know if she really was a Conservative.

'You are now, darling,' said Jims.

After dinner he took her into Westminster Hall and down into the Chapel of St Mary Undercroft. Even Zillah, who took very little notice of such things, had to admit that Sir Charles Barry's stonework was impressive and the lavish fittings magnificent. Obediently, she looked at the bosses showing St Catherine martyred on her wheel and St John the Evangelist boiling in oil, though she was squeamish about such things and St Lawrence being grilled made her feel a bit sick. She'd take care not to look up during the marriage ceremony. Against all this rich and brilliant colour, she decided, an ivory wedding dress would be most effective. Because she'd fixed on the single-woman option, she was determined to push aside the memory of her marriage and was almost reconciled to a church ceremony.

It was a pity the children couldn't be there. She rather fancied Eugenie as bridesmaid and Jordan as page. They'd have looked so chic in black velvet with white lace collars. Apart from these frivolous considerations, she was seriously concerned about her children. Their existence was one of those not exactly unpleasant, more disturbing, facts she couldn't banish, though she tried. That is, she tried not to think about them except as the two people she was closest to in the world, possibly the only people she loved, for her affection for Jims hardly came into that category. But the circumstances were too awkward to allow her to forget the troublesome aspects. For one thing, they constantly asked when they were going to see Jerry again. Jordan had a disconcerting habit of declaiming loudly out in the street or, worse, when Jims brought an MP friend to call, 'Oh, I do want to see my daddy!'

Eugenie, though less emotional, always spoke more to the point. 'My father hasn't been to see us for months,' or, quoting the babysitter Zillah now employed almost daily, 'Mrs Peacock says my father is an absentee dad.'

The last address Zillah had for him was in Harvist Road, NW10. Sometimes she got out the piece of paper on which he'd written it down and just stared at it, thinking. There was no phone number. At last she phoned Directory Enquiries. Without a name they couldn't or wouldn't help her. One afternoon, leaving Mrs Peacock with the children, she went up to Harvist Road on a Bakerloo Line train to Queen's Park. The place reminded her of her student days when she and Jerry had shared a room in a house near the station. They'd been very happy for a while. Then she got pregnant and they married, but things were never the same.

'Needles and pins, needles and pins,' said Jerry, quoting his old granny, 'when a man marries his trouble begins.' They were on their two-day honeymoon in Brighton. Then he said, 'I quite like being married. I may do it a few times more.'

She smacked his face for that but he only laughed. Now she was looking for him to find out if he was willing to stay dead. His name wasn't on a bell at the street number he'd given her. When she banged the lion head knocker an elderly woman came to the door and said, 'I'm not interested in double glazing,' before she'd even spoken.

'And I'm not selling it. I'm looking for Jerry Leach. He used to live here.'

'He called himself Johnny, not Jerry, and he doesn't live here now. Hasn't since last year. Months and months. The answer to your next question is no, I don't know where he's gone.'

The door was shut in her face. She walked across the road and sat down on a seat in Queen's Park, gazing at the green expanse. A black girl and a white girl, walking past, looked curiously at her short-skirted linen suit and high heels, put their heads together and giggled. Zillah ignored them. It was evident that Jerry didn't want his whereabouts known. She must make up her mind he'd gone for ever. What would he think when he saw her and Jims's photograph in the paper? Perhaps he didn't read them. But he'd be bound to find out sooner or later. If this thing Jims called a reshuffle took place, before the wedding. Because by then Jims might be a Minister and on account of his youth and good looks and *her* youth and good looks, a target for the media. Jerry was a rotten provider and generally hopeless with money, and unfaithful and callous, but not wholly bad. He was the last man to try and rubbish her chances. If he saw she'd made a good marriage and done well for herself he'd most likely laugh and say, 'Good luck, girl, I won't stand in your way.' Besides, he'd be relieved she wouldn't any longer nag him for child support. Not that he'd ever given her any, there being no blood in a stone.

That silly joke of his kept running through her head. She hadn't thought of it for years until Eugenie came out with it the other day. Adam and Eve and Pinch Me went down to the river to bathe. Adam and Eve were drownded. Who was saved? Perhaps he actually *was* dead. But no. She reminded herself that whatever she pretended or told Jims, Jerry was her legally wedded husband. She'd have been the first to be officially informed. He was her husband and she was his wife. Uneasily, she remembered that for some reason, now forgotten, Jerry had required and got the old form of marriage service from the *Book of Common Prayer*. There had been a bit about whom God had joined together let no man put asunder, and keeping only unto him as long as they both lived. Moreover, she was going to have to go through all that again at St Mary Undercroft where she didn't exactly know but could guess that they'd have the same old service. And the vicar (or whatever. The canon?) would say those awful words about answering as they would at the dreadful day of judgement that no just cause or impediment stood in the way of their getting married. Zillah didn't really believe in the dreadful day of judgement but the sound of it struck superstitious terror into her just the same. Jerry, wherever he was, was six feet and thirteen stone of just cause and impediment. Why did she always have to marry men who wanted their weddings to be in church?

After a while she got up and wandered back to the tube station. The trouble with thrusting unpleasant thoughts from your mind is that the thrusting can never be absolute and each time they come back it seems to be with redoubled threat. There were her parents to worry about too. She hadn't yet told them Jerry was dead. Nor had she informed them that the official version of their relationship was that they'd never been married at all. Ostensibly, they'd be giving the wedding reception. Jims, of course, would be paying. She wondered how she was going to stop her mother telling the Leader of the Opposition, not to mention Lord Strathclyde, how she used to take little Zillah with her when she went making beds and washing dishes up at the big house and the five-year-old was sometimes allowed to play with seven-year-old James.

The train came. The carriage she got into was full of yardies from Harlesden drinking lager out of cans, reminding her of the world she'd soon be leaving behind for ever. At Kilburn Park she moved carriages and went on to Oxford Circus. The best remedy she knew for nerves and depression was shopping, a taste she'd never till now been able to indulge. It was amazing how quickly she'd taken to it and how much she enjoyed it. Already, after only a few weeks, she knew the names of all the designers, was beginning to get a good idea of what their clothes looked like and how one differed from another. If only academic subjects were so easily learnt she might have got herself some qualifications by this time. Married to Jims she wouldn't need them.

Emerging from Browns some hour and a half later, laden with bags, she felt enormously happy and carefree, wondering why she'd been down in the dumps earlier. She took a taxi back to Battersea. The children were having tea, the table presided over by the babysitter.

'Mrs Peacock says you're going to marry Jims,' said Eugenie, 'but I said you can't because you're married to Daddy.'

'My mistake, Mrs Leach, I thought they knew.'

'Mummy marry Daddy,' said Jordan. 'Marry him tomorrow.' He picked up his plate and banged it on the table, overturning a mug of orange juice in the process, which set him off screaming, 'Jordan wants Daddy! Wants him now!'

Zillah fetched a cloth and began mopping up the mess while Mrs Peacock sat tight, her eyes travelling from Zillah to the Browns and Liberty bags and back again. 'Is there any tea left in the pot, Mrs Peacock?'

'It'll be cold by now.'

Chapter 8

This would be the first wedding Minty had ever been to. She was never beset by the ordinary woman's anxieties, so she worried not at all about what to wear and whether she ought to buy a hat. If Jock hadn't stolen her savings she'd have bought Josephine and Ken a present but now she had only her wages with nothing left over for luxuries, which included gifts. Would he have paid her back if he'd lived? Was he returning, his ghost appearing the way it did, not to take her away with him but because he wanted to pay his debt?

She hadn't seen him again since that night in the cinema, but she'd brooded about the things Sonovia and Laf had said. The cat walking on her grave. She couldn't help thinking about it, her burial ground maybe up in that huge, awful cemetery in the far north of London where Auntie'd once taken her to her sister Edna's funeral. It wouldn't be like Auntie's resting place, nice and cosy under the big dark trees and near to her home, only just the other side of the high wall, but one of a bleak row of white tombstones, each indistinguishable from the rest, her name that had been engraved upon it obliterated by the wind and rain. But would it be engraved on it? Who would do that for her? There was no one now Auntie was gone and Jock was gone.

She dreamed of the grave. She was lying in it under the earth but not in a box. They couldn't afford the cost of a coffin. She lay under the cold wet earth, the worst place she'd ever been in, and she was coated all over with dirt, on her skin, in her hair, in her fingernails. Mr Kroot's old cat came and scratched the earth, scraping with its paws the way they do. She saw it above her, looking down through the hole it had dug, its grey muzzle all bared teeth, and angry flashing eyes and shaking whiskers. Then it scraped back all the earth into her mouth and nose, and she awoke fighting for breath. After that dream she had to get up and have a bath, though it was the middle of the night.

What Laf had said about her muttering and her eyes being shut and Josephine saying talking to yourself was the first sign of insanity, she hadn't liked that either. She hadn't been muttering, she never did, and she'd had her eyes shut because she was scared. They'd been laughing at her all the time they were in that pub. Next time she wanted to see a film, she'd decided, she'd go on her own. Why not? She used to go on her own and she could again. She'd buy herself a packet of Polo mints. Or a banana because *he* didn't like them – but no, not that, she'd have to dispose of the outside of it somewhere.

In the bus on the way back, a man came and sat next to her. She wouldn't look round because she was sure it was Jock's ghost and she could hear a voice whispering, 'Polo, Polo.' But when she edged her head very cautiously and slowly towards the right, an inch at a time, she saw it was someone quite different, an old man with white hair. Jock must have sneaked off when she wasn't looking and made this old man sit there.

People didn't often go to the three-thirty showing. The multiplex cinema was always nearly empty then. Immacue closed at one on a Saturday, so in the afternoon Minty went to see *The Talented Mr Ripley*.

She bought one ticket and was told which theatre to go in. There were only two other people there and she had the whole row to herself. Jock didn't appear. She hadn't seen him for a week, for you couldn't count that meeting on the bus. It was nice being alone, you didn't have to keep saying thank you when someone passed you the popcorn or a chocolate, or have the person behind you telling you to shut up.

The evenings were getting light now. She could buy flowers for Auntie from the man at the cemetery gate and walk down to the grave in sunshine. There was no one about. It had rained so much lately that the vase was brimming over, though the flowers in it were dead. Minty threw them away under a holly bush and put her daffodils into the water. Then she took two tissues from her bag, laid them on the slab and knelt down on them, holding the silver cross between her forefinger and middle finger. Her eyes tight shut, she prayed to Auntie to make Jock go away for ever.

Sonovia was at her front gate saying goodbye to Daniel who'd come in for a cup of tea. Minty hadn't seen him for months, not since she got the letter saying Jock had been killed.

'How are you today, Minty?' he said in his busy doctor's voice, all breezy and bedside manner. 'Feeling a bit better?'

'I'm all right,' she said.

'Been somewhere exciting?' Sonovia asked it in the sort of tone that implies a person only does dull things, a tone with laughter somewhere underneath it. Minty didn't answer. She was aware of the bum bag with the knife in it sliding round under her clothes. 'You want a lend of my blue dress and jacket for Josephine's wedding?'

How could she say no? She couldn't think of a way, but stood there nodding, feeling awkward. Daniel went off to his car that he could park anywhere because it had a doctor sticker in its window. Minty wanted to go home, have a good wash, check Jock wasn't in the house and shut all the doors. Instead she had to go into Sonovia's, have a look in her clothes cupboard and choose the blue dress and jacket, whether that was what she wanted or not, because it was the only thing to fit her.

'I haven't been able to get into it since I put on weight,' Sonovia said.

Minty tried it on. There wasn't a choice. She hated Sonovia seeing her bare skin, so pallid and soap-smelling, and staring at the bum bag, hanging round her thin waist. The dress was a bit big but it would do. She shuddered so much as she pulled it over her head – how did she know how many times it had been worn and whether it had ever been cleaned? – that Sonovia asked that regular question of hers: was she cold?

'You look ever so nice. You really suit it. You ought to wear blue more often.'

Minty studied herself in the mirror, trying to forget about the dress being dirty. It was a full-length mirror that Sonovia called a pier glass. Behind her, opening the door and walking into the room, she saw Jock's ghost reflected. He laid his hand on the back of her neck and bending his head, pressed his face against her hair. She lashed out at the thing behind her. 'Go away!'

'What, me?' asked Sonovia.

Minty didn't answer. She shook her head.

Sonovia said, 'Where were you this afternoon, Minty?'

'I went to see a film.'

'What, all on your lonesome?'

'Why not? I like being alone sometimes.' Minty pulled off the dress. Jock had disappeared. She handed it to Sonovia like a woman buying a garment in a shop.

Sonovia said in a voice Minty didn't care for, dry and tolerant, like someone talking to a naughty child, 'I'll put it in a bag for you.'

Downstairs again, Minty refused the proffered cup of tea and the alternative, a gin and tonic. 'I've got to get home.'

Mr Kroot was in his front garden and his sister was with him. She had a suitcase, it looked as if she'd just arrived. She wasn't called Kroot but something else, she'd married someone about a hundred years ago. Minty didn't look at them. She let herself into her house. The dress and jacket smelt of something. Stale scent mainly. There was a spot of grease on the jacket hem, a splash of fat maybe. She shuddered, glad Sonovia wasn't there to ask if she was cold. All the pleasure she'd taken in the film had gone, driven away by what had happened since. She felt vulnerable, endangered. Going upstairs, she touched wood all the way, the banister bars which were cream-coloured, the rail which was brown, the skirting board at the top which was pale pink. Auntie had liked variety in house decoration and Minty was thankful for it. What would have become of her if all the woodwork had been white like in Sonovia's place?

She ran a bath and got into the water holding the knife, she didn't know why. Except that lying in the water with the knife in her hands, she felt safer than she did anywhere else. Jock's ghost had never come into the bathroom and it didn't come in now. She washed her hair and lay in the water until it began to grow cool. She wrapped a towel round her body and another round her head while she dried the knife. Now there were three towels instead of two for the wash but she accepted that, all in the good cause of being spotless. Clean cotton trousers went on and a clean T-shirt. Before handling the contents of Sonovia's bag, she put on a pair of Auntie's black cotton gloves but she still held dress and jacket at arm's length. She'd take them to Immacue on Monday and dry-clean them herself, put them through the luxury valet service. Leaving the dress in the spare room, well away from anywhere she might be, she took off the gloves and washed her hands.

It was the purest chance that Sonovia went into Immacue. Usually she took any clothes she and Laf needed cleaning to the place in Western Avenue but he hadn't been very pleased with the job they'd done on his dinner jacket, and for her part she'd not been amused by the crack the manager had made about the policeman's ball.

Now he wanted his grey flannels and houndstooth check sports jacket cleaned. 'Take them round to Minty's place, why don't you? Give it a go.'

At Immacue, clothes ready for collection were hung on a coat rack. The rack stood on the left-hand side of the shop and extended from behind the counter to the rear wall. When Sonovia entered there was no one about, so she waited a while, letting her gaze rove from the various aids to cleanliness on sale on the counter to the stacked shirts on the shelves on the right to the coat rack on the left. She was about to give a discreet cough when she spotted the garment hanging at the very front of the rack. It was on a hanger with a styrofoam collar and sheathed in transparent plastic but still she had no difficulty in recognising her own blue dress and jacket. Angrily,

Sonovia slammed her hand on the bell on the counter.

Josephine came out. 'Sorry to keep you,' she said. 'How may I help you?'

'By fetching Miss Knox, that's how. I've got a bone to pick with her.'

Josephine shrugged. She went to the door at the back and called, 'Minty!'

Sonovia was growing crosser by the second. When Minty came out she was standing there fuming, with her arms folded. 'I'd just like to know who you think you are, Miss Araminta Knox, to be so fastidious. Borrowing a person's clothes and then deciding they're not clean enough for you. I suppose you had one of your famous baths after you'd tried them on. I'm surprised you'd keep them in the house, or did you put them out in the garden over Sunday?'

Minty didn't say anything. She hadn't thought of that, putting Sonovia's dress out in the garden. It would have been a good idea. She advanced towards the coat rack and peered at the clothes through their plastic sheath.

'I call it a disgrace, considering how long we've known each other. The times you've enjoyed our hospitality! That you'd think I'd keep dirty clothes in my wardrobe, that's what I can't get over. Laf says I spend more on dry-cleaning than I do on food.'

'You don't spend it in here,' said Josephine.

'I'll thank you to keep out of this, Miss O'Sullivan. As for you, Minty, Laf and me were going to treat you to *American Beauty* tomorrow night and drinks after, no doubt, but we've changed our mind; we'll be going on our own. Him and me might not be clean enough for you to sit next to.'

Sonovia, flouncing out, forgot to take her dress and jacket with her. Josephine looked at Minty and

Minty looked at her, and Josephine burst out laughing. Minty couldn't quite do that. But she was glad she could keep the dress. Sonovia might never want it back now and that meant she'd always have something to put on in case anyone else ever asked her to a wedding. She went back to her ironing.

Someone had once given Auntie a boxed set of stereo LPs of something called *Porgy and Bess*. Minty couldn't remember why, a birthday maybe, but Auntie hadn't anything to play them on even if she'd wanted to, so the records were as good as new. If Minty had been on speaking terms with Sonovia and Laf she could have asked their advice, they had a thing that played CDs, but she wasn't, so that was out. In the end, she bought wrapping paper with wedding cakes and silver bells printed on it at the paper shop next to Immacue, wrapped up the LPs and took them with her to Josephine's wedding.

The dry-cleaners didn't open that Saturday morning. They put a notice in the window that said: *Closed for Wedding of Proprietor*. The marriage ceremony in the Oecumenical Church of Universal God the Mother, Harlesden High Street, was followed by a reception at the restaurant where Ken cooked, the Lotus Dragon. It was all very enjoyable with dancing and tambourine-playing in the church and a four-woman rock band, while a smiling green dragon, operated on the principle of a pantomime horse, cavorted in when lunch was in progress and made a speech in Cantonese. Minty had quite a good time, at least at the start. She'd hoped to secrete the bum bag with the knife in it under Sonovia's blue dress, but the outline of it showed through and it looked funny. For some reason she expected Jock's ghost to turn up. Once she'd seen the empty chair next to hers she was sure of it.

'Why's there no one sitting there?' she asked Josephine's best friend from Willesden.

The best friend said Josephine's mother was supposed to be coming over from Connemara but she'd had a fall yesterday and broken her ankle.

'They oughtn't to leave that chair there,' said Minty but nobody took any notice.

Josephine said the empty chair reminded her of absent friends. She looked quite nice if a bit flashy in a scarlet chiffon salwar kameez and a big black ostrich feather hat. Ken wore a grey morning coat and topper. There were red lilies all the way down the table and green dragons on the napkins.

They ate prawn toast and spring rolls, followed by Peking Duck. Even Minty ate it, she had to. During a long argument as to why not 'Beijing Duck' between the best friend from Willesden and Ken's brother, who could speak quite good English, Jock's ghost came in and sat in the chair next to Minty. He was dressed as she'd sometimes wanted him to be but had never seen him, in a dark suit, white shirt and blue tie with white spots.

'Sorry I'm late, Polo,' he said.

'Go away.'

He never answered her. He just started laughing, as if he were a real living person. She wouldn't look at him but she heard him whispering, 'I went into the garden and met a great she-bear ...'

Someone a long way down the table was taking photographs. While the flash blinded them, she picked up from the table the knife you were supposed to use if you couldn't handle chopsticks. Holding it down by her side and between them, she thrust it upwards into his thigh through the suit trousers. She expected blood, ghost blood that might be red like living people's or might not, but there was none. Instead of vanishing speedily, he seemed to blur like a reflection shuddering when the water surface is disturbed, then to melt and trickle away. The chair beside her was empty once more.

So it worked. Even a blunt knife got rid of him. But would it be for ever? She laid the knife back on the table. It was quite unmarked as if it had passed through no more than air. People were looking oddly at her. She managed a bright smile for the cameras. Dozens of them seemed to have appeared, flashing and snapping. Would the ghost show on the photographs? If it did, filling the empty chair, they were sure to put it in the Sunday papers.

Ken's brother made a speech, and so did Josephine's sister. More and more drink came out. Minty thought it was time to leave, though no one else did. She'd seen a sign saying Ladies, so she followed the arrow, passed through a room where all the wedding presents were laid out on a table, though she couldn't see hers, and escaped by the back door into a dirty yard. It took her quite a long time to find her way back into the Harrow Road and by the time she did she was shivering, frightened of running into Jock's ghost.

Just as Laf and Sonovia had for years put their *Mail* through her letter box when they'd done with it, so Laf regularly popped round with the *Evening Standard*, the *Mail on Sunday* and the *Sunday Mirror*. Only he hadn't for the past two Sundays and Minty didn't expect he would this week.

Next door the Wilsons were arguing hotly over just this question. Both still in dressing gowns, lingering over a protracted breakfast of bagels, Danish pastries and coffee, they failed to see eye to eye as to continuing their quarrel with Minty, or 'sending her to Coventry', as Sonovia called it.

'I don't want you taking those papers in there this morning, my deah, and that's that. I want them for

Corinne. She's stopped taking a Sunday paper and I'm sure your own daughter's got more right than the woman next door.'

'And for another,' said Laf, 'you want to keep up this row you're having, though God knows why you do, with a poor girl who's daft as a brush and doesn't know whether she's coming or going.'

'I like "girl", I really do. Minty Knox is a mere nine years younger than I am, as you surely should know. As for "daft", she knows how to borrow a person's clothes and accuse her of keeping a dirty home. And I'll tell you something else, she's enough sense to wear a money belt under her clothes. I saw it when she tried my dress on, a bag on a belt round her waist.'

'Well, good luck to her. It's a pity more women don't in a neighbourhood like this. There wouldn't be so many handbags snatched and muggings and all. As soon as I've got my things on I'm going to take that page you want for Corinne out of the paper and pop the rest round to Minty. Bury the hatchet, that's what I say.'

'If you do that, Sergeant Lafcadio Wilson, you can find someone else to cook your roast pork for Sunday lunch. I shall take myself round to Daniel and Lauren and my dear little granddaughter. So you've been warned.'

The more she thought about it the more Minty wanted to see the *Mail* and the *Mirror*. No one would take all those photographs if they didn't mean to get them in the papers and one of them might have Jock in it, *must* have, even if in shadowy or transparent form. It would be proof to show people, she thought vaguely, people like those Wilsons and maybe Josephine. When she'd stuck the knife into Jock she'd seen Josephine looking at her under that big black hat as if she were mad, an awful stare with her lip curled up.

When it got to half past midday and Laf still hadn't come, Minty washed her hands, put her coat on and went round to the paper shop, the one opposite the cemetery gates. There she bought three Sunday papers. Going home, she passed Laf's and Sonovia's gate and smelt the rich, savoury aroma of roasting pork, inviting for others but enough to make Minty shudder. She dragged her thoughts away from the bubbling fat, the spitting crackling and the browning potatoes – you could never get a roasting pan really clean – went indoors and washed her hands. Maybe she'd have another bath in a minute.

That the papers contained no pictures of Josephine's wedding, not only none of Jock taking his seat in the empty chair but none at all, was a bitter disappointment. Minty had to content herself with front-page photographs (and more inside) of someone called James Melcombe-Smith MP to a Ms Zillah Leach. The bit of print underneath said,

James Melcombe-Smith (30), Conservative Member for South Wessex, marries his childhood sweetheart Zillah Leach (27) at the chapel of St Mary Undercroft in the Palace of Westminster. A likely candidate for promotion when the Party Leader reshuffles the Shadow Cabinet, Mr Melcombe-Smith and his bride will defer their honeymoon in the Maldives until the House of Commons gets up for Easter on 20 April.

Minty wasn't very interested in any of that but she admired the bride's looks, considering her far prettier and better-dressed in her ivory slipper satin with cream and crimson orchids than Josephine in that ugly bright red. Josephine's glare and curling lip still rankled, and Minty felt resentful. She turned to the inside page but it only showed this Melcombe-Smith person walking about in the country with a gun and the bride grinning like mad in a dirty old sweater with her hair all over the place, under a completely incomprehensible heading: OUTING? WHO HAS THE LAST LAUGH NOW?

The trouble with some newspapers was that the ink came off all over your hands. Minty went upstairs and had a bath. Jock's ghost would be back. If not today, tomorrow and if not tomorrow, next week. Because she hadn't killed it. That dinner knife was a hopeless weapon. It simply made a ghost slip away for a while, escape, like any live person would when a weapon was waved at it. Next time she must be ready with one of the long, sharp knives, if she wanted to be rid of him for ever.

Chapter 9

A production company had asked Matthew to go on a programme they were making for BBC2 Television. It was to be called *Living on Air* or something like that and he was to be – well – the star, really. That is, he was to talk to people with problems similar to his own, interview them and point up the differences between disparate attitudes to food. They'd make a pilot and if that was a success it might lead to a series. Michelle was delighted. Matthew was so much better-looking since he'd been on Fiona's regime and he had such a beautiful speaking voice.

'It always reminds me of that newscaster,' said Fiona. 'What's he called? Peter Sissons.'

'They must have picked him because he sounds so nice,' said Michelle.

Fiona doubted that. They'd obviously picked him because of his column and because he looked like one of those men you saw pictures of who'd been in Japanese prisoner of war camps. But she didn't say so. The two women were in Fiona's conservatory, drinking chilled Chardonnay, while Matthew was at his computer, writing this week's 'An Anorexic's Diary'. It was the prettier sort of conservatory, a white, curlicued crystal palace, with white cane furniture, blue cushions, a cane and glass table and a great many little bonsai trees and tall ferns and spider plants in blue ceramic pots. Beyond the glass could be seen Fiona's small walled garden in which spring flowers bloomed and a fountain played.

'Jeff will be home in a minute,' said Fiona, for all the world as if her boyfriend had a job and commuted like the neighbours. Then she went on, embarrassing Michelle, 'You don't like him, do you?'

'I don't really know him, Fiona.' Michelle was finding this very awkward, but asked so directly she had to speak out. 'I admit I have wondered – and Matthew's wondered – if you're not being . . . well, a bit precipitate, marrying someone you've only known for a few months.'

Fiona didn't seem put out. 'I know that this is the man I'm certain I want to spend the rest of my life with. Please try to like him.'

He lives off you, he's rude, he's insincere and cruel, thought Michelle. *He's a liar.* These feelings must have shown in her face, though she expressed none of them aloud, for Fiona had begun to look distressed. 'When you know him better you'll think differently, I know you will.'

'All right, my dear, I admit I don't much care for him. No doubt it's as much my fault as his. Since he's going to be your husband, I'll try to get on better with him.'

'You're always so reasonable and fair. Have some more wine?'

Michelle let Fiona pour another inch of Chardonnay into her glass. It was supposed to be fattening but she'd noticed that most of the people whose preferred tipple it was remained disconcertingly thin. She'd been strong and not eaten a single one of the salted almonds in the dish on the table. Resigned, she asked, 'Have you fixed a date for the wedding yet?'

'Believe it or not, we can't find anywhere to have our reception. Apparently, everyone wants to get married in millennium year. It was going to be June but we've had to move on into August. That's where Jeff is now, trying to find a venue.'

Surely he could have done that on the phone, thought Michelle. Still, she was delighted the wedding was to be postponed. As for trying to like him, it was more probable that every week which went by was likely to begin the eye opening she and Matthew hoped would enlighten Fiona as to Jeff's true nature. 'Church or register office?'

'Well, it doesn't have to be either now, does it? Jeff's been married before so it can't be church but the idea might be to have it in some hotel with the reception there afterwards.' She paused to listen to the front door opening and closing. 'Here's Jeff now.'

He came through the dining room and down the step. Smiling, as usual. An honest face like one of those American politicians, thought Michelle, perfect teeth, earnest frown lines and deep-blue eyes that looked straight into yours. He bent over Fiona and kissed her like some film actor coming home to his wife. Michelle, who didn't want it, got a kiss too, a light peck on the cheek.

'How's the Thin Man?'

'Very well, thank you,' said Michelle, angry but speaking in an equable tone because she wouldn't for the world offend Fiona.

'I hear he's going to be on TV.' Because there was no glass provided for him, Jeff took Fiona's almost empty one, filled it and knocked back half. 'You want to get on it too, Michelle, and see if you can be the new Little and Large. Oh, don't look like that, Fiona sweetheart, it's only my way. I ought to know better. Listen, I've found a wonderful place in Surrey where they'll marry us and serve a splendid dinner afterwards. Twenty-sixth August – how about that?'

'It sounds perfect,' said Michelle, thinking it was a

long way off. 'I must go, Fiona. Thank you so much for the lovely drinks.'

'I'll see you off the premises.' For some reason Jeff winked stagily at Fiona. He escorted Michelle to the door and sent, as was his peculiar habit, his 'kindest regards' to Matthew. The front door shut rather sharply before she was halfway down the path.

'That', said Fiona, who wasn't usually critical, 'was rather rude. You can be very hurtful, you know.'

Concern could entirely change his face. It became at once pained. Saddened, sympathetic. 'I know. I'm sorry, my sweet. I suppose I can't help thinking that people who allow themselves to get so fat must be stupid.'

'Michelle's not stupid.'

'No? Oh, well, you know best. Shall we have another bottle of wine?'

'It won't be cold.'

'Easily remedied by popping it in the freezer for five minutes.'

He remedied it. While waiting for the wine to cool, he decided to take her out to dinner, spend part of the rather large sum of money he'd won on a horse that afternoon. He got out two clean glasses, put them on a tray with the wine and went back. 'How about I call the Rosmarino and take you out to dinner, my darling? I mean *I* take you out.' Pouring the wine, he was inspired. 'I've been investing in the Net and I'm doing rather well.'

She knew all about that, as of course she would. 'I didn't know you had shares in anything. How clever of you. But be careful, won't you, Jeff? We don't know much about these companies yet – pipedream-@bankwell.co.uk and cashflow@marvel.com and whatever. Their profits may all be on paper.'

He changed the subject fast, veering on to the

matter he'd been thinking of mentioning since Sunday when seeing it in the paper had given him such a shock. If he could have avoided it altogether he would have, but he dared not. Still, he must go carefully. 'You remember that wedding in the paper on Sunday? Front page of the *Mail*?'

She never read the news, just the city pages. 'Sorry, I was only interested in that merger. Why?'

'I feel a bit odd about telling you, though I don't know why I should. It's not as if I've done anything wrong.' He looked at her, into her eyes. 'Hold my hand, Fiona. I wouldn't hurt you for the world.' His voice was solemn. 'Fiona, listen to me. My ex-wife got married. It was in the paper. She married an MP.'

She took both his hands, pulled him towards her. 'Oh, Jeff. Oh, darling. Why didn't you tell me at once?'

'I don't know. I should have. Somehow I couldn't.'

'It's made you unhappy, hasn't it? I do understand. I know you love me, I know that, but you can still be desperately hurt by something like this. It's absolutely natural. Kiss me.'

They kissed, gently at first, then more passionately. Jeff was the first to break away. 'I'll phone the restaurant.'

Fiona smiled to herself a little ruefully. It was, as she'd said, entirely natural that he should be a little unhappy. She thought of various men in her past, two of whom had subsequently married other women. Unreasonably, she'd been upset, though she hadn't wanted them, wouldn't have dreamt of remaining with them. When he came back she gave him a lovely warm smile, almost maternal. 'D'you want to tell me about it?' She took his hand again. 'You don't have to. Only if you want to.'

'I rather think I do. Her name's Zillah. Z-I-double L-A-H. She's a gypsy or likes people to think she is, a

Romany. We met at university. Of course, we were both very young. It was the old story, we grew out of each other. There wasn't anyone else or anything like that. Well, there was always this chap she's married, they knew each other as kids, but I used to think he was gay.'

'What about the children, Jeff?'

'I suppose they're with her.' He was wondering how much to tell her. 'That worries me too. Of course, she's done her best to keep my children from me.'

'I'd like children,' said Fiona in a small voice.

'Of course you would. Aren't I relying on that? Darling, by this time next year we may well have our first baby. I'll be the perfect house husband, stay at home and look after it.'

'What's her name?'

'Whose? Zillah's?' He thought fast. 'Her maiden name was Leach. The bloke she's married, the ex-queer, is called Melcombe-Smith. He's the MP for where she comes from down in Dorset.'

Fiona nodded. She didn't say any more but went upstairs to change. Jeff decided to finish the bottle. They could have a cab to and from the restaurant. He'd been very shaken by the wedding picture and accompanying story, so disturbed that now he'd told her he couldn't stay in the house with Fiona but had to go out and take himself for a walk up to Fortune Green and back. It was pretty obvious that the letter he'd written on Matthew Jarvey's computer and sent to Zillah had been taken seriously. He'd expected Minty to take hers seriously, she was thick enough, that was the point of it, but not Zillah. The whole idea had been to give her a signal that he intended to disappear, she wouldn't be troubled by him again. He hadn't intended to give her carte blanche to remarry, just as if they'd been properly divorced or he'd really died. In a few years' time, maybe, when she hadn't seen him for ages, but not after six months. Still, in a way, he decided, after he turned in at Fiona's gate once more, he had to hand it to her. She'd got a nerve marrying an upper-class rich git like that Melcombe-Smith and telling the paper she was childless Miss Leach. Or he supposed she had. They'd had to get it from somewhere and where else but her?

Drinking the last of the wine, he reflected briefly on his children and, as he did so, felt something quite alien to him, a pang of real sorrow. He'd never seen much of them, particularly Jordan, but when he'd been with them he'd loved them. It was just that he couldn't stand that domestic scene, Mr and Mrs, mummy and daddy sharing the household tasks, the weekly shop, the preparation of food, the kids always there, always hurting themselves and crying, making a mess. Being poor, never knowing where the next penny was coming from. Zillah was a good enough sort of mother, or he'd always thought she was, never going out in the evening and leaving them on their own, though he'd tried to persuade her. As if they weren't safe as houses in a country village surrounded by kindly neighbours. He'd felt quite secure about going off and leaving them all for weeks on end because he could trust Zillah to look after his children. But now?

He'd kept the pages of the paper with her pictures but he'd read the story so many times he knew it by heart. She hadn't told the reporter a word about being a gypsy – he'd never believed that anyway – or about a previous marriage or Watling not Leach being her maiden name. Most troubling of all, she very obviously hadn't mentioned the children's existence. He knew enough about reporters – he'd once been involved with quite a well-known free-lance journalist – to be aware that it's useless for an interviewee to implore the interviewer to keep a secret once disclosed, 'not to say anything about that'. What you've said is what you get. Leaving out bits of what you'd said was another matter, taking things out of context to change the sense. This was different. In a story of this kind there was no chance that if Zillah had told the *Mail* she had two small children, whether born inside or outside marriage, its reporter would have meekly agreed to keep quiet. So she hadn't told them. What had she done with his children?

Fiona came downstairs looking lovely in a white suit with a very short, tight skirt and high-heeled black patent shoes. He felt the stirrings of lust. An evening spent in bed would have done a lot to dispel his anxieties about Eugenie and Jordan, but it wasn't to be. His fault; he'd suggested dinner.

A taxi appeared, coming down Fortune Green Road. Just as well, since Fiona couldn't have walked another yard in those heels. He was going to have to meet Zillah and talk to her, see his kids, he'd a right to see his kids, they were *his*. Their paternity was something he'd never disputed. They both looked exactly like him, as reliable a guide, he'd always thought, as any DNA test.

'Try not to let it prey on your mind, Jeff.'

For a moment he was afraid she'd read his thoughts. Then he realised that, of course, she imagined he was brooding on his 'ex-wife' remarrying.

'You've got me now and we've a new life ahead of us.'

It might not be a bad idea to let Fiona go on thinking he was unhappy about his final parting from Zillah. In the future, if he seemed preoccupied or absent-minded or just silent, she'd attribute it to this. 'I know,' he said. 'Don't think I'm not absolutely content with that. I'm thinking of my son and my little girl. And it's just that . . . well, she was my first love.' He took her hand. 'And you're my last. First in my heart and last in my life.' The taxi turned into Blenheim Terrace and he felt in his pockets. 'Have you got any change, darling? I've only a twenty-pound note.'

Fiona paid the taxi driver. When they were at their table she asked him a bit more about Zillah. 'If you wanted a meeting with her, talk it through, that sort of thing, I wouldn't mind.'

In a way this was his opportunity. It would be wiser not to take it. She might want to come with him or meet Zillah herself. He nearly shuddered. Fiona, with her house, her money, her inheritance, her job, was (as he put it to himself) the best woman who had ever happened to him. 'No, my darling. I want to put it all behind me.'

He studied the wine list. In spite of what he'd told Fiona he wouldn't use the money he'd made on the horse called Website but instead would pay with the American Express card he'd found in another restaurant, fallen on the floor under a table in Langan's, where he'd been as the guest of a woman he'd picked up on the Duke of York steps. The card had belonged to one J. H. Leigh and it was this find of his which led to his assuming the name of Leigh when he first met Fiona. He was still Lewis with funny little Minty Knox at the time and for a new identity he'd been toying with the idea of Long or Lane, but Leigh it was to be. He'd used the card sparingly at first and for small items, always expecting to be told it had been cancelled. Nothing happened. He paid for meals with it, even bought clothes for Fiona with it, though he never dared indulge in jewellery.

Inevitably, he'd speculated as to why. Who was this Leigh who was so rich and profligate that he not only didn't bother to report the loss of his American Express card but continued to pay the bills for it that must arrive at his home each month? Then it came to him. This wasn't a man at all but a woman kept by a man, a wife or girlfriend, whose Amex accounts were paid for by husband or lover with no questions asked. Had she been afraid to tell him she'd lost the card? Perhaps been in some situation or place she shouldn't have been in when the theft or loss happened? Or had she so many cards that she didn't notice the disappearance of one of them?

He thought along these lines because underhand behaviour, deceit, pulling fast ones and getting something for nothing were practices dear to his heart. One day the card would be stopped but that might be a long way off and meanwhile he was cashing in.

'I said, are you going to have the grilled vegetables or the smoked salmon? Darling, you've not been listening.'

'Sorry,' he said. 'I was thinking – well, you know what I was thinking.'

Luckily, she didn't. How was he going to get hold of Zillah? Phone her? It wouldn't be hard to find her number. *Call round*? Once, years ago, while Zillah was pregnant with Eugenie and they were living in that dump near Queen's Park station, they'd been asked round to drinks by this Melcombe-Smith at his place in Pimlico and they'd gone. Ghastly, it had been and nearly turned him into a socialist. Jims, as he was called, might still be living there, it was only six or seven years. Aghast, he realised he didn't exactly know the age of his daughter. But he loved her, he knew that, she was his and he had to see her. 'Listen to this,' he said. 'Adam and Eve and Pinch

111

Me went down to the river to bathe. Adam and Eve were drownded. Who was saved?'

'Come off it, Jeff.' Fiona's patience had snapped. 'Save it for this baby we're supposed to be having next year. I'm grown-up.'

Chapter 10

The attention she was getting was in many ways attractive and flattering. Zillah hadn't expected all that publicity in the *Mail on Sunday*, and when she first saw the pictures and read the respectful story about herself and Jims, she'd been entranced. Other people had seen it too and rung up to congratulate her. Only one had asked why Eugenie and Jordan weren't mentioned and this woman had supplied her own answer: 'I suppose you want to protect them from media attention.'

That was exactly right, Zillah said. She'd had a few days in which to relax and enjoy living in Abbey Gardens Mansions, appreciate the comforts of her new home, so vastly superior even to the Battersea flat, and to decide it was time to fetch the children. They'd been staying with her parents in Bournemouth since two days before the wedding but she was beginning to miss them and she wanted them back. The publicity was past. She was realising the truth of what she'd guessed all along, that Jims wasn't famous, was a mere back-bench MP and an Opposition MP at that, and that all that had attracted the press were her and Jims's good looks. And maybe the fact that everyone had thought he was gay and about to be 'outed'.

The children could come back, go out for walks with her, be driven about by her in her nice new silver Mercedes, go to school in Westminster, and no one would take a blind bit of notice. So Zillah thought – until the first journalist phoned.

'I'm not disturbing your honeymoon, I hope?'

'We're not having a honeymoon till Easter,' said Zillah, who wasn't much looking forward to this sex-free excursion to an island in the Indian Ocean with nothing to do but drink and chat to Jims all day.

'Not even a tiny scrap of one?' the woman asked. She worked for a national daily. 'I'm calling to beg for an interview. Our Thursday slot. I expect you know what I mean.'

Zillah forgot all about Jims's instructions to refer all such requests to Malina Daz. She forgot her fear of journalists. They'd been so kind to her in the *Mail*. Why shouldn't she do it? The children weren't back yet. This would give her a chance to confirm everything that had already appeared in print and maybe get some more glamour shots. 'Will you take photographs?'

She must have sounded apprehensive for the journalist misunderstood. 'Well, yes, of course. A piece about someone as attractive as you wouldn't be much without photos, would it?'

Zillah agreed to it. Two hours later the features editor of a glossy magazine was on the phone. They'd left her alone for a few days but the time had come to have something appear that was more comprehensive than a few lines about her wedding. Zillah mentioned the other journalist.

'Oh, don't worry about that. Ours will be very different, I assure you. You'll love it. You're going to receive a great deal of attention, I can tell you, especially with the rumour going around that your husband was going to be outed.'

'There was never anything in that,' Zillah said nervously.

'You cured him, did you? Sorry, that wasn't very

PC of me. Maybe I should say, you brought about a change of heart. How's that? We'll say Friday at three, then, shall we? The photographer will come an hour earlier to get set up.'

By the time Zillah got around to telling Jims and, through him, Malina Daz, two more newspapers and another magazine had joined the queue. Malina belonged to the school of thought which holds that all publicity is good publicity. Jims was more cautious, urging Zillah to deny his reputed orientation as vehemently as possible. The night before the first journalist was due, the two of them invented a past girlfriend for Jims, her name, her appearance, her age and Zillah's jealousy of her. At the interview Zillah said this woman was now married and living in Hong Kong. For obvious reasons, her present identity couldn't be disclosed. When she talked to the magazine she forgot the former girlfriend's age and said she lived in Singapore, but Jims said it wouldn't matter, as newspapers got everything wrong anyway.

The children were still in Bournemouth. Their grandparents had agreed, though rather grudgingly, to keep them a week longer. Mrs Watling said on the phone she thought there was something ironical about Eugenie and Jordan staying in Bournemouth 'indefinitely' when for the first time in their lives they had a decent home, while she and their grandfather had never seen them from one year's end to the next when they'd lived in that dump in Dorset. Zillah said to bear with her a while longer – a phrase she'd picked up from Malina Daz – and she and Jims would be down to fetch the children the weekend after next.

The first interview appeared in print on Friday morning. The photographs came out wonderfully well and the feature itself was a chatty piece with nothing in it about Jims's prospective 'outing' and plenty about Zillah's lovely looks and dress sense. In another Malina phrase, the whole subject had been 'treated with sensitivity'. The invented girlfriend was mentioned with a few words about her 'long relationship' with Jims. Altogether it was highly satisfactory. Two more articles were 'in the pipeline', said Malina and several more interviews were to come.

Jims was happy with the piece but he knew the ways of the media as Zillah didn't. He could hardly have been in the Commons for seven years without knowing their ways. 'Tabloids are often OK until they've got their knife into you,' he said to Zillah. 'Magazines are fine, magazines are pussycats. It's national dailies like the *Guardian* you want to worry about.'

'It might be useful for me to put in a presence', said Malina, meaning she ought to be there, 'when Zillah meets with the print media, especially the quality broadsheets.'

'Good idea,' Jims agreed.

Zillah didn't like Malina. She hadn't been told the truth about the marriage but she guessed. Sometimes Zillah thought she'd caught her smiling secretly to herself. She was in and out of the flat in Abbey Gardens Mansions, popping into bedrooms, Zillah suspected, opening drawers and poking her long, slender fingers into desk pigeon-holes. Malina had a boyfriend who was a top cardiologist in Harley Street and she was thinner than Zillah, maybe two whole dress sizes thinner.

She didn't want Malina present when she talked to *The Times* and the *Telegraph*. It was bad enough having the photographer there, taking pictures when she was off her guard and had her mouth open or held her head at an awkward angle. Malina's secretive little smile and way of contemplating with admiration her own hands and silver-painted nails would be, in her own word, 'inappropriate'. So Zillah said nothing to her about the forthcoming interview with a freelance for the *Telegraph Magazine*. Jims would be absent too, in the Commons Chamber on that day for the Local Government Bill.

She was waiting for the photographer to come, standing in the window looking across towards Dean's Yard, when she saw a car draw up and park by the kerb on a double yellow line. A newspaper photographer ought to know better. They'd tow him away or clamp him. She opened the window, preparing to call out to him not to leave the car there, but instead of getting out, the driver stayed where he was behind the wheel. Zillah couldn't see very clearly, but in spite of the car being a BMW and a far cry from the ancient Ford Anglia he had driven away in after their last meeting, she was almost sure the man was her husband Jerry.

She put her head out of the window and stared. He was studying something, probably a map or plan. It looked a lot like Jerry but from this distance she couldn't be sure. If this photographer and journalist hadn't been coming she'd have gone down and made sure of his identity and, if it was Jerry, confronted him. If they weren't coming she wouldn't have been all dressed up in skin-tight purple trousers, shoes with three-inch heels and a black and white bustier. She closed the window. It was too far away to see properly. The man in the car looked up. It *was* Jerry. Surely it was. And whose was the dark-blue BMW? Not his, that was for sure. The doorbell rang.

The photographer had come from the Abbey direction, which was why she hadn't seen him. He had an assistant with him, the usual teenager, or

117

teenager lookalike, and the two of them started setting up, spreading ice-white sheets all over the furniture and opening and shutting a silver-lined umbrella. Zillah went back to the window. A traffic warden was talking to the man in the BMW. She hoped he'd get out so that she could have a proper look at him. He didn't, but drove off towards Millbank.

Zillah didn't enjoy the interview. The journalist was once again a woman but serious-looking and austerely dressed in a black trouser suit. She introduced herself as Natalie Reckman. Her features were severely classical and her fair hair was scraped back and fastened by a barrette. She wore no jewellery but a thick, heavy and curiously sculpted gold ring on her right hand. A businesslike notebook was taken out of her black leather briefcase and a recording device. Zillah, who had been feeling glamorously dressed, was suddenly conscious of the ornate oriental necklace she was wearing, amethysts in tooled silver, the fashionable dozen or so bead bracelets and the earrings dangling to her shoulders. And the questions put to her were more awkward than usual, more probing.

This woman was the first journalist to say nothing complimentary about her appearance. At first she seemed more interested in Jims than his new wife. Zillah did her best to talk about him as an ardent young bride might about her new husband. How clever he was, how considerate of her and what a wise move it was to marry one's best friend. As to his political career, he was so dutiful that they'd postponed their honeymoon until Easter. They were going to the Maldives. Darling Jims would have preferred Morocco, he was longing to go there, but he'd deferred to her choice of the Maldives. They'd go to Morocco in the winter.

118

Natalie Reckman yawned. She sat up straight and the interview took a different turn. After trying to find out what Zillah had done for a living before she married and being reluctant to accept her vague description of herself as an 'artist', she asked with some incredulity if she was expected to believe the MP's new bride had really lived by herself in a Dorset village for seven years without a job, a partner or any friends. Zillah, who was becoming angry, said she could believe what she liked. She was thinking quickly whether it was too late to mention the children, to bring them into the conversation somehow. But how to account for never before confessing to their existence?

The journalist smiled. She began asking about Jims. How long had they known each other? Twenty-two years? Yet they'd never been seen about together before their marriage nor, apparently, lived under the same roof.

'Not everyone agrees with pre-marital sex,' said Zillah.

The journalist looked Zillah up and down, from the earrings and the 'big hair' to her stilt heels. 'You're one of those who don't?'

'I really don't want to talk about it.'

'OK. That's fine. I expect you've heard your husband used to be grouped with several MPs that a rather censorious person who shall be nameless threatened to "out". What do you feel about that?'

Zillah was beginning to regret the absence of Malina. 'That's something else I'd prefer not to talk about.'

'Surely you'd like to say there was no truth in the rumour?'

'If you print anything about my husband being gay,' said Zillah, her control going, 'I'll sue you for libel.'

'Now, Mrs Melcombe-Smith, or Zillah, if I may, that's a very interesting thing you've just said. It seems to show you think it's an insult to suggest someone is gay. Do you? Is it likely to bring the subject into hatred, ridicule or contempt? Do you believe being gay is *inferior*? Or wrong? Is there a moral difference between being straight and being gay?'

'I don't know,' Zillah shouted. 'I don't want to say any more to you.'

Jims and Malina would have known that by now the interviewer had a wonderful story which she could hardly wait to get down on paper – or a hard disc. Zillah only wanted her to go and leave her alone. And eventually she did go, not in the least put out by Zillah's anger and refusal to say another word to her. Zillah felt shaken. It had all been so very different from the previous two interviews. She now regretted concealing the children's existence. Could she possibly leave them with her parents a little longer? They liked being there, they seemed to prefer it to being at home with their mother, but her parents weren't, in her mother's phrase, as young as they used to be, and were growing weary, worn out by Jordan's night crying. And why had that awful woman asked so many questions about what she'd been doing before her marriage? Zillah acknowledged that she hadn't adequately prepared herself.

One consolation was that the *Telegraph Magazine* wasn't like newspapers, the article wouldn't appear for weeks and weeks. Perhaps not even until she and Jims were in the Maldives. And perhaps it wasn't too late to stop it – if she dared ask Malina to intervene on her behalf. That would take some thinking about. She didn't say a word to Jims about it when he came home. That wasn't until 1 a.m., anyway. He'd been in the Commons chamber, but after the seven o'clock vote he'd slipped out and walked a hundred yards along Millbank where he'd taken a cab to visit his new friend in Chelsea.

Zillah was beginning to see that getting oneself into the newspaper might not be all fun and glamour. These journalists were cleverer than she'd expected. Jims could be left out of it for now but she had to talk to someone. She phoned Malina and the PR woman came round. 'I thought maybe you could call the *Telegraph Magazine* and say I didn't mean that about libel and I'm sorry I shouted at her.'

Malina was appalled but she didn't show it. 'That would be inappropriate, don't you think? I would have put in a presence if I'd only been notified. But you did give the interview of your own free will, Zillah. No one brought any pressure to bear.'

'I was hoping you could stop it altogether. Suggest I gave her another interview. I'd be more careful next time.'

'No next time would be the preferred option, Zillah.' Malina seemed to have changed her mind about all publicity being good. 'But I suppose it's too late for that.'

'You could call the other papers and just say I don't want to.'

'They'll want a reason.'

'Say I'm ill. Say I've got – gastroenteritis.'

'They'll think you're pregnant. You're not, are you?'

'Of course I'm not,' Zillah snapped.

'Shame. That would be the answer to all our prayers.'

But Malina cancelled three of the projected interviews and would have cancelled the fourth, scheduled for the next day, but the journalist she was trying to reach wasn't answering his mobile, ignored her e-mail and fax, and responded to none of the messages she left. In spite of not liking her, Zillah had such confidence in Malina that she didn't bother to dress up when the visit from the next broadsheet was due. Malina would have cancelled it. When the doorbell rang she thought, suppose it's Jerry? She ran to answer it without, for once, bothering to look in the mirror first.

Charles Challis was the sort of man Zillah would in other circumstances have described as 'dishy'. But the circumstances were all wrong because she hadn't been expecting anyone, particularly a man, and she looked a mess. 'You weren't supposed to come,' she said. 'We cancelled you.'

'Not to my knowledge. Is the photographer here yet?'

Then Zillah did look in the mirror, at her unmade-up face, unwashed hair and sweater that was a souvenir of six years in Long Fredington and had originally come from the British Home Stores. Numbly she led Charles Challis into the living room. He asked her nothing about Jims's reputed gayness nor what she did for a living and made no comment on her appearance. He was nice. Zillah decided it wasn't journalists she disliked but women journalists. She asked the photographer if it would be all right for her to put on some make-up. When she came back Charles, as he'd asked her to call him, edged his questioning on to politics.

This was a subject of which Zillah admitted to herself she knew little. She knew who the Prime Minister was and she said she thought him 'dishy', but she couldn't remember the name of the Leader of the Opposition. The journalist put to her the burning question of the hour. What was her opinion on Section 28?

She looked blank. Charles explained. Section 28

forbade local authorities to promote homosexuality; the provision proposed in the Local Government Bill was to repeal it. Their contention was that, due to the section, children uncertain of their orientation were confused and made the victims of bullying. What did Zillah think about it?

Zillah didn't want to get into any more trouble. Recalling what the Reckman woman had implied about homosexuals and heterosexuals being equal with no moral difference between them, she said hotly that Section 28 was obviously wrong. It should be got rid of and quickly. Charles wrote it all down and tested his recorder to check that Zillah's voice was coming across clearly. How about trial by jury? Was Zillah in favour of shortening court proceedings and thereby saving the taxpayer's money? The night before, Jims had been complaining at length about the income tax he paid, so Zillah said she was all for economy and people on juries weren't lawyers, were they, so what did they know?

She felt quite pleased with herself. The photographs wouldn't be too bad. She often thought the casual look suited her better than formality. Malina phoned after they'd gone and said she'd managed to cancel everything but Charles Challis. How had the interview gone?

'It was marvellous. He was so *nice*.'

'Good. Well done, you.' Malina didn't say that the journalist in question was known in the Groucho Club as Poisoned Chalice.

Zillah put the phone down and looked out of the window. Jerry was standing at the entrance to the underground car park. She rushed out of the flat and down in the lift but when she came out into Great College Street he'd gone. He must have put his car into the car park. She ran down the slope and into the depths. There was no sign of him and no dark-blue BMW. Perhaps he'd been on foot because of the difficulties of parking. He could have got on a bus or walked to the tube while she was leaving the flat. What did he want? He could be thinking of blackmailing her. *Five hundred a month or I tell all.* But as far as she knew Jerry had never descended to blackmail in the past and wouldn't begin with her. She went back across the road and, because she'd forgotten her key, had to get the porters to let her in.

The interviews over or cancelled, it was time to fetch the children. Jims and Zillah drove down to Bournemouth on the Saturday. It was a pleasant drive, for once the roads not congested and it wasn't raining. They stopped for lunch at a smart new restaurant in Casterbridge, down by the river and the millrace, because Jims didn't want to stay long enough to sample her mother's cooking. Neither Eugenie nor Jordan seemed pleased to see them.

'Want to stay with Nanna,' said Jordan.

His sister patted him on the head. 'We like the seaside. Children need fresh air, you know, not traffic plumes.' She meant 'fumes' but no one corrected her.

'I suppose there's no reason why you shouldn't stay a bit longer,' said Jims hopefully.

'I'm afraid there is, James.' Nora Watling was never afraid to speak her mind. 'I'm tired. I need some peace. I've raised one family and I'm not in the business of raising another at my age.'

'No one wants us,' said Eugenie cheerfully. 'It's not very nice to be an unwanted child, is it, Jordan?'

Jordan didn't understand but he burst into howls just the same. When Jims looked at his watch at three thirty and said they might as well be going, Nora was deeply offended. The children had had their lunch but she insisted on stuffing them with crisps, ice cream and Black Forest cake before they left. On the way back to London Jordan was sick all over Jims's grey leather upholstery.

But once they were home, Eugenie had started at her new school and a place in a fashionable 'progressive' nursery been found for Jordan, peace reigned. It was possible to leave Abbey Gardens Mansions very discreetly by taking the lift down to the basement car park and driving out by the exit into a turning off Great Peter Street. A journalist would have had to be very vigilant and an early riser to spot Zillah taking the children to school at nine in the morning, the silver Mercedes slipping out by the back way. But there were no journalists. The media seemed to have lost interest. A couple of weeks went by and the newspapers ignored young Mr and Mrs Melcombe-Smith. Zillah had expected to be pleased about that if it happened, but now she began wondering what had become of the piece that nice Charles Challis was writing. She and Jims were going on their honeymoon on Easter Saturday. It would be just her luck to be away when it appeared.

'What do you mean, just your luck?' Jims had been unreasonably irritable lately. 'I'd say you've been pretty lucky up till now.'

'It was just a figure of speech,' said Zillah pacifically.

'A highly inappropriate one, if I may say so. Have you arranged with Mrs Peacock yet?'

'I'll do it now.'

But Mrs Peacock wasn't able to stay at Abbey Gardens Mansions for the ten days Jims and Zillah would be in the Maldives, or indeed for any part of that time. Zillah, she said, had left it too late. Only the day before she'd fixed up to go on a coach tour of Bruges, Utrecht and Amsterdam.

'I hope she freezes to death,' said Zillah. 'I hope she poisons herself on tulip bulbs.'

'Tulip bulbs aren't poisonous,' said Jims coldly. 'Squirrels prefer them to nuts. Have you never noticed?'

She had to ask her mother. Nora Watling exploded. The children had been in London less than three weeks and now she was expected to have them back again. Hadn't Zillah understood what she'd said about not wanting to raise a second family?

'You and Daddy could come here. The children are at school all day. You could do some sightseeing, go on the Millennium Wheel.'

'We haven't been on the wheel,' said Eugenie. 'We haven't even been to the Dome.'

'Nanna will take you,' said Zillah, covering up the mouthpiece. 'Nanna will take you anywhere you want to go.'

Of course Nora Watling agreed to come. She could hardly do otherwise. Having remarked scathingly that some people would put their children in a kennel or a cattery if they had the chance, she said she and Zillah's father would arrive on Good Friday.

'I wish you wouldn't teach them to call their grandmother Nanna,' said Jims. 'It's highly inappropriate for the stepchild of a Conservative MP.'

'Not a stepchild, not a stepchild,' screamed Jordan. 'Want to be a real child.'

On Monday morning, a week later than expected, the Challis interview with Zillah appeared. Or something appeared. There was no photograph and the piece devoted to Zillah was about two inches long. It was part of a two-page feature on MP's wives, their views and occupations, and it was written in a breezy, satirical style. She was made to look a combination of feather-headed butterfly and ignoramus.

Zillah, new bride of James Melcombe-Smith, [Charles Challis had written] *shares her husband's interest in politics if not his persuasion. Not for her the retention of Section 28 or that ancient bastion of the law, trial by jury. Sweep them away, is her policy. Where have we heard that before? Why, from none other than the Labour Party. 'People on juries aren't lawyers,' she told me, tossing back a lock of raven hair. (Mrs Melcombe-Smith looks a lot like Catherine Zeta Jones.) 'My husband would like to see an end to this waste of the taxpayers' money.' He, of course, is the Conservative Member for South Wessex, known to his constituents and other pals as 'Jims'. They will be fascinated by his wife's views.*

Jims was less angry about this than might have been expected. He muttered a bit and predicted he'd shortly be due for an unpleasant interview with the Chief Whip. But these were not the sort of slips and revelations he feared and he doubted whether more than a handful of the landowners and (in his own phrase) peasants, read 'that rag'. Zillah said she was sorry but she didn't know anything about politics. Was there a book she could read?

Later that day she saw Jerry again. She was in the car, fetching the children from school and had just turned out of Millbank, when she spotted him outside the Atrium. Her first thought was for the children and the trouble that would ensue if they saw him. But both were looking in the other direction, admiring two orange-coloured dogs with curly tails like pigs.

'Can I have a dog, Mummy?' asked Eugenie.

'Only if you look after it yourself.' Zillah's mother had said the same thing to her when she asked that same question twenty-two years before. She had got the dog and looked after it for three days. Remembering, she went on, 'No, of course you can't have a dog. A dog in a flat?'

'We used to live in a house. It was nice and we had friends. We had Rosalba and Titus and Fabia.'

'Want Titus,' said Jordan, but instead of screaming he began quietly to sob.

As Zillah waited in the middle of the street to turn right into the car park under Abbey Gardens Mansions she saw Jerry running along the pavement towards her. Without looking to her left she began to turn, causing the van coming from the left to brake violently and the driver, already galvanic with road rage, put his head out of the window and let forth a stream of obscene abuse. Zillah went on down the ramp into the car park.

'Mummy, did you hear the word that man said? Nanna said that if I used that word I'd come to a bad end. Will the man come to a bad end?'

'I hope so,' Zillah said viciously. 'Stop crying, Jordan. Do you think you two could manage to call Nanna Granny?'

Eugenie shook her head slowly from side to side. 'That would make her into another person, wouldn't it?'

Zillah didn't answer. She was confirmed in her belief that her daughter would be called to the Bar at an early age.

There was no more sign of Jerry. Jims again came home very late. In the morning he told her his new friend Leonardo Norton would also be in the Maldives while they were there, staying, in fact, in the same hotel.

Chapter 11

'You could come with me to the Television Centre,' Matthew said. 'I'd like that.'

But Michelle said no, she wouldn't. 'You'll be better off without having me to worry about, darling.' The truth was she couldn't face the stares and surreptitious giggles of all those long-legged girls and young men in jeans. Jeff Leigh's Little and Large jibe still rankled.

It was heartening to see Matthew set off for the tube station, walking along almost like a normal person, his shoulders back and his head high. Michelle dusted the living room and vacuumed the carpet. As she lumbered around, breathless, her heart thudding, she tried to recapture what it had felt like to be a normal person herself, to have an ordinary body. Not like a model girl, not even like Fiona, but to be an average rounded woman, wearing a size fourteen. Usually, when Matthew was there, as he almost always was, she stifled such thoughts, pushing them away, pretending she wasn't thinking them. This was the first time in how long – five years? seven? – that she had been alone in the house. There's nothing like being on your own for having space to think.

Michelle stood still in the middle of the room and felt her body, really felt what it was like, from her three chins to the cushions on her upper thighs. First with her brain, then with her hands, growing at last fully aware of the mountain of flesh in which her delicate and fastidious mind and her loving heart had their being. She closed her eyes and in the darkness seemed to see Matthew as he might be if restored to health and herself as she was, or nearly as she was, when first they married. And into that dream came a hint, like a winged insect, a fragile wisp, fluttering across her closed lids, of the old desire they had once had for each other, the passion that sprang from physical beauty and energy. Could it ever be recaptured? The love was there, just the same. Surely with that love present, they could return somehow to *making* love . . .

It was a long time since Michelle had been able to bend down. They had had to get rid of the vacuum cleaner they used to have, the kind with a long hose you pull along like a little dog, because she couldn't bend down enough to fetch it out of the cupboard and put it back. The upright one they had now was better, but only marginally, because to connect the attachments, she had to make the huge effort of lifting the cleaner by its handle on to a chair and performing this operation at thigh level. Afterwards she had to stand still for a moment, one hand pressed against the mountain of her bosom. But once she'd got her breath back, she managed to screw in the nozzle on the brush hose and finish the cleaning of the room. Then she went out shopping.

Not to Waitrose this time but nearer home to the Atlanta supermarket at West End Green. She put kiwi fruit into the trolley, Ryvitas and a large pack of dry roasted peanuts, but as, almost automatically, she took a big bag of doughnuts from the shelf, her hand was stayed in mid-air and very slowly she put it back again. The same with the thick wedge of Cheddar cheese and the Cadbury's Milk Flakes. She was bracing herself not to succumb but to leave the cheesecake where it was in the chilled foods cabinet when a voice behind her said, 'Stoking up the boilers, are we? Maintaining the *avoirdupois*?'

It was Jeff Leigh. Strange things were happening to Michelle in Matthew's absence. Her mind was in a turmoil as she thought thoughts she hadn't had for a dozen years and looked at people she was used to with new eyes. For instance, she was seeing Jeff as if for the first time and perceiving him as very good-looking, that it was obvious why women found him attractive. And equally obvious that his charm was spurious and his looks skin-deep. Any reasonable person, not blinded by a love that must be mostly physical desire, would dislike and distrust him. She didn't answer his question but asked him where Fiona was.

'At work. Where else?'

'To keep you in the luxury to which you're accustomed, I suppose.' Michelle surprised herself, for she couldn't remember saying such a thing or using such a tone in all her life before.

'It always amazes me', he said, smiling genially, 'how you women scream for equality with men but you still expect men to keep you and never to keep *them*. Why? In an equal society some men would keep women and some women keep men. Like Matthew keeps you and Fiona keeps me.'

'Everyone ought to work.'

'Excuse me, Michelle, but when did you last set foot in a nursery for a living?'

After she'd walked off in silence he was sorry he'd said that. It was cheap. Also it would have been funnier to have said something more about her shape and weight. Something on the lines of applying for a post with the Fattist Society, if she was in need of a job. Jeff bought the half-pint of milk he needed for

131

his morning coffee and the smoked salmon sandwiches which would be his lunch and went home to
think about the hours ahead before Fiona came
home.

For years now Jeffrey Leach had planned each day
with care. He gave an impression of casual insou-
ciance but in fact he was meticulous, well-organised
and industrious. The trouble was that he couldn't
exactly tell people how hard he really did work, for
most of what he did was dodgy or downright illegal.
Yesterday, for instance, he'd driven himself to an
Asda store and, presenting at the checkout the J. H.
Leigh credit card he'd found to pay for their week's
groceries, had asked for cash back. The weary girl
who'd been on for three hours, asked how much and
Jeff, who'd been going to say fifty, asked for a
hundred pounds. She handed it over and he wished
he'd asked for two. Yet she'd looked long and hard
at the card before giving him the money, so that he'd
heard a little warning bell tinkling.

Now, resolutely but not without regrets, he took
the card out of his wallet and, with Fiona's kitchen
scissors, cut it into six pieces. These he put into the
waste bin, careful to cover them with an empty
cornflake packet and a pair of Fiona's laddered
tights. Better safe than sorry even if safety was going
to cost him. The card had served him well as cards
go, and as cards go it went. He'd get another
somehow or other. Maybe Fiona would get him one.
American Express were always writing letters telling
their clients to apply for cards for family members. A
live-in lover was a family member, wasn't he? For
the life of him he couldn't see how he was actually to
marry Fiona unless he got up his nerve and committed bigamy like Zillah. He'd give more thought to
that when August approached.

Jeff used his mobile as seldom as possible, making

most calls on Fiona's phone. He lifted the receiver and rang his bookmaker, placing a bet on a horse called Feast and Famine running at Cheltenham. His almost uncanny success on the racecourse owed more to instinct and serendipity than knowledge of horseflesh. It enabled him to pick up a nice little weekly income. He was in need, however, of a larger sum immediately. Fiona still hadn't got an engagement ring and the sort he usually picked up for twenty quid in Covent Garden market or off a stall outside St James's Piccadilly wouldn't do for this top-quality woman. Once he'd run a most successful scam offering, through an advertisement and on receipt of a five-pound note, a brochure on how to be a millionaire within two years. He'd made a small fortune before applicants began writing furious letters asking where their brochure was. But he couldn't repeat the exercise. Imagine the post he'd get and Fiona's face when she rumbled him.

Zillah had been right when she'd decided her husband would not blackmail her. To his credit, demanding money with menaces had never crossed Jeff's mind. The engagement ring would have to come from another source. Fleetingly, he thought of Minty. Funny little thing. She was the cleanest woman he'd ever slept with. Even if he hadn't met Fiona and quickly picked up on her wealth, he'd have had to drop Minty. What man would fancy the bed smelling of Wright's Coal Tar soap every time he'd had a bit of a cuddle? Still, he might have got her to take out that mortgage on the house before he left her. Why hadn't he? Because he was a decent bloke at heart, he told himself, and making one fiancée pay for another fiancée's engagement ring was too low even for him.

Jeff had a look around the house for money. There never was any, he knew that by now, but he never quite gave up hope. Fiona didn't seem to have any cash. It was what came of being in banking, he supposed, everything on paper, cards, computers. She'd once told him she dreamed of a day when cash as such would disappear and be replaced by paying and being paid by iridian means or a fingerprint. He looked in a tea tin in the kitchen which seemed to serve no purpose but to contain money, though it never did, and through the pockets of Fiona's many coats. Not even a twenty-pence piece. Still, he had enough to get along on and when Feast and Famine came in first, as it undoubtedly would, he'd net five hundred.

When he'd drunk his coffee and eaten his sandwiches, Jeff went out. Even on such a fine day it would take too long to walk to Westminster but he did get as far as Baker Street before taking a bus. He had no doubt that the woman he'd seen yesterday, driving and nearly crashing the silver Mercedes, was Zillah. This was the first time he'd been sure. The glimpses he'd caught of a dark woman at a window in Abbey Gardens Mansions might have been she and might not. When he'd last seen her in Long Fredington (and bade her farewell, though she didn't know it) her hair was scraped back and fastened with an elastic band, and she'd been wearing a sweatshirt and jeans. This woman, the one in Abbey Gardens, looked like an oriental princess, all big hair and jewellery, and some kind of low-cut satin top. It was a matter of chance that he'd seen her the day before. He hadn't brought Fiona's BMW, it was too much hassle parking it. He'd done it like today on foot and by bus and, after hanging about for a long time, ended up outside that flash restaurant and been leaning against the wall wondering what to do next. And she'd come along in that car out of Millbank.

Of course he'd given chase, trying to see if the kids in the back were his children. There were two of them, a younger boy and an older girl, of that at any rate he'd been sure. But they hadn't been looking in his direction, and they seemed too big to be his Eugenie and his Jordan. He thought with a pang that it was six months since he'd seen them and small children alter considerably in six months, growing taller, their faces changing. It couldn't be, could it, that this Jims had a couple of kids and it was his two in the car? Gay men did sometimes have kids before they decided women weren't for them. He had to be sure. Today he was going to find out.

Getting off the bus at Charing Cross, he went into a newsagent's and looked through the sort of newspaper that tells its readers what's happening in Parliament that day.

The newsagent watched him turning the pages, folding back the sheets. 'Like they say, if you don't want the goods don't mess them about.'

Jeff had found what he wanted. It was Maundy Thursday and the Commons sat at eleven. He dropped the paper on the floor, said like some character from Victorian fiction, 'Keep a civil tongue in your head, my man.'

The river sparkled in the sun. The spokes on the London Eye glittered silver against a cloudless blue sky. Jeff walked past the Houses of Parliament, crossed the road and turned into Great College Street. From the bus window he'd noticed that *The Talented Mr Ripley* was on at the Marble Arch Odeon. He might pop in later. Fiona wasn't keen on the cinema. He pushed open the art nouveau oak and glass doors of Abbey Gardens Mansions and was a little disconcerted to see a porter sitting behind a desk in the flower-decked red-carpeted foyer. 'Mr Leigh,' he said, 'to see Mr Melcombe-Smith.'

Zillah wouldn't know who it was but she'd let in a strange man who came to call on Jims. He hoped. However, the porter didn't attempt to phone through to her but indicated the lift with a surly nod. Up Jeff went and rang the bell of number seven. It was the old Zillah who came to the door, the unmade-up, hair-scraped-back, casual-clothes version, though the jeans were Calvin Klein and the top Donna Karan. She screamed when she saw him and clapped her hand over her mouth.

The children's schools had broken up for Easter and Eugenie and Jordan were out for a walk with Mrs Peacock while their mother packed for the Maldives. That they weren't there and nor was Jims gave her courage. 'You'd better come in,' she said. 'I thought you were dead.'

'No you didn't, my dear. You thought I was telling you I was dead. It's not the same thing. You're a bigamist, you know.'

'So are you.'

Jeff sat down on a sofa. He lived in comfortable and elegant surroundings himself so he had no need to comment on hers. 'You're wrong there,' he said. 'I've never actually been married to anyone but you. Admittedly, I've got engaged to three or four but marriage, no. You want to remember what they said to the old person of Lyme who married three wives at one time. When asked why a third, he replied one's absurd. And bigamy, sir, is a crime.'

'You're despicable.'

'I wouldn't call anyone names if I were you. How do you and Jimsy-wimsy get on about a bit of how's-your-father? Or is it a marriage of convenience?' He looked about him as if hoping for the missing pair to emerge from out of the cupboard or under the table. 'Where are my children?'

Zillah blushed. 'I don't think you've any right to ask. If they'd depended on you they'd be in care by now.'

He couldn't deny it and didn't try. Instead, 'Where's your loo?' he asked.

'Upstairs.' She couldn't resist saying there were two. 'One's the door facing you and the other's in my bathroom.'

'Jims, Jims, the rick stick Stims, round tail, bobtail, well done, Jims.'

Jeff didn't open that door but the one to the right of it. Two single beds, two bedlamps with coloured butterflies on their shades, otherwise almost without furniture and very tidy. He nodded. Next to it was a room the same size but rather austere, not quite a monk's cell but in that category. The door at the end of the passage opened on to what he suspected an estate agent would call the master bedroom. On the double divan were two open suitcases, the kind that unmistakably come from Louis Vuitton. The crocodile handbag beside them was also open. Jeff put his hand inside. Feeling in a side compartment, he came upon a Visa card, still in the name of Z. H. Leach. Then he went back into the living room and offered Zillah a Polo mint.

'No, thanks, as always.'

'I see you're packing. Going somewhere nice?'

She told him, adding sulkily that it was their honeymoon. Jeff burst out laughing, roaring uncontrollably, tickled to death. He stopped as quickly as he'd begun. 'You didn't answer my question. Where are my children?'

'Out for a walk.' She invented, 'With their nanny.'

'I see. A nanny. Jims-oh isn't short of a penny or two, is he? And will you be taking them to the Maldives?'

Zillah would have liked to say yes, but Mrs

Peacock and the children might return at any time. She'd already had enough stick from Eugenie because she wasn't taking them. 'I told you,' she said, 'it's a honeymoon. My mother will be here to look after them.'

Jeff, who hadn't sat down again but had been roving about the room, said, 'I won't stay to see them. It might be upsetting for them and me. But I don't like the sound of what you've been saying, Zil. It strikes me neither you nor Jims really want my kids. You didn't say a word about them to those newspapers, not a hint to that magazine that you'd got any kids – oh, yes, I read it, I made it my business to read it.' He paused. 'Now, Fiona loves children.'

This casual remark had the effect he hoped for. 'Who the hell's Fiona?'

'My fiancée.' Jeff smiled wolfishly. 'She's a merchant banker. She's got a very nice house in Hampstead.' He left out the 'West'.

'I suppose the BMW belongs to her.'

'As you say. Her house would be an ideal home for children. Four bedrooms, garden, everything the heart could wish for. And I'm home all day to look after them while she earns the moolah to keep them in luxury.'

'What are you saying?'

'Frankly, my dear, I'm not sure yet. I haven't thought it through. But I will and I very likely may come up with a plan. Like applying for sole custody, right?'

'You wouldn't stand a chance!' Zillah shouted.

'No? Not if the court heard you'd committed bigamy?'

Zillah began to cry. There was a notepad on the table with tear-off pages in a silver case. He wrote down Fiona's address and gave it to Zillah, pretty sure he could retrieve any letter that came to Jerry

Leach. Then he left, whistling 'Just Walk on By'. As he closed the front door behind him he could hear her loud sobs. Of course he'd no intention of taking the children away from her but the threat was a useful weapon. And he wouldn't mind getting his own back on Jims, who was certainly using Eugenie and Jordan as pawns in the game he was playing to prove himself an exponent of family values. Should he tell Fiona about it? Perhaps. A doctored version at any rate.

Still, where were his children? That story about the nanny might be an invention. If Zillah had dumped them, where had she dumped them? With her mother? He didn't like it. Perhaps he'd call again next week when Nora Watling was there and find out the truth. If she was there, if that wasn't a lie too.

Now for lunch at the Atrium. On Zillah's credit card? A bit dangerous. She and Jims might be regular visitors. Jeff had an idea that a credit card had some sort of code on it that betrayed the sex of the customer using it. In an Italian restaurant in Victoria Street he put it to the test and had no problem. All was well. Imitating Zillah's signature was no problem either, he'd often done it in the past. *The Talented Mr Ripley*, the three-fifteen showing, had just begun when Jeff got to the cinema. The small intimate theatre was almost empty, just himself, two other men on their own and a lone middle-aged woman. It always amused him to see how they'd placed themselves, as far apart as possible, one of the men near the front on the extreme right, another, who looked very old, on the left halfway down and the third in the back row. The woman sat next to the aisle but as far as possible from the old man. It seemed to Jeff that human beings didn't like their own kind much. Sheep, for instance, would all have huddled together in the centre. He took his seat behind the woman – just to be different.

Matthew came home in the middle of the afternoon. Naturally, he'd had no lunch. Without Michelle to look after him and coax him, he'd never eat at all. But he looked well, very nearly a normal thin man. The recording for the television programme had been highly enjoyable. 'I loved it,' he said, just like the old Matthew she'd married. 'I didn't really expect to. I was full of gloomy forebodings.'

'You should have told me, darling.'

'I know but I can't unload all my burdens on to you.'

She said in an unusually bitter voice, 'You could. My shoulders are broad enough.'

He looked at her with concern, sat down next to her and took her hands. 'What is it, my love? What's wrong? You're pleased for me, I know that. This programme may be the start of many. We'll be richer, though I know you don't care about that. What is it?'

She came out with it. She could no longer keep it to herself. 'Why do you never say I'm fat? Why don't you tell me I'm gross and bloated and hideous? Look at me. I'm not a woman, I'm a great obese balloon of flesh. I said my shoulders are broad enough – well, I hope yours are for what I'm saying. That's my burden, my size, my awful, huge, revolting size.'

He was looking at her, but not aghast, not in horror. His poor, thin, wizened face was softened and changed by tenderness. 'My darling,' he said. 'My sweet, dearest darling. Will you believe me when I say I've never noticed?'

'You must have. You're an intelligent man, you're perceptive. You *must* have noticed and – and hated it!'

'What's brought this on, Michelle?' he asked seriously.

'I don't know. I'm a fool. But – yes, I do know. It's Jeff, Jeff Leigh, every time I see him he makes some sort of joke about my size. It was – well, this morning it was "stoking up the boilers?" and the other day he said - no, darling, I can't tell you what he said.'

'Shall I speak to him? Tell him he's hurt you? I will, I shan't mind doing that. You know me, aggressive bastard when I'm roused.'

She shook her head. 'I'm not a child. I don't need Daddy to tell the boy next door to stop it.' A little smile transformed her face. 'I never thought I'd say this about anyone but I – I hate him. I really do. I hate him. I know he's not worth it but I can't help it. Tell me about the television.'

He told her. She pretended to listen and made encouraging noises, but she was thinking how deeply she disliked Jeff Leigh, how certain she was that he was a petty crook and she wondered if she could find the strength to warn Fiona. As if she were her mother. Did people ever heed that kind of warning? She didn't know. But she wasn't Fiona's mother and that would make a big difference.

When she had made a meal for Matthew (milkless tea, a ryvita, two slices of kiwi fruit and twelve dry-roasted peanuts) she went upstairs, of necessity holding on to the banisters with both hands, puffing at the top as she always did, and entered the bathroom. The scales were for Matthew. She had never stepped on them. How delighted they both were when Matthew weighed himself last week and the scales registered seven stone two instead of the needle quivering on the six-stone mark as it once had. Michelle kicked off her shoes, looking down at her legs and feet. They *were* beautiful, as lovely in shape as any of those models', if not as long. Taking a deep breath, she stepped on to the scales.

At first she didn't look. But she had to look, that was the point. Slowly she lowered her closed eyes, forced herself to open them. Her breath expelled in a long sigh, she took her eyes away from what it came to in kilos, in pounds. She weighed three times what Matthew did.

What had happened to her to make her do what she'd just done? Jeff Leigh had happened. That made Michelle smile. It was absurd to think of the person you hated as doing you good. For he had done her good. She put on her shoes, went down to the kitchen again and tipped the food she'd prepared for her tea, a big bread roll (in the absence of doughnuts) with strawberry jam, two shortcake biscuits and a slice of fruitcake, down into the waste bin.

Chapter 12

The horrible thing was that she'd begun to fancy Jims. Really to fancy him, a different matter altogether from the feeling she'd had when they were both teenagers. In those days it had been just an itch, coupled with resentment that here was one boy among all those she knew who wasn't attracted by her. That in itself was enough to make her try to seduce him. But now things had changed.

Paradoxically, as she started to want to go to bed with him, so she liked him less. When they'd just been seeing each other every few weeks, having a drink together, talking over old times, Zillah would have said Jims was her best friend. Sharing a home with him made a huge difference. His peevishness was apparent, his selfishness and, when there was no one else present, his absolute indifference as to whether she was there or not. If anyone called, one of his parliamentary pals, for instance, he was all over her, holding hands, looking into her eyes, calling her darling, pausing as he passed the back of her chair to drop a kiss on the nape of her neck. Alone with her he barely spoke. But this coldness, along with his appearance, his grace, his dark slenderness and those large, dark eyes, fringed with black lashes like a girl's, contributed to his appeal. Every day, it seemed, she sank deeper into wanting him very much.

In the Maldives it was worse. They shared a suite

in which there were two bedrooms and two bathrooms, but Jims was seldom there, spending his nights in suite 2004 where Leonardo was. Ever cautious, he would sometimes return at eight in the morning, to be sitting opposite her at the glass table on the balcony, both in their white towelling robes, when the waiter brought their breakfast at nine.

'I wonder why you bother,' she said.

'Because you never know who else may be staying here. How do you know that red-headed woman we saw on the beach yesterday isn't a journalist? Or that the very youthful couple, the topless girl and her boyfriend, aren't media people? Of course you don't. I have to be ever vigilant.'

Most women would be overjoyed, she thought, if their husbands could talk about a young girl going topless without a flicker of lust in their eyes, without the least deepening of their tone. In the mornings Jims lay on a sun lounger on the silver sands and Leonardo lay on another sun lounger beside him. But Zillah was there too on a third one. When she protested, saying she'd rather go in the pool or take a look at the village, such as it was, he reminded her of his reason for marrying her. And for giving her two homes, almost unlimited spending money, a new car, clothes and security. He'd also, he said, become a father to her children. Zillah was beginning to understand that she'd taken on a job rather than a husband, while in exchange for all those worldly goods she'd abandoned her freedom.

Leonardo worked for a stockbroker in the City and was a high flyer at twenty-seven. From a family that, on the father's side, had been staunch active Conservatives for the past hundred and fifty years, he was as mad about politics as Jims and the two talked Conservative Party history, House of Commons procedure and personalities all day long, swapping anecdotes about Margaret Thatcher or Alan Clark. Leonardo was enthralled by John Major's autobiography and constantly read bits out of it aloud to Jims. Zillah thought bitterly how unlike their dialogue was to the received opinion among the party mandarins she'd met, as to the style in which gay men conversed.

She was worried as well. As to his vaunted role as Eugenie's and Jordan's father, so much for his saying he loved children. He'd barely spoken to either of them since their return from Bournemouth. When she'd mentioned this, he said he supposed Eugenie would be off to boarding school in a few months' time. Then they'd get a live-in nanny for Jordan and he'd have the fourth bedroom converted into a nursery. She hadn't said a word to him about Jerry. How could she? They were supposed never to have been married and he to have no rights over the children at all. Suppose Jerry did try to get the children? Suppose he renewed his threat to expose her as a woman who'd married one man while still married to another? Oh, it was so unfair! He'd utterly deceived her, sending her that letter saying he was dead.

And now, just to crown everything, she'd succumbed to Jims's charms. In the dining room last evening, for the benefit of the other diners, he'd put his arm round her while they were waiting to be shown to their table and, once there, when he'd pulled out her chair for her, given her a soft little kiss on the lips. She'd actually heard some old woman nearby whisper to her companion how nice it was to see a couple so much in love. That kiss nearly finished Zillah off. She'd have liked to go upstairs and have a cold shower but she had to sit here with Jims looking into her eyes and holding her hand across the table. Leonardo always took his dinner in

his suite while watching, Zillah suspected, porno-
graphic movies. Or maybe only videos of some Tory
by-election coup.

The *Daily Telegraph Magazine*, the one with her
interview in it, hadn't yet come out. Unless it had on
Easter Saturday. Zillah's mother had strict instructions to look out for it and keep it if it appeared
while she was away. The day before they left she'd
written to Jerry at the Hampstead address he'd given
her, only it wasn't Hampstead proper but West
Hampstead, as she could tell by the postcode.
Obscurely, this discovery made her feel a little better.
   Zillah wasn't accustomed to writing letters; she
couldn't remember when she'd written the last one.
It had probably been to thank her godmother for
sending her a five-pound note when she was twelve.
The first effort she made looked very threatening
when she read it over, so she started again. This time
she threw herself on Jerry's mercy, appealing to him
not to expose her as a criminal, to remember what
she'd been through, how he'd left her alone to fend
for herself. That wouldn't do either. She tore it up
and finally wrote simply that he'd frightened her.
She hadn't meant to keep the children from their
father. He could have access and visiting rights and
anything he wanted if only he wouldn't tell anyone
she'd done what he knew she'd done. Without
actually writing 'bigamist' in case the letter fell into
the wrong hands, she asked him please not to use
'that word' any more. It was cruel and unfair. This
she sent.
   The trouble with the Maldives was that beautiful
though the island was, it was really only the sort of
place you went to with someone you were having a
big, sexy and romantic affair with and wanted to
make love all the time. Like Jims and Leonardo. For

anyone else it was just a yawn. She read paperbacks she'd bought at the airport, she had a massage and got her hair done three times, and because Jims, sustaining his role of devoted husband, took photographs of her, she took some of him and a few times included Leonardo. But it was a relief to be going home on Sunday.

The newspapers that were brought round in mid-air were yesterday's, thick Saturday papers stuffed with supplements. Zillah took the *Mail* while Jims opted for the *Telegraph*. She was reading a very interesting piece about fingernail extensions when a choking sound from Jims made her look round. He had gone dark red in the face, a change which made him a lot less attractive.

'What's the matter?'

'Read it for yourself.'

He screwed up the newspaper, tossed the magazine at her and got up, turning right down the aisle and making for where Leonardo was sitting in the back row.

The article about her filled nearly three pages, the text liberally interspersed with photographs. At first Zillah concentrated on the pictures, they were so beautiful. The *Telegraph* had done her proud. What was Jims making a fuss about? The big glamour shot really did make her look like Catherine Zeta Jones. Zillah had been contemplating breast implants now she could afford it, she'd always felt herself lacking in this area, but this photograph showed her with a deep cleavage overflowing out of the bustier.

The big headline didn't present her in a light she much liked: GYPSY SCATTERBRAIN, it read, and underneath that, 'A New Breed of Tory Bride'. Then she began to read the text, her heart gradually sinking and sweat breaking out all over her face and neck.

Gypsy, scatterbrain and firebrand, Carmen to the life, Zillah Melcombe-Smith belongs to the new kind of trophy wife politicians are increasingly acquiring. At 28, she looks like a model, talks like a teenager and suffers, it seems, from various neuroses. Her dark good looks and fiery eyes support her assertion of having Romany blood, as so maybe do her wild statements. We had been in her Westminster flat (suitably close to the Houses of Parliament) for no more than ten minutes when she was threatening to sue us for libel. And why? Because we had dared question her astonishing left-wing beliefs, not to say double standards. Zillah bitterly opposes Tory opinion on homosexuality, that it isn't equal to heterosexuality and is a matter of choice, yet calling someone gay is an insult she looks capable of duelling about.

Odd when you remember [Natalie Reckman went on] *that Zillah's husband 'Jims' Melcombe-Smith had attracted recent speculation as to his possible sexual orientation. All that, of course, has been proved wide of the mark by his marriage to the gorgeous Zillah. But if his past is no longer a mystery, hers may be. The new Mrs Melcombe-Smith had apparently lived the first 27 years of her life in total seclusion and isolation in a Dorset village, an existence she made sound like being walled up in a convent. No job? No training? No former boyfriends? Apparently not. Strangely, Zillah forgot to mention a few small interruptions to this cloistered existence, her ex-husband Jeffrey and their two children, Eugenie 7 and Jordan 3. True, there were no children about when we visited on a sunny spring day. Where has Mrs Melcombe-Smith hidden them? Or has their father custody? If so, this would be a highly exceptional decision on the part of the divorce court. Custody is only given to a father if the mother proves unfit to care for them, which high-spirited, handsome Zillah very obviously is not.*

148

Zillah read to the end, by now feeling sick. Natalie Reckman devoted two long paragraphs to describing her clothes and jewellery, suggesting that Jims ought to be able to afford real stones if she had to adorn herself in the daytime, not the kind of thing you could pick up from the souk in downtown Aqaba. Everyone wore high heels with trousers these days but not stilt heels with leggings. Reckman had a successful technique of insulting her subject by levelling at her hurtful abuse and immediately following it up with a sweetly gentle compliment. So she described Zillah's outfit as more suitable for hanging about King's Cross station, but added that even soliciting gear couldn't spoil her lovely face, enviably slim figure and mane of raven hair.

By this time Zillah was crying. She threw the magazine on the floor and sobbed in the manner of her son Jordan. The stewardess came up to her and asked if there was anything she could do. A glass of water? An aspirin? Zillah said she'd like a brandy.

While she was waiting for it Jims came back, his expression stormy. 'A fine mess you've made of things.'

'I didn't mean to. I was doing my best.'

'If that's your best,' said Jims, 'I wouldn't care to see your worst.'

The brandy made her feel a little better. Jims sat there, austerely drinking sparkling water. 'It makes you look all kinds of a fool,' he continued, 'and by extension, since you're my wife, me as well. What on earth did you mean by threatening to sue for libel? Who do you think you are? Mohamed Fayed? Jeffrey Archer? How did she know your – er, Jerry's name?'

'I don't know, Jims. I didn't tell her.'

'You must have. How did she know the children's names?'

'I really didn't tell her. I swear I didn't.'

'What the devil am I going to say to the Chief Whip?'

Jeff Leigh, alias Jock Lewis, once Jeffrey Leach, read the *Telegraph Magazine* by chance. Someone had left it on the bus he was taking back from reconnaissance in Westminster. He only looked at it because a line in white letters on the cover told him that one of his ex-fiancées was writing inside, *Natalie Reckman Meets a Modern Carmen*. He still had a soft spot for Natalie. She'd kept him without complaint or resentment for nearly a year, got engaged without expecting a ring and parted from him with no hard feelings.

She'd been tough on Zillah and serve her right. Why was she keeping the children's existence dark? During the past week he'd twice been back to Abbey Gardens Mansions, but there had been no one there. The second time the porter told him Mr and Mrs Melcombe-Smith were away but he had no idea where the children were. Jeff tried to press him but he must have become suspicious because he wouldn't even say if there were any children living in apartment seven. Could Natalie be right when she implied Zillah had somehow disposed of them? Yet in that hysterical letter she'd written him – he'd picked it up off the doormat in the nick of time before Fiona got there – said he could have access, see them when he wanted. The way, of course, to settle all this would be for him to write to Jims and simply tell him that Zillah's husband was alive and well, and still married to her. Or even write to that old bat Nora Watling. But Jeff was reluctant to do this. He was aware of how much Jims disliked him, a feeling that was mutual, and this antipathy was shared by Zillah's mother. They might simply disregard his letters. And if they didn't and everything came out into the open, Fiona would very probably find out.

For all his wedding plans, organising the ceremony and reception, talking happily about the forthcoming event, Jeff hoped not to have to marry Fiona while still married to Zillah. He vaguely planned putting off the wedding, finding a reason for postponing it till next year. And although he wanted to know that his children were safe and, come to that, happy, he shied away from having them to live with him. That would be too extreme a step. If he exposed Zillah as a bigamist and Jims abandoned her, as he surely would, the powers-that-be – police? Social Services? the court? – might well take the children from her. The obvious place for them to go would be their father's home. Especially with a broody future stepmother pining to look after them.

Jeff remembered the ridiculous promise he'd made to Fiona, while light-headed on Chardonnay, that he'd be a house husband, stay at home and look after their baby. That could mean looking after Eugenie and Jordan too. Closing his eyes for a moment, he pictured his life, shopping in West End Lane with a baby in a buggy, holding Jordan's hand, hastening to be in time to fetch Eugenie from school. Jordan's constant tears. Eugenie's didactic speeches and general disapproval of everything. Getting their tea. Never going out in the evenings. Changing nappies. No, having the children wasn't feasible. He would have to think of a reason for continuing to live with Fiona without marrying her. Was it too late to say he was Catholic and couldn't be divorced? But Fiona thought he was divorced already . . .

He got off the bus and walked slowly down Holmdale Road. In all his six-year-long quest to find a woman who was young yet rich, a home owner, out at work all day, good-looking, sexy and loving, willing without demur to keep him, he'd never come across one who satisfied the criteria as well as Fiona. Sometimes, especially when he'd had a drink, he even felt romantic about her. So how was he going to juggle the three slippery balls of keeping her in love with him, obtaining access to his children and avoiding marrying her?

He let himself into the house and found her watching Matthew Jarvey's television show. He kissed her affectionately and asked after her parents, whom she'd been visiting while he was out. On the screen Matthew, looking like a famine victim, was gently interviewing a Weight Watchers woman who'd lost twenty pounds in six months.

'Must be nuts, that guy,' said Jeff. 'Why doesn't he just get himself together and eat?'

'Darling, I hope it doesn't upset you, but did you know there's a big piece in the *Telegraph Magazine* about your ex-wife?'

'Really?' This would solve his dilemma of whether to tell her or not.

'Mummy kept it for me. She thought it terribly naff – I mean, the people who write this stuff! What kind of a woman would be such a bitch?'

For some obscure reason, this innocent attack on Natalie Reckman made Jeff angry, but he didn't show it. 'Have you got it, darling?'

'You won't let it upset you, will you?'

Fiona handed him the magazine and returned to watching Matthew chatting to a man who failed to put on weight no matter how heartily he ate. On rereading, the bits about Zillah's clothes and her souk jewellery restored his good temper and made him want to laugh. He assumed a gloomy expression. 'I admit I'm anxious about my children,' he said

152

quite truthfully when the programme ended and Fiona switched off the set.

'Perhaps you should consult a solicitor. Mine's very good. A woman, of course, and young. High-powered, doing very well for herself financially. Shall I give her a ring?'

Fleetingly, Jeff considered it. Not because he had any intention of involving the law – nothing could be more dangerous – but he liked the sound of this woman: young, high-powered, rich. Good-looking? Richer than Fiona? He could hardly ask. Regretfully, he said, 'Better not, at this stage. I'll fix up a meeting with Zillah first. What shall we do this evening?'

'I thought we might stay in, have a quiet time at home.' She edged closer to him on the sofa.

Zillah also had a quiet time at home. Jims had dumped the suitcases in her bedroom and gone off to spend the night with Leonardo. A note by the phone informed her that her mother had removed the children to Bournemouth, being unable to stay in London because Zillah's father had had a heart attack and was in hospital there. Zillah picked up the phone and, as soon as it was answered, got a mouthful of abuse from Nora Watling. How dare she go off without leaving the phone number of the hotel she and Jims were staying in? And never to call once from the Maldives! Had she no concern at all for her children?

'How's Dad?' asked Zillah in a small, wretched voice.

'Better. He's home. He might be dead for all you care. I may as well tell you here and now that I never in my life read anything so disgusting as that article in the *Telegraph*. I haven't kept it for you. I burnt it. More or less calling you a prostitute! A gypsy! When you know perfectly well your father and I come from

153

good West Country stock for generations back. And that picture! As good as topless you were. And calling poor James a pervert!'

Zillah held the receiver at a distance until the cackling ceased. 'I don't suppose you'll feel like bringing the children back?'

'You ought to be ashamed to ask. I'm worn out with nursing your father. And I don't know what to do about Jordan's crying. It's not natural a child of three crying at the least little thing. You'll have to fetch them yourself. Tomorrow. What do you have a car for? I'll tell you something, Sarah, I didn't know my luck all that time we barely had any contact. Since you went to London I haven't had a moment's peace.'

In Glebe Terrace, in Leonardo's tiny but extremely smart Gothic house, he and Jims were reclining on the huge bed that filled Leonardo's bedroom but for a few inches between it and the walls, listening to *The Westminster Hour* on the radio. They had eaten their dinner (gravad lax, quails with quails' eggs, *biscotti*, a bottle of Pinot Grigio) in that bed and made some inventive love afterwards. Now they were relaxing in their favourite way, Leonardo having comforted Jims by telling him not to worry about the *Telegraph*. There was nothing offensive about him in it, rather the reverse. It was Zillah who got all the stick.

A couple who had been spending the evening in a similar way were Fiona and Jeff. Their lovemaking had also been inventive and satisfying, but their dinner had consisted of papaya, cold chicken and ice cream with a bottle of Chilean Chardonnay. Fiona was now asleep while Jeff sat up in bed rereading Natalie Reckman's piece. After a while he got up and, treading softly, went downstairs to find the address book he kept in an inside pocket of his black leather jacket. Fiona, as she'd no hesitation in telling him, was far too honourable ever to look in jacket pockets.

There it was: Reckman, Natalie, 128 Lynette Road, Islington, N1. She might have moved, but it was worth a try. Why not give her a ring for old times' sake?

Chapter 13

Nearly a month went by before Minty got to see Josephine's wedding photographs and then she was expected to pay if she wanted a set of her own. She hadn't the money to waste on things like that, but she carefully scrutinised the photos for a hint of Jock's presence before handing them back. Auntie had had a book with amazing spirit photos in it, taken at seances. Sometimes the spirits looked solid like Jock and sometimes transparent, so that you could see the furniture through them. But there was nothing of either sort in Josephine's pictures, only a lot of drunk people grinning and shrieking and hugging each other.

For a week, while Ken and Josephine were on a deferred honeymoon in Ibiza, Minty had been in charge of Immacue on her own. She didn't like it but she had no choice. Once, when she was in the back ironing and she heard a man's voice, or rather, a man's cough from the shop, she thought Jock had come back again, but it was Laf, his kind face looking doleful and apologetic.

He was in uniform, an imposing figure, all six foot two of him and, it seemed to Minty, exaggerating, nearly six foot two round his middle. 'Hallo, Minty, love. How are you?'

Minty said she wasn't so bad, thanks. Josephine would be back next day.

'It's not Josephine I want. It's you. To be honest

156

with you, it's no good me popping in next door with Sonovia the way she is. She's got a nasty tongue when she likes, as you know. But I thought – well, me and Sonny are going to see *The Cider House Rules* tonight and I thought – well, you might like to come along. No, don't say anything for a minute. I thought, maybe you'd meet us there and sort of come up to us and say hello or whatever and Sonn would – well, she wouldn't make a song and dance of it in a public place, would she?'

Minty shook her head. 'She'd ignore me.'

'No, she wouldn't, love. Believe me, I know her. It'd be a way of putting things right between you. I mean, it's not right the way things are, never being able to pop next door, me not allowed to pass on the papers and all that. I reckon if you did that, she'd apologise and then maybe you would and everything'd be grand again.'

'I've nothing to apologise for. She ought to be glad I had her outfit cleaned. I've still got it, did you know that? *And* I've had it cleaned again since I wore it. If she wants it back she can fetch it.'

Laf tried more persuasion about the cinema visit but Minty only said, no, thanks. She'd been going to the pictures on her own lately, it was quieter and there was no one whispering at her. Because she had no quarrel with Laf she didn't say anything about the popcorn. He went off, shaking his head and saying she hadn't heard the last from him, he'd mend the rift if it was the last thing he did.

Anyway, she didn't want to see that film. She didn't care for the sound of it. Jock had once bought her a half-pint of cider and she'd had to leave it, it tasted so sour. Jock. She'd seen him several times since the wedding, so she knew sticking a blunt knife in him hadn't got rid of him. Again he came into the cemetery when she was putting tulips on Auntie's grave, called her Polo and said he preferred narcissi because they had a lovely scent. All the rest of that day, though she couldn't see him, he kept whispering 'Polo, Polo' at her. The next sighting was in her own house. Once more he was in that armchair. He got up when she came in and, lifting his shirt, showed her the bruise the dinner knife had made in his side, a purplish-blue blotch. Minty went out of the room and shut the door on him, though she knew closed doors couldn't keep him in just as they couldn't keep him out. But when she went back again he was gone. She'd been trembling so much she'd been walking through the rooms touching one colour wood after another but there weren't enough different colours to do any good.

Bruising him wasn't much use. The knife she carried was too small as well as too blunt. She needed one of Auntie's long carving knives. As a police sergeant, Lafcadio Wilson had had to be an observant man and when he came into Immacue to reason with Minty he'd noticed something like a bar or wooden baton lying horizontally across her waist. But it was mostly concealed by the loose garment she wore and it was only when she was backing away from him and turning her body round to face the other way that he saw the end of it push out the hem of her sweatshirt. He thought no more about it. Minty was eccentric, everyone knew that. He never suspected the truth, that what he detected was a fourteen-inch-long butcher's knife with a sharp point and a bone handle.

Minty had sharpened it on Auntie's old-fashioned oilstone and she was surprised at the edge she'd achieved. She laid it against the skin on her forearm. One touch and the blood leapt from her arm in a string of beads. She wrapped the knife in one of Auntie's linen table napkins, securing it in place with

158

elastic bands, then, with more bands attached it to the bum bag. Provided she wore really loose tops, it wouldn't show.

Often now she heard his voice, but it never said more than 'Polo, Polo'. Not so Auntie's, which had joined his. All the time she'd been praying to Auntie at the grave she never got an answer and she didn't now. It seemed to her that Auntie spoke when days elapsed since she'd been to the cemetery, as if she protested at neglect. The first time she heard the voice she was frightened, it was so clear, so plainly Auntie's. But in life she'd never been afraid of her and gradually she became used to this new invisible visitor from beyond the grave, she'd even have liked to see her, as she saw Jock. Auntie never appeared. She only talked. The way she had when she was alive, about her sisters Edna and Kathleen, about her friend Agnes who'd brought the baby Minty to be looked after for an hour and had never come back, about the puréed prunes and the Duke of Windsor and about Sonovia not being the only person on earth with a son a doctor and a daughter a lawyer.

Then, one day, while Minty was having a bath and washing her hair, Auntie's voice came very clearly and said something new. 'That Jock's evil, Minty love, he's really evil. He's dead but he can't ever come where I am because he's an imp of Satan. If I was back on earth I'd destroy him but I can't touch him from this holy place. I'm telling you it's your mission to destroy him. You've been called to destroy him and then he can go back to hell where he belongs.'

Minty never answered Auntie because somehow she knew that though she could speak, she couldn't hear. She'd been deaf for a couple of years before she died. The voice persisted for most of the evening. From her front room Minty watched Sonovia and Laf go off to the cinema. The evenings were light now, the sun still shining. But it had always been rather dark inside this house, perhaps because Auntie and now Minty only drew the curtains back halfway across the windows. For inner London and in parts a rough area, it was also very quiet. Mr Kroot on one side lived in dim silence while the Wilsons weren't keen on television or loud laughter. Into the absence of any sound Auntie's voice came back, telling her to destroy Jock and rid the world of his evil spirit.

Next day the top she put on was tighter and shorter, and the knife showed through, sticking out like some sort of frame. She tried other ways of carrying it and finally found that wearing it under her trousers against her right thigh, strapped in place by a belt, answered best.

A lecture awaited Zillah in the morning. Jims was dressed as she hadn't seen him for the past ten days. Perhaps she'd never seen him so svelte and elegant. He wore a charcoal suit, impeccably cut, for which he'd paid £2000 in Savile Row, a frostily white shirt and a slate-coloured silk tie with a vertical saffron stripe. Zillah belonged to that school of taste which holds that a man is never so attractive as when dressed in a dark formal suit and gloom descended on her. She hadn't slept well and her hair needed washing.

'I've something to say to you. Sit down and listen, please. Recriminations are quite useless, I realise that. What's done is done. It's the future I'm concerned about.' All of Eton and Balliol were in his tone. 'I don't wish you to speak to any journalists at all, Zillah. Do you understand what I'm saying? Not any at all. There must be no exceptions. Frankly, I had no idea when you began on your press campaign that you would be as rash and uncontrolled as you have

160

been. I expected a modicum of discretion, but I've said there are to be no recriminations, so let that be an end to them. The key phrase for you to remember is, no contact with the media. Right?'

Zillah nodded. She was remembering the charming boy of her adolescence who had been such a sweet and funny companion, and the gracious man who visited her in her loneliness at Long Fredington and who always seemed close to her in a happy and intimate conspiracy, Zillah and Jims versus the world. Where had he gone? Her heart sank like a stone when she thought: *this is my husband.*

'I would like to hear you say it, Zillah.'

'I won't talk to the media, Jims. Please don't be so angry with me.'

'I shall tell Malina Daz to hold you to that. Now you're off to fetch the children today, I think you said. It would be a good idea if you were to stay a few days with your parents.'

'In Bournemouth?'

'Why not in Bournemouth? It's a very pleasant watering place and the children like it. It will give you an opportunity to check on your father's health. How do you suppose it would look if it got about – if it got into a newspaper – that (a) you failed to return from the Maldives when your father had had a coronary and (b) you failed to rush post-haste to his bedside once you did return?'

'But I didn't know he'd had a coronary till last night!'

'No, because you didn't once take the trouble to phone your mother while you were away, although your children were with her.'

It was unanswerable. Even Zillah could see that. 'How long do you want me to stay there?'

'Until Friday.'

It was a lifetime.

The traffic was heavy and it was nearly six by the time Zillah reached her parents' house. Her father lay on the sofa, boxes and bottles of medicaments on the little table beside him. He looked perfectly well, his eyes bright and a rosy flush on his face.

'Poor Grandad fell down on the floor,' said Eugenie importantly. 'He was all alone. Nanna had to bring me and Jordan down to save his life and I said, "If poor Grandad dies, we must get someone to bury him in the ground," but he didn't die.'

'As you see,' said Charles Watling, grinning.

'We went to the hospital and Nanna said to Grandad, "Your daughter's gone to the ends of the earth and I don't know her phone number."'

Nora Watling had packed up the children's things and prepared sandwiches for them to eat in the car on the way home. When Zillah said they would be staying till Friday she sat down heavily in an armchair and said flatly that they couldn't. Even one more day of Jordan's crying and Eugenie's officiousness would be too much, not to mention the presence of Zillah herself.

'No one ever wants us,' Eugenie said calmly. 'We're just a burden. And now our poor mummy is too.'

Weakening, Nora put an arm round her. 'No, you're not, my darling. Not you and your brother.'

'If we can't stay here,' said Zillah, 'where are we supposed to go?' Had she known the passage, she might have said that the foxes have their holes and the birds of the air their nests, but she had not where to lay her head. 'To a hotel?'

'Your husband had enough of you, has he? That's a good start, I must say. I suppose you'll have to stay, if that's what you want. But you'll have to help me. Do the shopping, for one thing, and take the children out in the afternoons. Never mind about

162

Eugenie's schooling. That's the last thing on your mind. But you mark my words, there's no doubt one never gets rid of one's children. No matter how often you think they've gone for good this time, they always come back. Look at me with you.'

'You see, you'll never get rid of us, Mummy,' Eugenie said happily.

Zillah had to sleep in the same room as the children. Jordan went to sleep crying and woke up in the night crying. This began to worry her and she wondered vaguely if she should take him to a child psychiatrist. In the daytime the three of them spent the mornings food shopping and fetching prescriptions, and in the afternoons, because the weather was fine, they went to the beach. It was as bad as being back in Long Fredington. On Thursday morning Charles Watling became ill again, breathless and with a pain down his left side. The GP came and he was rushed into hospital.

'It's no good, you'll have to go, Sarah. I can't stand the worry and the noise, not with your father like this. I wouldn't be surprised if it was hearing Jordan crying all the time that set this second attack off. You can stop tonight in a hotel. Goodness knows, it's not as if you were short of money.'

At five that afternoon Zillah checked them into a hotel on the outskirts of Reading. Eugenie and Jordan were tired and after they'd eaten pizza and chips, went immediately to bed and to sleep. For once, Jordan didn't cry but nevertheless Zillah slept badly. Yawning and rubbing her eyes, she remembered to phone her mother in the morning, was told her father was 'comfortable' and would probably be having a bypass at the end of the following week. At just after eight she started the drive home in heavier traffic than she'd ever experienced and it was past eleven when she drove into the Abbey Gardens Mansions car park.

Once in the flat she phoned Mrs Peacock. Would she have the children? Take them somewhere for lunch and then maybe to the zoo or Hampton Court or something? Please. She'd pay her double her usual rate. Mrs Peacock, who'd spent a lot more than she'd meant to while in the Netherlands, readily said yes. Zillah rang the porters, told them she wasn't to be disturbed on any account, unplugged the phones and fell into bed.

The quest for his children Jeff might have postponed for a while had it not been for Fiona's urging. It must have been seeing his dilemma down in black and white in the newspaper that affected her, for she'd spent most of Monday evening encouraging him to arrange a meeting with Zillah, demand to see his children and, if such attempts failed, consult her solicitor. Jeff knew it wasn't the plain sailing it seemed to her. Too much of this sort of thing and his marital status would come out. He couldn't exactly promise he'd free himself from Zillah, for how could you divorce a woman who'd already married someone else? How could he say he was a Catholic when he'd never mentioned it before?

On Tuesday he'd taken the Jubilee Line tube from West Hampstead to Westminster and walked down to Abbey Gardens Mansions. No one was at home in number seven and this time the head porter said he'd no idea where Mrs Melcombe-Smith was. Someone must have warned him to be discreet, for he denied all knowledge of any children living in the flat. For all he knew, as he said afterwards to his deputy, that chap might be a kidnapper or a paedophile.

It was a lovely day. Jeff sat on a seat in the Victoria Tower Gardens and called Natalie Reckman on his mobile. At first he got her voice mail but when he rang again ten minutes later she answered.

Her tone was cordial. 'Jeff! I suppose you read my piece in the magazine?'

'I didn't need that to remind me,' he said. ' I think about you a lot. I miss you.'

'How nice. All alone, are you?'

'You could say that,' Jeff answered carefully. 'Have lunch with me. Tomorrow? Wednesday?'

'I couldn't before Friday.'

He had the five hundred he'd won on Website. Unashamedly he said, 'I'll pay. Where shall we eat? You choose.'

She'd chosen Christopher's. Well, he could use Zillah's Visa card and hope he hadn't already gone over its limit with the handbag he'd bought Fiona for her birthday and the roses for the six months' anniversary of their moving in together. These cards should have their limit printed on them for the sake of people like him. He'd crossed the street and tried the Melcombe-Smith flat again but Zillah still wasn't in.

On Thursday, a bit recklessly, he'd backed a horse called Spin Doctor to win and it came in first. The odds had been long and he'd picked up a packet. Next day he went back to Westminster and got to Abbey Gardens Mansions just as Zillah and the children were coming off the M4 at Chiswick. He rang the bell, got no answer, made more enquiries of the porter and was told the man didn't know, he couldn't keep tabs on all the residents and no one expected him to. As it happened, Jims had gone down to his constituency on the previous afternoon, by chance passing Zillah outside Shaston. Neither saw the other.

Jeff wondered how he could consult a solicitor without its coming out that he was still married to

165

Zillah. Dared he confess this to Natalie? Probably not. She was a very nice woman, clever and good-looking, but she was above all a journalist. He wouldn't trust her an inch. The only person he could confess to was Fiona. As he wandered along the Embankment in the sunshine, he pondered the possibility of this. The danger was that she wouldn't forgive him, she wouldn't say something on the lines of, 'Darling, why didn't you tell me sooner?' or 'It doesn't matter but you'd better set about it now,' but would throw him out of the house. She was strictly law-abiding, he'd never known such rectitude in a woman or man either, come to that. Whatever she advised or whatever she warned him about, she'd want those Melcombe-Smiths told the truth, she'd want to know his intentions. Jeff didn't care much for Zillah and he actively disliked Jims but he stopped short at making her destitute and wrecking the man's career. No, he couldn't confess to anyone. Except perhaps to a solicitor? What he told such a person would be in confidence. There might be some way of serving divorce papers on Zillah without Jims or anyone else being any the wiser. But what about the children? Would it be possible to get a divorce without mentioning the children's existence? After all, they didn't need anyone to support them, they had Jims. One of those postal divorces. . .

With these thoughts rotating in his head, he bought himself a cup of coffee in the Strand, a half of bitter in a pub in Covent Garden and arrived at Christopher's at five to one. Natalie came in at five past. As always, she was severely dressed, this time in a grey pinstriped trouser suit, but with her upswept blonde hair – she had that kind of stripy fair hair, gold and flaxen and light brown, which no dye can emulate and which Jeff admired – and discreet silver jewellery, she looked very fetching.

After some small talk and, in Jeff's case, a lot of lies about his recent past, he grew mildly sentimental about what might have been.

'I don't know about that,' said Natalie sharply. 'You left me.'

'It was what they call constructive desertion.'

'They call it that, do they? And by that they mean, presumably, a certain amount of questioning on my part as to why I always paid the rent and bought the food?'

'I'd explained I was between jobs, you know.'

'No, you weren't, Jeff. You were between women. Just in a spirit of enquiry, who came after me?'

Minty had. Looking back, Jeff thought he'd never sunk so low. But he'd been impoverished and desperate, living in that dump in Harvist Road. The Queen's Head barmaid Brenda had told him Minty had her own house and a lot of money, her aunt had left her God knew how much. A quarter of what rumour said, if he knew anything about it, but as he'd put it to himself, any port in a storm. He might as well be more or less honest about it with Natalie.

'A funny little thing, lived up near Kensal Green Cemetery. I called her Polo because of her name.' He hesitated. 'I don't think I'll tell you what that was. I owe her some money actually, only a thousand. Don't look like that. I mean to pay her back as soon as I can.'

'You never paid me back.'

'You were different. I knew you could afford it.'

'You're incredible, you really are. She came after me. Who was before me?'

The chief executive of a charity and a restaurateur, but he could leave them out. He'd told enough of the truth for one day. 'My ex-wife.'

'Ah, the tarty Mrs Melcombe-Smith. You should have cured her of decorating herself like a Christmas tree. I suppose she never had the chance while she was with you. Funny I remembered your children's names, wasn't it? I must have been fond of you.'

'I was hoping you still are.'

Natalie smiled as she finished her double espresso. 'Up to a point, Jeff. But I've got someone, you see, and I'm very happy with him. You didn't ask, though I asked you. Does that say something about us?'

'Probably that I'm a selfish bastard,' said Jeff cheerfully, though he wished she'd told him before he'd asked her to lunch and was on the way to forking out eighty pounds. One thing about Jeff, as women were to say later, was that he'd no false pride. He didn't try to put himself on her level by mentioning Fiona.

'Where are you off to now?' she asked when they were out in Wellington Street.

'Movies,' he said. 'I don't suppose you'd feeling like coming too?'

'You don't suppose right.' She kissed him on the cheek, one cheek. 'I've work to do.'

He'd told Natalie he was going to the cinema but this was because it was the first thing that came into his head. It wasn't what he'd intended. Revisiting Abbey Gardens Mansions was what he'd had in mind. But getting back to Westminster wouldn't be easy from Kingsway. He'd done enough walking for one day and there was no bus or tube from here that went that way. A taxi with its light on came along and he almost stepped off the pavement and put up his hand. The driver began to pull in. Jeff thought of the money he'd spent on Natalie's lunch and the credit card that was probably over its limit and shook his head. Thus he sealed his fate.

Or he almost sealed it. The seal was poised and it wavered above the hot fresh wax and he was given one more chance. At Holborn he got into a west-bound Central Line tube train. As it approached Bond Street, he thought he might as well get off, change on to the Jubilee Line and go home. But being at home on his own was something he'd never much cared for. He needed a woman there and some food and drink and entertainment. The train came into Bond Street and stopped, the doors opened, a dozen people got out and much the same number got in. The doors closed. Instead of proceeding, the train waited where it was. As usual there was no explanation for the delay offered over the public address system. The doors opened. Jeff got up, hesitated, sat down again. The doors closed and the train started. At the next station, Marble Arch, he got out.

He went up the steps, turned right and made his way to the Odeon. One of the films showing was *The House on Haunted Hill*. He picked it because it started at three thirty-five and the time was now a quarter past three. For some reason, when he'd bought his ticket, he thought of what his mother used to say, that it was a shame to go to the pictures when the sun was shining outside.

Chapter 14

It would have been more interesting, Minty sometimes thought, if the shirt colours and designs had
been more varied. If there hadn't been a preponder-
ance of white ones, for instance or if more had had
button-down collars and pockets on them. She
thought the white ones were getting more common,
there must be a fashion for absolutely plain white
shirts. This Friday morning it had meant ironing
three white ones before she did a pink stripe and two
more before coming to the blue with a navy stripe
and button-down collar. She'd arranged them in
order before starting. Just leaving it to chance was
fatal. Last time she'd done that she'd ended up with
six white ones and it was weary work getting
through six shirts that all looked the same. Apart
from being, in her estimation, unlucky. That morning, when she'd had the white ones left over, had
been the last day she'd seen Jock, and it had to have
something to do with the shirts being out of
sequence.

His ghost had been in the hall when she'd got
home last evening, standing there looking out for
her, waiting for the sound of her key in the lock.
She'd pulled up her sweatshirt, undone her trousers
and tugged the knife out of the strap that held it
against her leg, but he'd slipped past her and run
upstairs. Though she was shaking with fear, she'd
run after him, chasing him into Auntie's bedroom.

Just as she'd thought she had him cornered he vanished through the wall, the way she'd heard spirits could but had never seen before. Auntie's voice had said, 'You nearly had him there, girl,' and said a lot more while Minty was having her bath, all about Jock being evil and a menace to the world, the cause of flood and famine, and the herald of the Antichrist, but it wasn't the first time she'd said that and Minty knew it already. She was beginning to get as impatient with Auntie's talking as she was with Jock's appearances.

Drying her hair, strapping on the knife again, pulling on clean T-shirt and trousers, she shouted out as the voice persisted, 'Go away! I've had enough of you. I know what to do!' She went on saying it as she went downstairs and heard the doorbell ring. Sonovia's younger daughter Julianna, the one who was at university, was outside.

'Were you talking to me, Minty?'

'I wasn't talking to anyone,' said Minty. She hadn't seen Julianna for about a year and only just recognised her, what with a gold stud in one nostril and her hair in about ten thousand braids. It made her shiver. How often could she wash it and how did she get that stud in and out? 'Did you want something?'

'I'm sorry, Minty. I know you and Mum aren't speaking, but now Mum wants her blue outfit back, she'd lost a lot of weight to get into it, and she's going to wear it to a christening on Sunday.'

'You'd better come in.'

Serve her right if Jock came and talked to her, Minty thought as she went upstairs. She might be one of those people who could see him. It would be a relief to get rid of the blue dress and jacket. In spite of dry-cleaning it twice, she couldn't rid herself of the idea that it was still dirty and contaminating the house. 'Polo, Polo,' Jock whispered to her as she went into Auntie's room. He was still there, then, though she couldn't see him any longer.

She'd zipped the outfit up inside a dry-cleaner's bag, taken it downstairs and handed it over to Julianna. 'It's a bit gloomy in here,' Julianna said. 'Why don't you pull the curtains back?'

'I like it that way.'

'Minty?'

'What?'

'You wouldn't come back with me, would you, and say hello to Mum and sort of make things all right? It'd really please my dad if you would. He says it gets up his nose not being on good terms with the neighbours.'

'Tell your mum', said Minty, 'it's her fault, she started it. She can say she's sorry and then I'll start speaking.'

From the window she watched the girl go. She thought of all this while she was ironing and Josephine said, 'Did you ever make it up with what's-her-name that lives next door to you? The one that made all that fuss about her dress?'

'She's called Sonovia.' Minty slipped the last white shirt but three into its plastic bag, tucked the cardboard collar round its neck and took the last striped one from the pile. 'Her husband came in here begging me to apologise but I said I'd nothing to apologise about, it was all her. It was all her, wasn't it? You were there.'

'Of course it was. I'd say that in any court of law.' Josephine looked at her gold and rhinestone watch, a wedding present from Ken. 'I tell you what, Minty, when you've finished that lot you can take the afternoon off if you want. And tomorrow morning. It's only what you deserve, looking after the place while me and Ken were on honeymoon.'

Minty thanked her and managed a half-smile.

She'd rather have had a rise but thought it was hopeless asking. The last three shirts were always a drag to do, but she'd finished them by five to one.

At home again, she took her second bath of the day, feeling fresh resentment against Jock when she thought how he'd done her out of the money she could have spent on a shower cabinet. Sometimes, while in the bath, she thought of the dirt that came off her floating about in the water and getting back on her again. The dirt from her body into her hair and the dirt from her hair on to her body. It might be the reason for her never feeling clean enough. Would she ever be able to afford a shower now?

She ate one of her clean hygienic lunches: carefully washed chicory leaves, a skinned chicken wing, six small boiled potatoes, two slices of white bread with good unsalted butter on them. Then she washed her hands. She'd spend her afternoon off at the cinema.

It was a beautiful, hot, sunny day. Even Kensal Green had smelt fresh and floral as she walked home from Immacue. Beyond the high wall the trees of the cemetery made it look as if some verdant park lay behind. Auntie used to say it was a wicked shame going to the cinema on a fine day, you ought to be outside enjoying it. But she didn't say it now, though Minty listened for her voice to come. Should she go to Whiteley's or to the Odeon at Marble Arch? The Whiteley's complex was nearer, but to reach it she'd have to go through one of the underpasses below the Westway. An underpass was just the sort of place Jock might be waiting for her and she didn't want to see him today, she didn't want him spoiling her time off. So Marble Arch on the 36 bus. *The House on Haunted Hill* was showing there and she quite liked the sound of it. Ghosts in a film weren't frightening when you had a real ghost of your own.

*

Ages passed before the bus came, or it seemed like ages, though it was only ten minutes. As if making up for time, it raced along the Harrow Road and down the Edgware Road, dropping her off at the bottom at exactly three o'clock. By this time she was an old hand at buying her own ticket, showing it to the usher and making her way alone to a seat. Ten people were sitting in the auditorium. Minty counted. She sat in a seat at the end of a row, so that no one could sit next to her on the right, and unless the place filled up, which it wouldn't, nobody would choose to sit on her left. The present occupants of the cinema all looked older than she and were isolated except for a couple of pensioners, man and woman, seated in the very front row. She was pleased to find herself almost alone in the whole block of seats on the right-hand side. It was much better going to the cinema in the afternoon than with Laf and Sonovia in the evening.

The auditorium darkened and advertisements appeared on the screen. Minty had often before watched such commercials with puzzlement, for she understood not a word of them and not an image. The noise they made was loud and the voices that uttered incomprehensible words raucous, while music pounded and brilliant colours and explosive lights flashed across the screen. They were succeeded by something romantic and dreamy, accompanied by a soft sonata: the first trailer of films to come.

To her annoyance, a man had come in and was edging along the row in front of her. He probably couldn't see where he was, the place was dark as pitch but for the pastel colours on the screen. He turned light-dazzled eyes in her direction and she saw it was Jock's ghost. There seemed nowhere she could go where he wouldn't follow her and haunt her. He wasn't wearing his black leather jacket today, it was too warm for that, but a stripy shirt like one of those she'd ironed that morning and a linen jacket that looked new. Where did ghosts get new clothes from? She'd never thought of that before.

He sat down, not directly in front of her, but in the seat in front of the one next to hers, and took a packet of Polo mints out of his pocket. How long would he stay? Would he get up again and vanish through the wall as he'd done the night before in Auntie's room? Minty was more angry than she'd been for a long time, perhaps than she'd ever been. Fear of him had almost gone, it was all anger now. He half turned his head, then looked back at the screen. The romantic film trailer faded away and a violent one came on, the sort that shows high-powered cars in brilliant colours and blazing lights crashing into other cars and careering over precipices while maddened men craned out of their windows, firing guns. The ghost took a mint out of the packet and put it in his mouth. Carefully and silently Minty lifted her T-shirt, unzipped her trousers and pulled the knife stealthily from its plastic sheathing and the strapping round her leg. She laid it on the seat beside her, zipped up her trousers and pulled down her T-shirt. She thought she'd been quiet but she must have made a little sound.

Jock's ghost turned round again, more fully this time. As he looked into her face in the dimness and the roaring noise, his eyes opened wide and he began to get to his feet as if he were afraid of her instead of her of him. More swiftly than she could have believed she'd do it, she snatched up the knife and, rising, thrust it into where she guessed his heart was. If a ghost had a heart, if a ghost could die.

He didn't cry out, or if he did she couldn't hear it above the car crashes and the guns and the beat of the music. No one could have heard anything with that noise going on. But maybe he hadn't made a sound, perhaps ghosts didn't. It took both hands to pull the knife out. There was something reddish brown on it that looked like blood, only it couldn't be, ghosts didn't have blood. It must be whatever ghosts had in their veins that made them able to walk and talk. Ectoplasm maybe. Auntie had talked a lot about ectoplasm in her last years. Minty wiped the dirty knife on the upholstery of the seat next to her. It still wasn't clean, of course it wasn't, it would have to be put in a pan of water and the water brought to the boil before it was really clean. But there was no water here, no stove and no gas. Shuddering, she unzipped her trousers and pushed the knife back against her leg, thankful for the plastic wrapping which kept it from contact with her skin.

Jock's ghost had fallen to the floor and disappeared. Or at any rate, she couldn't see what remained of it. She didn't want to. And she didn't care to remain where she was with the dirty stuff wiped off on to the seat next to her, but she did want to see this film. Fastidiously, shrinking away from contact with that seat as she passed it, she moved to the aisle end of the row, walked a few yards up the aisle and picked herself another seat. It was in the central block and there was no one in front of her and no one behind.

Sleepy Hollow hadn't frightened her and this one didn't. It was a disappointment. If these film people had had her experience of ghosts they'd know more about making things frightening. She wished she'd gone to *The Green Mile*, but it was too late now. Anyway, if she had, Jock's ghost mightn't have been there and she wouldn't have had the chance of banishing him once and for all. When the film was about three-quarters of the way through she got up and left. The man in the back row left too, so she wasn't the only one who hadn't liked it.

Outside it was still hot and sunny. She looked at her hands to see if there was any mess on them but she'd wiped what there was off on the seat when she'd wiped the knife. Still she shivered because when she lifted her fingers up to her nose she could smell something that was like blood but stronger, she thought, more bitter and *unholy*. Spots and splashes of it were all over her clothes but they weren't noticeable to anyone but herself because her trousers were dark red and her T-shirt was a red and blue and yellow pattern. Not that Minty much worried about anyone seeing, it was for herself that she cared. She'd never been concerned about what other people thought of her. They ought to be thinking about what *she* thought of *them*.

But she didn't want to get on a bus. Sitting with that ghost juice on her would somehow be worse than walking in the fresh air. For one thing, it would be all around her, close to her, pressing on her, and for another she'd smell it more. The stench of it began to make her miserable, to make her want to tear her clothes off and plunge into water, any water. That wasn't possible. So she walked. Up the Edgware Road in the heat and the smell from the Middle Eastern takeaway restaurants, along the start of the Harrow Road and through the underpass into Warwick Avenue. There was no longer any fear of meeting Jock there.

This was familiar territory, home ground. The people you passed never took any notice of you and they never sniffed, trying to smell you. Everyone sweated, there was no escaping it, but she hated it happening to her, the feel of the beads of moisture breaking out on her upper lip and forehead, the trickle of it dripping down her chest like tears. It wouldn't smell, not with all the deodorant she used. But how could you be sure you hadn't missed out a little bit of skin surface? She imagined the sweat leaking out of that little bit inside her armpit and that awful meaty, oniony smell breathing on to the air. Almost crying now with the filth that covered her, her own perspiration and the splashed ghost juice, she let herself into the house. She ran upstairs and fell into the bath. It was half an hour later that she boiled the knife. The clothes she'd worn were beyond saving, far far beyond washing. She wrapped them in newspaper, then in plastic, and put them into a black waste bag. Knowing they'd be there, albeit outside, for another four days, sent her out again. The heat met her, it was like opening an oven door. She walked slowly, shrinking her body to keep the sweat in, and dropped the bag into the big council rubbish bin a few yards up the road.

Chapter 15

Michelle set out wineglasses on the coffee table, a heart-shaped dish filled with vegetable crisps that would neither thin down nor fatten up and a rather larger oval one with dry-roasted peanuts. Fiona had said she liked them and she hoped to persuade Matthew to eat a few as well. She, of course, would eat nothing, not even the pink and orange slivers of root vegetable, and would go sparingly on the wine. After her shower that morning she had stood on the scales, hardly daring to look, but found she'd lost three pounds. The week before it had been four pounds. Could there be any greater tonic to an overweight woman than to find she'd lost half a stone in a fortnight? She'd been singing while she dressed herself and Matthew had smiled lovingly at her.

He and she had been out shopping in the afternoon and bought the wine. Michelle knew nothing about wine but Matthew did – in her opinion he was an expert on everything – and he'd chosen a Meursault. Fiona was coming and Michelle knew she preferred white wine over any other alcoholic drink. There wasn't much food to buy, just the few things Matthew would eat, and today he'd agreed to try a bit of chicken, another suggestion of Fiona's, the kind you get at a delicatessen counter and which looks like a close-textured white loaf, from which the assistant saws wafer-thin slices. It would do for her too, along with some green leaves. The shopping bags were about twenty pounds lighter than usual.

It was such a lovely day that Michelle had suggested she drive them both up to the Heath, where they could sit in the sunshine and look at the view. So she'd done this and they'd stayed up there a long time, talking about Matthew's TV successes. He was due to have lunch with a producer who planned to make a short series on the lines of the pilot programme.

'When he said "lunch",' Matthew said, 'I started laughing, darling, I couldn't help it. I thought, *me* having lunch with someone. In a *restaurant*. He thought I was laughing with pleasure at the idea of a series.'

'Can you do it?' Michelle was all concern. 'Eat with someone in a restaurant, I mean? I know you can do the series.'

'I'm going to try. Before we start I'm going to remind him what I am and just why I got the job. And then I'll eat salad and a bit of dry bread. By "eat" I mean nibble and leave three-quarters.'

When Michelle looked at her watch it was past four and they had to get back. She hadn't given Fiona a definite time, just said to come in for a drink when she returned from work. Jeff hadn't been mentioned but Michelle knew that when people were a couple you had to accept the uncongenial one along with the one you liked.

'Still, I hope he's out somewhere and not expected home till seven,' she said to Matthew as she put the two bottles of wine in the fridge.

Matthew looked up from his computer. 'I don't think he'll be rude to you in my presence, darling. If he is I shall tell him to watch his tongue.'

'Oh, Matthew, we mustn't upset Fiona.'

'He mustn't upset you,' said Matthew.

Still, if it hadn't been for Jeff, Michelle thought, she wouldn't be losing weight now. Every time she was tempted by a croissant or a slice of quiche she remembered his hurtful words and turned away from the dangerous food. It was rather odd, to dislike someone yet feel indebted to him.

A little after five thirty Fiona rang the bell. 'You should have come in the back way,' said Michelle. 'No need to be formal.'

'All right, I won't next time. Jeff's out somewhere. He's gone for a job interview. Well, actually, two job interviews, one over lunch and the other at four this afternoon.'

Michelle said nothing. She didn't believe in these possible jobs, but she thought Jeff Leigh perfectly capable of saying he'd found lucrative employment; this in order to get himself out of the house for regular periods each day while pursuing whatever nefarious occupations provided him with an income.

'I've left him a note telling him to come in here when he gets home. I hope that's all right.'

'Of course.'

There was a chill in Michelle's tone and Fiona noticed it. But she smiled uncertainly, told Michelle she was looking remarkably well and wasn't she right in thinking she'd lost weight?

'A few pounds,' said Michelle comfortably.

Matthew shut down his computer and poured the wine. He passed Fiona the dish of peanuts and ate two himself. Michelle had sparkling water. She watched in amazement as Matthew poured himself half a glass of wine and sipped it like a person who hadn't an eating problem, raising his glass to Fiona and saying, 'To your future happiness!'

The talk turned to Fiona's wedding, who'd be invited, what she'd wear, where they'd go for their honeymoon. Michelle noticed she still had no engagement ring and then castigated herself for being a censorious bitch. Maybe engagement rings were no longer fashionable or Fiona just didn't like them. Fiona began talking about a vegan she knew who was bringing up her children as vegans which she, Fiona, didn't think was right. How could she be sure they'd get enough protein? But she'd wondered if Matthew would think the vegan woman suitable to go on his programme.

Matthew laughed and said it was early days yet. 'I haven't got a programme till I've talked to the producer and perhaps not even then.'

'Oh, everyone knows you will have. That first one was so good. Well, I don't know where Jeff's got to. Did you hear my phone ringing a minute ago? That may have been him.'

Michelle occasionally heard the ringing of Fiona's phone through the wall but she hadn't this time. She saw Fiona to the door and kissed her as they said goodbye.

'There you are, darling,' Matthew said. 'He's no more keen on our company than we are on his.'

Because it was past seven when she let herself into her house, Fiona checked her answering machine for messages and then she checked her mobile. Nothing. Jeff might have phoned, of course, and not left a message. That would mean he'd soon be home. She'd very little food in the house and didn't feel like going out to buy some, so she called a restaurant they both liked at Swiss Cottage and booked a table for dinner at eight thirty.

'Wake up,' said Eugenie, shaking Zillah. 'If you go to bed in the daytime you won't sleep tonight.'

Zillah opened her eyes sluggishly and sat up with a groan. It was half past five and she'd slept since eleven. For a moment she hardly knew where she was or why she was there. Then she heard Jordan crying. 'Where's Mrs Peacock?'

'You gave her a key and she let us in. If you hadn't I expect we'd have been out there on the doormat all night. In the cold. Why don't you give me a key, Mummy?'

'Because seven-year-olds don't have keys. And it isn't cold, it's probably the hottest day of the year. Where's Mrs Peacock?'

'Out there.' Eugenie pointed to the door. 'I wouldn't let her come into your bedroom because you might not have any clothes on.'

Zillah got up and, noticing she was wearing only a bra and knickers, put on her dressing gown. Outside the bedroom door, Jordan sat on the floor in tears. She picked him up and he buried his wet face in her neck.

Mrs Peacock was sitting in the living room, in the window seat with its magnificent view of the sunlit Palace of Westminster, drinking from a large glass of what was evidently cream sherry. 'I helped myself,' she said, not at all abashed. 'I needed it.'

'Mrs Peacock took us to McDonald's and then to a movie,' said Eugenie. 'We saw *Toy Story* 2. And please don't say you shouldn't go to the cinema when the sun's shining because we did and we *loved* it, didn't we, Jordan?'

'Jordan cried.' He dug his fingers into his mother's neck till she winced.

'I must owe you a lot of money.'

'Yes, you do rather. I'll just have another Bristol Cream and then we'll tot it up, shall we?'

Zillah paid Mrs Peacock double her usual rate as well as for the cinema and the lunch. Somewhat unsteady on her feet by this time, she meandered into the lift. Zillah shut the front door. Where was Jims? With Leonardo, no doubt. Or had he gone down to his constituency? Most likely he was in Fredington Crucis and had Leonardo with him. She wondered how on earth she was going to pass the weekend. It was as bad as being in Long Fredington. Because there was no Annie or Lynn here, no Titus and Rosalba, it was worse.

The body of Jeffrey John Leach lay on the floor of the cinema, on the right-hand side between rows M and N, for nearly two hours before it was discovered. No one leaving a cinema looks along an empty row even if the lights are on. The next performance of *The House on Haunted Hill* was due to begin at six ten and there would be a final screening, the most popular, at eight forty-five. But the six-ten showing was fairly well attended – or would have been if the two eighteen-year-old girls hadn't entered row M at a quarter to. They told no one what they saw. They screamed.

Immediately the cinema was cleared and patrons' ticket money refunded. An ambulance came, but it was too late for that. The police arrived. Jeffrey Leach had taken a little while to die, it came out later at the inquest, as his lifeblood seeped away into the carpet. Police noticed the blood all over one of the seats, as if the perpetrator had wiped the weapon on its upholstery. It was at this point that the whole cinema, not only this particular theatre, was closed to the public.

Within an hour they knew that Jeff had died between three and four thirty. None of the staff remembered who had sat in that row nor any patron leaving early. One said he thought he recalled a man leaving around five and another vaguely remembered a woman slipping out at ten past. Both were unable to describe these people or even make a guess at their ages. The cinema was searched for the weapon, a long, sharp carving knife. When that yielded nothing the search was extended and the Edgware Road closed from Marble Arch to Sussex Gardens, causing the worst traffic jam in central London for ten years.

The body was removed. The bloodstained seat and those on either side of it were also taken away for DNA testing, in case the perpetrator had left behind a hair, a flake of skin, a drop of his or her own blood. The police might have saved themselves the trouble. All the hairs that ever fell from Minty's head came out when she washed it, as she did once or twice a day, and disappeared down the plughole. Any flakes of skin had been scrubbed off with a nailbrush and a loofah in hot soapy water. She left no more DNA behind her than would a plastic doll fresh from its manufacturer's. The principle that every murderer leaves something of himself behind at the crime scene and takes some trace of it with him, Minty had disproved.

When it got to nine and Jeff hadn't come home, Fiona was so worried she went next door. Not because Michelle or Matthew would know any more than she did, not that they could give her any advice she couldn't give herself, but simply for their company, for the comfort and reassurance they might give her. To have someone else with whom to share her anxiety. Long before, she'd cancelled that dinner reservation, made herself tea and tried unsuccessfully to eat a sandwich.

Afterwards, when they were in bed, Matthew and Michelle confessed to each other that they'd both had the same thought: that Jeff had deserted Fiona. Of course, they said not a word of this at the time. When a woman is out of her mind with worry you don't tell her that maybe the man she met only eight months before and of whose past history she knows nothing, has walked out on her. You don't say he's obviously a villain and a conman who's alarmed by the prospect of marriage. You give her a brandy and tell her to wait a little and then you'll start phoning hospitals.

Fiona went home twice just to check he hadn't come back in the meantime. She returned to the Jarveys twice, by now shaking with fear. It was past ten. If that man's somewhere with another woman, thought Michelle, I'll find some way to punish him. Never mind his teaching me to slim, that was me, not him. I didn't have to take notice of what he said, but I will make life hard for him if he's betrayed her. I will find him and tell him what I think of him. I will set a private detective on his track, I *will*. Her unaccustomed vindictiveness alarmed her and she forced herself to give Fiona an encouraging smile. Should she make tea? Another drink? Fiona stood up and threw herself into Michelle's arms. Michelle hugged her and patted her shoulder, and held her against her big, soft bosom while Matthew phoned the Royal Free and the Whittington, and half a dozen other hospitals. Then he phoned the police.

They knew nothing about a Jeff Leigh. Matthew spelt the name for them.

'You said Leigh, not Leach?'

'No, Leigh.'

'There's been no accident to anyone of that name.'

For by now they knew whose was the body they had on their hands. In the breast pocket of its linen jacket they found a bloodstained driving licence in the name of Jeffrey John Leach, of 45 Greta Road, Queen's Park, London NW10. It had been issued nine years ago and a long time before new British driving licences were required to contain their holders' photograph. Also in the pocket were a photograph, in a plastic pack, of a long-haired young man with a baby in his arms, a bloodstained letter from a woman called Zillah, a doorkey of a common kind and unnumbered, three hundred and twenty pounds in twenty- and ten-pound notes, a Visa card in the name of Z. H. Leach and a half-used packet of Polo mints.

It took no more than a few hours to establish that Jeffrey John Leach was married to Sarah Helen Leach, née Watling, who also had a driving licence and lived at an address in Long Fredington, Dorset.

Chapter 16

Arriving in his parliamentary constituency late on Friday afternoon, Jims had first had a meeting with his agent, Colonel Nigel Travers-Jenkins, and then, accompanied by him, gone as guest of honour and principal speaker to the annual gala dinner of the South Wessex Young Conservatives at the Lord Quantock Arms in Markton. Contrary to Zillah's belief, Leonardo wasn't with him. While he was speaking, on the subject of the Party's future hope and inspiration being in the hands of its youth, whose idealism and fervour had already been manifested to him that evening, Zillah was sitting in the Abbey Gardens flat watching a *Rugrats* video with the children, Jordan grizzling on her lap.

Jims, who had been casually fond of her for years, had always used her rather as a screen for his natural activities than as a friend. She was the kind of woman whose appearance led the South Wessex Conservatives to put her down as a female of loose morals. Any Fredingtonian seeing him call at Willow Cottage, particularly in the evenings, believed – again in their phrase – the worst. But they were the sort of people who held to a double standard, condemning the woman in this situation but attaching no blame to the man. Rather the reverse, as Jims well knew, for someone had reported back to him that Colonel Travers-Jenkins had been overheard calling him 'a bit of a lad with the birds'. For this reason, though he used her, he had always felt grateful to Zillah and persuaded himself this was affection.

Now he was married to her he felt quite differently. She was a nuisance and, if not kept under surveillance, might damage his career. Jims thought about these things as he drove back to his house in Fredington Crucis. What a pity it was that once you'd been through a marriage ceremony, you had to live under the same roof as your bride! What a misfortune you couldn't give her a lump sum and a little house somewhere, and never see her again! Still, he knew this was impossible. He must be married and manifestly be seen to be married. And his wife must be Caesar's wife. There was no other way. When he got home on Monday morning he would set about educating Zillah in her duties as helpmeet to the Member for South Wessex. He would teach her about the boards and committees she must chair, the garden parties she must attend, the baby shows judge, Conservative Women's gatherings address, the canvassing she must do and the suitable clothes she must wear. No skirts above the knee, nothing low-cut, no sexy shoes, tight trousers – maybe no trousers at all – but afternoon dresses and big hats. A supposed mistress may look like a loose woman but not an MP's wife.

Jims had phoned Leonardo and then gone to bed. In the morning he held his surgery at nine sharp in Casterbridge Shire Hall, where he made earnest promises to his constituents that he would personally improve the education of their children, the National Health Service, transport and the environment, while undertaking to retain at all costs hunting with dogs. Jims didn't say 'dogs', though that was the term that appeared in the title of the new Bill proposed on the subject. To please the people in the Shire Hall he referred always to 'hounds'. Talk of the hunt, a constant subject of conversation and discussion in South Wessex, reminded him that on Saturday evening he would be addressing the local branch of the Countryside Alliance at Fredington Episcopi village hall. The meeting would be so well attended that the largest hall in the neighbourhood had been chosen as its venue.

His speech he had brought with him. It was still in his briefcase, which he hadn't even opened while at Fredington Crucis House. In calling it a speech, Jims was rather underrating himself, for of course he had no intention of *reading* to the assembled members. But there were all sorts of details of a previous Private Member's Bill that he had noted down on paper, along with statistics, reports on research into cruelty to stags and stress levels in foxes and, most important, assessments of the hardship which would be suffered by locals should hunting be banned in what Jims was careful to call 'England' and occasionally 'this blessed plot', but never 'the United Kingdom'. Also with his notes was the Burns Report in its dark-blue cover, the findings of Lord Burns's investigation into hunting. When he was leaving his surgery and was once more in his car, he opened his briefcase to check that he had it and his notes with him.

Jims intended to have lunch at the Golden Hind in Casterbridge with a close friend, the predecessor, in fact, of Leonardo. The decision to end their relationship had been mutual and there were no hard feelings. Moreover, Ivo Carew was chairman of a charity called Conservatives Target Cancer, so being seen with him could only win approval. But he couldn't find his Countryside Alliance notes. He emptied everything out of the briefcase on to the passenger seat. Before he started he knew they weren't there and he also knew very well where they were. Inside a transparent blue plastic folder which matched the cover of the Burns Report, and he would have spotted them at once. He knew they weren't there and he knew where they were: in Leonardo's house.

But precisely where? That he couldn't remember. He did remember, though, that Leonardo had told him on the phone the evening before that he was taking Friday off and would be going to see his mother in Cheltenham. These visits were frequent and enjoyable, for Giulietta Norton, born in Rome just after the Second World War and a hippy and groupie in the sixties, was a fascinating woman and about as unlike a mother as could be. Leonardo might even decide to stay the night. Of course Jims had a key to the flat, that was no problem. Even if he could remember exactly where the blue folder was and could persuade one of Leonardo's neighbours to let his messenger in, whom could he trust? Was there anyone he could rely on to go to Glebe Terrace, find the notes and fax them to him, without thinking it funny, without thinking it suspicious that James Melcombe-Smith MP left important papers in the home of a young and very good-looking stock jobber? In, very probably, that young man's bedroom? Zillah, perhaps. He called his home number on his mobile. No answer. In fact, Zillah, deeply asleep, heard the phone ringing in a dream about Jims changing his sexual orientation and falling in love with her. She thought the ringing was her mother and she ignored it.

How useless she was! An encumbrance, not even a helpful companion. Jims called Ivo Carew and cancelled their date.

'Thanks a bunch,' said Ivo. 'Did you have to wait till five to one?'

'It's unavoidable. D'you honestly think I wouldn't rather see you than drive back to bloody London?'

He stopped en route at a Merry Cookhouse where, shuddering, he tried to eat chicken in a basket and chips. With plenty of time to spare, he could have lunched with Ivo and set off a couple of hours later, but he was becoming nervous about the whereabouts of that folder. His mind must be set at rest as soon as possible. But not before he'd complained about the soggy chips and the chicken, which he was sure was high. The manager was a man with a temper easily roused and the two of them engaged for a minute or two in a slanging match.

The traffic was heavy and grew heavier as Jims approached London. A pile-up near a motorway and a road junction caused a nose-to-tail queue extending for several miles, while roadworks near Heathrow airport reduced cars to a single lane. It was close to eight o'clock before he parked the car in Glebe Terrace. His mind must be going, he thought. Having mislaid his notes, he was now unable to find the key to Leonardo's house. He looked on his Abbey Gardens Mansions key ring and his car keys ring, then went through his pockets. It wasn't there. The woman next door, Amber Something, had one. He prayed she'd be at home and she was. She gave him a funny look in which there was a lot of snide amusement but she gave him the key, saying to be sure to let her have it back in the morning. He let himself into Leonardo's house.

Mounting the little staircase to the bedroom, he thought how ghastly it would be if he opened the door and found Leonardo in bed with someone, maybe that guy in the Department of Education and Employment he said was attractive. A lot of men wouldn't mind, though he wasn't one of them. But the room was empty.

Jims searched for the folder. It was nowhere to be found. Seriously worried, he went back downstairs and after hunting – hunting! – for ten minutes, found it and Burns at the back of a rather elegant rosewood filing cabinet. Put there, no doubt, by Leonardo's obsessively tidy busybody of a cleaner.

He'd go out to dinner, then come back here to sleep. There was a chance Giulietta had a date, in which case Leonardo might come back. Anyway, he couldn't face his own home, not with Zillah there and those kids.

While Jims was searching for his notes and Zillah was watching television in Abbey Gardens Mansions with Jordan on her lap, two policemen, a sergeant and a constable, were calling at Willow Cottage, Long Fredington.

After she had left, Zillah's landlord, who during her tenancy had been afraid she'd never go but stay for ever and eventually establish children's rights for her girl and boy, had decided to sell the place. Accordingly, he was having it redecorated and a new kitchen and bathroom fitted. Although the builders had started soon after Christmas, their task was still incomplete. Scaffolding covered the front of the house, the windows were boarded up and a builders' sign proclaiming the workmen as Construction Designers stuck up in the garden. The police could see no one lived there. They tried the neighbours and were told Mrs Leach had left in December and got married again. The woman next door could even tell them whom she'd married: the local MP, Mr Mel-combe-Smith.

It was, of course, imperative that the late Jeffrey Leach's wife be told as soon as possible of his violent death. But it now appeared she was his wife no longer. She had remarried, and into a social class far above what the investigators had calculated was Jeffrey Leach's.

Zillah had just got up on Saturday morning when the policeman rang the bell at Abbey Gardens Mansions. It was only half past eight, an early hour for her, but she'd been unable to lie in, for Eugenie's prediction proved true, that having slept most of the day she wouldn't be able to sleep at night. The children were already up and watching cartoons on television. Zillah came out in her dressing gown and began making toast and pouring cornflakes into bowls. She caught sight of herself in a mirror and backed away from it, she looked so terrible, her hair in rats' tails and dark smudges under her eyes. A spot, the like of which she hadn't had for fifteen years, was erupting in the middle of her chin.

'Who on earth's that?' she asked when the bell rang.

'You'll know if you open the door,' said Eugenie. 'What a stupid question.'

'How dare you be so rude!'

Jordan, who was always upset by shouting, began to snivel. The doorbell rang again and Zillah went to answer it.

'Mrs Melcombe-Smith?'

'That's right.'

'May I come in? I have some distressing news for you.'

There was no one in the world not in the flat at that moment whom Zillah cared enough for to mind whether they were fit or injured, alive or dead. But she couldn't hide her shocked response when the caller told her of the death of Jeffrey Leach. 'I don't believe it!'

'I'm afraid it's true.'

'What did he die of? Some sort of accident?'

This may have given the man the impetus to come straight out with it. 'He was murdered yesterday afternoon. I'm sorry.'

'Murdered? Who murdered him?'

There was no reply to that. The policeman wanted to know where she'd been between three and four thirty and Zillah, still amazed at the news, said she'd been here.

'Alone?'

'Yes, quite alone. My children were out with their – er, nanny.'

'And Mr Melcombe-Smith?'

Zillah couldn't exactly say she didn't know. It would look very odd in a bride of two months. 'In his constituency. That's South Wessex, you know. He's been there since Thursday afternoon. I can't believe Jerry's been murdered. Are you sure it was Jerry?'

'Certainly it was Mr Jeffrey Leach. Is this him?'

Zillah looked for the first time in nearly seven years on the photograph she herself had taken in those happier times – though she hadn't thought them so then – of Jerry with the three-week-old Eugenie in his arms. 'My God, yes. Where did you find it?'

'That's not important. You identify it as Jeffrey Leach?'

She nodded. 'I'm amazed he kept it.'

Then came the question of questions, the one that brought the blood to her face and made it recede again as rapidly: 'When exactly were you divorced, Mrs Melcombe-Smith?'

She knew it would be a mistake to lie but she had to. Still, she hesitated. 'Er – it must have been last spring. About a year ago.'

'I see. And when did you last see Mr Leach?'

It had been two days before, here, in this flat. She

195

remembered how he'd called her a bigamist. The time before that had been six months ago, in October, in Long Fredington, when he'd come for the weekend. And driven away in the boneshaker, ten minutes before the express and the local train crashed. 'October,' she said. 'It was while I was living in Dorset with my children.' For the sake of verisimilitude, she felt the need to insert some circumstantial detail. 'He drove down on the Friday evening and stayed the weekend. The first weekend in October. He left again on the Tuesday morning.'

He held something out to her. It was a Visa card. 'Is this yours?'

'Yes, no, I don't know.'

'The name on it is Z. H. Leach and those are not common initials.'

'Yes, it must be mine.'

It was the card Jims had arranged for her to have last December when she'd accepted his proposal. She saw that its starting date was December and expiry date November 2003. After she was married and Jims gave her two new cards in the name of Mrs Z. H. Melcombe-Smith, she'd forgotten all about the existence of this one. How had Jerry got hold of it? That day in the flat he'd wandered about when he was supposed to be going to the loo, she'd heard his stealthy footsteps, thought she heard him go into her bedroom, but attached no importance to it. After all, she was used to visitors prying into her things, Malina Daz, Mrs Peacock . . .

'Did you give it to Mr Leach?'

'No, yes. I don't know. He must have taken it. Stolen it.'

'That's an interesting conclusion to come to, especially since this card wasn't issued until December and the last time you saw Mr Leach was in October. Are you sure you haven't seen him since?'

Then Zillah uttered the time-honoured phrase so often on the lips of old lags up in court yet again. 'I may have done.'

The policeman nodded. He said that that would be all for now but he'd be in touch. When did she expect Mr Melcombe-Smith's return? Zillah didn't but she said Sunday evening. Eugenie came into the room, holding her brother's hand, both fully dressed and looking clean and neat. The policeman said in the kind of voice childless men use when talking to children they've never met before, bluff, interrogatory, embarrassed, 'Hello. How are you?'

'Extremely well, thank you. What have you been saying to my mummy?'

'It was just a routine enquiry.' The policeman suddenly realised the late Jeffrey Leach must have been their father. 'I'll see myself out,' he said to Zillah.

A famous Italian novelist and professor had just published a new book to great acclaim and Natalie Reckman was off to Rome to interview him. Her flight left from Heathrow in the late morning. She bought the novelist's first book in paperback and three newspapers at an airport bookstall but they told her only that a man had been murdered in a London cinema and this didn't much interest her.

While in the aircraft she read her paperback. The *Evening Standard* was brought round but Natalie shook her head, she'd seen enough newspapers for one day. She thought she might stay in Rome till Monday, have a look at a new theatre that was being built, maybe see what all this fuss was about someone desecrating the graves in the English Cemetery. With luck she'd get three stories for the price of one.

*

When it got to midday on Saturday and Jeff still hadn't come back, Fiona feared he had left her. She searched the house for a note, looked under tables and behind cabinets in case it had fallen on the floor from where he'd left it. There was nothing. To go without a word was to add insult to injury, but gone he had.

Michelle helped with the search. She pointed out that if Jeff had really left, he'd taken nothing with him. All the clothes but those he'd gone out in were in the cupboard, including the black leather jacket he was so fond of. His four pairs of shoes, apart from those he was wearing, were in Fiona's shoe rack, his underpants and socks in the drawer. Would he have gone without his electric shaver? Without his *toothbrush*?

'I'm afraid he must have met with some sort of accident,' Michelle said, her arm round Fiona. 'Now, Fiona darling, was he carrying anything to identify him?'

Fiona tried to remember. 'I don't know. You wouldn't go through Matthew's pockets, would you?'

'I never have.'

'No, and nor do I. I trust Jeff. D'you think I should now? I mean, look in the pockets of the leather jacket?'

'Yes, I do.'

There was nothing helpful, only a pound coin, a supermarket bill for groceries and a ballpoint pen. Fiona tried the pockets of Jeff's raincoat. A tube train ticket, a button, a twenty-pence piece. 'Where's his driving licence?'

'Where did he usually keep it?'

'I suppose it might be in the car.'

The two women went out to Fiona's dark-blue BMW, which she was obliged to leave parked in the street. Michelle, who was finding it less difficult these days to climb into a car than it had been, got into the back and searched the pockets, while Fiona, in the driver's seat, examined the glove compartment. A road map, a pair of sunglasses, a comb, all belonging to her. No gloves, of course, there never are. Michelle found another road map, a half-empty box of tissues, a chocolate paper and a single Polo mint. This might have been a valuable clue for the police if they'd known of it and known how to read it. Fiona dropped it down the drain in the gutter.

Michelle stayed with her, made lunch, salad and cheese and crispbread. Neither felt like eating. At mid-afternoon Matthew joined them. Michelle had left his lunch on a tray and to please her and divert Fiona, he told her he'd eaten it all, three slices of kiwi fruit, a dozen salted almonds, half a bread roll and a sprig of watercress. By this time Fiona's mood had changed. They'd been unable to find Jeff's driving licence, so he must have it on him and if he'd met with an accident could have been identified by it. The anger which had been suspended when she realised all his clothes were in the house, to be replaced by the anxiety of the night before, returned. He'd left her. No doubt he intended to come back one day for his possessions or he'd even have the nerve to ask her to send them on.

The *Evening Standard* was delivered to the house in the late afternoon. Matthew heard it drop on to the doormat and went into the hall to fetch it. Fiona was on the sofa with her feet up, Michelle in the kitchen making tea. The newspaper had a big headline: MOVIE MURDER and under that: 'Man Stabbed in Cinema'. A large photograph showed the interior of the theatre where the body had been found, though nothing of the body itself, and there was no picture of the dead man. His name wasn't disclosed. Matthew took the newspaper back into the living room but Fiona was asleep. He showed it to Michelle.

'There's no possible reason to think it's Jeff, darling.'

'I don't know about that,' said Matthew. 'He likes the cinema and Fiona doesn't. It wouldn't be the first time he's gone in the afternoon on his own.'

'What shall we do?'

'I think I'll call the police, darling, and see what I can get out of them.'

'Oh, Matthew, what are we going to do if it *is* Jeff? How terrible for poor Fiona. And why would anyone want to murder him?'

'You can think of a few reasons and so can I.'

Leonardo had returned from his mother's just as Jims was going out to get his dinner. The two men went to a new and fashionable Tunisian restaurant together, came home again at ten thirty and Jims spent the night in Glebe Terrace. Both were far too discreet to suggest Leonardo accompany Jims to Dorset, so he set off alone at about ten in the morning.

Once it was possible, when driving to the West Country, to stop in some little town of great antiquity and beauty, and there eat lunch in the White Hart or the Black Lion or whatever ancient hostelry graced the place. But since the coming of arterial roads that bypassed every urban habitat this pleasant custom had disappeared, unless you made a twenty-mile detour, and all that now existed to provide refreshment to the traveller were motorway cafés and huge complexes of restaurant, shops and lavatories. Into one of these Jims was obliged to go, having parked his car among several hundred others, to eat a limp salad, two samosas and a banana. One good thing: he'd avoided the Merry Cookhouse. By three he was back in Fredington Crucis where he had a bath and dressed in his country-go-to-meetings suit, a well-cut tweed outfit with waistcoat, a tan-coloured shirt and knitted tie. A crowd of anti-hunt protesters were assembled outside Fredington Episcopi village hall, all carrying banners with words like 'barbarians' and 'animal tormentors' on them. Dreadful photographs of tortured foxes in their death throes and stags escaping hunters by plunging into the Bristol Channel were set up along the short driveway. A horrible baying sound, not unlike that of hounds in full cry, went up from the protesters as Jims walked in, but inside he was greeted by sustained applause. The place was packed, with chairs in the aisles and people standing at the back.

The chairman of the local branch introduced him and congratulated him on his recent marriage. The audience cheered. Jims addressed them as 'Ladies and Gentlemen, friends, Englishmen and Englishwomen, you who uphold our Dorset way of life, you the backbone of our land, this land of such dear souls, this earth, this realm, this England'.

They clapped and cheered. He told them at length what they already knew; what a glorious sport hunting with hounds was, how it had been part of English rural life since time immemorial, that it was a hallowed tradition which preserved the countryside and sustained thousands in employment. Though in fact he rather disliked riding, he went on to say what a pleasure it was for him, toiling all week in the murk and bustle of London, to go out with the South Wessex on a fine Saturday morning. The fresh air, the wonderful countryside, the sight and sound, surely the finest of all rural experiences, of the hounds on the scent. Foxes, he said, suffered very little in the chase. Lamping by night and shooting by the unskilled with a gun was far more cruel. In fact, he corrected himself, hunting wasn't cruel at all, considering that only six per cent of hunted animals were actually killed. The real pain would be suffered by those employed in various ways by the hunt – he quoted the alarming statistics in the notes he'd gone back to London to find – and who stood to lose their livelihoods if this pernicious bill became law.

He continued in this vein, though he was preaching to the converted and had no doubters to persuade. Just before he came to the end he recalled that he hadn't responded to the chairman's congratulations on his nuptials, so he finished by thanking him and saying how much he looked forward to setting his two charming stepchildren on horseback and introducing them to the joy of the chase.

The tremendous applause went on for nearly two minutes, with foot-stamping and shouts of approval. People queued up to shake his hand. A woman said she'd nearly not voted for him at the General Election but now she thanked God nightly in her prayers that she had. The local branch of the Alliance took Jims out to dinner in a horrible little restaurant called the Warming Pan, but he managed to escape at ten and drove himself home to Fredington Crucis House, fearful all the way that due to the amount of a rather disgusting Armenian red he'd drunk he might be over the limit.

Zillah had spent the sort of afternoon that wasn't at all to her taste, first taking the children to a playground on the south side of Westminster Bridge, then walking them along the South Bank past the London Eye and the National Theatre and the bookstalls, as far as Tate Modern and Shakespeare's Globe. It was sunny and warm, and it seemed to her as if everyone in London was down there on the traffic-free embankment. Strange, then, that this walk reminded her of life in Long Fredington. The loneliness of it, perhaps, with no one else to talk to but two people under eight, no man in her life, not even Jerry. She hadn't brought his pushchair, so after a while she had to carry Jordan. She bought ice cream and Jordan's dripped down on to her Anne Demeulemeister jacket. 'Sometimes I think I'll still be carrying you when you're eighteen.'

Her cross tone set him off snivelling. Neither child had made any comment on the policeman's visit, for which Zillah supposed she should be thankful. She was praying she'd heard the last of him and of Jerry. Perhaps, on the next visit he'd threatened, he'd only want to talk to Jims. Bigamy, she thought, when she was home again getting the children's tea, bigamy. Why had that policeman asked her for the date of her divorce? But even though Jerry had been alive when she married Jims, she reminded herself, he was dead now. He'd died within two months of the wedding. Hold on to that, she said to herself, hold on to that, you haven't got two husbands, you had two for only a few weeks. You can't be a bigamist when you've only one husband.

At nine thirty that night the police phoned. They wanted her to identify the dead man and would send a car to fetch her. Tomorrow morning at nine? Too frightened to protest, she phoned Mrs Peacock. Could she come in the morning and look after the children while she went out?

'On a Sunday?' said Mrs Peacock in an icy tone.

'It's business. Very important business.' Zillah didn't want to tell her she was off to identify a corpse in a mortuary. 'I'll pay you double.'

'Yes, I'm afraid you'll have to.'

Eugenie, who had come out from her bedroom in her nightdress and overheard this, said in nearly as cold a voice, 'Don't you *ever* want to stay at home and look after us?'

The police officer was a woman, plain-clothed. She looked about Zillah's own age and rather like one of those women detectives in TV dramas, tall, thin, with long blonde hair and a classical profile, but her voice was an unpleasant near-cockney, high-pitched and brisk. She sat in the back of the car with Zillah, who had dressed herself soberly for this solemn occasion in a black suit and white blouse. On the way to the mortuary there was no conversation between them.

Zillah had never seen a dead body before. Feeling queasy, she saw that Jerry looked more like a waxwork of himself than a real person no longer alive.

'Is that your former husband, Jeffrey Leach?'

'Yes, that's Jerry.'

The woman, who was a detective inspector, asked Zillah in her strident uncompromising tone as they left the mortuary and walked across a yard to the police station, why she called the dead man that.

'He was usually known as Jerry. Some people called him Jeff and his mother called him Jock. On account of his second name being John, you know.'

The detective inspector looked as if she didn't know. She took Zillah into an office, functionally furnished, and asked her to sit down on the opposite side of the desk from her own. Her dislike was palpable, it seemed to beam out of her in waves. 'Did you write this, Mrs Melcombe-Smith?'

She passed across the desk a sheet of paper with writing on it. If Zillah hadn't been sitting down she thought she'd have fainted. It was the letter she'd written to Jerry begging him not to reappear and, above all, not to brand her a bigamist. Her head was swimming too much for her to read it. Had she used the word 'bigamist'? Had she? She couldn't remember. She closed her eyes, opened them again and made the sort of effort of will she was seldom called upon to attempt. A deep breath and she managed to read the letter. *Dear Jerry*, she had written,

> *I am writing to you to beg you not to come back, to really go away and disappear out of my life. You did write that letter telling me you were dead, and though I didn't believe that, I thought you meant me to act as if you were. Please do that. Please. I thought you were not fond of the children because you did not want to see them for months and months. If you want to see them sometimes we could arrange that. I could bring them somewhere to you. Jerry, I will do anything if you will only not try to see me or come here and please, please, don't use that word about me. It frightens me, it really does. You must believe I don't wish you any harm but rather the reverse. I just want to get on with my life, so please, if you have any pity for me, stay away.*
> *Yours, Z*

'Did you write it?' the detective inspector repeated.

'I may have.'

'Well, Mrs Melcombe-Smith, there aren't many women with first names that begin with Z, are there? A few Zoes maybe. I can't say I've ever met a Zuleika but I believe there are some about.'

'Bigamist' wasn't in the letter and nor was 'bigamy'. It didn't exactly reveal anything, it was quite discreet. 'I wrote it,' Zillah said.

'To what address? The envelope is not in our possession.'

'I don't remember. Yes, maybe – it was somewhere in NW6.' She might as well tell her the rest. 'He's been living with a woman called Fiona. She works in a bank.'

'You were very anxious never to see Mr Leach again. What did you mean, "to act as if he was dead"?'

'I don't know,' Zillah said in a small voice. 'I don't remember.'

'You write that you were frightened. Had he ever abused you?'

Zillah shook her head. She supposed she must look frightened now. 'If you mean did he hit me, no, he never did.'

'What was the word you didn't like him using? Some insult, was it? Some term of abuse? "Bitch" or "cow", something of that kind?'

'Oh, yes, that was what it was.'

'Which one?'

'He called me a cow.'

'Ah. A frightening word, cow. That will be all for now, Mrs Melcombe-Smith. We'll call in the morning and see your husband.'

Much as he disliked Jerry Leach on the few occasions he'd spoken to him, he'd rather fancied him and thought he'd detected an answering gleam in Jerry's eye, for Jims was one of those gay men who believe that all men are secretly gay at heart. This, then, as he said to himself when Zillah told him, was a turn-up for the books. But he couldn't see how it would affect himself and Zillah, Jerry being a thing of the past in his life and hers. That the dead man had also been the father of Eugenie and Jordan didn't at the time cross his mind. Family relationships meant very little to him. But when he'd walked into the flat in Abbey Gardens Mansions just after one, he was quite shocked by Zillah's haggard face and shaking hands.

'The police are coming back tomorrow morning. They want to talk to you.'

'Me? Why me?'

'He wanted to know where I was on Friday afternoon when Jerry was killed. He'll want to know where you were.'

Michelle identified the photograph in the Sunday paper as that of Jeff Leigh. Hatred, or something approaching it, confers much the same powers of acute observation as love. When she saw that face, younger, the features smudged and cloudy, she nevertheless knew who it belonged to and heard again that voice saying, 'Little and Large, Michelle, Little and Large. Stoking the boilers, Michelle?' He was holding a baby in his arms and for some reason that made her shiver.

To tell Fiona? Matthew phoned the police first. He said he thought Jeffrey John Leach, so-called, was really Jeffrey Leigh, the man who'd been the partner of his neighbour. His wife had identified him from a newspaper photograph. Where did he live, they wanted to know. When Matthew said West Hampstead they were interested. They'd come. Would 4 p.m. suit him?

Then Michelle went next door to tell Fiona what they feared, what they more than feared, and that the police were coming.

Chapter 17

Jock was gone. A couple of days passed before Minty could really believe it. Especially when she'd been out and came back into the house, she was fearful, always afraid he'd be sitting in a chair or waiting for her in the shadows behind the stairs. She dreamt about him. But that wasn't the same thing as a ghost, just someone who came into your dreams. Sonovia and Laf came into them, and Josephine sometimes, and Mr Kroot's sister and Auntie, always Auntie. The dream Jock, not the ghost Jock, walked into a room where she was and offered her a Polo mint or said 'Good-oh' and once even said those words that were halfway between a joke and a tease, about pinch, punch, first of the month. In the dreams he always wore his black leather jacket.

Auntie's voice she heard much more often than she once had, but she never saw her. Yesterday she, or her voice, had come in while Minty was in the bath, which was something Jock's ghost had never done. 'It's a whole two weeks since you put flowers on my grave, Minty,' said Auntie. She kept over by the door, not looking in Minty's direction, which wouldn't have been nice. She was just a disembodied voice, without eyes. 'It's not very pleasant being dead but it's worse if you're forgotten. How d'you think I feel with my last resting place all bare but for a bunch of dead tulips?'

It was no use answering because they couldn't

hear you. Jock's ghost had never taken a blind bit of notice of anything she said. But that afternoon she'd gone into the cemetery where the evergreen leaves seemed fresher now and the new leaves a dazzling green, where the grass was bright and glittering with raindrops from a shower, and taken out the dead flowers, replacing them with pink carnations and gypsophila. The carnations had no scent but, like Josephine said, you couldn't expect it, not with plants forced up in hothouses. Usually, when she'd visited Auntie's grave, Minty had knelt down on a clean piece of paper or plastic and said a little prayer to her, but she hadn't yesterday. Auntie didn't deserve it, not the way she was going on, she'd have to be content with the flowers.

Sunday was the day Minty did her washing. Her major wash, that is. A certain number of clothes got washed every day. But on Sundays the week's sheets and towels were done and considering no towel was used more than once and no sheet slept on more than three times, a great quantity mounted up. While the first batch was whirling and bouncing about in the machine, gladdening her heart with the soap bubbles and the clean smell – those moments spent watching the washing were the only time Minty felt really content with life – she went out into the garden to put up the clothes line.

Some of the neighbours left their clothes lines out all the time, in all weathers. Minty shuddered when she thought of the black deposits of diesel fumes that must form on them. Her own plastic-covered rope was scrubbed and rinsed and dried each time she took it down. She checked that the posts were firm and attached the clothes line to the bolt on top of the one at the end of the garden, unrolling it carefully as she walked across the paving towards the house.

Next door Mr Kroot's sister was pulling out

weeds. His garden was overgrown with weeds for months, he never did anything out there, and it was only when his sister came that anyone got rid of the dandelions and stinging nettles and thistles. She wasn't wearing gloves and her hands were covered with dirt, the fingernails black. Minty shuddered. She went indoors and washed her own hands, as if she'd absorbed some referred dirt from Mr Kroot's sister. What was she called? Auntie had known. She'd called her by her name until that day they stopped speaking for ever over something to do with the fence. Minty couldn't remember the name but she remembered the quarrel and it all came back to her, though it was a good fifteen years ago.

It was when Auntie had had a new fence put up between their gardens. Mr Kroot never said a word about it but his sister that must once have been a Miss Kroot accused Auntie of stealing six inches of ground from next door. If she didn't move the fence, the sister said, she'd chop the wire down herself with wire cutters, and Auntie said not to threaten her and if there was any chopping of wire, so much as a single snip, she'd call the police. No one cut anything and the police weren't called but Auntie and Mr Kroot's sister never spoke again, and Minty was told not to speak to her either. Then Sonovia stopped speaking to her out of loyalty.

Minty wished she could remember the sister's name. Maybe Auntie would tell her next time she started talking. Not that she wanted to know that much, not enough to welcome ghost voices. She took the first batch of washing out of the machine, put the next lot in, and carried the damp towels outside in a large basket she'd lined with a snowy white sheet. Mr Kroot's sister was standing up now, staring at her. She was a stocky, stoutish old woman with dyed ginger hair, who wore glasses in violet-coloured frames. When she put one earth-covered, black-nailed finger up to her face and scratched her cheek, Minty turned away shuddering.

The morning was bright and sunny but fresh with a sharp wind blowing. A good drying day. She pegged out the towels, using plastic pegs she'd scrubbed and dried along with the clothes line. Mr Kroot's sister had gone indoors, leaving weeds lying about all over the path. Minty shook her head at such fecklessness. She too went indoors and started thinking about what to have for lunch. She'd bought a nice piece of ham at Sainsbury's and she was going to cook it herself. Buying cooked meat, in her opinion, was very risky. You never knew where it had been or the state of the pot it was boiled in. When she'd got the meat on maybe she'd go up the road and get a Sunday paper now Laf never brought theirs in to her.

First she went into the front room to look out of the window and see who was about. It was just as well she did, for as she lifted the half-drawn curtain she saw Laf and Sonovia come out of their house, wearing the serious expressions they always did when on their way to church. Sonovia had the blue dress and jacket on with a white hat and Laf a striped suit. Minty waited a bit to let them get out of the way, then she went off in the opposite direction to the paper shop.

It was quite a coincidence, she thought when she looked at the front page of the *News of the World,* a man murdered in that same cinema where she'd got rid of Jock's ghost. The paper didn't say when it was, only that the man was called Jeffrey Leach.

'There are more and more murders about these days,' Auntie's voice said suddenly. 'I don't know what the world's coming to. They're all in gangs, them as get murdered, murdered by other gangs.

You go down Harlesden High Street and it's all gangs when it's not Yardies.'

Minty tried to ignore her. She sat down in the front room to read the paper. When she heard the machine stop she went to the kitchen and took the sheets and pillowcases out. One more sheet and a duvet cover still remained. She put them into the machine and carried the damp washing outside to the clothes line. Mr Kroot was putting a colander full of potato peelings into his wheelie bin. All unwrapped, they were, just as they came off the potatoes. It made Minty feel quite sick, thinking of that bin having to be wheeled through the house in time for Brent Council's waste disposal men to come and empty it. She kept her own bin in the front, padlocked to the wall – this was such a rough area, people were even capable of stealing your rubbish – and having scoured it, scattered emerald-green disinfectant powder all over the inside.

'The Duke of Windsor's son was murdered,' Auntie said. 'Him as should have been Edward the Ninth. Only when it's someone famous they don't say "murdered", they say "assassinated". It was in France. If he'd been in his rightful place it never would have happened.'

'Who cares?' said Minty, but knowing it was useless. 'Go away, can't you?'

More boiling water needed adding to the ham in the pot. She'd have boiled potatoes with it and frozen peas. Once when Jock was around he'd got her to buy organic broccoli and when she'd washed it a pale-green caterpillar the same colour as the stems had dropped out. Never again. She opened the knife drawer and there on the top was the one she'd used to get rid of Jock's ghost. She'd boiled it and spoiled the colour of the handle in so doing, it must be as clean as a knife could be, but somehow she

212

couldn't fancy slicing meat with it. She'd never fancy it, no matter how long she kept it. It would have to go. Shame, really, because she thought it was one of a set given to Auntie for her wedding in 1961.

'Nineteen-sixty-two,' said Auntie.

John Lewis – that had been Jock's name. Just like the Oxford Street store. How funny, she'd never thought of it like that before. If he'd lived she'd have been Mrs Lewis and it would have been on envelopes, Mrs J. Lewis. But she need not think of it, for he was gone. She put on her rubber gloves, washed the knife again and dried it, wrapped it up in the sports pages of the paper, the ones she didn't want to read, and then put it in a plastic carrier bag. Better not leave it in her wheelie bin. If no one could steal the bin they could steal what was inside it and what those gangs wanted was knives.

'That's what they use,' said Auntie's voice. 'Guns aren't easy to get hold of, you have to pay a lot of money for a gun, but knives are another thing. They all carry knives. That's why there are all these murders. Gangs going after gangs. Good riddance to bad rubbish, if you ask me. It was a bomb killed Edward the Ninth, but he was different.'

'Go away,' Minty said, but Auntie went on muttering.

Maybe she should take the knife up to one of the big bins in the street. The one where she'd put her stained clothes would do. She was taking the third batch of washing out of the machine when the doorbell rang. Who could that be? Now Laf didn't come round with the papers, no one ever called on her unless it was Jehovah's Witnesses. Auntie had liked the Jehovah's Witnesses, she'd bought that *Watchtower* from them and agreed with everything they said, but she drew the line when it came to going about with them, knocking on people's doors.

Minty washed her hands and was drying them when the bell rang again. 'All right, I'm coming,' she said, though no one could hear her out there on the step.

It was Laf and Sonovia. Minty stared. She didn't say anything.

'Don't shut the door in our faces, Minty love,' said Laf. 'We've come in a spirit of goodwill and loving your neighbour as yourself, haven't we, Sonny?'

'Can we come in?'

Minty held the door open wider. Sonovia tripped as she stepped on to the mat, her heels were so high. The blue dress that had hung loose on Minty was still a bit tight across the hips. She and Laf followed Minty into the front room where it was gloomy as usual, even on a sunny day.

'It's like this,' Laf began in the tone he used to teenage criminals who had reoffended. It sounded more like sorrow than anger. 'Neighbours mustn't go on not speaking. It's not right and it's not Christian. Now Sonn and me have just listened to this sermon all about loving your enemies, especially your neighbours, and we reckoned we'd come in here on the way back in a spirit of humility, didn't we, Sonn?'

'I'm sure I'm not anybody's enemy,' said Minty.

'And we're not. Sonny has got something to say and it's not easy for her, being somewhat puffed up with pride like the pastor said some folks are, but she's going to humble herself and say it, aren't you, Sonn?'

Sonovia said in a low, grudging voice that she hoped things would be all right now. 'We could let bygones be bygones.'

'Say it, Sonn.'

She screwed up her face in agony at the prospect of an apology passing her lips. The words came out one by one and slowly. 'I'm sorry. About the dress, I mean. I didn't mean to upset anyone.' She looked at her husband. 'I – am – sorry.'

Minty didn't know what to say. This was a situation she'd never before been in. Auntie had quarrelled with a lot of people but she'd never made it up afterwards. Once you stopped speaking to someone you'd stopped for good. She nodded at Sonovia. As if all the words were new to her, as if in a foreign language she learnt as a child but never since then used, she said, 'Sorry. I'm the same as you. I mean, about bygones.'

The two women looked at each other. Sonovia took a step forward, with a helpful push from Laf. Awkwardly, she put her arms round Minty and kissed her cheek. Minty stood there and let herself be hugged and kissed.

Laf gave a sort of cheer and held up both his thumbs. 'Mates again?' he said. 'Pals? That's the stuff.'

'My deah,' said Sonovia, her normal vitality restored, 'to tell you the truth, I was actually quite glad to have this outfit cleaned, I should have had it done myself. After I'd let you have it I remembered there was this nasty ketchup stain on the hem.'

'That's all right,' said Minty. 'That soon came off.'

Laf smiled broadly. 'So what we want is that you come to the pictures with us tonight. Not Marble Arch, not after that poor chap getting murdered, but we thought Whiteley's and *Saving Grace*. How about it?'

'I don't mind. What sort of time?'

'We reckoned on the five-fifteen showing and then we can all have a pizza afterwards. Now, how about a kiss for me?'

The knife she'd wrapped up she put into a carrier bag, one of the anonymous plain blue ones the corner

215

shops gave you, and walked the hundred yards to the bin in the Harrow Road where she'd put her stained clothes. But the bin was full to overflowing, as it often was on a Sunday, bags of rubbish all round it, spilling out their contents on to the pavement. Minty wasn't going to contribute to that, it was disgusting. She went home again and had her lunch, washing her hands before and after she ate it.

She seemed to remember a group of bins somewhere down Kilburn Lane and she walked a long way up there looking for them. In the end she had to make her way quite a distance down Ladbroke Grove, past the tube station, before she found what she was looking for: clean bins and no mess spilling from them. She opened the lid of a bin. It smelt nasty owing to people like Mr Kroot not wrapping their rubbish up properly. On the top was a bright green Marks and Spencer's carrier with nothing dirtier in it than something wrapped up in tissue paper, a couple of cereal packets and an unused loaf of bread still in its cellophane packing. She didn't too much mind being associated with any of that, so she thrust the knife in its blue bag in between the loaf and the cornflakes, and closed the lid.

On the way back she stopped for a while and looked down over the bridge to the railway track. The tube wasn't really a tube at all here but underground trains doing this bit of the track above ground, and it was also the main line to places in the west of England. Here, she knew, just down there below her, the local train and the Gloucester express had collided. Many people had died in that crash, including her Jock. One of the trains caught fire and that was the one, she supposed, he'd been in.

He'd been visiting his mother. Minty thought of her as very old and bent, with wispy grey hair, walking with a stick, or maybe someone like Mr

Kroot's sister. She ought to have been in touch with Jock's fiancée, ought really to have come to see her. Minty imagined a nice letter from old Mrs Lewis, saying how sad it was and inviting her to come and stay. She wouldn't have gone, of course she wouldn't. The house was very likely dirty and without much hot water. But she should have been asked. Of course, it was plain why she hadn't been asked. Once she was in that house or even once she'd answered a letter, Mrs Lewis would have had to give back the money.

It had begun to rain. Minty shook her head at it, though she knew it would take no notice. As soon as she got home she ran a bath. She scrubbed her fingernails and her toenails and Auntie's voice said, suddenly coming out of nowhere, 'Rain's filthy stuff. It comes down through miles of dirty air.'

Minty said, 'When I'm in here I'm private. Leave me alone,' but Auntie took no notice.

'Getting rid of that knife was wise,' she continued. 'It was harbouring untold millions of germs.' Was Auntie actually addressing her at last? She seemed to be. 'I've just seen Jock's mother. You didn't know Mrs Lewis was here with me, did you?'

'Go away.' Minty thought she'd die if Mrs Lewis manifested herself.

The rain was coming down in sheets when she went downstairs. The house seemed empty. It felt cold, the air grey like twilight. Laf came round at four under a big umbrella with palm trees on it and said he'd be taking the car, it was pouring so. God knew where he'd park but he'd do his best. Auntie's words had upset Minty. Auntie and Mrs Lewis might come into the cinema. She started feeling nervous. And there was no wood to touch in a cinema, it was all plastic and cloth and metal.

Kind and gracious, proud of her new-found

humility, Sonovia went ahead into their row, smiling over her shoulder. 'There you are, my deah, you sit between us. You got the popcorn, Laf?'

He had and it was clean and dry, quite fit for Minty to eat. The cinema was filling up, all the seats in front of them occupied. There was no room for Auntie and Jock's mother. The lights dimmed and suddenly the screen was filled with the bright flashing colours and ear-splitting noises she associated with her banishing of Jock. Minty delicately picked out the smaller pellets of popcorn and relaxed.

When she did get to see Mrs Lewis she'd ask what had happened to her money and *make* the old woman answer. Maybe she'd write it down. They never answered when you spoke to them but they might if it was all down on paper. As the big picture started she was planning what she'd write, how she'd push the paper in front of Mrs Lewis's face, and it was quite a long time before she lifted her eyes to the screen.

218

Chapter 18

Jims gave very little more thought to what Zillah had told him of the police's intention to call on him on Monday morning. He'd be at home, so of course he'd see them, it was his duty as a citizen; he'd answer their routine questions and later he'd stroll across to the Commons. Unaccustomed to spending much time at home, he found this Sunday evening almost unbearably tedious. Leonardo had invited him to a gay club, the Camping Ground in Earls Court Square, and Jims would have loved to accompany him but he knew where to draw the line. Instead, with Eugenie sitting beside him making critical comments, he watched as much of a Jane Austen costume drama on television as he could bear and went to bed early.

Something woke him at four o'clock in the morning. He sat up in bed in his solitary and rather austere bedroom, remembering that he hadn't spent the entire weekend in Casterbridge and Fredington Crucis, as last evening he had taken for granted and sent to the back of his mind. Now it resurfaced, but in a different form. On Friday afternoon he'd driven back to London to recover the mislaid notes for his hunting speech. And he couldn't simply tell the police that because the notes hadn't been in his own home in Abbey Gardens Mansions but in Leonardo's house in Chelsea. A faint but consistent sheen of sweat broke out across Jims's face, down his neck and across his smooth golden chest. He switched the light on.

They would want to know why those papers were in Glebe Terrace and even if he could somehow satisfy them on that point, would enquire why, having recovered them, he failed to go home and spend the night with his new wife in Westminster. It wasn't as if she was away somewhere, they knew she was at home because they had phoned her there, as she'd told him last night. They'd want to know why, instead, he'd passed the night under the same roof as Leonardo Norton, of the well-known London and Wall Street stockbrokers, Frame da Souza Constantine. Various options presented themselves. He could omit to tell them he'd returned to London. Or he could tell them he had returned in the afternoon, found Zillah asleep and, unwilling to disturb her, had recovered the papers and gone straight back to Dorset. Or he could say he'd come home late in the evening, found the papers, spent the night with Zillah and left again very early in the morning before the police came. This would necessitate Zillah's lying for him. He thought it likely she'd agree and the children didn't count since they'd both have been in bed asleep.

Jims hadn't much in the way of morals; he was generally unprincipled and unscrupulous and quite capable of telling a 'white lie' to the police. But when he thought of asking his wife to lie for him, to tell a detective inspector of the Murder Squad (or whatever they'd changed its name to) that he had been here when he hadn't, his blood ran cold. He was a Member of Parliament. Last week the Leader of the Opposition had smiled on him, patted his shoulder and said, 'Well done!' Other MPs referred to him in the Chamber as the Honourable Member for South Wessex. The *Honourable* Member. 'Honour' wasn't a word Jims often much considered but he considered it now. In his position and capacity, honour was supposed to be attached to him, it was as much invested in him as in any mediaeval knight or servant of the sovereign. Sitting up in bed, wiping the perspiration off himself with a corner of the sheet, Jims told himself he couldn't ask someone else to lie for him.

What he'd do was forget all about having come home for those notes. Between now and nine when the police were arriving, it would slip his mind. After all, he hadn't really needed them and could easily have delivered a successful speech without them. It was only that he disliked going unprepared to any function at which he had to speak. He made an effort to get back to sleep but he might as well have tried to turn time back a couple of days, which he would also have liked to do. At six he got up and found that Eugenie and Jordan had already destroyed the peace of his living room by switching on the television to a noisy and very old black-and-white Western. By the time the police came he was cross and moody, but he contrived to sit on the sofa beside Zillah, holding her hand.

The detective inspector was the same woman who had gone with Zillah to the mortuary. She had another plain-clothes officer with her, a sergeant. Zillah asked her if she minded Jims's wife being present and she said not at all, please stay. Zillah squeezed Jims's hand and looked lovingly into his face, and Jims had to admit to himself that some-times she could be an asset to him.

He was asked about the weekend and he said he'd spent it in Dorset. 'I went down to my constituency on Thursday afternoon and held my surgery in Casterbridge on Friday morning. At the Shire Hall. After that I drove back to my house in Fredington

Crucis and worked on a speech I was making on Saturday evening to the Countryside Alliance. I spent the night there and the following day, made my speech later on and dined with the Alliance. I drove home here on Sunday morning.'

The sergeant took notes. 'Is there anyone who can confirm your presence in your Dorset house on Friday, Mr Melcombe-Smith?'

Jims put on an expression of incredulity. It was one he'd often worn in the House of Commons when some Government Member made a remark he thought it would become him to regard as ludicrous. 'To what are these questions tending?'

He knew the answer he'd get. 'They are a matter of routine, sir, that's all. Is there someone who can confirm your presence? Perhaps a member of your staff?'

'In these degenerate days', drawled Jims, 'I do not have a staff. A woman comes up from the village to clean and keep an eye on things. A Mrs Vincey. She provides food in the fridge for the weekend when I'm going to be there. She wasn't there that day.'

'No one called on you?'

'I fear not. My mother spends part of the summer there but mostly she lives in Monte Carlo. She was here, of course, for our wedding' – Zillah's hand received a squeeze – 'but she went back a month ago.'

The police officers looked rather puzzled by this unnecessary information, as well they might. 'Mr Melcombe-Smith, I'm not questioning what you say, but isn't it rather odd for a young and active man like yourself, a very busy man and newly married, to pass what must have been about thirty hours on his own indoors with nothing much to occupy him but the sort of speech he was well used to making? It was an exceptionally fine day and I believe the countryside around Fredington Crucis is beautiful, yet you didn't even go out for a walk?'

'You certainly are questioning what I say. Of course I went for a walk.'

'Then perhaps someone saw you?'

'I am unlikely to know the answer to that.'

Later in the day Jims was walking across New Palace Yard towards the Members' Entrance. He felt reasonably satisfied with what had happened and was sure he'd hear no more. After all, they couldn't possibly suspect him of making away with Jeffrey Leach, not *him*. He had no motive, he hadn't seen the man for at least three years. In the worst-case scenario, if they found out about his return to London – and they couldn't – he'd brazen it out, say he'd forgotten. Or give story number four, the one he hadn't thought of in the small hours, that he'd returned in the night after Zillah was asleep, slept in the spare room so as not to disturb her and left again before she was awake. That would cover everything.

When Michelle told her the murdered man in the cinema was Jeff, Fiona had suffered that momentary loss of consciousness once apparently common in women but which is now rare. She fainted. Michelle, who a few weeks ago couldn't have got down to the floor, did so with ease, sat beside her stroking her forehead and whispering, 'My dear, my poor dear.'

Fiona came to, said it wasn't true, was it? It couldn't be true. Jeff couldn't be dead. She'd seen a paper which said it was someone called Jeffrey Leach. Michelle told her the police were coming. Would she feel able to see them? Fiona nodded. The shock had been so great, she couldn't take much else in. Michelle got her on to the sofa, helped her put her feet up and made milky coffee with plenty of sugar in it. A better remedy for shock than brandy, she said.

'Was he really called Leach?' Fiona asked after a moment or two.

'It seems so.'

'Why did he tell me he was called Leigh? Why did he give me a false name? He'd been living with me for six months.'

'I don't know, darling. I wish I knew.'

At her interview with the police – the same woman who had taken Zillah to the mortuary and would speak to Jims next morning – Fiona suffered the beginnings of disillusionment to add to the pain of her loss. That his name was truly Jeffrey John Leach was confirmed, that he was in touch with his former wife and that he appeared to have had no employment for several years, not perhaps since his student days. The police asked her where she'd been on Friday afternoon and to that she gave very little thought. She could easily name half a dozen people who saw and spoke to her at her merchant bank between three and five. 'I wouldn't have harmed him,' she said, a tear running down her face. 'I loved him.'

They examined Jeff's clothes and what they called his 'personal effects'. As a result of watching television programmes, Fiona asked tentatively if she would be needed to identify Jeff. They said that wouldn't be necessary as Mr Leach's former wife had already done so. Fiona found this more upsetting than anything she'd so far heard and she began to sob. Through her tears she made it known that she'd like to see Jeff and they said that could be arranged.

When they'd gone she fell into Michelle's arms. 'There's never been anyone I felt about the way I did about him. He was the man I'd been waiting for all my life. I can't live without him.'

224

Most people would say eight months' acquaintanceship wasn't enough for life, and Fiona's sorrow would pass, but Michelle had known Matthew for only two when she married him and what would she have felt if he'd died? 'I know, darling, I know.'

Fiona thought how unkind she'd been to Jeff that evening in the Rosmarino when she'd told him to save his silly stories for their baby, she was grown-up. She remembered how she'd reproved him for not being as nice as he might have been to Michelle. Oh, why hadn't she loved him as he'd deserved?

Responsibility for the recycling and rubbish bins in the neighbourhood of Ladbroke Grove station was not Westminster's or Brent's but that of the Royal Borough of Kensington and Chelsea. The men who came to empty them on Monday regarded anything in them worth having as their especial perks and discarded goods were generally picked over with an eye to unconsidered trifles.

The green Marks and Spencer's bag was still fairly near the top of one of the bins and the younger of the recycling men spotted inside it something wrapped in tissue. It looked as if whoever had used it as a waste receptacle – it was sure to be a she, he said scornfully to his mate – had forgotten she had left a newly bought item inside. And so it was. Investigation revealed a pale-blue cashmere sweater, which would do admirably as a birthday present for the recycler's girlfriend.

Something else was in the bag. They unwrapped it. By that time everyone in the country who read a newspaper or watched television knew the police were looking for the weapon used by the Cinema Slayer. This might well be it.

The cemetery desecration made an even better story

than Natalie Reckman had expected. Witchcraft appeared to have been involved, and an interview with an English resident in Rome revealed the possibility of satanic rites carried out near the burial place of Shelley's heart. Building a new theatre was a project she thought she might work up into an article if she described what was happening on the Palatine Hill and recommended something similar for London as a sort of follow-up to millennium celebrations. It might be called the Millennium Theatre or even, thought Natalie, her imagination running away with her, the Natalie Reckman Theatre.

Before getting on the plane home on Monday morning, she bought an English newspaper. It was, of course, a paper from the day before, the *Sunday Telegraph*, and there she read that the dead man, victim of a murderer becoming known as the Cinema Slayer, was Jeffrey Leach.

Most people, however tough and however experienced, feel some pang, frisson or tremor of nostalgia on learning of a former lover's death. Natalie had never loved Jeff but she'd liked him, enjoyed his company and admired his looks, even when quite aware he was using her. In the prime of life, he had met a horrible death at the hands of some madman. Poor old Jeff, she said to herself, what a thing to happen, poor old Jeff.

That horrible death must have taken place no more than an hour or so after leaving her in Wellington Street. Sitting in the aircraft, that morning's paper delivered to her and on her lap, Natalie remembered, as they left the restaurant, how Jeff had asked her to go to the cinema with him. If she'd gone, would things have been different? Maybe she'd have chosen a completely different cinema to go to. But another possibility was that she'd have been killed too.

The someone she'd told Jeff she was very happy

with was at Heathrow to meet her. They had lunch together and Natalie told him all about it. A journalist himself, though of rather a different kind, he saw what she meant when she said there might be a story in it. 'Poor Jeff looked a bit funny when I talked about this Zillah woman. Guilty, I felt. Well, maybe not so much guilty as having something to hide. There's been something fishy going on. I'm wondering if they were never divorced at all. That would be just like Jeff.'

'It's easily checked.'

'Oh, I shall check it. Never fear. I've already put my researcher on to it. I called her on the flight.'

'You are a fast worker, my love.'

'But first I think I'll be good and contact the Bill and tell them Jeff had lunch with me last Friday.'

Natalie wasn't alone in believing something fishy had been going on. The investigating officers had never been satisfied by Zillah's explanation of the letter she had written to Jeffrey Leach. The word he had used to her on some unspecified visit he'd paid to Abbey Gardens Mansions when he'd stolen her credit card wasn't 'cow', whatever she might say. Zillah Melcombe-Smith wouldn't be fazed by that. And she had been fazed, she'd been very frightened. Such a woman, doubtless, seldom wrote letters to anyone, she wasn't that sort; but she had written to Leach under great pressure of – what? Guilt? Extreme fear? Terror of some sort of discovery? Perhaps all those.

When they interviewed Natalie they were glad to be further on with piecing together the ways Leach had spent the day prior to his cinema visit. And she was able to contribute to the history of him they were starting to compile, something of his past. That, for instance, he'd been newly married when he'd first lived in Queen's Park, that besides his wife there had been many women before her, all owning their homes and able to keep him. Natalie told them things they already knew about Fiona Harrington and Zillah Melcombe-Smith and something they didn't know: that when she split up from Leach rather more than a year before he had moved back to Queen's Park, this time to Harvist Road, and there doubtless had found himself another woman. They returned to their scrutiny of the letter.

Mrs Melcombe-Smith had remarried in March. Her divorce had taken place in the previous spring. Or so she said. There were children involved, questions of custody and child support, so the divorce could hardly have been a simple quick affair. If the word Leach had used to her had aroused so much terror, might it not perhaps have something to do with that divorce, some factor which had come out in the proceedings or resulted from the process? To check would be easy and uncomplicated, starting with January twelvemonth and going on from there.

The sergeant's wife still had a copy of the *Daily Telegraph Magazine* in which Natalie Reckman's piece had appeared; she was one of those people who seldom throw anything away. He hadn't looked at it the first time round but he did now. He read with particular interest the passage where Natalie wrote that Mrs Melcombe-Smith appeared to have lived the first twenty-seven years of her life in jobless, manless isolation in Long Fredington, Dorset. No mention of a former husband, no talk of children.

Both those Melcombe-Smiths were behaving oddly, to put it mildly. No one could be found who had seen the MP in Fredington Crucis on Friday or Saturday, but two people had told the local constable that his distinctive car, which he always left parked outside the front door of Fredington Crucis House, wasn't there after 9 a.m. on Friday. The postman who delivered a package at 8.45 a.m. on Saturday took it away again because no one answered the door. Irene Vincey, coming in to clean half an hour later, found the house empty and no sign that Jims's bed had been slept in.

No porter at Abbey Gardens Mansions had seen him between midday on Thursday and Sunday afternoon. The most damning thing for Jims was when the manager of the Golden Hind in Casterbridge called to say that Mr Melcombe-Smith had cancelled his table reservation for lunch and someone had told him this was information to interest the police. The chairman of a cancer charity called Ivo Carew reluctantly confirmed this, using a few choice epithets about the Golden Hind manager.

With no idea of what might lie in store for him, Jims made a speech in the Commons about the Conservatives being the party of old-fashioned values but new-fashioned kindness, consideration and true freedom. Quentin Letts quoted it in the *Daily Mail* (wittily and with a few snide comments) and rumours began running around the Palace of Westminster that the Member for South Wessex was tipped for an Under-Secretaryship. Shadow, of course, which rather reduced the glory.

Jims thought the police fools, anyway, and probably too much in awe of him, landed gentry as he was, to trouble him again. He was so young, so good-looking and so *rich*. That night he dreamed a new version of a dream he'd sometimes had in the past, but this time when he came down the steps of Number Ten Downing Street to the waiting cameramen he had Zillah on his arm, the youngest and most beautiful First Lady in living memory. God was in His heaven, thought Jims, and everything more or less right with the world.

Chapter 19

Zillah rather surprised herself by discovering how little she cared about Jerry's death. Could she ever have loved him? It made the years she'd spent more or less with him seem a waste of time. Of course, she'd got the children out of them, there was that. Back into the routine of driving them to and from their schools, she felt a sublime indifference towards everyone but herself and them. With a free morning before her to do as she liked, she put the police out of her mind, she even forgot Jims and the difficulties he seemed deliberately to create for her, and revelled in just being alone for three hours. She celebrated by buying a Caroline Charles dress and a Philip Treacy hat to wear at a royal garden party.

Whenever she bought clothes, Zillah formed a picture in her mind of herself wearing the new garment in some particular, usually glamorous, scenario. Sometimes she would be accompanied by a man – up until she married him it was often Jims – and sometimes, very occasionally, by her children dressed in equally ravishing outfits. It was an innocent form of fantasising that gave her a lot of pleasure. As she alighted from a taxi in Great College Street, the rosebud-sprigged dress in a bag in one hand, the pink straw hat in a bandbox, she was imagining herself on a sunny lawn with a glass of champagne in her hand. She had just curtseyed with exceptional grace to the Queen and was listening to the admiring words of a young and handsome hereditary peer who was obviously deeply attracted by her. The events of the past few days had almost been erased from her mind.

It was twenty past eleven. She just had time to go up to flat seven, hang up the dress, put the hat away and have a quick cup of coffee before driving off to fetch Jordan. She ran up the steps to the art nouveau double doors, pushed them open and tripped into the foyer. There, sitting on one of the gilt and red velvet chairs, was the journalist who had been so rude to her and had written that horrible piece for the *Telegraph* magazine.

Zillah could hardly understand how a woman would choose to wear the same black suit on two consecutive visits to the same person. And not even vary her shoes or her jewellery. That same curiously shaped gold ring was on her right hand. 'Were you waiting for me?' She barely paused in her rush to the lift. 'I have to go out again immediately to fetch my son from school.'

'That's quite all right, Mrs Melcombe-Smith. I'll wait.'

Zillah went up in the lift. While she was hanging up the dress she thought maybe she ought to have asked the woman – Natalie Reckman was her name. How could she have forgotten even for a moment? – to come upstairs and wait for her. But journalists really weren't the sort of people to leave alone in one's home. They might do anything, pry into one's private drawers, read one's letters. They were worse than Malina Daz or, come to that, poor Jerry. She no longer fancied coffee. A brandy would have been more beneficial but she wasn't going to start down that road. Instead of returning to the foyer, she went all the way down in the lift to the basement car park, and fifteen minutes later had picked up Jordan and brought him back.

It was now half an hour since she'd seen Natalie Reckman and she was tempted simply to carry on with her day as if she hadn't seen her. She microwaved a couple of chicken nuggets for Jordan's lunch, poured him a glass of orange juice and sat him at the table. While she was making herself a sandwich the house phone rang. The porter's voice said, 'Shall I send Miss Reckman up, madam?'

'No – yes, I suppose so.'

The journalist might not have changed her outfit but her manner had undergone a transformation. Gone was the cool intellectual approach and in its place a warm friendliness. 'Zillah, if I may, I'm very anxious to have another chat with you. It's so good of you to see me.'

Zillah thought she hadn't had much choice. 'I was just going to have my lunch.'

'Nothing for me, thank you,' said Natalie, as if she'd been asked. 'But I wouldn't say no to a glass of that delicious-looking orange juice. Is this your little boy?'

'That's Jordan, yes.'

'He is so exactly like his father, the spitting image.'

Zillah tried to remember if there had been any photographs of Jerry in the papers, apart from the one she took of him with baby Eugenie, but she was sure there hadn't been. He'd never allowed anyone to take his picture. 'Did you know my – Jerry – that is, Jeff?'

'Very well indeed at one time.'

Natalie was sitting down now, nursing her orange juice. Her tone was subtly changing again and her manner sharpening. She gave Zillah one of the searching stares that had been so much a feature of her previous visit. 'How otherwise do you think I knew you'd been married to him and had two children? You did read my article about you, Zillah?'

'Oh, yes, I read it.' Zillah took a hold on her courage. 'If you want to know, I thought it very unkind.'

Natalie laughed. She drank the juice and set the glass on the table. It was rather too near Jordan for his taste and he pushed it out of his way with a petulant shove. The glass fell on to the floor and broke. He let out a howl of dismay and, picked up by his mother, beat his fists against her chest, shouting an emotional demand he hadn't given expression to for weeks, 'Jordan wants Daddy!'

Rather in the manner of a social worker, a children's officer perhaps, Natalie shook her head sorrowfully. She got down on her knees and began picking up broken glass.

'Oh, leave it!'

Natalie shrugged. 'As you like. I only read of your husband's death yesterday. I've been in Rome, working.'

What did she care? She set Jordan down on the floor with a box of bricks and two miniature cars but he immediately got up and ran to her, embracing her knees with sticky hands. Then Zillah took in what Natalie had said. 'He wasn't my husband.'

'Are you sure?'

Zillah forgot the stickiness on her legs, the pool of orange juice on the floor, the mess on the table, the time, Jims, her new dress and hat – everything. A cold shiver, like an ice cube dropped on the back of her neck, ran down her spine. 'I don't know what you mean.'

'Well, Zillah, it's a funny thing but I spent a long time yesterday, I and my assistant actually, looking through quite a lot of records. We were trying to trace your divorce from Jeff and the extraordinary thing was that we couldn't find it.'

'What business was it of yours, I'd like to know?'

'Goodness, your teeth are chattering – are you cold? It's very warm in here.'

'I'm not cold. Oh, for God's sake go and play with something, Jordan. Leave Mummy alone.' Zillah lifted up a white face in which frightened eyes glittered. 'I asked you what business you had to go rooting through my private affairs?'

'Do you really think your affairs, as you quaintly call them, are so private? You've been in all the papers. Don't you think your readers have a right to know what you get up to?'

'You journalists are all the same, you'll do anything and say anything. Now I'd like you to go, please.'

'I shan't be staying much longer, Zillah. I was just hoping you could help me, perhaps give me a firmer date for when your divorce actually took place. I – and, incidentally, the police – had the idea it was some time last spring but that doesn't seem to be so.' Natalie had no idea whether the police were pursuing the same line of enquiry as her own and it was only by chance that she was right. 'Still, I'm sure you can set us right. Was it perhaps the year before?'

Jordan sat on the floor and gave tongue, howling like a puppy. 'I don't remember the date.' Zillah was driven beyond exasperation now. She wanted to scream and afterwards hardly knew how she'd controlled herself. 'You just have to accept it. What's it to do with you, anyway?'

'It's in the public interest. Hadn't you thought of that? You're – er, married to an MP, you know.'

'What do you mean, "er, married"? I *am* married. My first husband is dead.'

'Yes,' said Natalie above Jordan's squalling. 'I'd

noticed. I'll get out of your hair now. There seems to be something wrong with your little boy. Isn't he well? I'll let myself out.'

Going down in the lift, she remembered how, a few years back, she'd been in some American city in the Midwest where she'd interviewed a police chief. She was talking to him about crime statistics, various kinds of crime, and she'd asked him about some woman she'd heard of who'd remarried without first being divorced.

'Lady, we have nine murders a week in this city,' he'd said, 'and you're asking me about *bigamy*.'

But would the police here take the same attitude? Hardly. Jeff had been murdered and his wife or whatever she was had married an MP. Natalie decided not to write anything yet, for she was very much alive to the risks involved in saying in print that Zillah wasn't legally married, just in case it turned out that she was. Some day soon she'd write a magazine piece about all Jeff's women, it would be quite sensational. But first she had to go and talk to the Violent Crimes Task Force and at the same time make sure she got in with her exclusive story before anyone else did. In a thoughtful frame of mind she took a cab home.

Zillah had always deplored and clicked her tongue over those people who were up in court for cruelty to children. They belonged, she'd believed, to a different breed from herself. Now, walking up and down with her heavy, screaming, damp child in her arms, as if he were three months rather than three years old, she began to understand. She'd have liked to throw him out of the window. Anything to stop that noise and stem those ever-ready tears.

As she paced, she told herself over and over that things would be all right, it was all right now, because Jerry was *dead*. You couldn't be a bigamist if your husband was dead and you'd married again. It was really only a matter of having said she was single when in fact she was a widow, or was soon to be one. She'd never actually said she was divorced until today, she just hadn't mentioned Jerry at all – had she? She didn't have to be divorced if her husband was dead. Anyway, none of it was her fault. It was these journalists poking their noses in where they weren't wanted. And the main thing was she was a widow now, or would have been if she hadn't married Jims.

To her surprise, Zillah found that Jordan had fallen asleep. He looked lovely when he was asleep, pink-flushed roseleaf skin, incredibly long dark eyelashes, damp curls clustering across his forehead. She laid him down on the sofa and eased his shoes off. He rolled away from her and stuck his thumb in his mouth. Peace. Silence. Why had she agreed to get married in that fancy crypt place? Why had she wanted to? She couldn't remember. Somehow it wouldn't be so bad if she and Jims had fixed it up in a hotel or a town hall. In a place like that she wouldn't have had to hear those awful, or perhaps she should say awesome, words. Yet they hadn't seemed awe-inspiring at the time, she hadn't really taken them in, she'd been thinking about her dress and what the newspaper photographs would be like. . . . *As ye shall answer at the dreadful day of judgement, when the secrets of all hearts shall be revealed, that if either of ye know any just cause or impediment why ye should not be so joined, ye are to declare it.* And then there came a bit about as many as are married without declaring it weren't really married at all, *neither is their matrimony lawful.* Jims would kill her if he found out his matrimony wasn't lawful. But it must be lawful, Zillah thought, this unhappy merry-go-round circulating in her head, because her husband was dead and if he hadn't been dead in the middle of March he soon was, only a few weeks later.

She had to wake Jordan to take him with her and meet Eugenie from school. He whimpered and whinged. He was wet too. She took his jeans and underpants off. There was a big smelly stain on Jims's cream silk sofa. It was terrible having to put a three-year-old into a napkin but she didn't dare not to. On the way back she'd stop at a chemist and do something she'd sworn she never would do, buy a dummy to stuff in his mouth. And then she *must* phone her mother.

For once she was early. The school was a big Georgian house in a lane off Victoria Street. The car parked on a yellow line – but a single line and she wouldn't be there long – she got out and got Jordan out, and was leaning against its nearside in the sunshine, thinking once more about her marriage service and those words, when a man got out of the BMW behind and came up to her.

'Zillah Watling,' he said.

He was very attractive, tall and thin and fair, with a hooky nose and a nice wide mouth, and dressed in what Zillah thought the most flattering uniform a man could wear, blue jeans and a plain white shirt. The neck was open halfway down his chest and his sleeves were rolled up. She'd seen him somewhere before, long ago, but where she couldn't remember. 'I'm sure I know you but I can't think . . .'

He reminded her. 'Mark Fryer.' They'd been students together, he said. Then he'd left and Jerry had come . . . 'Is this your boy? I'm here to pick up my daughter.'

'I'm here to pick up mine.'

They exchanged news. Mark Fryer didn't appear

to be a newspaper or magazine reader, for he knew nothing about her marriage to Jims. And he didn't mention a wife, partner, girlfriend or anyone that might be the mother of this child who, by a happy coincidence, came down the school steps with her arm round Eugenie.

'Look, we've got so much to say to each other, can't we meet up again? How about tomorrow? Lunch tomorrow?'

Zillah shook her head and silently indicated Jordan.

'Then say Friday morning. We could have coffee somewhere.'

She'd love to. He pointed across the street. How about that place? Zillah thought it rather too near the school for comfort and he named another in the Horseferry Road. He waved as she drove off, calling, 'I'm so glad we ran into each other.'

Eugenie, in the passenger seat, was staring censoriously at her. 'What does he mean, "ran into each other"? Did he hit our car?'

'It's just an expression. It means "met by chance".'

'He's my friend Matilda's father. Did you know that? She says he's a womaniser and when I said, what does that mean, she said he chases after ladies. Did he chase you?'

'Of course not. You're not to talk like that, Eugenie, do you hear me?'

But Zillah was already feeling better. It was wonderful what a little male admiration could do. As to the other thing that was always coming back to haunt her, *no one can do anything to me,* she said to herself, *because I'm a widow.*

Police officers were back again, talking to Fiona. Although they never came out and said so, she was sure they thought she couldn't have been deeply affected by Jeff's death because they hadn't known each other for very long. It didn't stop them expecting her to know all about his past, his family, his friends and everywhere he'd lived since he left art school nine years before.

She'd told them everything she could think of but great gaps existed in her knowledge. His marriage, as she told them, was a closed book to her. She didn't know where he'd lived with his wife, whether or not she'd ever been in Harvist Road or the ages of the children. She thought it very hard on her that she couldn't be left in peace to mourn quietly and by herself – or maybe with Michelle. As for the ex-wife, 'I don't even know where she lives.'

'That's OK, Miss Harrington, we do. We'll see to that.'

Did she imagine the flicker that crossed the man's face at the word 'ex-wife'? Perhaps. She didn't know. She could never banish from her mind what they'd told her about Jeff not booking that hotel for their wedding on the appointed day or any other day. Why had he lied to her? Was it that he'd never meant to marry her? She'd tried to talk about it with Michelle but her neighbour, usually so warm and affectionate, grew remote and impenetrable when expected to reassure her about Jeff's shortcomings. Fiona wanted excuses made for him, not suggestions, however gently put, that she should try to look to the future instead of dwelling on a man who was – well, she'd never even hinted at this but Fiona knew the missing words were 'after her money'.

'You've told us about friends and family, insofar as you can. Now, how about enemies? Did Jeff have any enemies?'

She didn't like the way they referred to her as Miss Harrington but to him as Jeff, as if he were too much of a villain to be accorded the dignity of a surname.

What do they say to each other about me when they get out of here, she often asked herself. 'I don't know that he had any,' she said wearily. 'Do ordinary people have enemies?'

'They have people who don't like them.'

'Yes, but that's different. I mean, my neighbours, the Jarveys, didn't like Jeff. Mrs Jarvey admitted it. They both disliked him.'

'Why was that, Miss Harrington?'

'Jeff was – you have to understand he'd got an enormous lot of vitality. He was so full of life and energy . . .' Fiona couldn't keep back a little sob when she said this.

'Don't upset yourself, Miss Harrington.'

How could you help upsetting yourself when you were forced to talk about things you'd have liked to keep locked up inside you for ever? She wiped her eyes carefully. 'What I was going to say was, Jeff came out with things that – well, that sounded unkind, but he didn't mean them, they just sort of brimmed over.'

'What kind of things?'

'He made digs, sort of jokes, at Michelle – Mrs Jarvey. About her size. I mean, he called her husband and her Little and Large, things like that. She didn't like it and her husband *hated* it. If it had been left to her I don't think she'd ever have had anything more to do with Jeff.' Fiona realised what she was saying and tried to make a better impression. 'I don't mean they did anything about it, they didn't even say anything. Michelle's been an angel to me. It was just that they didn't understand Jeff.' She made herself put Michelle's point of view, though she'd never faced up to it before. The lie Jeff had told about the hotel booking returned to her mind. 'I suppose the truth is Michelle didn't want me to marry Jeff, she thought he was bad for me. And – well, Michelle

240

thinks of me as a daughter really, she told me so. My happiness is very important to her.'

'Thank you very much, Miss Harrington,' said the inspector. 'I don't think we'll have to trouble you again. You won't be needed at the inquest. Be sure to give us a call if you think of anything you haven't told us.'

In the car he said to his sergeant, 'The poor cow's having a rude awakening.'

'D'you want me to keep on searching for that divorce decree?'

'There are some things you can search for, Malcolm, that you're never going to find. Because they don't exist, right?'

'So do we do her for bigamy?'

'I reckon we leave it to the DPP to sort out. We've got enough on our plate without that.'

'I shall be going down to the constituency this afternoon,' said Jims, 'but I'll delay it till after four so that you have time to fetch Eugenie from school first.'

Zillah gave him an aggrieved look. 'Don't bother. I'm not coming.' How could she? She was meeting Mark Fryer for coffee in Starbuck's at eleven on Friday. 'What made you think I'd be coming?'

Jims had forgotten that dream of himself as Prime Minister with Zillah as his consort. 'I'll tell you what made me think it, *darling*. We made a bargain, remember? So far you've got everything out of this marriage and I've got fuck-all. You're my wife, at least you're the ornament I chose to impress my constituents, and if I choose that you accompany me to Dorset, you do it. In case, as is more than likely, you never read a newspaper or watch anything on television above the level of a hospital soap, there's a by-election in North Wessex next week and I intend to be there on Saturday to support our candidate. With you. Dressed in your best and looking lovely and gracious and *devoted*. With the kiddiwinks, trusting that little devil doesn't bawl the place down.'

'You bastard.'

'The children are yours, not mine, but you'd be wiser not to use language like that in front of them.'

'What about you saying "fuck-all" then?'

Jordan had taken the new dummy out of his mouth and flung it across the room. 'Fuck-all,' he said thoughtfully. It seemed a better panacea to stop him crying than the dummy. 'You bastard.'

'Anyway, I'm not coming. I never want to see Dorset again. I saw all I wanted to while I was living there. Take that Leonardo. I bet you were going to.'

'I hope I know something about discretion, Zillah, which is more than you do. By the by, have you remembered to enquire after your father?'

Next morning neither of them saw Natalie Reckman's article, Jims because he woke up late and had to rush to get to his surgery in Toneborough on time, Zillah because she went off straight from dropping the children to have a facial and make-up done at the Army and Navy Stores. At just after eleven, a vision of loveliness in Mark Fryer's words which didn't sound as if he meant to be sarcastic, she was drinking cappuccino with him in the Horseferry Road, where he told her all about his broken marriage, recent divorce – a sensitive word to Zillah at the moment – and was disbelieving when she said she had to go and pick up Jordan.

'Let me come with you.'

Afterwards Zillah could never imagine how she'd come to get out of the car with Jordan and Mark Fryer and, instead of going up to the flat in the lift, walked round to the front of the block. Could it have been because the building was beautiful from the front and a dingy concrete nightmare in the basement? Had she wanted to impress him? Perhaps. But there it was. They all walked along Millbank and turned the corner into Great College Street.

A crowd had gathered outside Abbey Gardens Mansions, made up mostly of press photographers and young women with notepads. They turned as one when they saw Zillah approaching and closed in upon her, strident voices bombarding her with questions and bulbs flashing. She tried to cover her face with her hands, then, she hoped, with Mark's jacket which he'd been carrying over his shoulder.

He snatched it back, said hastily, 'This is no place for me. See you,' and disappeared. Jordan began to scream.

Chapter 20

It was Laf's day off. At eleven in the morning the Wilsons were sitting outside their french windows, drinking coffee and reading the *Mail* and the *Express*. Sonovia kept her small garden as she often said a garden should be, 'a riot of colour', in contrast to next door where everything was neat, sterile and flower-free. Tubs held shocking-pink azaleas, scarlet and pastel-pink geraniums were coming into bloom, while trailing plants in Oxford and Cambridge boat race colours spilled out of hanging baskets and over the rims of stone troughs. A bright-yellow climber no one knew the name of blazed against the far fence.

Laf laid down his paper and said appreciatively to his wife that the garden was a treat to look at. 'Those blue things are a lovely sight. I don't think you've had those before.'

'Lobelias,' said Sonovia. 'They make a nice contrast to the red. I got them on the mail order but to tell you the truth, I never thought they'd turn out like the picture. Have you seen about this woman who used to be married to that man that was murdered in the Odeon marrying someone else without being divorced? It says here she thought she was divorced. I don't see how she could have, do you?'

'Don't know. There's people about as will do anything, as I have good reason to know. Maybe he showed her some false papers.'

He wasn't going to let on to Sonovia that this latest

bit of news in the Cinema Slayer case hadn't yet reached Notting Hill police station. The knife was different, he knew all about that, how it was found in a recycling bin and someone said it looked as if it had been boiled and the lab couldn't tell if it was the murder weapon or not. Who'd boil a knife? That was what the DI had said and Laf had thought, Minty would. He'd had to laugh at the idea of little Minty harming anyone.

'D'you reckon this Zillah Melcombe-Smith'd done wrong,' he asked his wife, 'marrying again when she wasn't divorced? I mean, if she thought she was divorced and she married that MP in good faith?'

'Oh, I don't know, Laf. Maybe she ought to have checked up before she actually stood at the altar.'

'Well, d'you reckon anyone does wrong if they don't know it's wrong?' These matters sometimes troubled Laf as a responsible policeman. 'I mean like, if you attacked someone, killed them, because you thought they were a demon or Hitler or something, really believed it? If you thought you were ridding the world of an evil – an evil entity? Would that be wrong?'

'You'd have to be nuts.'

'OK, more people are nuts, as you call it, than you'd think. Would it be wrong?'

'That's too deep for me, Laf. You'd better ask the pastor. D'you want another coffee?'

But Laf didn't. He sat in the sun, thinking that what he'd outlined to Sonovia would be wrong for the person who got killed and all their friends and family, it would be just as wrong if the killer had meant it. But it wouldn't be wrong for the person who did the killing, they wouldn't have committed murder like the Commandment said thou shalt not, they'd be innocent as a lamb; they'd have nothing on their conscience and perhaps they'd be proud to have been Hitler's or the devil's assassin.

Laf, who was a deeply religious man and an Evangelical, asked himself if they'd go to heaven. He *would* ask the pastor. And he was pretty sure he'd say that since it was God who had made them mad He ought to let them inside the gates of paradise. He looked back at the garden. Those pale-pink geraniums were a lovely colour. It was a great thing to be a happy man, to sit under his vine and his fig tree, as the Bible said, under his may tree and his lilac really, with a good wife and his quiverful of children.

Sonovia had gone into the house to phone Corinne. In the afternoon they were going to the Dome, taking their granddaughter with them. He'd wait until a quarter past one, by that time they'd have had their lunch, and then he'd take the papers in to Minty. Maybe she'd like to come with them. Mending the rift between Minty and Sonovia had been the most worthwhile thing he'd done for a long time, Laf thought. His wife was a good woman, if a shade quick-tempered. He leaned his head back and closed his eyes.

Minty wasn't surprised to be haunted by old Mrs Lewis, she'd expected it. She couldn't see her and she hoped she never would, but her voice came as often as the other voices. At any rate it proved she was dead and Jock's words she'd heard whispered in the night were true. The living didn't come back and speak to you, they were here already.

She knew the new voice was Mrs Lewis's because Auntie told her. Auntie didn't introduce her, she didn't bother to, which Minty thought rather rude. She just called her Mrs Lewis. It was quite a shock. Minty had been ironing at the time, not at Immacue like now, but at home in her own kitchen, when

Auntie had started talking to her. She didn't say a word about the flowers Minty had put on her grave the day before and they'd cost a lot, over ten pounds, but started criticising her ironing, saying the washing was too dry, the creases would never come out. And then she'd asked Mrs Lewis for her opinion. 'What do you think, Mrs Lewis?' she'd said.

The new voice was gruff and deeper than Auntie's, and it had a funny accent. Must be West Country. 'She wants one of them sprays,' it said. 'They've got a lot of it at the dry-cleaners where she works. She could borrow one of them.'

They knew everything, the dead. They could see into everything, which made it funnier, really, that they couldn't hear what you said to them. Mrs Lewis had lived in Gloucester, which was hundreds of miles away, while she was alive and she'd never have known about Immacue and Minty working there, but she knew now because she was dead and secrets were revealed to her. The two of them were talking to each other while she went on ironing, chattering away about washing powders and stain removers. Minty tried to ignore them. She couldn't understand why Mrs Lewis had come back to haunt her. Maybe the old woman had died when she'd heard her son Jock was dead, given way under the shock. She needn't suppose Minty was going to tend her grave, wherever it was. It was bad enough with Auntie's, not to mention the expense.

The ironing was done, everything folded and laid in the laundry basket on a clean sheet. Minty picked it up.

'You don't need to use that basket,' Auntie said. 'That's not a very big pile. You could carry it, it'd be easier.'

'Go away,' said Minty. 'It's nothing to do with you

and I'm not putting any more flowers on your grave. I can't afford it.'

'You can understand her feelings,' said old Mrs Lewis. 'That son of mine got all her money off her. Mind you, he'd have given it back if he hadn't met his end in that train crash. Every penny he'd have restored to her.'

'If you want to tell me things,' Minty shouted, 'you can tell me to my face, not tell *her*. And it's down to you to give me my money back.'

But Mrs Lewis never did talk to her. She talked to Auntie. By a miracle Auntie had got her hearing back and Mrs Lewis had been talking to her this morning while Minty was ironing for Immacue customers. They could get anywhere, these ghosts. Auntie said she was looking pale, been picking at her food no doubt, but Mrs Lewis intervened then and said her Jock had made Minty eat, he was a trencherman himself and he liked a girl to be a hearty eater.

'Go away, go away,' Minty whispered, but not quietly enough, for Josephine came out, wanting to know if she'd been talking to her.

'I didn't say anything.'

'Oh, I thought you did. Have you seen the papers this morning? There's a woman was the wife of that murdered bloke who's gone and married someone else.'

'I never see the papers till I get home. Why shouldn't she if he's dead?'

'He wasn't dead when she did it,' said Josephine. 'And what d'you think, her and this MP got married on the same day as me and Ken. Look, I've got the *Mirror* here. D'you like her outfit? Jeans can be too tight, I don't care what anyone says. And her hair's all over the place. That's some guy she was with, it doesn't say who he is, not the husband, and that's her little boy, sobbing his heart out, poor mite.'

'It's wicked to murder people,' Minty said. 'Look at the trouble it causes.' She finished the last shirt and went home.

She'd only been in five minutes when Laf came round with the papers. He wanted her to go to the Dome with him and Sonovia and Daniel's little girl, but Minty said no, thanks, not this time, she'd got too much to do at home. She'd have to have a bath, she couldn't go out again dirty, and they were off in ten minutes. Besides, there were the papers to read and the dusting to do and the floors to vacuum.

'Not in the afternoon,' said Auntie the moment Laf was gone. 'A good housewife gets her work done first thing in the morning. The afternoon's for sitting down and catching up on the sewing.'

Mrs Lewis had to put her oar in. 'She'll say she's got her job. You wouldn't want her cleaning the place on a Sunday, I'm sure. Sundays are a day of rest or should be. There was some in my day as would get up at the crack of dawn and get the dusting and hoovering done before they went to work, but not any more.'

'Go away,' said Minty. 'I hate you.'

For some reason she thought they wouldn't follow her out of doors and she was right. Maybe it was too bright for them or too hot or something. Ghosts faded away in sunshine, she'd heard that some-where. She got out the mower and cut the little lawn, then the long-handled shears to do the edges. Mr Kroot's sister came out into the garden next door, dropping lumps of bread with green mould on it to feed the birds. Minty wanted to say it wouldn't be birds that would come but rats, only she didn't because she and Auntie had sworn never to speak to Mr Kroot or the sister or anyone to do with them again.

Auntie spoke to her at last, the minute she came

into the kitchen. 'I'd have had a bone to pick with you if you'd said a word to Gertrude Pierce.'

That was her name. The dead knew everything. Minty remembered it now, though she hadn't heard it for a good ten years. She didn't answer Auntie. The two of them went on muttering somewhere in the background. She'd just have to put up with it until they got tired and went back to wherever they came from. They wouldn't like her hoovering, the noise would drown out their voices. Let them grumble all they liked. At least she couldn't see them.

She always did the dusting first. While Auntie was alive she'd had a lot of opposition from her over that. Auntie vacuumed first, but Minty maintained that if you dusted afterwards all the dust went on to the clean carpet and if you were thorough you'd have to hoover it all over again.

Sure enough, Auntie started as soon as Minty took the clean yellow duster out of the kitchen drawer. 'I hope you're not going to use that before you've done the floor. I don't know how many times I've told her, Mrs Lewis. It goes in one ear and out the other.'

'Might as well talk to a brick wall,' said Mrs Lewis, for by this time Minty had begun moving all the ornaments on the little table and spraying the surface with liquid wax. 'That stuff she's using just swallows up the dirt and leaves a nasty deposit.'

'My very words. I'd like a five-pound note for every time I've said that.'

'It's not true,' Minty shouted, moving on to the sideboard. 'Not if you keep the place clean like I do. And it's five-pound notes you ought to be giving *me*.'

'She's got a nasty temper, Winifred. You say a word to her and she bites your head off.'

'I'd like to bite yours off! I'd like to get a big police dog to come and bite it off.'

'Don't you speak to Mrs Lewis like that,' said Auntie.

So they could hear her. Maybe it was only when she got angry. She'd remember that. She cleaned the whole house. Up in the bathroom she plugged her ears so as not to hear, but she still heard their voices through the cotton wool. Only while she had a bath and washed her hair was there silence. Lying in the water, she tried to picture what Mrs Lewis looked like. She'd be very old. Somehow Minty had got it into her head Mrs Lewis had been knocking fifty when Jock was born. Her hair would be white and wispy, so thin that patches of bald pink scalp showed through, her nose a hook and her chin another hook coming up to meet the nose, with a mouth like a crack in a piece of coarse-grained brown wood in between. She looked like a witch, bent and very small because she'd have shrunk, and when she walked she took little stumbling steps.

'I don't want to see her,' she said aloud. 'I don't want to see her and I don't want to see Auntie. They don't need me, they've got each other.'

No one answered her.

Clean and in clean clothes, light grey Dockers from the charity shop and a white T-shirt with Auntie's silver cross on the chain round her neck, Minty sat in the window reading the papers and from time to time looking up at the street outside. It was after five and the Wilsons hadn't come back. Gertrude Pierce came out of Mr Kroot's with a letter in her hand. Her orange hair was quite white at the roots. She had a purple coat on with a fake fur collar, a winter coat on a warm summer afternoon. Minty watched her cross the street and walk down to the postbox on the corner of Laburnam. Now, returning, she was facing this way and Minty saw that she'd covered her face with make-up, coats of it, and scarlet lipstick and black stuff on her eyebrows. It made you shudder to think of wearing all that muck on your skin, and she must have been seventy-five if she was a day.

The ghost voices didn't comment. They hadn't spoken for the past couple of hours. Minty made herself a cup of tea in a nice clean white mug and had a Danish pastry with it that she'd personally watched the man, wearing gloves, pick up with stainless-steel tongs from under a cover, on a white plate with a white doily on it. Then, when she'd washed up the mug and the plate and dried them, she put on a clean white cardigan and went across the Harrow Road to the cemetery. On the way she passed Laf and Sonovia and the little girl and Daniel's wife Lauren coming home in Laf's car. They waved to her out of the open windows. Lauren had her long black hair done in what they called corn rows and pictures of flowers on her fingernails, which wasn't right in a doctor's wife.

The cemetery was very green and lush, buttercups and daisies growing among the grass and fresh gleaming moss climbing over the old stones. The full gasometer loomed on the far side of the canal. Sometimes, when it was nearly empty, it was just the bones of itself, like the skeletons that lay everywhere here in mouldering boxes under the ground. She went along the path between the ilexes and conifers where ivy clambered over mossy fallen angels and lichened mausoleums. Some of the gravestones had stone ivy carved on them with real ivy climbing over it. No one was about. It was just here, where the two paths intersected, that she had seen Jock coming towards her in his black leather jacket. She was sure she'd never see him again. She'd never pray to Auntie again, not after the way she'd been treated, and there'd be no more flowers on the grave.

It was hard because Auntie had been all she'd got, really, until Jock came along. Sonovia had once said Auntie was like God to her and Laf, who'd been there, was shocked and said not to talk like that, Minty didn't worship Auntie, she didn't pray to her. The truth was she did but she couldn't say so, though when she went home she got down on her knees and prayed. She was muddled, she didn't know what to do, to thank Auntie for dying and leaving her the house and the bathroom or to wish her alive again. Well, in a way, that second wish had come true.

The carnations and gypsophila she'd put on the grave a couple of weeks ago were dead now and brown. The water in the vase was brown too and only about an inch of it was left. She pulled out the dead flowers, threw the water on the ground and put the vase back where she'd found it, on the slab in front of some old man's tomb. The sun warmed her and she lifted up her face to its gentle evening light. She'd expected Auntie and maybe Mrs Lewis to say something. Auntie must know by now that she'd meant it when she'd said there'd be no more flowers. Removing the vase would have told her that. The dead knew everything, saw all. But no voices came, they'd gone away somewhere, back to where they'd come from.

That done, she'd go to the pictures. On her own. Walk it, it wasn't that far to Whiteley's. If she was going to see them anywhere, she thought, it would be in the underpass by Royal Oak station, though she'd no special reason to associate either of them with tunnels under roads. And they weren't there, not even their muttering voices. Something called *The Insider* and something else called *The Beach* were the choices before her. She chose the latter and had to sit through a story about a bunch of teenagers in some foreign place.

A man came and sat beside her and offered her a Polo mint. She shook her head and said no, but of course it reminded her of Jock, and when the man put his hand on her knee she remembered how she'd told Jock she was his and would be for ever. There'd never be anyone else. It made no difference that Jock had stolen all her money. She picked up the man's hand, digging her nails into the back of it until he cried out. Then she moved three seats along the row and after a minute or two he left.

When she came out of the cinema it was dark and no longer very warm. She walked up towards the Edgware Road and waited for a 36 bus. It was while she was standing there, quite alone, in a dreary isolated place near Paddington Basin, that she saw Auntie sitting on the seat under the bus shelter. She wasn't as clear as Jock had been but a shape that you could see through, a semi-transparent entity that was nevertheless unmistakably Auntie from her iron-grey hair in a coil on the back of her head and her rimless glasses to her sensible black lace-up shoes.

Minty wasn't going to speak to her, she wouldn't give her the satisfaction, but she did wonder if taking the vase away and throwing out the dead flowers was what had brought her back in visible form. Of Mrs Lewis there was no sign. Minty stared at Auntie and Auntie purposely looked away towards the bridge over the canal. Within a few minutes the bus came. I'm not getting on it if she does, Minty said to herself. But when the bus stopped Auntie got up and went away towards the underpass.

'Good riddance to bad rubbish,' Minty said as she passed her money to the driver.

'You what?'

A lot of people were staring at her.

'I wasn't talking to you,' she said to the driver, and to the rest of them, 'or any of you.'

She went upstairs to the top, to escape them.

Chapter 21

Never in his life, as far as he could recall, had Jims been so angry, and his anger was compounded in part of rage and in part of fear. Up to a point he was an imaginative man and he saw his career lying in smithereens while ever before him loomed the ogre-like shape of the Opposition Chief Whip.

He was lying in bed in Fredington Crucis House, having dutifully listened to an hour of the *Today* programme on his bedside radio. At eight thirty Mrs Vincey brought him up a cup of tea – something she'd never done before – and two tabloid newspapers. They must have been her own, for Jims took no papers in the country and, if he had, would never have chosen these. He'd often thought she hated him and now he was sure of it.

This was the day he was supposed to go over to Shaston and support the Conservative candidate. He pictured the media with their cameras and recording devices waiting for him and was just making up his mind not to go because it would do more harm than good to the Party, when the phone rang.

It was Ivo Carew. 'Look, lovey, I've got a confession to make. I told the cops about you skiving off our luncheon. I more or less had to. They asked me.'

How they could have when he hadn't even mentioned Ivo's existence to them, Jims couldn't imagine. 'Have you seen the papers?'

'Who hasn't?'

'What am I going to do?'

'Well, my old love, in your place I'd pretend I didn't know. I mean, about the husband still being the husband.'

'I *didn't* know.'

Ivo plainly didn't believe him. 'I'd simply maintain my innocence. *Stoutly* maintain it. A bridegroom' – he sniggered nastily at the word – 'can't be expected to scrutinise his bride's divorce papers. She said she was divorced and you accepted it.'

Jims said nothing.

'Why on earth did you marry her?'

'I don't know,' said Jims. 'It seemed a good idea at the time.'

'Shall I come over, lovey?'

Get into bed with him, no doubt, and further complicate things, not to mention old Vincey, downstairs but with her ears on stalks. 'Better not. I'm going home.'

Showered and dressed, Jims felt slightly better, though in no fit state to eat the plateful of fried eggs, bread, bacon and potatoes swimming in fat, unaccountably prepared for him. He drank a cup of Nescafé and reconstituted milk. Were things quite so bad as he'd thought at first? As a politician, Jims believed that there were few situations in public life that couldn't be remedied with the right strategy, few errors that couldn't be made good by (apparent) frankness, sincere apology and an earnest air of innocence. And he *was* innocent. What more likely than that two people like Zillah and Jerry Leach, feckless and sloppy, had shacked up together and had two kids without ever marrying? Of course he'd believed her. He could say something about her first marriage being too painful for her to wish it commemorated in any document. That would do. Well, no, it wouldn't do, but it would help.

Probably the best line to take would be that he hadn't known. Zillah believed herself divorced and, now Jeffrey Leach was dead he, Jims, would make everything good by immediately remarrying the widow. Did he really want to do this? Of course not. He'd rather never see her again. But he didn't have a choice. Needs must when the devil drives, and the devil had never driven harder and faster than this. They could always get divorced when the fuss died down. Perhaps he should issue a statement. Call Malina Daz now and get her to help him word it. It would still be too late for the *Evening Standard*. Best go home first, work out the statement in his head on the way, and talk to that unspeakable little bitch Zillah he wished he'd never set eyes on in the first place. He'd call Malina on his car phone and then he'd call Leonardo.

But perhaps he did have a choice. Perhaps there were other options. He picked up the phone and dialled Ivo's mobile. When all was said and done, Zillah wasn't very bright.

Michelle didn't much care about her and Matthew being suspected of murdering Jeffrey Leach, as she'd had to learn to call him. That was an exaggeration. Of course she would care if they really suspected them, if all that questioning hadn't been just routine. They had to ask questions, it was their job. She and Matthew were still treating it as a joke. They'd even given jokey names to the principal police officers, calling the woman Miss Demeanour and the man Violent Crimes. But even if they'd truly put Mr and Mrs Jarvey of Holmdale Road, West Hampstead on their list of suspects and had real suspicions about them, that would be nothing to Fiona's betrayal.

When they'd called yesterday morning, and wanted to know where she and Matthew had been a week ago on the day Jeff was killed, when they'd said she understood they'd disliked Jeffrey Leach and made it plain they did, she'd asked them how they knew that. Of course, they wouldn't tell her; they'd said they weren't able to divulge that information. But she knew and the knowledge lacerated her. Only Fiona could have told them, for no one else had heard of their dislike. She and Matthew were barely acquainted with anyone else, apart from her sister and his brother, whom they hardly ever saw and would never have confided in. Fiona knew the Jarveys didn't like her fiancé, she and Michelle had discussed it and, when asked if Jeff had any enemies, named the people next door. Her friends. The woman who loved her as a mother might and who thought herself loved in daughterly fashion in return. It was monstrous. Didn't Matthew think it was, asked Michelle in tears.

'You can't be sure, darling. They may only have assumed we disliked him because it seems that most people did except these poor women he strung along.'

'No. Fiona told them. How would they know no one liked him? They don't know anyone he knew. His past life is a blank, Fiona said. She's betrayed me and I hate to say this, but I can never feel the same about her again, never.'

'Don't cry, darling. I can't bear to see you cry.'

Miss Demeanour and her twin – it was two women this time – wanted something Michelle had always believed wasn't a real requirement but only a feature of detective stories and television sitcoms. They asked her and Matthew to provide an alibi. At first this shocked her. Living in a sheltered world where honesty was taken for granted, she believed the senior of the two women would take her word.

'My husband and I were out shopping together.

First we went to Waitrose at Swiss Cottage and then, because it was such a lovely day, I drove us up to the Heath.'

'Hampstead Heath?' Miss Demeanour asked this as if there were dozens of open spaces in London known familiarly as the Heath. Michelle nodded. 'You parked and sat in the car? Where exactly was that?'

Everyone must surely know how difficult it was to park anywhere in the vicinity. You could no longer go where you chose, as was the case when she and Matthew first came to Holmdale Road, but had to settle for wherever you could find a space.

'It was by the Vale of Health pond.'

'What time would that have been, Mrs Jarvey?'

She couldn't remember. All she could say was that they'd left and gone home soon after half past four because Miss Harrington was coming in to have a drink with them at five thirty.

Matthew said, 'We went out shopping at half past two and were at the Vale of Health by a quarter to four. We stayed there for three-quarters of an hour.'

Surely they must have been impressed by his beautiful voice. Was that the voice of a thug who went about murdering people with knives? Michelle hadn't expected the next question.

'Did anyone see you? Would anyone remember you at Waitrose?'

'I shouldn't think so.' Matthew looked faintly amused, his lips twitching. 'Hundreds of people were in there.' And we don't look as funny as we used to, Michelle thought. I'm still fat and he's still thin, but the contrast isn't so great. Lots of couples look like us. 'I can't remember seeing anyone at the Vale of Health. People don't go out for walks any more, do they?'

No one answered him. It was then that Michelle

260

had asked how they knew she and Matthew had disliked Jeff and the two officers said they were unable to divulge that information. Matthew said he couldn't understand this insistence on an alibi. They alibied each other, they'd been together all the time. Miss Demeanour's colleague smiled pityingly. Ah, yes, but they were married. The inference was that each would readily lie to save the other. That was absurd when you remembered how many husbands and wives were at loggerheads.

Michelle reverted to the subject next morning. Sleep had been slow in coming to her last night and when at last it did she dreamt of her unborn children, those children that would now never be born. There were three of them, all girls, all clones of Fiona, each one turning their back on her and walking away, saying they'd never loved her because her heart was full of hatred.

Wanting to raise the subject again with Matthew, she lighted upon it obliquely. 'I can't believe they'd seriously think of us as people capable of murder.'

'Well, if you think that, darling, you've nothing to worry about. So cheer up. Come and give me a kiss.' Michelle kissed him. 'You know, you look lovely today, you look years younger.'

Even that was no comfort to her. She could hear Fiona saying the words. The people next door, she'd have said, we'd got quite friendly with them, but they made it plain they disliked Jeff. It got uncomfortable being with them. Sometimes Mrs Jarvey had the most awful vindictive expression on her face. All Jeff did was imply that she's fat. Well, for God's sake, she *is* fat and she knows it perfectly well.

'You can't tell if she said those things, Michelle. It does no good conjuring up these scenarios. It's a very dangerous kind of fantasising. After a while you stop distinguishing between the fantasy and what really happened; you don't know the reality any more.'

Michelle knew that there could be only one kind of reality, that Fiona had led the police to believe she and Matthew, the gentlest and most civilised of men, hated their neighbour's partner so much that they were capable of killing him. In a neutral voice she said, 'I'd better think about getting our lunch.'

Not that she would eat anything. Since Jeff's death she had lost her appetite and often felt that food would choke her. In death as in life, he had given her invaluable help. What would the police think if she told them that? That she was mad or that she'd killed Jeff to make sure she'd lost her appetite? Matthew, on the other hand, had discovered the pleasures of a new food, ciabatta, the best thing he'd tried for years. Or Fiona had discovered it for him last week. Before Jeff died, before she betrayed me, Michelle thought, as she cut two slices of the Italian bread and put them on a plate with cottage cheese and twelve salted almonds.

For Zillah it had been a terrible day, an awful night and a worse morning. First, of course, the media crowding her, the flash bulbs going off in her face, the bombardment of shouted questions.

'How does it feel to be married to two men at once, Zillah?' No one called her Mrs Melcombe-Smith any more. 'Why didn't you get a divorce, Zillah? Did you get married in church both times? Will you and Jims marry again? Properly this time, Zillah? Is this your little boy, Zillah? What's your name, darling?'

It was then that Mark Fryer, the rat, had deserted her and run off. Several young women with note-pads pursued him. Zillah had put her hands up in front of her face, leaving a gap in the mouth area, through which she shouted, 'Go away, go away, leave me alone!'

She'd scooped up Jordan who was crying as usual, and not just crying but sobbing, bellowing, shrieking in fear. One of the porters had come down the steps, not looking sympathetic but with a dreadful expression of disapproval as if he were silently saying, this isn't the kind of thing we expect in Abbey Gardens Mansions, here under the shadow of the Houses of Parliament. But he provided her with a coat to cover herself and escorted her into the building, the other porter doing his best to keep the crowd back. Zillah was very nearly pushed into the lift. The doors closed.

The moment she entered the flat the phone started ringing. Ten minutes later she knew better than to answer it but this first time she lifted the receiver.

'Hi, Zillah,' a man's voice said. 'The *Sun* here. Come out into the sun, right? Can we have a few words? Now, when did you first . . .'

She slammed down the receiver. It rang again. She lifted it tentatively. It might be her mother, it might be – God forbid – Jims. But she'd have to speak to him. Jordan sat in the middle of the floor, rocking from side to side and screaming. This time the caller was the *Daily Star*. He must be on a mobile, she could hear the traffic in Parliament Square, Big Ben chiming.

'Hi there, Zillah. How d'you like being the centre of attention? Fame at last, right?'

Having unplugged the phone and the one in Jims's bedroom and the one in her bedroom, she went to bed with Jordan in her arms, hugging him close and pulling the covers over her. Later on, she reconnected her bedside phone and called Mrs Peacock. Would she fetch Eugenie from school?

'I will this once, Mrs Melcombe-Smith. But I'm not

going to be able to carry on with this much longer. If you're happy with that I'd like to pop in tomorrow morning about ten and have a frank chat about things, talk it through.'

Zillah wasn't happy about anything but she felt too broken to say so.

Eugenie came in half an hour afterwards, saying Mrs Peacock had brought her to the flat door, rung the bell and gone down in the lift without waiting for it to be answered. 'Why are the phones all pulled out? My friend Matilda is going to phone me at six and she won't be able to get through.'

'You can't have phone calls at your age, Eugenie.'

'Why not? I'm seven and seven is the age of reason. Miss McMurty told us.'

I haven't reached it yet, thought Zillah with unusual humility, *and I'll be twenty-eight next month*, but she refused to plug in the phones and Eugenie sulked all evening. That night Zillah was awakened by Jordan screaming in an apparent frenzy. He was soaked in urine and so was his bed. She changed his nappy and his pyjamas, brought him into bed with her. What was wrong with him? She ought to do something about it, take him to that child psychiatrist. At his age his sister had left babyhood behind, was clean, dressed herself, chatted away about anything, only cried if she fell over.

True to her word, Mrs Peacock arrived at ten sharp.

'We're not going to have to be looked after by her *again*, are we?'

'No, Eugenie, you're not,' said Mrs Peacock. 'Never again, if I may so put it. Have you looked out of your window this morning, Mrs Melcombe-Smith? A rat pack is outside. I believe that's the current expression.'

Zillah went to the window. The media people

looked like the same lot as yesterday. They were waiting patiently, most of them with cigarettes and a couple with flasks of something. A lot of merriment was going on, they all seemed on the best of terms. As if in protest, Jordan began to cry.

'I brought some papers for you, in case you haven't seen them. You're in them, on all the front pages.'

'Thank you. I prefer not to see.'

'Frankly, I'm not surprised. May I sit down? It's rather early, but all this has been a shock to me and if you don't object, I'd like a glass of Bristol Cream.'

Zillah poured it, a large schooner. She could quite clearly hear the laughter and chatter from the street two floors below. The phone rang. She pulled out the plug, watched closely by Mrs Peacock.

'Now, Mrs Melcombe-Smith – though to be honest with you I doubt if you've any right to that name – when I phoned you yesterday I was, as you might say, in a state of innocence. Things have changed. I've read the newspapers. As you may imagine, I could hardly believe my eyes. Abbey Gardens Mansions is no place for you, Maureen Peacock, I said to myself.'

'There are two sides to this,' said Zillah. 'I can explain everything.'

The innocent never utter these words and perhaps Mrs Peacock knew it. 'We need not go into that. Who touches pitch shall be defiled. I shall be reluctantly forced to terminate our agreement. You owe me fifty-seven pounds, twenty-five pee, and I'd like cash. You never know with some people whether cheques won't bounce.'

A little of her old spirit returned to Zillah. 'Don't you dare speak to me like that!'

Mrs Peacock ignored this. She got slowly to her feet, emptied the sherry glass and wiped her lips with a small lace handkerchief. 'Just one other thing before I go.' She pointed to Jordan who, by this time, was lying on his back, writhing and weeping. 'There's something seriously amiss with that child. He needs help without more ado. I knew a child like him twenty-five years ago, always crying and screaming. And what d'you think? Nothing was done and he grew up to be a psychopath. He's in prison now, in a straitjacket, one of those places where they put violent people who are a threat to the community.'

But Zillah had gone to her bedroom to fetch the money. The amount was more than she had in the flat and she had to take a five-pound note out of Eugenie's piggy bank. Eugenie, who was really a very strange child, perhaps a genius, started laughing as soon as Mrs Peacock had gone. Zillah could hardly believe she'd understood what the woman had said but something had made her laugh and after a second or two Zillah joined in. She put her arms round her daughter, preparing to give her a hug, something she hadn't done for a long time. Eugenie stiffened and pulled away.

Jims might have been trying to get through to her but it didn't matter much. She knew he'd be here by lunchtime. He'd have cancelled his engagement in Casterbridge and driven straight home. There was very little to eat in the flat and obviously she couldn't go out shopping. If Mrs Peacock hadn't been so abominable and rude and defiant, she'd have asked her to get a few things in. The children could have scrambled eggs, though they'd had rather a lot of these lately, and Eugenie had already told her eggs were stuffed with cholesterol and did she know?

It was just after twelve when Jims came. Unlike her, he wasn't so foolish as to run the gauntlet in

Great College Street, he'd have seen what was going on when driving past in the car, but still there was no escape for him. Media people were round the back as well. Zillah, shaking with nerves, heard the lift come up and its doors open. Malina Daz was with him, wearing a sea-green salwar kameez and with her hair done like a Japanese geisha's.

Jims opened the living-room door, took a step inside and surveyed his little family the way uncharitable people look at asylum seekers. To the children he said not a word. He addressed Zillah in an Arctic voice. 'Malina and I are about to prepare a statement for the media. I will show it to you when we've finished.'

Malina brought the statement in to her. It was short, prepared on a word processor.

My wife Zillah and I fully understand the sensation recent circumstances – the tragic death of Mr Jeffrey Leach taken in tandem with our marriage – have occasioned in the media. While absolutely concurring in the opinion of national newspaper editors that this matter is in the public interest and should not be kicked into the long grass but openly aired, we would nevertheless like to assure those kind enough to take an interest in us, that we were totally innocent of any offence.

My wife sincerely believed that her marriage to Mr Leach had been dissolved twelve months ago. She had implicit trust in Mr Leach as did I. Not for a moment did either of us believe we were guilty of wrongdoing. If we had, in spite of our love for each other, we would of course have deferred our marriage until we had secured a formalisation of the divorce and could start afresh with a level playing field.

Needless to say, we shall remarry as soon as this is feasible. We would both like to extend our best wishes to

*those good enough to be concerned for us and ask them
for their understanding, indulgence and, indeed, forgiveness.*

'It's a bit formal,' said Malina, 'but we deemed that
suited to the seriousness of the subject matter. Jims
decided it might be best not to mention your
husband's passing setting you free. It looks bad. And
we were minded not to use the word "bigamy". It
sounds terribly twentieth century, don't you think?'

Because she dared not ask Jims, Zillah asked
Malina, 'What will they do to me?'

'What, for being married to two men at the same
time? Not a lot, I should think. After all, your
husband's dead, isn't he? It'd be different if he were
still alive somewhere. They'll be focusing on the
murder.'

Malina went off to do whatever she did to
disseminate the statement. Jordan cried himself to
sleep. Eugenie said that if someone would take her
there she'd like to go round to her friend Matilda's
for the afternoon but first she was starving.

'There is no food in the house,' said Jims.

'I know there isn't. I couldn't go out shopping,
could I? Not with all that lot outside.' Zillah very
much wanted to placate him. 'I could now if I go
through the basement. They aren't in the back.'

'They are. They nearly flattened my car when
Malina and I came in.'

'Miss McMurty says that if you don't have enough
to eat you'll get a vitamin deficiency. Your eyes will
go blind and your teeth drop out,' Eugenie said.

'I will get one of the porters to shop for us,' said
Jims.

Zillah wondered when the showdown would
come, when he'd ask her why she'd deceived him
over the non-existent divorce. She prepared lunch.

268

The porter had bought inferior quality food from some corner shop, besides getting all the things the children didn't like. The lettuce was wilted and the tomatoes soft. Jordan screamed when he was expected to eat corned beef.

'Can I phone Matilda and get her to come here?' Eugenie suggested.

'I'm surprised you condescend to ask.'

'Well, can I?'

'I suppose so. You'll have to play in your bedroom. I've got a splitting headache.'

Too late Zillah remembered Matilda's father would probably bring her. But when the child arrived half an hour later she was in the care of a very young and beautiful au pair. She supposed she ought to be thankful Eugenie's friend was allowed to come at all, permitted to associate with the Melcombe-Smiths, after what had been in the papers.

'I'll come back for you at six, Matilda.'

They'd to have her for three whole hours? That meant Zillah must find something to feed them on. She watched them go off towards Eugenie's room, chatting happily, her daughter giggling like a normal child. The phone began to ring. Zillah lifted the receiver fearfully. It was her mother, saying nothing this time about newspapers but asking if she was so indifferent to her father's fate that she had forgotten he'd had a heart bypass that morning. After making wild promises she knew she'd never carry out, once Nora Watling had slammed down the phone she was left alone with Jims.

He took from the bookcase an as yet unread biography of Clemençeau, returned with it to his armchair and, in total silence, opened it at the preface. Zillah picked up a glossy magazine and tried to read a piece about collagen lip implants. Suppose he never spoke to her again? What would she do? She remembered, back in December, how she'd foreseen this marriage as the chaste and charming companionship of two best friends, two people who would have fun together, enjoy life and at the last have a greater affection for each other than either had for any lover.

'What do you want me to say?' she asked him when she could bear the silence no longer.

He looked up, a shade of irritability crossing his face. 'I beg your pardon – what?'

'I asked you what you wanted me to say.'

'Nothing,' he said. 'There is nothing to say. The newspapers have already said it.'

'We can get through it together, can't we, Jims? All the fuss will die down. You've done nothing wrong. The statement will stop it, won't it? Oh, Jims, I'm so desperately sorry. I'd have died before I let something like this happen, I'm so *sorry*.'

'Don't be ridiculous. Abjectness doesn't suit you.'

She'd have gone down on her knees to him but for the phone ringing at that moment. 'Don't answer it, let it ring.'

He got up, crossed the room to where the phone was and lifted the receiver. His expression changed subtly as he listened. 'Yes,' he said, and 'yes' again. 'May I ask why?' She couldn't remember ever having seen him dismayed before. 'I would like to phone my lawyer first,' and then, 'Half an hour, right.'

'What is it, Jims?'

'They want me at the police station. Here won't do. They're coming to fetch me.'

'My God, Jims, but why?'

Instead of answering he lifted the receiver and dialled the home number of his solicitor.

Eugenie came in, trailing Matilda behind her. 'You owe me five pounds, Mummy. You'd better write it down or you'll forget.'

Chapter 22

Alone at home, Fiona hadn't set foot in her garden or conservatory since the news reached her of Jeff's death. Nor had she been back to work. She had barely been out. When Violent Crimes and Miss Demeanour weren't there, and their visits grew shorter and shorter until they no longer happened, she sat in her living room, not reading, not watching television nor listening to the radio, but just sitting. Her hands were usually folded in her lap, her knees close together. It was days now since she'd cried. She'd phoned no one and when the phone rang she left it to ring.

Michelle, who had been with her every day up until Thursday, hadn't been back since. She'd have liked to see her, for her next-door neighbour was the only company she wanted. But Michelle, she supposed, had grown tired of comforting a grief-stricken woman and had doubtless run out of things to say.

Fiona marvelled at the intensity of her own sorrow. She was as wretched as any widow after a twenty-year marriage. Her heart was broken. In the past she had laughed at the absurdity of this phrase and others like it: heartbreak, heartbroken. 'You will break my heart,' her mother had said to her over some minor offence she'd committed while at university. What nonsense. So she'd thought then but now she understood. Her own heart was broken, shattered to bits, and she told herself that since Jeff died she hadn't been able to feel it beating. When she placed her hand under her left breast there was no fluttering movement, nothing but a dull ache. Sometimes, sitting alone, she worried over this and took her own pulse, not knowing whether to be relieved or not at its gentle regular throb.

Every day the newspapers had a fresh story in them about Jeff. His marriage, his idle life. Fiona swore not to look at these articles but she couldn't help herself. They'd said everything they could about the murder and now they were on to Jeff's womanising activities, his failure ever to have worked for his living, the base advantage he took of women who kept him and were then abandoned. Reading about this brought her an intense physical pain, which fetched little sobs and moans from her. One woman he'd moved in with five years ago had parted with her savings amounting to two thousand pounds, had later lost her job and was living on the benefit. Fiona, still believing herself the great love of Jeff's life, the one to change him, felt she ought to compensate this woman for her losses.

All this added to her grief. Next week she would have to go back to work. She had grounds no longer for staying away. It wasn't a close relative she had lost, not a husband or partner in a long, steady relationship, not even really a fiancé. That word had become a dirty one to Fiona, who would never again read it on the page or hear it spoken without recalling how Jeff had not given her a ring and had lied to her about their wedding date. That knowledge did nothing to reduce the strength of her love, but it tinged that love, loss, sorrow, with bitterness.

At work they would all, of course, say they were sorry about her boyfriend, what a shock, what a ghastly thing to happen, and that would be it. Until the police caught the person who'd done it, when their sympathy would be revived and her boss would tell her to take the day off. She'd be a curiosity, to be pointed out as the woman whose boyfriend had been murdered. For ever, probably. Fiona imagined herself at fifty, still single, of course, still alone, the middle-aged solitary whom people got to know, wherever she might live, as the cinema victim's girlfriend.

She forgot to eat. Having shared an almost nightly bottle of wine with Jeff, she could no longer bear the pain of tasting it. A woman who lost weight easily and quickly, she felt her hip bones protruding, her elbows sharp. At this rate – and she managed a wry joke with herself – Matthew would want her on his programme. If only Matthew would come to her! If only Michelle would come! The phone had stopped ringing. Something hindered her from lifting the receiver and making a call herself; she couldn't physically perform the actions. As for going to them, she had a vision of herself stepping out of her front door, ringing their bell and, when the door opened, two people staring at her as if they'd never seen her before, as if she were some stray caller wanting to promote a product or give away a tract.

At night she took sleeping pills, Temazepam. They sent her to sleep but it was an uneasy sleep and full of dreams. Always of Jeff. In one he came back from some foreign trip he'd been on. She'd thought he was dead and felt boundless joy at their reunion, as he promised he'd never go away again. Waking to reality was one of the worst experiences of her life.

The newspapers continued to be delivered and thrown into the recycling bin. She'd need to take it out to the street one day before it got too heavy to lift, but she'd have to leave the house on Monday anyway, somehow get herself to the tube and the City and London Wall. Taking the papers from the doormat on Saturday morning, though hating them, though determined as ever not to look, she caught sight in the front-page photograph of a woman she recognised. It was, surely it was, Jeff's ex-wife.

Only she wasn't his *ex*-wife. They'd never been divorced. Fiona felt a shaft of intense pain run through her body as if she too had been stabbed with a long, sharp knife. She was indifferent as to whether Zillah Melcombe-Smith had knowingly committed bigamy or not. Jeff had lied again and this lie was infinitely worse than telling her he'd booked a wedding date when he hadn't. He couldn't book a date, he was married already.

Fiona dropped the paper. She lay face-down on the hall floor in an agony of grief and, strangely, shame.

'I shall sue these trashy rags for libel,' Jims said when, for five minutes, Violent Crimes left him alone with his solicitor. He had completely forgotten deriding Zillah for making much the same threat.

'Have you got a million pounds to spare?' Damien Pritchard was a little older than his client, but not unlike him to look at, being also tall, dark, classic-featured and gay. 'A million you wouldn't mind dropping down a drain or giving to a beggar?'

'Of course I haven't. I wouldn't need to. I'll win.'

'Oh, please. Do me a favour. Let me tell you something. A solicitor came to live next door to my parents when I was a kid. I've always remembered my father saying to my mother, he's a lawyer, don't touch his ears. Actually, I think it had a lot to do with making me want to be one. Well, the same goes for newspaper editors. Don't touch their ears.' Damien shook his head in exasperation. 'And now, can't you really come up with a better alibi than what you expect the Plod to swallow? Oh, God, here they are, coming back.'

Jims could, of course, improve on his alibi. He could have told the truth. But that seemed almost the worst thing he could do and its results the worst that could happen to him. Once more he sat down at that bare table with Damien next to him and Violent Crimes and Miss Demeanour facing them. They all sat in the kind of chairs Jims wouldn't even have had in his garden shed. At least they were still calling him by his surname and style, though he wondered how long that would last.

'The difficulty is that no one confirms your presence at Fredington Crucis House during Friday afternoon and evening, Mr Melcombe-Smith. Two callers at the house noticed that your car was absent.'

'Who?'

'You know I'm not at liberty to tell you that. You still maintain you spent Friday evening there? And stayed over Friday night?'

'My client', said Damien, 'has already told you so. Several times.'

Jims was starting to get cross. 'Why would I have killed the guy, anyway? For what possible reason would I have stuck a knife in him?'

'Well, Mr Melcombe-Smith,' said Miss, or Detective Inspector, Demeanour, 'he was married to the lady with whom you'd been through a form of marriage.' She smiled very faintly as Jims winced. 'It would have been very much in your interest to have him out of the way, especially if he'd threatened to reveal the truth to, say, a newspaper.'

'So what? Everybody else reveals it. Anyway, he wasn't blackmailing me. I thought Zillah and he had never been married. I hadn't seen him for years.' Like many in his position, Jims was anxious to be scrupulous about telling the truth in every area of questioning except one. 'Well, two years.'

The words 'so you say' were plainly written on the woman's face. 'You came back to London on Friday afternoon, didn't you, Mr Melcombe-Smith?'

Jims was silent. He was hesitating. He could feel doubt, a loss of confidence in his friend and client, by some strange means emanating from Damien. Violent Crimes was looking at him. Behind them, on the ochre-coloured wall, a crack in the plaster ran from ceiling to skirting board. It was shaped, Jims thought, like the silhouette of a man with an erection. He looked away.

Damien, who was a good guy, a real friend in need despite his wavering trust, said softly, 'If you don't mean to charge Mr Melcombe-Smith, and I don't think you do, you're obliged to let him go home now.'

Violent Crimes knew a trick worth two of that. 'You drove back to London to fetch something. Something you'd forgotten. I've been wondering if it was the notes for your speech to the Countryside Alliance. It's a coincidence, but the Chief Constable of Wessex happened to be there.'

Jims tried to remember if he'd referred to the missing notes and his return to retrieve them when he was making that speech. He couldn't remember. *And it wouldn't matter whether he'd referred to them or not.* It was enough that this policeman had the sense, the skill, if you like, to suggest that he had. It didn't even matter whether it was true about the Chief Constable. He looked at Damien in despair and Damien said nothing.

'Mr Melcombe-Smith?'

They contrived by the tone of their voices to make his name ridiculous. Jims thought of appealing to them to keep what he might confess to them a secret.

Would they agree? Or should he trust to luck? He considered the procedures he read about in the newspapers which preceded murder trials, or any court cases come to that. The police never told the media how they arrived at arresting someone or charging someone or how they agreed to or exploded alibis. There must be something in law which forbade their doing so. Not for the first time he wished he'd read law instead of history and practised for a while at the criminal bar.

'Mr Melcombe-Smith?'

'All right, I did come back to London.' He dared not look at Damien. 'I had, as you say, forgotten my notes. I started the drive back soon after one and had something to eat at a – well, a sort of café on the A30.' A sound, something between a sniff and a grunt, came from Damien. Or maybe not, perhaps he'd imagined it. 'I'm not sure where. They might remember me. The traffic was bad. I didn't get – home till seven.'

It was interesting, it was almost disconcerting, the way they accepted that up till now he'd lied. They didn't comment. Neither said, 'So you've been lying to us' or 'Why didn't you tell the truth before?' It was as if they were entirely used to a kind of endemic mendacity, it was what they expected. Jims began to feel sick.

'So you went home, Mr Melcombe-Smith?'

Nothing but the truth would do now. 'I'd left the notes at a friend's house.'

'Ah,' said Inspector Demeanour. 'And where might that be?'

He gave her Leonardo's address. Beside him Damien seemed to swell and palpitate, though when he turned to look at him the solicitor was sitting there, immobile and calm. Jims wanted to fall on his knees before them and beg them to say nothing, to tell no one, to accept his word, just as Zillah had wanted to kneel to him. He stayed where he was, his face expressionless.

'And Mr Norton will confirm what you say?'

The truth once told starts a train of truth. 'I didn't see him until eight thirty. As I was going out to eat I met him coming in.'

'So you left Casterbridge at – what? Half past one?'

'About that,' said Jims.

'And you reached Glebe Terrace at seven? Five and a half hours to drive a hundred and fifty miles, James?'

Something he'd said, or simply because he'd admitted to lying, had reduced him in their eyes. He'd taken away his own dignity and thereby lost the privilege of being treated courteously. 'I know it took a long time,' he said. 'I've never taken so long before. There were miles of roadworks. That bit took me nearly an hour to get through. Then there was a pile-up near Heathrow.'

They would check, of course, and find it was true. It hardly helped him. 'The Merry Cookhouse' – it pained him to utter the words – 'where I had lunch was just before the roadworks, if that's any use.'

'It may be. The relevant time is between 3.30 and 4.30 p.m. Did anyone see you enter the house in Glebe Terrace?'

How could he have forgotten, even for a moment? Relief flooded him. It was like drinking something warm and sweet when in a state of shock. 'The woman next door – it's 56a, I think – she gave me her key.'

'And now', said Damien, 'perhaps you'll let Mr Melcombe-Smith go.'

When the phone rang or when someone came to the front door, every time these things happened,

Michelle thought it was the police. The joke aspect of being treated with suspicion had gone. She'd got it into her head it would be impossible to find witnesses to her and Matthew's whereabouts that Friday afternoon and, though she wasn't usually a nervous woman, she saw them both high on the list of suspects. Miscarriages of justice did happen, people were mistakenly tried and falsely imprisoned. She'd only once encountered the police before and that was when the Jarveys' car was broken into and the radio stolen.

Matthew did his best to reassure her: 'Darling, I think you must believe that when they say an enquiry is routine it *is* routine.'

'I hated being questioned like that. It was the worst thing that's ever happened to me.'

That made him laugh, but not unkindly. 'No, it wasn't. The worst thing that's ever happened to you was when you thought I was going to die through my stupid food fads.'

'Not stupid,' Michelle said hotly. 'You don't mean that. You mean your illness.'

'Well, it's not really fear of being arrested that's upsetting you, is it? It's not being suspected of a crime or interrogated, it's indignation at Fiona's behaviour.'

'More than that, Matthew.' She went close behind the chair where he sat reading the *Spectator*, and put her arms round his neck. He looked up into her face. 'It's real pain over what she did. I'll never be able to think of her, let alone speak to her, without remembering what she did.'

He said very seriously, 'You'll have to get over that.'

'Yes, but how? I wish I weren't the sort of person who remembers for ever hurtful things people have said or done. But I am. I do. I don't like it, I know I

279

ought to forgive and forget. If only I could. I remember unkind things people said to me when I was at school. I mean, thirty years ago, darling. The words they used are as fresh in my mind as when they first said them.'

Although he knew it already, she'd told him before, he said to her in a light amused tone, 'I shall have to be very careful what I say to you then.'

She was vehement, intense. 'You never *never* say those sort of things. You never have. It's one of the reasons I love you and go on loving you, because you never hurt my feelings.'

Again he lifted to her his wizened, skeletal face. 'Not because I'm so sexy and charming?'

'That too. Of course.' She was entirely sincere, unsmiling. 'And the thing about Fiona is, it was true what she told the police, that I disliked Jeff, that I hated him, if you like. I hated him because he said those cruel things. He's dead and he died in a horrible way, but I don't care. I'm glad. It won't matter how I try, I shall never forget the things he said.'

Matthew covered her hands with his. 'Not even if you get thin and I get fat?' He knew now that she was trying to lose weight and he supported her, though without admonition for the past or congratulations for the present. 'Not even when I'm Large and you're Little?'

As she was trying to answer him the doorbell rang. Michelle put up her hands to her face, her eyes suddenly bright and staring. 'They've come back. On a Sunday. They don't care when they come, they don't even let us know they're coming.'

'I'll go,' Matthew said.

He walked quite quickly these days and could stand almost upright. The bell rang again before he got there. Fiona was on the doorstep, a new unattractive Fiona, her dirty hair in rats' tails, her face swollen from weeping and her eyes red. The trousers she wore were several sizes too big for her and looked like a man's. A shirt which should have been white, tucked into the waistband, showed how thin the past week had made her.

'Come in.'

She put her face close to his and kissed him on both cheeks. It was the kind of kiss the recipient isn't required to return. 'I have to see you. I can't be alone any longer. I'm going back to work tomorrow. I think it will kill me.'

Michelle blushed brightly when they came into the living room. She got up and took two, then three, awkward steps towards the visitor. Matthew wondered what she'd say, if she'd even refer to her contention.

Fiona stepped towards her, they met, and the bereaved woman threw her arms round Michelle, breaking into sobs. 'Why haven't you come to me? Why have you deserted me? What have I done?'

The silence was profound. Then Michelle said, in a voice Matthew had never heard before, 'You know what you've done.'

'I don't, I don't. I needed you and you left me alone. I've no one I care about but you. What have I done? Tell me, you must tell me. I swear I don't know.'

'You don't know that you told those police people that Matthew and I disliked Jeff? You told them that and now they suspect us? You don't know that?'

'No, darling, they don't suspect us,' Matthew said firmly. Fiona had broken into fresh tears. She threw out her arms wildly, her face streaming. 'Sit down, Fiona. Come on now, calm yourself. I'll make some tea.'

'Not until Michelle says she'll forgive me. I didn't know what I was doing or saying. I said anything that came into my head. I'd give everything I've got to take it back now.'

Michelle was looking at her sadly. 'The difficulty is that you can't take things back.'

'Then say you'll forgive me. Say it can be as if it never happened.'

'I've forgiven you already,' Michelle said drily and went into the kitchen to switch on the kettle. *But I haven't forgotten*, she thought. *Why is it so much easier to forgive than to forget?*

Violent Crimes interviewed Leonardo Norton on Sunday evening. He was very shocked that Jims, whom he thought the most discreet and laid-back of men, had given them his name. A sense of grievance sounded in his voice. 'It was at least eight thirty before I saw him, probably nearer nine. I'd spent the day with my mother in Cheltenham.' This rang in his own ears as the most innocent and blameless of ways to spend a day. 'I really can't account for what Mr Melcombe-Smith may have been doing in the afternoon.'

They didn't ask him where Jims had spent the night. Presumably, they hadn't much interest in what happened after 4.30 p.m.

The next question was rather near the bone. 'Did he have a key to this house?'

'To my house? Certainly not.' Jims, after all, would never admit to such a thing.

'But the lady next door has?'

'Amber Conway? Yes, she does. As I have a key to hers. It seemed wise. I understand Mr Melcombe-Smith borrowed her key.'

According to her sister, whom they tracked down, Amber Conway had gone to Ireland but not until

Saturday. She had been at home on Friday night but the sister knew nothing about a key. Violent Crimes told Leonardo they'd come back. Leonardo phoned Jims at home. When the receiver was lifted he could hear a child screaming, another one laughing and something that sounded like a Disney video bleating and crooning from the television.

'You *are* a one,' said Leonardo when he heard Jims's morose tones. 'Quite a little devil when you like. Did you really stick a knife in your wife's husband's guts?'

'Of course I fucking didn't.'

'You'll be taking bribes in brown envelopes next.'

'I don't allow even you to say that.'

Leonardo laughed. 'Want to come over?'

Jims told him coldly that he didn't think so. He'd had a grilling that had lasted most of the day and he was tired. Besides, he'd have a fresh confrontation next morning.

'Nothing to worry about,' said Leonardo. 'The papers will only say a Westminster man has been helping them with their enquiries. Or maybe "a well-known Tory MP".'

'Leave it out, would you?' said Jims.

Chapter 23

On the opposite side of Glebe Terrace to Amber Conway and Leonardo Norton lived a woman Natalie Reckman had got to know. She was the sister of her boyfriend's flatmate's girlfriend, a rather distantly removed relationship but one whose branchings were instantly simplified by most of the parties meeting for a dinner arranged and cooked by the flatmate. His sister-in-law-to-be told the company how the peace of her street had been disturbed all day by the comings and goings of the police, some in uniform and some, she was sure, plain-clothed. Their quarry appeared to be the woman opposite or it might instead be this woman's neighbour, a young banker or stockbroker or something whom she'd always supposed perfectly law-abiding. Someone had told her that a frequent visitor to his house – and she'd seen him call there herself – was that MP whose wife was a bigamist. She recognised him when she saw his picture in the paper.

Natalie was so excited she could barely eat her dinner. Unfortunately, she had to eat it and she was going to have to stay the night there too or put her relationship with her boyfriend in jeopardy. He'd already complained she was always away and thought more of getting a scoop than of him. Anyway, there wasn't much that could be done before the morning. But by nine next day she was in Glebe Terrace, her car in the underground NCP to avoid all risk of towing away or clamping, and Natalie was ringing the bell on a pretty little house which was the right-hand half of a joined-up pair. No police were about. Just as it began to look as if Amber Conway was still away and Natalie had rung the bell three times, the door was opened by a half-asleep woman with tousled hair and sleep dust in her eyes, wearing a short dressing gown over baby doll pyjamas.

'Amber Conway?'

'Yes. Who are you? I only got home at three this morning. Are you the police?'

'Certainly not,' said Natalie. 'What an idea.'

'They've been phoning me. I told them not to get here till ten.'

'That's why I got here at nine.' Natalie put one foot over the threshold. 'Can I come in?'

Jims had spent the evening lecturing Zillah on what he called her 'disgusting and criminal behaviour'. If he was to continue to share his life with her it must be on the strict understanding that she did what she was told, starting with a marriage ceremony, quietly carried out this time at an hotel or some such place, anywhere licensed for weddings. After that it would be more sensible for her to live permanently at Fredington Crucis House, only coming to London when her presence was required at some Conservative function, say a party hosted by the Leader of the Opposition. Eugenie must go to boarding school and Jordan follow her in three years' time. Meanwhile he would attend a nursery school of Jims's choosing.

'I won't,' Zillah said. 'I've only just left the bloody place and I'm not going back.'

'I'm afraid you must, my dear. If you don't I shall have no option but to leave you, or rather, turn you out. Because if we aren't married and haven't even lived together for more than two months, I shall be under no legal obligation to support you. Jerry can't, if he ever did to any extent. He's dead. So you either toe the line or go on the benefit. I don't know where you'll live but I dare say Westminster would put you in bed and breakfast accommodation.'

'What a bastard you are.'

'Calling names won't help. Thanks to some crafty string-pulling, I've arranged for us to be married on Wednesday. All right with you?'

That had been Monday. Neither of them had much sleep that night. Even though he hadn't revealed his state of mind to Zillah, Jims was seriously worried about the police investigation. One never knew when they would pounce again, for pounce he was sure they would. The Chief Whip had as yet said nothing to him and neither had the Leader of the Opposition, but from each he fancied he'd received chilly looks. The idea that they were biding their time was inescapable.

Zillah, too, lay awake but, oddly enough, her state of mind was far more cheerful and forward-looking than his. That afternoon, before he came home, she'd had a phone call from a television channel called Moon and Stars asking her if she'd be willing to go on their *A Bite of Breakfast* show and talk about her experiences. She'd said she'd think about it and get back to them on Tuesday. If she played her cards right, she could maybe have a career in television. It might be wisest to get married first, just to be on the safe side. She'd ring Moon and Stars in the morning and ask them to wait just one more day when she'd be able to give them a positive answer.

Jims worried also about the newspapers. That remark of Leonardo's about describing the man who'd been 'helping the police with their enquiries' as a well-known Tory MP still rankled. He was pretty sure they couldn't do that, they wouldn't dare, it would be *sub judice* or whatever the term was, and once again he wished he had some legal training. Probably there would be nothing anyone could link with him – but when would they come back for him? Could he find the courage to make an appointment with the Chief Whip before the tiresome man sent for him? Once he'd have said his nerve was limitless, but now he wasn't so sure. He couldn't understand why he'd had no invitations from the *Today* programme or Jeremy Paxman's *Start the Week*. They came fast enough when he had nothing to say.

The newspapers flopped on to the mat at six thirty in the morning. Jims had only slept for about an hour. He was up drinking coffee. If he grabbed the papers with unseemly haste, there was no one to see him. He sighed with relief for there was nothing more about him than the usual 'man helping'. So far, so good. A pity, really, that there was no point in going back to bed at this hour. He could have slept at last.

The manager – he called himself the chief executive - of the Merry Cookhouse on the A30 remembered Jims, identifying him from a photograph without any trouble. Indeed, he'd already known who he was when first he entered the restaurant, the MP husband of that woman who'd married him while married to someone else. It had been all over the newspapers. Then when he'd come into the Merry Cookhouse all problems of recognition, if there'd been any, disappeared. He was the rudest and most difficult customer the man behind the counter had come across for some time. When he'd finished insulting the décor and the service, he'd said the food wasn't fit for pigs, it was a suppurating sore on the fair face of

England and the staff were morons who couldn't tell a chicken breast from a pig's balls.

That had been at three o'clock on the Friday afternoon. Violent Crimes reasoned, rather to their disappointment, that with the state of the traffic, Jims couldn't possibly have got from this point in Hampshire to Marble Arch in under two hours, more likely three. They didn't bother to tell him so. Why not let him sweat for a bit? He was obviously guilty of something, if not murder. Once they'd got the evidence of the Merry Cookhouse man, they didn't take the trouble to call on Amber Conway, though they might have done so if they'd known Natalie Reckman had forestalled them.

'This MP chap, he was a mate of Leonardo Norton, was he?' Natalie was asking this question at the very moment Violent Crimes's visit was due. 'What you'd call a close friend?'

'More than that,' said Amber. 'You won't mention my name, will you?'

'Absolutely not.'

'I suppose I'm naïve, but I thought for a long time it was politics. We're all very political in Westminster, you know.'

Natalie switched off the recording device Amber hadn't noticed she was using. 'Often borrowed your key, did he?'

'I've never known him do it before. He had a key of his own.'

Back at home, Natalie found a message waiting for her on her answering machine. It was from Zillah Melcombe-Smith and for a start it sang, rather well and in tune: 'I'm getting married in the morning.' This was followed by spoken words: 'Sorry if I wasn't very nice to you last time. I was under a lot of pressure. Once I'm legally married to that sod I'll have a story for you. Would you like to come round on Wednesday afternoon, say about three?'

Natalie put everything on hold. The inquest having taken place and been adjourned, Jeff was getting himself cremated that afternoon at Golders Green. She might as well go. After all, she'd been attached to him for longer than most of his other women and though she'd finally thrown him out, their parting had been as amicable as possible in the circumstances and her fondness for him had endured until his death. That was probably because she'd never been under any illusions about him.

At two o'clock she dressed herself in a black skirt and jacket. Some precept lingering from years ago when she'd lived at home with her mother made the idea of a trouser suit worn to a funeral seem indecent. Natalie didn't like hats and only had one, an unbleached straw with a big brim she'd bought for a holiday in Egypt. It wouldn't do, so she went bare-headed. So did Zillah Melcombe-Smith, whom she hadn't expected to see. She smiled at her across the chapel, and waved in a discreet and funereal way, suitably subdued to be appropriate for the occasion. Zillah had a child with her, the little boy who was always crying and was Jeff Leach's son. No doubt, there was no one around for her to leave him with. The voluntary set him off and he was screaming at the top of his lungs by the time the coffin was carried in.

The weeping woman in deepest unrelieved black must be the current girlfriend, or rather, the most recent past girlfriend. Fiona Something. Blonde, as usual, with the exception of the one he'd married. She cried all through the perfunctory service. The fat woman who'd come with her put an arm round her shoulders, then pressed her to the biggest bust – you couldn't call it 'breasts' – Natalie had ever seen. That man who'd made such a success of a TV programme about anorexia was with them, singing hymns in rather a good baritone. Natalie hadn't sent any flowers. She'd been feeling guilty about that, but now felt worse, there were so few wreaths. Those there were lay on a paved courtyard outside the crematorium, gerberas and lilies and ranunculus mostly, and Natalie thought how flowers sold in Britain had changed in the past ten years. Before that, it would have been all roses and carnations. A card on the biggest sheaf read: *In adored memory of my darling Jeff, Your Fiona.* Next to it was a wreath of white dianthus, tightly packed, that looked uncannily like a large Polo mint. The 'In loving memory' card said, *From Dad and Beryl.* Nothing from the widow. No other former girlfriends there.

Natalie, who'd split up from Jeff just after the Christmas before last, found herself wondering who had come between her and this Fiona. There must have been someone – or had he made do with his wife? She couldn't imagine Jeff being content for sex and comfort and a roof over his head, not to mention money, with a woman who lived in the depths of Dorset. If she was going to write an intimate story about all of them she'd have to discover this missing woman's name as well as that of the girlfriend who came before her and maybe the one before that.

The mourners had all left the chapel by this time and were standing about admiring the flowers, some of them tearfully. Not one among them looked even remotely likely to have been her successor and Fiona's predecessor. The plump lady with the pretty face was impossible – too old and the wrong shape. A blonde, not unlike Fiona to look at, she recognised as a detective inspector. Natalie introduced herself to a tall thin woman of sixty who said she'd been Jeff's landlady in Harvist Road, Queen's Park.

'He was a lovely man, dear. Never gave a moment's trouble.'

'I bet he got behind with his rent.'

'There was that. Fancy his wife going and marrying someone else while she was still married to him. Is that her? I think I've seen her somewhere before.'

'Was he away much overnight while he was living in your house?'

'For days on end and often at weekends, dear. But it was all above board. He used to go to Gloucester to see his mother. I was ever so worried he might have been on that train that crashed.'

Not likely, thought Natalie, considering he was driving his old banger back from Long Fredington at the time. Jeff's mother, she knew for a fact, had died in 1985 and his father was living in Cardiff with a woman Jeff disliked, the Beryl of the Polo mint wreath. They hadn't spoken for years. 'That was at weekends. Was he away much in the week?'

'In the summer he was and maybe September too. "I think you've found yourself a lady friend," I said and he didn't deny it.'

Natalie went over to have a word with Zillah. 'Congratulations on your impending nuptials.'

'You what? Oh, yes. Thanks.'

'I'll see you tomorrow.'

Who could the other woman, the intervening woman, be? Well-off, naturally, either with money or in a well-paid job. Owning her home and that home somewhere in London. North London, Natalie thought. Jeff had been one of those people who treat south London as alien territory for which you probably needed a passport. Once he'd boasted that he'd never even crossed a river bridge. That made her wonder what had become of his car, that twenty-year-old Ford Anglia he'd never cleaned while he

was with her. She imagined it in a pound somewhere, having been clamped or grabbed from wherever he'd abandoned it in one of the myriad
interlaced streets that lie between the North Circular
Road and the Great Western line.

Back home, she made a few phone calls to check
that Zillah (aka Sarah) Leach and James Melcombe-
Smith were indeed due to be married in the City of
Westminster next morning, but found nothing. Jims
must be doing the deed in South Wessex. She
wondered what chance she had of securing an
interview with Leonardo Norton but decided to wait
until she'd talked to Zillah, who might have revelations for her beyond anything she'd yet dreamt of.

Compared with her last one and even her first, the
wedding was a drab affair. When the new rule or
law had come in, Zillah had thought it a brilliant
idea that you no longer had to be married in a church
or register office but could fix things up in a hotel, a
country house or anywhere, really, provided it was
licensed for the purpose. She changed her mind
when she saw the place Jims had chosen, a 1930s
roadhouse just off the A10 near Enfield. Dressed in
the white suit and wearing a new cloche hat with
curly black and white feathers, she thought she
might as well not have bothered but stayed in jeans
and sweater.

The ceiling was half-timbered in black *faux* beams
and the walls hung with equally *faux* linenfold
panelling. Rustic chairs and tables stood about, and
sofas upholstered in chintz covered in half-blown
pink and red roses. Zillah had never before seen so
much harness or so many saddles, bridles, spurs and
horse brasses, not even in the depths of Dorset. She
was introduced to the owner of the place, a slightly
superannuated pretty boy with a cockney voice who

had once been Ivo Carew's lover. Saying he was pleased to meet her, he winked rudely at Jims over her shoulder.

The registrar was a woman, young and good-looking. Zillah, for once anti-feminist, wondered if she'd feel properly married with a woman performing the ceremony, though she knew registrars were mostly female these days. Ivo and the pretty boy were witnesses, and the whole thing passed off swiftly. Zillah had expected lunch even in this dump, some kind of celebration, but Jims, who hadn't spoken to her except to say 'I will', quickly said goodbye to everyone and drove her back to Westminster.

At last he addressed her. 'Now we shall have to make arrangements for you and your children to decamp to Fredington Crucis.'

Chapter 24

This week, though Josephine wouldn't remember, Minty would have worked at Immacue for twenty years. The end of May, it had been, and she was eighteen. As she started on the shirts, she tried to work out how many she must have ironed in those years. Say three hundred a week for fifty weeks a year, two being taken off for holidays, times twenty made a hundred thousand shirts. Enough to dress an army, Auntie had said when she'd done ten years. White ones, blue and white striped, pink and white, yellow and white, grey and blue, there was no end to it. She picked the first one off the pile. It was light and dark green, a rare combination.

As often happened when she let herself think about Auntie, the ghost voice spoke to her. 'It's not a hundred thousand, you're wrong there. You never did shirts on a Saturday, not when you first went there. Not for a good two years. And there was days when you never did fifty on account of there wasn't fifty to do. That figure's more like ninety thousand than a hundred.'

Minty didn't say anything. Answering Auntie relieved her feelings but it caused trouble, too. Yesterday, when she'd shouted back, Josephine had come running out, wanting to know if she'd burnt herself. As if a person who's ironed a hundred thousand shirts would burn herself.

'She ought to have a celebration for you just the

same. She's bone selfish, never thinks of anyone but herself and that husband of hers. If she has a baby you'll find yourself looking after it. She'll bring it in here and ask you to keep an eye on it while she goes to the shops or pops round the Chinese. That Ken, he may be over the moon, but he'll not babysit. Men never do.'

'Go away,' said Minty, but very quietly.

'Now Mrs Lewis knows more about these things than me. She's had the experience. Giving birth, I mean. I had all the trouble and expense of rearing you but I never had the labour pains. If Jock hadn't been killed in that train crash you'd maybe have had a baby yourself. You'd have liked to be a grandma, wouldn't you, Mrs Lewis?'

This time Minty couldn't restrain herself. 'Will you shut up? I wish you'd stayed deaf. She's not going to have a baby and neither am I. Take that old woman out of here. I don't want her near me.'

Josephine came out, as she was bound to. 'Who were you talking to, Minty?'

'You,' Minty said boldly. 'I thought you called me.'

'When do I ever call you when you're doing the ironing? Now look, I'm going to nip out for a while and I'm leaving you in charge, right? I want to have a bit of lunch with Ken. Can I bring you anything back?'

Minty suppressed a shudder. She eat food someone else had touched? Food she hadn't seen being bought? Josephine would never learn. 'No, thanks. I've got my own sandwiches.'

She didn't start on them till she'd finished the shirts. They were chicken sandwiches, made with white bread she'd sliced herself – you could never tell who or what had done the slicing with cut bread – fresh Irish butter and chicken she'd cooked and carved herself. She'd used the remaining big knife, twin of the one she'd had to get rid of because you could never tell how clean boiling made anything. If she ever saw that Mrs Lewis she might need to use the big knife as she'd used the one that got rid of Jock's ghost.

But she'd never seen Mrs Lewis. Auntie manifested herself every so often, though she was never as clear and solid as Jock had been. Furniture and doors were always visible *through* Auntie. Sometimes she was no more than an outline, the middle part of her just a watery shape that shifted and waved like the mirage on the road she'd seen from the bus last week. Minty thought she might go away altogether if she resumed putting flowers on her grave. If she went back to praying to her. But why should she? She'd never defied Auntie while she was alive but she thought it was time to assert herself. Why should she be tied to that for the rest of her life, spending all that money and arranging those flowers, just to please a ghost?

She wasn't even particularly afraid of Auntie. That must be because she'd known her so well and known, too, that Auntie wouldn't do her any harm. Jock, after all, had already harmed her, helping himself to her money like that. And when he came back as a ghost he'd sometimes glared fiercely at her, opening his eyes wide and baring his teeth. But it was Mrs Lewis showing herself that she really feared and she didn't know why. If the old woman ever actually addressed her instead of always speaking to Auntie, she felt she might not be so alarmed by the thought of it. Mrs Lewis had never done this, but attached herself to Auntie like her shadow and, like a shadow, was only there at certain times and on certain days. For instance, this morning there had been no word from her and when Auntie asked her a question she hadn't replied. That might mean she wasn't there and Auntie, for purposes of her own, had been speaking to the empty air. On the other hand – and this was what frightened Minty in a way she couldn't have entirely explained – she might have accompanied Auntie from wherever they lived, a heaven, a hell or an unknown, unnamed abode of shades, yet kept silent. This was hateful to Minty, who imagined her lurking unseen behind Auntie, taking Auntie away from her, noting everything Minty did, making judgements on her appearance and her home. Biding her time, but for what she couldn't tell.

With the arrival of Josephine in the ironing room Auntie had disappeared and she hadn't come back. Minty finished her sandwich and went to wash her hands. She washed her face as well because she couldn't be sure she hadn't got an invisible smear of butter on her chin. While she was in the washroom the bell rang on the outer door. She could hardly believe her eyes. Mr Kroot's sister was standing in the middle of the shop, clutching an armful of dirty clothes she'd pulled out of a very old and worn carrier bag.

Gertrude Pierce – was that her name? – was as surprised to see Minty as Minty was to see her. 'I'd no idea you worked here.' Implicit in her remark was the unspoken, 'If I had I'd never have come in.' Her voice was low, with a sort of growl in it and an accent Minty couldn't place. Very recently, perhaps on the way here, she'd had her hair colour touched up and it was as red and glossy as the scarlet satin jacket she deposited on the counter along with a green woolly jumper and a pair of purple trousers. Minty could smell them from six feet away. She wrinkled up her nose, a change of expression Gertrude Pierce wasn't slow to notice. 'If you don't want to do them I'll take them elsewhere.'

Josephine wouldn't like her to turn away business. 'We'll do them.' Minty had to answer her but the thought of Auntie finding out that she'd actually spoken to Mr Kroot's sister made her tremble. Her hand shook as she worked out the cost of dry-cleaning, wrote the sum down on a card and the name 'Mrs Pierce', and passed it across the counter. 'Ready by Saturday.'

Gertrude Pierce studied the card with suspicion and something like wonder. It was as if she speculated as to what divining powers or superhuman insight Minty must possess to have known her name. 'I'll have my carrier back, thank you.'

It lay on the counter, a black bag bruised and scratched by the hundred occasions on which it had been used since the assistant at Dickins and Jones put newly bought goods into it for the first time. Minty pushed it an inch or two nearer Gertrude Pierce. Mr Kroot's sister waited, perhaps for her to bring it over and curtsey, Minty thought. She went into the ironing room and slammed the door. Presently she heard heavy footsteps and the exit bell ring.

'I told you not to speak to her,' said Auntie. 'I could hardly believe my ears. You should have pretended she wasn't there, not given her the satisfaction.'

'I'd like to pretend you're not there.' With Josephine absent, she could answer back as much as she liked. 'I want you to go away for good and take Jock's old mum with you.'

'You put *nice* flowers on my grave like you used to and I'll think about it. Tulips are over, whatever the florist may say. I suppose roses are too much money.'

'Nothing'd be too much to get rid of you,' said Minty rashly.

And when she left for home at five thirty she

bought roses, a dozen white ones, expensive enough but cheaper than they would have been at the cemetery gates. It was a dull evening and just inside the gates, the building she'd never noticed before with its pillars and porticos in weathered grey stone looked as if it had been there for hundreds, maybe thousands, of years. Minty, who'd last week seen a television programme about ancient Rome, wondered if it dated from that time. It was a smaller version of the great gloomy crematorium and, like it, its doors were shut. Inside, the air would be dark and smelly and always cold. She shut her eyes and turned her back on it. She didn't know why she'd come down this way at all, this wasn't the way to Auntie's grave.

That was because she'd come in by the eastern entrance instead of the western. She'd never done that before. For once, she'd bought flowers at a shop, not at the gates. Suddenly it seemed very important to her to 'give' Auntie the flowers. Auntie had asked for them and specifically for roses. Was the grave up along this aisle or that? The cemetery was so big with so many paths, some of them winding, so many tombs that looked the same. Some of the trees were evergreens that might more suitably have been called everblacks, their leaves were always dark and dull. Others had limp green leaves hanging down. Only the grass and the tiny flowers in it, yellow and white, were bright and varying from season to season.

It was still broad daylight and would be for hours, even if that light was half obscured by cloud. She should be heading for the crematorium and the western gate but she didn't know how. She walked down one aisle and up another, turned right and then left again. She'd know the grave when she saw it, by the name on it of course, but first by the angel, covering his eyes with one of his hands and in the other holding the broken violin. The trouble was that the cemetery was full of stone angels, every other tomb seemed to have an angel on it, some holding scrolls, some stringed instruments, though these were mostly harps, some on which the angel wept with bowed head. Minty began to feel like weeping herself. She knew she ought to go out of the gate she'd come in by and re-enter by the other, but that would mean passing the man who sold flowers. He might think she'd stolen hers when he wasn't looking or even taken them from someone else's grave, a not uncommon proceeding, she'd heard.

Maisie Julia Chepstow, beloved wife of John Chepstow, who departed this life December the 15th, 1897, aged 53. Asleep in the arms of Jesus. She knew the inscription by heart and she remembered telling Jock the corpse or the bones or the dust which lay below had been those of Auntie's grandmother. None of that mattered. All that did was that she had buried Auntie's ashes in that grave. By now she was down by the canal with the small Roman place ahead of her, and she turned once more. There were so many graves in here and so few people to look after them that grass and moss and ivy crept over and covered everything, hiding stone and obscuring engraved names. She had never seen a cat in here, though she imagined them invading the place by night, but now one appeared, long, thin and grey, picking its way delicately over anonymous mounds, diving into an ivy-tangled cavern between the roots of a tree when it saw her.

An angel holding something loomed ahead of her at the point where the aisle met a path at right angles. This must be it, this was where, kneeling on the earth, she had looked up and seen Jock's ghost approaching. Even before she had reached it she saw that the angel was the same, with the same covered eyes and holding the same broken violin. But when she pushed aside ivy tendrils and read what was engraved on the stone she saw that it was different. This wasn't Maisie Julia Chepstow, beloved wife of John Chepstow, but *Eve Margaret Pinchbeck, only daughter of Samuel Pinchbeck, fled to her Saviour, October the 23rd, 1899.* Adam and Eve and pinch me, thought Minty. Have a Polo, Polo. How could two graves be so alike yet not belong to the same person? Maybe the person who made statues all that long, long time ago, maybe in those Roman times, made lots of them the same.

Perhaps it would do. And if Auntie's ashes weren't here that might not be so important. Something different on this woman's grave was the stone vase that was part of the moulding round the base of the platform the angel stood on. It was dry and green moss crept close up to its lips. As she had done before, Minty found flowers on a nearby grave, flowers that were withering, threw them into the bushes and used the water they had been standing in to fill the mossy bowl. She arranged the roses, breaking off their stems to shorten them, and in doing so tore her hands on their thorns. The blood-letting relieved her in a strange way she hadn't experienced before, though the dirt that must be on the rose stems was distressing. There should be a water tap somewhere in here, there probably was, but she didn't know where.

She stood up and turned round, walking on, away from the gasometer. That must be the right direction for the western gate. Yet it wasn't. She began to be frightened. Suppose she could never find the way out, but must wander on for hours, searching searching for years maybe, for ever among the overgrown graves with cats walking over them and making live people shiver. This was surely a place of

301

ghosts, with the myriad dead lying everywhere beneath the ground, but hers weren't here. There was only dimness and a kind of heavy peace, and in the distance the hum of traffic on the Harrow Road. No other people, alive or phantom, no birds singing. She came suddenly into an open place with the huge colonnaded temple that was the crematorium before her. It was always frightening but from this angle more so with its high blank wall and the gathering grey clouds behind it, the wilderness of the neglected place coming close up to its footings. Minty imagined its great door swinging open, its stained-glass window shattering and ghosts coming blindly out, their hands upraised and their robes streaming. She began to run.

Notices directing you were everywhere but they never seemed to point to what she wanted, never to Auntie's grave. She read the one ahead, she didn't know why, as she pounded along, afraid to look back in case she was pursued. It said: *Exit*. The relief was enormous. She knew where she was now, approaching the western gate that was opposite her own street and where the flower seller was. By the time she reached it she was walking quietly, managing a smile and nod for the flower man. And there was no one and nothing behind her.

It was rare for Minty to feel happy. Fear drives away happiness as much as sorrow does and she was mostly afraid. She lived in a climate of unnameable fears, terrors that could only be kept within bounds by strict routines. Something else had allayed them, had once or twice entirely banished them, and that had been what she'd never known in her first thirty-seven years, the feeling she'd had for Jock. When she'd told him, after he'd made love to her, that she would never be like this with another man, for she was his for ever, she was expressing for perhaps the first time in her life her true and honest feelings, unaffected by cleanliness or tidiness or eating prejudices. And what he gave her back, or she thought he did, had given her a strange unfamiliar sensation she didn't know how to name. Happiness. She felt it now, returned in some small measure, as she left the cemetery and walked towards Syringa Road.

With Jock it had been relatively long-lived. If he hadn't died, she sometimes thought dimly, not knowing quite what she meant or wanted, if he'd stayed alive and with her, those feelings she'd had and he'd inspired might have changed her into a different woman. This present scrap of happiness was doomed to be short, she knew it while it was with her, succeeding raw terror, for fear was returning as she approached her front door. She was afraid of what awaited her inside and she even thought of knocking on the Wilsons' door, spending half an hour with them, having a cup of tea, a chat, maybe telling them about her experience looking for Auntie's grave, of which, now it was over, she could see the funny side. What, a woman who'd lived a stone's throw from the cemetery all her life, unable to find her own auntie's grave! If she went into Sonovia's house she'd only have to come out again and enter her own. She couldn't stay in next door all night.

She put the key in the lock and turned it. Although it wouldn't be dark for hours, she switched the hall light on. Nothing. Emptiness. She went upstairs, fearing to meet Auntie on the way, but there was no one, nothing. Very faintly, through the dividing wall, she could hear music, the kind of music very young people like. That wouldn't be Mr Kroot's radio, it must be Gertrude Pierce's. A strange woman she was, playing teenager's music. Minty ran a bath, using the kind of gel that makes foam, washed her hair in it, scrubbed the blood off her hands with a

303

nailbrush. The punctures the thorns had made were a hundred tiny wounds. The music was turned off and silence followed. Minty dried herself, dressed in her usual clean T-shirt, clean trousers, socks. She never wore sandals, even in hot weather, because the streets were dirty. Things could burrow their way into your feet and give you a disease called bill-heart-something, she'd read about it in Laf's newspaper. That was in Africa but she couldn't see why it wouldn't happen here.

She wasn't hungry. Those sandwiches had been very filling. Maybe later she'd have a scrambled egg on toast. You never knew where the egg came from but it must be out of a chicken and, anyway, she'd cook it very thoroughly in a clean saucepan. Out of the kitchen window she could see washing sagging on the line in Mr Kroot's garden. It looked bone dry, had probably been there since before Gertrude Pierce came into Immacue. Minty went outside. It hadn't been hot all day, there was too much cloud for that, but it had been gently warm and still was. She studied next door's washing. So much sagging had taken place, one of the poles that supported the line leaning over at an angle of forty-five degrees, that the edges of the sheets and towels were on the ground, actually touching the dry, dusty grass. Minty was shocked but there was nothing she was prepared to do about it.

Sonovia's voice called to her over the other fence, 'Minty! Long time no see.'

In fact, it wasn't very long. No more than two or three days. Knowing it would please, Minty told her, with many glances over her shoulder, about Gertrude Pierce coming into the shop, not realising she worked there. Sonovia laughed, especially at the bit about her being amazed Minty knew her name. Some twenty years ago Mr Kroot was reputed to have made a racist remark, though where and to whom he'd made it no one seemed to know, but it was enough for Laf who'd never addressed a word to him since. Sonovia was often heard to say that she wished it hadn't been so long ago but now instead and she'd have him up in court.

'Someone told me she's going home on Saturday week. We'll all be glad to see the back of her.' She listened, smiling, while Minty told her what had happened in the cemetery. The smile didn't waver but when Sonovia went back into her own house, she said to Laf, 'If Winnie Knox is buried in Kensal Green Cemetery it's the first I've heard of it.'

'She isn't buried at all. She was cremated. You ought to remember that, you and I were there.'

'Of course we were. That's why I said that was the first I'd heard of it. Minty had the ashes in a box on the shelf for months, but I noticed they'd gone. She's just told me she got lost in the cemetery looking for Winnie's grave. White roses she'd bought because she said her auntie was fed up with tulips. What d'you make of that?'

'We've always said Minty was peculiar, Sonn. Remember all that stuff about ghosts?'

Minty had for a moment forgotten all that stuff about ghosts. She went back into her kitchen and through to the living room thinking about Gertrude Pierce and the washing and the evil-smelling clothes she'd brought to be dry-cleaned. In the doorway she stopped. Two women were standing between the fireplace and the sofa, Auntie and an old bent person with a humped back and a witch's face. Minty couldn't speak. She stood there on the threshold, still as one of the cemetery statues, and closed her eyes. When she opened them again they were still there.

'You know very well that wasn't my grave, was it, Mrs Lewis? You put those roses on a stranger's grave. How d'you think that makes me feel? Mrs Lewis was disgusted.'

Auntie had never talked like this to her while she was alive, though Minty had often thought she'd like to but for some reason had resisted. There had been anger in her eyes, this anger that was now coming out, while she said nice things. Mrs Lewis stood quite still, not looking at Auntie nor in Minty's direction, staring at the floor, her gnarled old hands clasped.

'Can't even manage a word of apology. She never could say she was sorry, even when she was little, Mrs Lewis. There was never a word of regret passed her lips.'

Minty found a voice. 'I'm sorry. It won't happen again. There, will that do?' Her tone strengthened, though her fear hadn't lessened, and the words came out in a throaty croak. 'Go away, will you? Both of you. I don't want to see you again. You're dead and I'm alive. Go back to where you came from.'

Auntie went but Mrs Lewis stayed. Minty could see Jock's face in hers, the same features but wrinkled and aged as if by a thousand years. His eyes had looked like hers, defeated and tired, when they'd been to the racing and the dog he'd put money on came in last. One day he might have come to look like her if the train crash hadn't taken him. The old woman raised her head. She was less solid than she'd been when Minty first saw her and again she was aware of that mirage effect, the watery waviness that made Mrs Lewis's loose cardigan and floppy skirt shiver as in a breeze. They stared at each other, she and Jock's mother, and she saw that the eyes were not blue as she'd first thought but a dull, cold green amid the wrinkles, each one like a bird's egg in a nest.

If she turned and walked away the old woman

would follow her. For the first time, she wanted a ghost to speak, in the midst of her fear she wanted to hear what kind of a voice Mrs Lewis had. 'Say something.'

As she spoke, the ghost vanished. Not immediately but like smoke disappearing into the neck of a bottle. And then she was gone and the room empty.

Chapter 25

When Jims arrived in Glebe Terrace, Natalie was waiting for him in a bedroom in a flat on the other side of the street. It belonged to Orla Collins, whom she'd met at the dinner party. Orla had had some qualms at first but these vanished when Natalie explained she was spying on a Member of Parliament who'd married his wife bigamously while at the same time carrying on an affair with a man on the opposite side of Glebe Terrace. Thursday was the third evening she'd been there, but she wasn't surprised he hadn't turned up the previous night. Even Jims might jib at making an assignation with a lover on his wedding day.

In her own words, Zillah had spilt the beans. When Natalie arrived on Wednesday afternoon she was still in the white suit she had worn for her wedding. 'I thought you might not be able to take a photograph of me,' Zillah said, 'on account of your union or whatever, so I did a polaroid.' As Natalie was looking at it, she said, 'And now I'm going to tell you everything.'

She had. It was the best story Natalie had secured in fifteen years of journalism. For all that, she didn't quite dare take Zillah's word for Jims's adventures with Leonardo Norton. That would have to be confirmed. She sat in a wicker armchair by the window at Orla Collins's, eyeing, not for the first time, the photographs Zillah and Jims had taken on their honeymoon. His were of little use to her, for they were only of island views but for a single shot of Zillah bathing in the Indian Ocean. Hers, on the other hand, were a revelation. She admitted to having taken them because even then she felt jaundiced by this mock marriage. Jims and a young man whose face was turned away lay on adjoining recliners, they sat side by side on spread towels on a beach and, best of all, most damning of all, sat at a table *alfresco*, Jims's hand resting on the young man's thigh. It was interesting that Jims was always smiling at him and once into the camera, while Leonardo contrived to hide his face from view. These photographs would make it an easy matter to recognise the MP when he came down Glebe Terrace or stepped out of a car. How would he come? As time passed, as her watch told her seven thirty, eight, eight fifteen, Natalie considered the possibilities. Sloane Square was only three stops on the Circle Line from Westminster. He could take the tube and then a cab. Or a cab all the way. Reputedly, he had a large private income. He could drive himself and, since it was past six thirty, park anywhere on a single yellow line. The idea of a bus Natalie dismissed as too plebeian for the likes of Jims. As for a bicycle . . .

At twenty minutes to nine he came by the only means she hadn't considered. On foot. He was even better-looking in the flesh than in the Maldives pictures. Natalie, like many women taking a view never shared by homosexual men, said to herself, what a waste! To her delight, he produced a key from his pocket and unlocked Leonardo Norton's front door. A blind was down in the window she took to be that of a living room but an upstairs window was uncovered except for an inch or two of curtain showing on either side. Any picture she might take Natalie had grave misgivings about, but she was ready with her camera. Within minutes she almost wished she hadn't brought it with her, for the shot she got no newspaper editor would dare to use. In the two-foot-wide gap between the curtains Jims and Leonardo were locked in a passionate embrace.

Almost immediately Leonardo, dressed only in a pair of red and white candy-striped briefs, drew the curtains. Natalie remained. She was resolved to stay the entire night in that chair if necessary, eating the sandwiches she'd brought and sipping from the half-bottle of Valpolicella.

But at eleven thirty Orla wanted to go to bed. 'There's no point in you staying,' she said. 'He always stops the night.'

If the police had never reappeared in Holmdale Road, Michelle might have extended her forgiveness of Fiona to forgetfulness. She might have taken the advice Matthew gave her and excused her neighbour on the grounds of her grief, her shock and the almost unbearable pressure she had been under. After all, she and Matthew had shown their support by accompanying Fiona to the funeral of a man they had both disliked and distrusted. But the police came back on Friday morning to say they'd been unable to find any confirmation of the Jarveys' presence on the Heath on that crucial afternoon. On the other hand, a car of the same make and colour as theirs had been seen parked on a meter in Seymour Place, W1 at the relevant time and Seymour Place, as they must know, was only a short distance from the Odeon, Marble Arch.

Matthew said, in a cool, almost detached voice, 'That was not our car.'

'The witness wasn't able to take the number.'

'If he or she had, it would not have been the number of our car.'

Michelle, glancing at her husband and then down at her own plump hands that lay in her bulky lap, marvelled that anyone looking at the two of them could even momentarily suspect them of committing a crime. A fat (if no longer obese) woman of forty-five who couldn't climb half a dozen steps without gasping and – as much as she loved him, she had to put it like this – a poor skeleton crippled by his own grotesque phobia. That was the last realistic and level-headed thought she was to have for days.

She drew in her breath when the woman asked her, 'Can you give us something firmer to establish that you were in your car on the Heath at that time?'

'What kind of thing?' She heard her own voice grown thin and hoarse.

'Or even in Waitrose? The staff don't remember you there. Well, they remember you' – Michelle thought she detected the suspicion of a grin – 'but not which day. Apparently, you often go there.'

The implication was plain, that she and Matthew had purposely planned frequent visits to the supermarket in order to confuse witnesses about the only day they *weren't* there.

'And about the Heath, Mrs Jarvey?'

'I told you, there were other cars there with people in them, but I didn't know any of them and they didn't know us.'

After the officers had gone, she clutched hold of Matthew and looked piteously into his face. 'I'm so frightened, I don't know what to do. I thought – I thought, Fiona's got us into this, she ought to get us out.'

'What does that mean, my darling?'

'I thought, we could ask her to say she saw us on the Heath, she drove up there as soon as she got home – I mean, she could say she got home an hour sooner than she did – and saw us and spoke to us. Or

– and this would be better – she could get a friend of hers to say she saw us, someone from down the street, she knows the woman at a hundred and two, I've seen them together, and she could –'

'No, Michelle.' Matthew was gentle as always but tough too, as he used to be long ago. 'You'd be inciting her to perjury. It would be wrong. And apart from the morality of it, you'd be found out.'

'If she can't do a little thing like that for us I'll feel like never speaking to her again.'

'You don't know. Maybe she would do it. You haven't tried her – and, Michelle, you're not going to.'

'Then what will become of us?'

'Nothing,' he said. 'Innocent people don't find themselves in court on a murder charge,' though he was by no means sure of that. 'You're being silly. This is simply hysteria.'

'It is not!' She began sobbing and laughing at the same time. 'It's not, it's not!'

'Michelle, stop it. I've had enough.'

She looked up at him, the tears streaming down her face. 'And now she's made us quarrel. We never quarrel.'

Fiona had returned to work on the previous Monday. People said how sorry they were about Jeff, but those who couldn't remember his name referred to him as 'your friend', and Fiona thought this reduced him to the status of someone she'd happened to know at college. But she faced more curious glances and inexplicable silences than she would have done if Jeff had died of cancer or a heart attack. Murder marks its victim's loved ones for ever. Fiona knew her name would never again be mentioned among acquaintances without some qualifying phrase defining her as the woman 'who lived with that chap who was murdered in a cinema'. Added to this was her bitter regret that she'd mentioned the Jarveys' names to Violent Crimes. She no longer knew why she had and was driven to the conclusion that, as is often the case in these circumstances, she had come out with it because she had nothing to say, knew nothing and could think of no real help to offer.

Michelle's declaration of forgiveness hadn't been accompanied by much warmth. This quiet, sad woman wasn't the affectionate and demonstrative maternal creature she'd known, but subdued, retired into herself. Fiona had been into the Jarveys' house three times since Sunday's contretemps, so often, she now believed, in the ever-renewed hope that this time Michelle would have changed back into her familiar self, but though perfectly courteous and hospitable, she never had. This Friday afternoon Fiona was there again, using the back door to demonstrate an intimacy she desperately wanted to re-establish. And for a moment it looked as though she was approaching it, for Michelle came out to meet her and kissed her cheek.

Matthew's manner seemed heartier than usual. It was Michelle, not he, who generally offered her a glass of wine. He fetched a bottle he'd had on ice, filled a glass for her and one for his wife. To her dismay she saw that Michelle's eyes had filled with tears. 'What is it? Oh, what is it? If you cry you'll have me crying too.'

Michelle made the effort. 'The police were here this morning. They don't believe we were where we said we were that – that day. Someone saw a car like ours parked near the cinema. They want us to prove we were up on the Heath and we – we can't, we can't. We'll never be able to.'

'Yes, you will. I'll help you. It's the least I can do. I can't say I saw you there because the people in my office have already told them I was there till five. But I can find someone who'll say it. I know someone – I mean, I know her well – who lives in the Vale of Health, and she'll say you were there, I know she will. She's just the sort of person who'd go to the police and tell them she'd come to offer evidence to support your story. Let me do it, please. I know it'll work.'

Michelle was shaking her head, but Matthew had begun to laugh as if he hadn't a care in the world.

Because he was holding his surgery in Toneborough on Saturday morning instead of Friday, Jims had postponed his trip to his constituency by twenty-four hours. In spite of an announcement of his marriage appearing in Thursday's newspapers and the evident loss of police interest in him as a murder suspect, a good many of his fellow Conservatives in the Commons still cold-shouldered him. But the Chief Whip had said nothing more. That morning, the Leader had nodded to him and even managed a slight smile. Jims was beginning to be confident that the people who mattered believed he'd been ignorant of his wife's marital status when first he married her.

His drive down to Dorset was uneventful. All the roadworks had been completed and the cones and speed limit signs taken away. He reached Casterbridge in time to have a reconciliation lunch with Ivo Carew. Ivo's sister Kate joined them for a drink and had a good laugh over a little bit of help the two of them, with Kevin Jebb, had given Jims on the previous day. Jims spent the afternoon visiting a retirement home, housed in a neo-Gothic mansion, where elderly gentlefolks of his own political persuasion ended their days in luxury suites. There, he talked to each resident in turn, toured the library and the film theatre, and made a little speech – not to encourage them to vote Conservative, which exhortation would be unnecessary, but to vote at all, and he assured them of the comfortable transport available to take them to the polls. Before they sat down to their four-course dinner, he drove to Casterbridge station on the Great Western line, where he picked up Leonardo off the London train.

This was indiscreet. He'd never done it before, but he told himself no one could possibly find out. Of course they wouldn't dine out together. Jims had brought a cold chicken, a game pie, some asparagus and a *Livarot* with him. Fredington Crucis House was always plentifully stocked with drink. By the time he got home the cheese was stinking the car out, for it had been a warm day, but this only served to make them laugh companionably. On the following afternoon, after Jims's surgery was over, they thought they might drive down to Lyme where Leonardo, a Janeite, wanted to renew his acquaintance with the spot from which Louisa Musgrove jumped off the Cobb.

There was no need to be in Toneborough next morning until ten thirty, so they stayed in bed till nine and would have stayed later still but for sounds from outside which alerted Jims. Leonardo slept on. He was accustomed to hearing traffic noise from his bedroom, to voices shouting, taxi engines pulsing and lorry drivers applying squeaky brakes. So was Jims but not here, not in the grounds of Fredington Crucis House where, if anything awakened him, it would be birdsong. He sat up and listened. Mrs Vincey's radio? But no. He'd expressly told his cleaner not to come. Besides, the noise was coming from outside. It was a mingling of voices with a crunching on the gravel drive. A car door slammed. Jims got up, put on a dressing gown and went to a window. The floor-length curtains were drawn but there was a gap perhaps half an inch wide between them. He put his eye to the gap and leapt back with an exclamation. 'Oh, my God!'

Leonardo stirred, turned over, muttered sleepily, 'What is it?'

Without replying, Jims threw off his dressing gown, pulled on the jeans he'd changed into the night before and a dark sweatshirt. He went upstairs to the second floor where, at these smaller windows, the curtains remained undrawn. Jims knew that, unless you are staring purposefully, it is almost impossible to see anything from a distance through a window with no light behind it. He advanced on all fours and pushed his head above the sill, up to the level of his nose.

About fifty men and women were outside, some wielding cameras, others with notebooks and recording devices. Their cars were there too and they were leaning against them or sitting inside them with the doors open. A woman, accompanied by two others and a young man, was pouring something from a flask into plastic cups. All were chattering and laughing. Even from this distance Jims could see his drive was already littered with cigarette ends.

It was a dull morning but by no means dark. These small rooms up here had once been servants' bedrooms and were always rather dim. Still, there was no excuse for what Leonardo did. Entering the room behind him, dressed only in boxer shorts and exclaiming, 'What the hell are you doing, crawling about like a dog?' he switched the overhead light on.

A roar went up from the crowd, bulbs flashed and the whole mob surged forward as one, towards the front steps.

The newspaper which had bought Natalie's story

was not one that was normally delivered to 7 Abbey Gardens Mansions. Zillah had put in a special order for it. She woke up very early on Saturday morning, about two hours earlier than usual, happily anticipating the arrival of the papers. On the previous afternoon, having checked that her generous monthly allowance from Jims had been paid into her bank account, she had phoned Moon and Stars Television. They would send a car for her first thing on Monday morning so that she could appear on *A Bite of Breakfast*. Mrs Peacock having dismissed herself, Zillah had made an arrangement with the young Iranian girl who cleaned at number nine to stay over Sunday night and be there for Eugenie and Jordan in the morning. At the same time, putting her house entirely in order, she'd fixed an appointment with a child psychiatrist.

Thinking about Jims being stricken by disaster brought her a lot of pleasure. She knew for a fact he had no morning papers delivered to Fredington Crucis House and wouldn't, in any case, have seen this one, which he habitually referred to as a 'backstreet rag'. The likelihood was that he'd be ten minutes into his surgery before he found out. Some hard-done-by citizen of Toneborough, anxious about his council tax, his hound puppy-walking or his incapacity benefit, would be bound to bring a copy of the rag with him. She hadn't felt so happy since she walked up the aisle to marry him at St Mary Undercroft.

Just as the newspaper dropped on to the doormat at seven o'clock, Jordan woke up and started crying. Zillah picked him up, stuck him in his high chair – surely he shouldn't still be in a high chair? – gave him orange juice and what he ought not to have, what would rot his teeth and set him on the path to obesity, a chocolate bar. Then she lay on the sofa and looked at the paper.

The front page almost frightened her. A very large headline read: THE GAY MP, TWO WEDDINGS AND A FUNERAL. The picture of her was one she hadn't seen before. It must have been taken in those halcyon days when she was being photographed all the time and had perhaps been previously rejected because it was unflattering. For once, Zillah didn't mind. She looked distraught, as if she hardly knew which way to turn. Her face was half covered by one hand and stray locks of hair, greasy looking, protruded between the splayed fingers. That was the day, she remembered now, when she hadn't been expecting the photographer. To the left of it, in a kind of 'before' and 'after' arrangement, was the pre-first wedding picture of her and Jims, both of them smiling, relaxed, happy.

There was virtually no text. For that she had to turn to page three. There, too, was one of her own Maldives shots, Jims unmistakably Jims, his hand on the bare thigh of an unrecognisable young man with his face half turned away and in shadow. The trickle of fear returned. What would he do when he read it? What would he do to *her*? Was he reading it now or was he still blissfully asleep at Fredington Crucis House, unaware of what awaited him? She read her own words: *'I honestly thought I was free to remarry. Poor Jeff'* – she'd never called him that in all their life together –

'told me we were legally divorced. Then when he was killed and I found out my mistake I realised I was – tragically – freed by his death. Our marriage had not been a happy one, down to his frequent affairs with other women. Just the same, his murder was a devastating blow, as was discovering the other side to

318

James's nature. That happened when he brought his lover on our honeymoon . . .'

Mrs Melcombe-Smith cries a lot these days. She was once more in tears when I asked her what she thought the future held for her and the MP for South Wessex. 'All this has been horrendous but I will stand by him,' she said. 'I don't care what he's done. I love him and I truly believe that in his heart he loves me.'

There was a good deal more but that line about standing by Jims, words she had certainly uttered to Natalie Reckman, she now reread with new eyes. When she said them she hadn't given much thought to what she meant. It was just what wives in her sort of position traditionally said. She'd read it repeated in newspapers many times over the years. But now she thought of the reality. She rather liked the idea of seeing herself in the role of devoted and supportive wife, a woman who has been bitterly ill-used but who forgives and pours out renewed love. Not that this new part she contemplated playing would deflect her from appearing on *A Bite of Breakfast*. She wasn't bound to forgive immediately . . .

In the few short months that had passed since her first wedding to Jims she had almost entirely lost her ignorance of how the media operate, but she still wasn't aware that the newspaper she didn't see until 7 a.m. might be read by rival journalists the night before. So she believed she had several hours in which to prepare herself before the pack of reporters and photographers presented themselves on the doorstep of Abbey Gardens Mansions. Jordan was crying again. She gave him cereal and a mug of milk. He put his hands into the milk as if it were a finger bowl and began a low keening that was halfway between a moan and a song.

Eugenie came down from her bedroom, demanding to know why everyone was up so early and what were all those people doing outside in the street. Zillah went to the window. They were here already, waiting for her. She wouldn't attempt to exclude them this time, she wouldn't hide herself or escape via the garage. They were welcome. She thought of all the women she'd heard of recently who'd broken into television or modelling careers or simply become celebrities of unspecified talent, through nothing more than getting themselves into the media for taking their clothes off in public or demonstrating against something or being victims. How much more success could a beautiful bigamist, widow of a murderer and wife of a newly outed gay MP, hope to enjoy?

But the pack mustn't see her yet. Give her an hour in which to transform herself. Zillah ran her bath and took Jordan into it with her to shut him up.

Chapter 26

All Saturday morning Sonovia kept her eye on the street and Mr Kroot's in particular but Gertrude Pierce didn't go home. She kept darting into her front room to look in case she missed her.

Laf came, carrying a mug of coffee. 'Why are you sitting there looking out of the window?'

'Nothing exciting ever happens in Syringa Road.'

'You should be thankful. What d'you want to happen?'

Sonovia ignored him. Mr Kroot's front door was opening. The old black cat came out and the door shut.

'D'you want to go out tonight?'

'Anything you like, only don't bother me now, you're spoiling my concentration.' Sonovia often reproached herself for not having been more vigilant when Jock Lewis was on the scene. How she regretted not ever seeing his face!

Laf looked up films in the paper. There was nothing on he and Sonovia would fancy. Besides, though he'd been a few times, he'd never enjoyed the cinema like he used to since the Jeffrey Leach murder. It was a funny thing for an officer of the Metropolitan Police to think, he ought to be hardened and indifferent, but the fact was that he always expected the flash of a knife when the person in front of him or behind got up, or thought he might trip over a body in the dark. Why not go to the theatre instead? Laf had only been twice in his life, once to *The Mousetrap* when he was a kid and later on, for his fortieth birthday, to *Miss Saigon*. How about *An Inspector Calls*? It sounded as if it might be about the police and therefore he'd get irritated if they got the police procedure wrong. On the other hand, he'd be able to tell Sonovia afterwards just how inaccurate it had been. There were little bits of description of the play for each theatre. Laf read that this one was an 'acclaimed psychological thriller'. It didn't sound bad. He got on the phone and booked three seats for eight fifteen. Sonovia would be *amazed* and as for Minty . . . Laf looked forward to seeing Minty's face when he told her.

Just as Sonovia was on the watch for Gertrude Pierce, so Minty was waiting for the reappearance of Mrs Lewis. She was ironing. The light-green and dark-green striped shirt was on the top of the pile. It couldn't be more than ten days since she'd ironed it. The man it belonged to must be very fond of it, maybe it was his favourite. She spread it out on the ironing board, feeling the cotton. It was just damp enough but not so damp that steam rose from it when she applied the iron.

She'd ironed shirts for Jock, not many and not often, but when he'd stayed the night she wouldn't let him put the same one on in the morning. Next time he'd come over she'd handed him the clean shirt and he'd said he'd never seen such good ironing as hers. That was the day he'd taken her bowling. It was the most amazing evening of her life. She slipped the cardboard collar round the neck of the green shirt and as she slid it into its cellophane bag, a tear slipped down her cheek and splashed on to the shiny transparent stuff. Minty wiped it off and washed her hands. On second thoughts, she washed her face as well. The poky little room smelt of detergent and heat, a scent she couldn't define because it wasn't a burning smell but something like a really hot summer's day. She was alone, there was no one watching her and arguing about her. The ghosts had been absent all the morning. She started on the last shirt but two, a white one with a very pale pink check.

Sonovia got bored with waiting. It wasn't as if anything else happened down the street that was worth looking at, apart from those two yobs revving up their motorbikes for an unnecessarily long time and that Iranian woman coming out in the *chador* that enveloped her from head to foot in black folds, leaving only her tired eyes free. Her three children looked like anyone else's, dressed in jeans and T-shirts and sandals. Sonovia couldn't understand it.

'When in Rome do as the Romans do,' she said when Laf came in.

'Pardon?'

'Our mothers never got themselves up like that after they came here. They adapted.'

'Your mum never dressed like a nun either,' said Laf sarcastically, 'so far as I recall. In case it's of any interest, Mrs Pierce is sitting in the old man's back garden in a deckchair. So you can come off watch. Want a beer? I'm going to have one.'

Sonovia accepted the beer but sat there ten minutes longer, just to prove she was relaxing, not waiting for Gertrude Pierce. She was just getting up, thinking about making lunch for her and Laf, when Minty came along. The last thing she wanted was for Minty to find out for herself Gertrude Pierce was still here, which she would do as soon as she looked out of her kitchen window, so she waved and mouthed, 'She's not gone. She's in the back.'

Minty nodded and made a face, a sympathetic face

that registered disgust and fellow feeling at the same time. Inserting her key in the lock, she felt the usual apprehension and braced herself. There was no one and nothing there. It was funny, she was getting to be able to tell if the house was empty of them the minute she came into the hall. Anyway, they weren't her immediate worry. For some reason, Josephine had kissed her when she left and she could still feel her scent on her skin and the smear of her lipstick as well as her own tears. But first she went through to the kitchen and looked out of the window at the two of them next door, Gertrude Pierce and Mr Kroot in old-fashioned striped deckchairs. They'd put a rickety table with a green baize top between them and on it they were playing cards. The black cat with its aged grey muzzle lay on the grass, looking as if it were dead. But it often looked like that and it never was dead. Minty could hardly remember a time when that cat hadn't been there, its face like an old whiskered person's, its walk growing stiffer. A bumble bee drifted down close to its ears. They twitched and its tail flicked. Gertrude Pierce swept up the cards into a pack and shuffled them.

Had Mr Kroot's cat been in the cemetery again, walking over where her grave would be? Or trailing arthritically over Auntie's two graves? Upstairs now, Minty ran her bath. She hardly ever had a bath these days without thinking about her money and how she could have bought a shower with it. She dropped her clothes on to the floor in a heap. They'd been clean on that morning, of course, but to her they smelt of Josephine and the litter-strewn street and the diesel fumes from lorries and taxis and all the cigarettes people smoked between here and Immacue and the fag ends they left on the pavement. She scrubbed herself with the nailbrush, not just her hands but her arms and legs and feet as well. The skin was bright pink under the water. Then she used the back brush. She dipped her head in and shampooed her hair, digging into her scalp with her fingertips. Kneeling up, she rinsed her head under the running tap. If only she had that shower!

As she was drying herself, another towel wrapped round her head turban-wise, something told her they were back. Not in here. To do her justice, Auntie wouldn't bring a stranger in, she had her own ideas of modesty and Minty hadn't been seen without her clothes since she was nine. They were outside the door. Let them wait. Minty used her deodorant not just under her arms but on the soles of her feet and the palms of her hands, because it was summertime now. She dressed in white cotton trousers and a white T-shirt with pale-blue stripes. Both were 'left-behinds' from Immacue, among those garments which their owners for some reason failed to collect and which, after six months, Josephine sold at two pounds apiece. Minty got a discount and only paid two for both. She wouldn't have dreamt of doing it if they'd only been dry cleaned but these were wash-able, had many times been washed and the trousers she'd boiled, which reduced their size and made them fit better. She combed her hair, wrapped up her soiled clothes in the towels and, drawing a deep breath, flung open the door.

They were outside, a couple of yards away in the doorway of Auntie's bedroom. Minty touched all the wood she could reach, pink wood and white wood and brown, but they didn't go away. Mrs Lewis was much clearer and more solid today than Auntie was. She looked like a real person, the sort of old woman you might see in the street, coming back from the shops. In spite of the warmth of the day she wore a winter coat of dark-red wool, a colour Minty particu-larly disliked, and she had a dark-red felt hat jammed down over her ears. So they could change their clothes wherever it was they came from, Minty thought, marvelling.

Auntie, behind Jock's mother and much taller than she was, appeared rather shadowy, something you only thought you saw and had to look at again to make sure. But she thickened and grew sharper as Minty's eyes fixed on her. Minty remembered once, when she was a child, some relative or friend, it might have been Kathleen's husband or Edna's, who took photographs and developed his own films. It was Edna's, she remembered now, recalling him for other mysterious, never fully understood reasons. She'd seen him develop the films and watched the blank sheet in its pool of liquid gradually turn into a picture. Auntie was like that, growing from a vague shapelessness into a picture of herself.

Her arms full of damp towels and clothes, Minty stared at them and they stared back at her. This time she was the first to speak. She addressed Auntie. 'You wouldn't have anything to do with her if you knew what she owed me. Her son borrowed all my money and yours too, what you left me, and she could have paid it back; she had the time, but she never did.'

Auntie said nothing. Mrs Lewis went on staring. Shrugging, turning away, Minty went downstairs. She put the clothes and the towels in the washing machine, started it and washed her hands, thinking how she'd have held that stuff at arm's length if it hadn't been for encountering those two on the landing. Mrs Lewis had come down behind her, but she'd come alone. Auntie was gone. Had she taken Minty's words to heart?

Minty wasn't going to eat her lunch with that old woman watching her. She'd rather starve. Mrs Lewis moved about the kitchen, looking down at the cupboards and up at the shelves. If she was thinking Minty wasn't a good enough household manager, wouldn't have made a suitable wife for her son, she had another think coming. Everything in that kitchen was spotless.

Mrs Lewis lifted the lid off the teapot and looked inside the bread bin. 'She keeps it nice, I will say.'

'Say what you like,' said Minty. 'I couldn't care less. Why didn't you give me back my money?'

No answer, of course. The old woman was close beside her now. Minty had a brilliant idea. She pulled open the cutlery drawer and seized the knife, the twin to the one she used in the cinema. The knife in her hand, she drew back her arm and lunged, but Mrs Lewis had gone, faded into the wall or been swallowed up by the floor.

It seemed then that just threatening got rid of them. But Minty didn't immediately put the knife back. She washed the blade because she felt it was contaminated, though it had touched nothing. Then she carved some slices from a piece of ham and chopped some lettuce and tomato. The knife needed washing again and this time she put it right into the sink with plenty of hot water and detergent. It might be necessary, she thought as she dried it, to carry this knife with her as she had the one she'd used, find a more efficient way of carrying it, though wrapped up and laid along the side of her leg under her trousers would do. She poured herself a nice fresh glass of cold milk.

Her lunch was just finished and all the crockery in hot water when the doorbell rang. Laf, it would be, with the papers. 'You want a cup of tea?' she asked, letting him in.

'Thanks, love, but I won't stop. Where d'you think we're going tonight, me and Sonny and you? We're going to a show. In the West End.'

'In a cinema, d'you mean?' She wasn't going back to that Marble Arch one, whatever he said. That was just the place Mrs Lewis and Auntie were likely to be, haunting the spot where Jock had last appeared. 'I don't know, Laf.'

'In a theatre,' he said. 'It's a thriller about the police.'

'Well, I can't say no, can I?'

'Of course you can't. You'll love it.'

She wouldn't be able to wear those clothes, that was for sure. Not after carrying those dirty towels and the trousers and top she'd taken off. Shame, because these white trousers were really nice. Anyway, she'd have to undress to put the knife down the side of her leg and once she'd got that far it was only another step to have a bath. She washed the dishes, took the papers outside and sat in a clean cane chair she'd scrubbed, and with a cushion whose cover she'd washed and ironed. This made her feel very superior to Mr Kroot and Gertrude Pierce who'd stopped playing cards and eaten their lunch on the green baize table, sandwiches and Fanta by the look of it, for they'd piled up the dirty dishes on a tray and left it on the grass right by the cat's nose, a real magnet for flies. Minty looked once but never again.

It would have been nice to go in the car, but Laf said where was he supposed to park? Down there, finding somewhere to put your vehicle was a nightmare. Taking the tube to Charing Cross meant you'd nothing to worry about. But the Bakerloo Line train was jam-packed and the streets were almost as bad.

Like many suburb dwellers, though their suburb wasn't far out, Sonovia and Laf had only a sketchy knowledge of inner London. Laf occasionally drove through the Park to Kensington or even past Buckingham Palace. He knew roughly where the big streets led, while she had her shopping trips to the West End, and both, as inveterate picture-goers, visited the Odeon Metro and Mezzanine. But Sonovia had no idea of the way places linked up and couldn't have told you how to get from Marble Arch to Knightsbridge or Oxford Street to Leicester Square. As for Minty, she hadn't been down here for years, she'd had no occasion to come, and the big buildings of Trafalgar Square intimidated her with their rows of tall pillars and flights of stairs. It was as if she'd never seen them before or that she'd found herself transported to some foreign city. At the same time they reminded her of those Roman temples in the cemetery.

'Why is he up there?' she said to Laf, pointing to Nelson on his column. 'He's so high up you can't see what he looks like.'

'I don't know why, love. Maybe he wasn't much to look at and it's better not to see him close to. I like the lions.'

Minty didn't. Crouching there like that, they reminded her of Mr Kroot's cat. Maybe in the middle of the night they got up and walked about, treading on tall buildings and stamping on trees. She was glad when she and the Wilsons had pushed their way through the crowds and were seated in the Garrick Theatre. Laf bought a programme for her and one for Sonovia and a box of Dairy Milk. Minty didn't want a chocolate, it stood to reason they couldn't come in those shapes unless someone handled them, but she took one so as not to be rude and felt funny for the next half-hour as the germs ran about inside her stomach.

An Inspector Calls wasn't a bit like they'd imagined, though there was a policeman in it, or perhaps not a real one, perhaps a ghost or an angel. Minty didn't want it to be a ghost, she had enough of those in reality, and sometimes she had to shut her eyes. The set was the best thing, they all agreed on that, not like something made to be the background to a play but like a real house in a real street, transported inside the stage. When it was over and Minty got up to go the point of the knife pushed against the stuff of her trousers at the knee, but she adjusted them quickly before Laf or Sonovia saw.

It was quite late but cafés and restaurants were open everywhere; she had never seen so many all together and it made her wonder how they could make enough money to exist on. They went into a little one in a side street and ordered pizzas. Minty wouldn't have had salad or cooked meat or anything she couldn't see being cooked but a pizza was all right, you could watch the man take it out of an oven with a pair of tongs on to a clean plate. *And* he was wearing gloves. They had a couple of glasses of wine each and that reminded her of Jock.

'Adam and Eve and Pinch Me,' she said.

'You what?'

They'd never heard it before. 'Adam and Eve and Pinch Me went down to the river to bathe. Adam and Eve were drownded. Who was saved?'

'Well, Pinch Me, of course,' said Sonovia and Minty pinched her.

Laf laughed uproariously. 'You had her there, Minty. I didn't know you had it in you.'

'Yes, well, the joke was on me,' said Sonovia and, in a patronising tone, 'But it's not "drownded", my deah. You're wrong about that. "Drowned" would be correct.'

'Jock said "drownded".' Minty finished her pizza. 'It was him told me.'

She shivered. Thinking about him often had that effect.

'Not cold, are you? It's very warm in here. I've been asking myself why I didn't put a thinner jacket on.'

But by this time it was growing colder outside, whatever Sonovia said. They passed a pub and then another, and Laf asked if they wanted a drink, one for the road, a nightcap, but Sonovia said no, enough was enough and it'd be one in the morning before they were in their beds as it was. The tube train came and it was so full that Laf said, 'Let's wait for the next one, it's due in one minute,' so they waited and it came and it was nearly empty. A lot of people got in at Piccadilly, a lot got out at Baker Street and one old woman got in. It was Mrs Lewis.

The empty seat nearly opposite Minty was one of those intended for the old or disabled. Not that many took much notice of that, but it happened to be empty and Mrs Lewis sat down in it. She was still in her dark-red coat and hat. Auntie was nowhere to be seen. Evidently she'd taken to heart what Minty had said about not associating with Mrs Lewis on account of her being Jock's mother and never paying Jock's debts. Minty stared fixedly at Mrs Lewis, who refused to meet her eyes. She had settled herself carefully to avoid sitting on the knife, though it was wrapped first in plastic and then in a clean white rag, but she was very aware of it now.

'What are you staring at, my deah? You're giving me the creeps.'

'She's not real,' Minty said. 'Don't you worry, she's only a ghost, but she's got a nerve coming after me here.'

Sonovia looked at her husband, shaking her head. Laf raised his eyebrows. 'Must be the wine,' he said. 'She's not used to it. They gave you really big glasses in that pizza place.'

Mrs Lewis got up to go at Paddington. For the first time Minty noticed she had a holdall with her. She must be catching a train to Gloucester, back to the old home she'd had when she was alive. 'Can you get a train to Gloucester at this time of night?' she asked Laf.

'I shouldn't think so. It's gone half past midnight. What d'you want to know for?'

Minty didn't reply. She was watching Mrs Lewis leave the train and make her way along the platform. A bad walker, shuffling more than walking. Then she remembered some of the money Jock had borrowed had been to pay for his mother's hip operation. 'She never had it,' she said aloud. 'I don't reckon she lived long enough to have it.'

Again the Wilsons exchanged glances. As Laf said to his wife later, all the people in the train were looking uneasily at Minty. You got used to seeing some funny sights in the underground – he'd once seen a chap racing maggots across the floor – but Minty looked crazy, her face as white as chalk and her wispy hair standing on end. Besides, anyone could tell she'd been talking to the empty air. They got out at Kensal Green and walked home; it wasn't far. The only people in the streets were groups of young men, black and white and Asian, all around twenty years old, all looking somehow like a threat.

Sonovia put her arm through Laf's. 'I wouldn't feel all that comfortable if you weren't with us, love.'

'Well, I am,' said Laf, gratified. 'They won't mess with me.'

On the corner of their street was a seat with a sort of flowerbed behind it. The flowers had to compete with empty beer cans, fish and chip paper and fag ends, and the rubbish was winning. Mrs Lewis hadn't gone home to Gloucester. She was sitting on the seat, the holdall open beside her. Laf and Sonovia probably thought she was the old bag lady who sometimes sat there at night, but Minty knew better. In the ten minutes since Mrs Lewis had left the tube at Paddington she'd changed her clothes again for a black coat and headscarf, and somehow got up here. But ghosts could do anything, get through walls and floors, travel long distances at the speed of light. She was here now but before Minty could get there she'd be in her house, waiting for her.

Down here there was no one else about. The boys in gangs stuck to the Harrow Road. Sonovia and Laf said goodnight and see her soon. Minty was so preoccupied with Mrs Lewis that she forgot her manners and all the things Auntie had taught her, and didn't say thanks for taking me to the theatre or anything. She didn't even say goodnight.

The Wilsons went indoors and Sonovia said, 'I've never known her so peculiar. Talking to herself and seeing things that aren't there. D'you reckon we ought to do something?'

'What can we do? Send for the men in the white coats?'

'Don't you be silly, Laf. It's not funny.'

'She just had too much wine, Sonn. People can have hallucinations when they've had too many. If you don't believe me you can ask Dan.'

Mrs Lewis wasn't waiting for her. Minty searched the house. She wasn't anywhere and nor was Auntie. She'd still be on that seat, fumbling about in that holdall, planning something, laughing maybe because she'd managed to die before she had to pay that money.

Minty knew what she had to do. She patted the knife, opened the front door and closed it quietly behind her. The street was deserted, silent. The lamps were out. Only in the flat opposite was there a light, a gleam in one of the windows like a candle flame. It looked as if the Wilsons had gone straight to bed, for their bedroom light went out as Minty looked upwards. She walked up to the corner, suddenly sure Mrs Lewis would have gone and the seat be empty.

But she was still there. She'd decided to sleep there, Minty couldn't think why. She'd put the battered holdall under her head for a pillow. What did a ghost want with a holdall? The flowers behind her had closed up for the night, their leaves faintly gleaming from among the crumpled cartons and polythene bags and cigarette packets. Mrs Lewis would never give her back her money now, it was gone for ever. Minty, drawing out the knife from its strapping, was suddenly consumed with righteous anger. This would show Auntie that she meant business, teach her to be more careful in future.

It was quite silent in the street now. Mrs Lewis didn't make a sound. If she'd been real Minty would have thought her heart had stopped the minute the point of the knife touched her.

Chapter 27

Alone in the car, Jims escaped from Fredington Crucis House, pursued for several hundred yards down the lane by reporters and photographers. Leonardo he had left behind to fend for himself. They had had a row.

Half an hour had passed before he understood why the reporters and cameramen were there. During that time, having berated Leonardo for being such a fool as to put the light on, he had showered, shaved and dressed, and braced himself to go outside and meet them. But that had to be postponed, for first he looked out of a window. The eyes and cameras of the crowd were turned on to the front door and he was able to observe them for a moment or two without being seen. 'Predators,' he said to himself, 'vultures,' and, rather outmodedly, the legacy of a classical education, 'harpies.'

Then, as one, they turned towards the gates. Mrs Vincey was shutting them behind her and had started up the drive. The reporters closed in upon her, but not before Jims had seen she was carrying a newspaper, the only word of which he could read from this distance in the large-lettered headline was 'MP'. Since he'd asked her not to come this morning, the idea was inescapable that the newspaper and curiosity had fetched her. He could see she was quite willing to talk to them and if they weren't all that anxious to take her photograph this wasn't for her want of readiness to pose for them. What was she saying? And what was it all about, anyway? He soon knew.

She let herself in, and herself alone, by the front door. Jims met her in the hall and found himself in a situation comparable to that Zillah had experienced with Maureen Peacock. Mrs Vincey held up the newspaper's front page in both hands and told him she'd never been so disgusted in all her life. For the first time, she didn't call him Sir or Mr Melcombe-Smith. In the words of Cleopatra when her power is waning, he might have asked, 'What, no more ceremony?' Instead, he stood in silence, reading the headline over and over: THE GAY MP, TWO WEDDINGS AND A FUNERAL.

'Aren't you ashamed of yourself? A Member of Parliament! I wonder what the Queen thinks about you.'

'Mind your own fucking business,' said Jims, 'and get out. Don't come back.'

He went upstairs. At that moment, immediately, he couldn't bring himself to read more. But he had seen the photographs on page three, notably the one of himself and Leonardo in the Maldives, and he blamed Leonardo for all of it. Leonardo had talked, gossiped perhaps, at any rate told someone, had given their picture to a gutter rag. He found him in the bedroom, sitting on the bed fully dressed but looking very hangdog and, to Jims's mind, guilty as hell. Jims began to shout and rave at him, waving the newspaper, accusing him of treachery, perfidy and barratrous betrayal – his once successful career was in part due to his command of language – and not listening to his indignant defence.

Leonardo stood up. 'I haven't talked to anyone. You're mad. I've got my career to think of as much as yours, remember. Let me see that.'

336

They struggled with the paper, pulling it this way and that until the front page was torn in half. Leonardo finally got possession of it. 'If you'll read it instead of ranting like a maniac you'll see it's your precious wife who's been talking, not me. And talking, my God!'

Jims half believed him but he refused to look in his presence. He grabbed the paper and shouting, 'You can get yourself back to London. Walk to bloody Casterbridge, it's only six miles,' ran downstairs.

Mrs Vincey had gone. The pack was still outside. Jims put the newspaper in his briefcase, his wallet and car keys in his pocket and, like General Gordon solitarily confronting the Mahdi's soldiery at Khartoum, opened the door and stepped outside. The pack roared with pleasure and flash bulbs popped.

'Look this way, Jims!'

'Give us a smile, Jims!'

'I'd like just two words, Mr Melcombe-Smith.'

'Is it true, Jims?'

'If you'd like to make a statement . . .'

Jims said in his patrician tones, 'Of course it isn't true. It's all lies.' He embroidered, recalling Leonardo's words, 'My wife is having a mental breakdown.'

'Did you know you were a bigamist, Jims? Will your wife stand by you? Where's Leonardo? Do you expect to lose your seat?'

This last, which they all seemed to take as some sort of ghastly and obscene pun, raised a roar of laughter. Jims, in what was nearly a reflex because he'd felt his face grow hot and therefore red, put up his briefcase to hide it. Bulbs flashed. One exploded almost in his face. He tried to grab the camera, failed and plunged for his car. They were all over it, he thought, like monkeys in a safari park. He pushed a girl off and she fell over, shouting she'd get him for assault. He got the door open, squeezed in and shut

337

it, hoping to slam a man's fingers in it but the hand was snatched back in the nick of time. As he drove down the drive he could see ahead of him that the gates were closed. That bitch Vincey had shut them after her on purpose, he thought, when nine times out of ten she left them open, in spite of his admonitions.

'Open the bloody gates!' He shouted it out of the window but they took no notice. Or rather, one of them stuck a camera in through it.

He got out and they clustered about him, plucking at his clothes, cameras in his face. Someone was actually sitting on the top bar of the left-hand gate.

'You off to London, Jims?'

'What'll you say to Zillah when you get there?'

'Was it a contract killer murdered Jeff Leach?'

'Will Zillah stick by you, Jims?'

Jims pulled open both gates. The reporter sitting on one of them tumbled off and lay on the ground, shouting that he'd broken his leg. He shook his fist and said he'd get Jims for that if it was the last thing he did. While they were trying to bar his exit Jims, resigned to sacrificing his expensive oak gates if necessary, drove straight at the pack and forced them to jump out of his way. Most of them pursued him into the village, only giving up when they saw that the Crux Arms was open. He drove through Long Fredington, eyeing with bitterness Willow Cottage, where his courtship, such as it was, had begun, and then with a glimmer of interest, for he saw it was up for sale. He was reminded of what Leonardo had said about his 'precious wife' talking. There was nothing for it but to stop being a coward and read that newspaper. He pulled off the road at Mill Lane where Zillah, on her way to Annie's house, had once dreamt of her future with him, its affluence and its glamour, and read the story.

It was even worse than he'd expected, but now, after making his getaway from the pack and, thanks to them, becoming somewhat inured to a rain of onslaughts on his privacy, his proclivities and his reputation, he was more able to take it. Plainly, Zillah was entirely responsible. He had underrated her, had treated her in a way he thought she would tolerate but had not. This was her revenge. There were imponderables in the story, though, things for which she could surely not be blamed. He turned back to page one and saw Natalie Reckman's byline. It was she who'd done that snide article about Zillah in the early days of their marriage! Jims could easily imagine her watching Leonardo's house, spying on his arrival, probably bribing the neighbours. Ah, the world was a wicked place and those caught in the fierce light that beats upon its high shore, exposed to perpetual threat and peril.

For all that, everything was over between Leonardo and him. If he'd fancied himself in love for a few short weeks, all that had vanished in the blink of an eye. He never wanted to see Leonardo again. Jims was nothing if not a snob and he asked himself what sort of a fool would walk about a gentleman's house wearing only a pair of vulgar underpants from Cecil Gee. And not have the sense to know a light in an uncurtained room showed up the occupants clearly to anyone outside? He wouldn't be at all surprised if Leonardo's mother lived on a council estate. That it was in (or more probably well outside) Cheltenham meant nothing. Congratulating himself on his escape, both from Fredington Crucis and Leonardo, Jims drove eastwards and left the road to mount the steep escarpment that rises out of the Vale of Blackmoor and on which Shaston stands. Even today the view from Castle Green over 'three counties of verdant pasture' is almost unchanged from Hardy's time and still a sudden surprise to the unexpectant traveller, but Jims didn't linger to look at it. He put the car in Shaston's pay-and-display car park and walked along Palladour Street to an estate agent's. The woman seated behind the desk was probably the only person in the United Kingdom, thought Jims, who hadn't read the story in the newspaper and who didn't recognise his name when he gave it. That was all to the good. His business transacted, he returned to the car and headed back to the London road.

On the journey he turned over the facts in his mind and saw that, come what might, his career was in ruins. There was nothing left to salvage from the wreck. He was branded a bigamist, which he could perhaps feebly deny, and a practising promiscuous homosexual, which he couldn't and no longer wanted to. And he had been questioned as a suspect in a murder case. All those years of campaigning, accepting the offer of a hopeless candidature in the industrial Midlands before getting at last a safe seat, all those Fridays or Saturdays spent in his surgery, all that rattling about the county in a Winnebago, all that speech-making and fête-opening and baby-cuddling – how he disliked children! – and lying to pensioners and huntsmen and pro-vivisectionists and hospital patients and schoolteachers, all of it an utter waste of time. The Party would probably expel him, take away the Whip, send him to Coventry. There was no possibility of his ever making his way back. He was done for. He could only be thankful that he had an unbreakable alibi for the Friday afternoon when that miscreant Jerry Leach was killed. And that, whatever she might think, he'd pulled a fast one on Zillah.

At an exit leading to a couple of villages he pulled off the main road. It was three-quarters of an hour past noon. He drove to an hotel he knew – in the

340

days when he was carefree, he and Ivo Carew had once spent a pleasant weekend there – and ordered lunch. But his appetite failed him and he couldn't eat a thing.

Before she went down to the reporters Zillah had dressed herself and the children with great care and forethought. She'd devoted a lot of time to planning it the night before. Eugenie and Jordan wore the uniform of fashionable upper-middle-class children in summertime at the turn of the millennium: white trainers, white shorts, white T-shirts, with stripes in Jordan's case and modish spots in Eugenie's. Zillah herself was in white trousers and a blue shirt with plunging neckline. Remembering what some awful journalist had said about her shoes, she'd put on flat sandals.

Eugenie hadn't wanted to wear shorts and at first had refused flatly: 'I'm not that sort of girl. You ought to know by now. I either wear long trousers or a dress. You ought to know.'

'I'll make it worth your while,' said Zillah recklessly. 'Five pounds.'

'Ten.'

'You'll come to a bad end.' Zillah used the same words her mother had used to her twenty years before.

Jordan snivelled. Zillah had thought of quietening him in some positive and dramatic way, such as by giving him a tot of whisky, but she'd lost her nerve and had resorted to junior aspirin instead. It had had no effect.

She smiled charmingly at the reporters and posed, holding a hand of each child, for the photographers. Jordan stopped crying for five minutes, fascinated by the biggest dog Zillah had ever seen that one of the cameramen had brought with him. She said she'd something for them all and passed over copies of a statement she'd done on Jims's computer the night before. It said that everything in that morning's paper was true and she'd only like to add that she'd be standing by her husband and supporting him through thick and thin. She and he had spoken several times on the phone that morning and she'd assured him of her devotion and her determination to be a rock for him to cling to. She answered only one question before retiring into the building with dignity.

A young woman with a Yorkshire accent asked her if Jims was bisexual.

'I'm sure he won't mind my saying that yes, he is. Everything has to come out into the open now.' In one of Malina's favourite phrases, she added that trust and caring 'must be the building blocks of our new relationship'.

Jordan burst into fresh tears. Satisfied with what she had done, Zillah carried him up in the lift. After the interviews and the photographs she felt rather flat. She was in the position of having absolutely nothing to do. When would Jims get back? It was a lie she'd told the newspaper people when she'd said she and Jims had spoken several times that morning. She knew he wouldn't phone and she'd no intention of phoning him. But he'd be home and she wasn't going to be there when he came if she could help it. When she'd rejected the idea of the cinema, swimming pools and the various entertainments on offer at the Trocadero, she took the children out to lunch at McDonald's and then on a river boat to the Thames barrier. The water was calm and the motion slow, but Jordan was sick and he cried all the way home.

They returned to the flat at six and Jims still wasn't back. Unless he'd come in and gone out again. She suspected this wasn't so and was proved right within ten minutes. By that time she'd changed into a pair of beach pyjamas she'd bought at a shop at The Cross, remembered her father was ill but didn't phone her mother and put both children in the bath. The front door opened and closed. When she turned round she saw Jims standing in the doorway. His face was pale and he looked racked with anxiety.

'I'm just going to phone my mother,' she said nervously.

'Not now,' he said, and 'May I get you a drink?' in the silky tones he used when he was either very pleased or very angry.

She didn't know whether to say yes or no. She rinsed her hands under the tap and dried them. 'A gin and tonic, please.' Her voice came out rather timidly. She followed him into the living room.

He brought her the drink and stood over her for a moment or two. There was nothing threatening in his stance but he himself was a threat to her and she flinched. He laughed, a bitter, dry laugh. 'I've seen the newspaper,' he said, sitting down. 'I suppose it's a newspaper, I don't know what else to call it. And I've talked to the media. A bit OTT, wasn't it?'

'Wasn't what?'

'The things you said to La Reckman. And the photograph you gave her. Did I really deserve that?'

'Of course you did, the way you've treated me.'

A wail came from the bathroom and Eugenie walked in, wearing her nightdress and dressing gown. She looked at Jims as a householder might look at a dog turd on the doorstep but said nothing. 'I'm not getting him out of the bath,' she said to Zillah. 'He's your responsibility, as I keep telling you. He says his tummy hurts.'

Zillah went. So, after a moment or two, did Eugenie, returning in a few seconds with a book.

Jims's world had ended but he meant to die bravely, triumphantly exacting vengeance. He took out of his pocket a packet of cigarettes and lit one. It was the first he'd had for six months and it made him feel a bit faint, but he savoured it and thought he might start smoking seriously again. Nobody would admonish him now, no one would ask questions in the Commons Chamber about disgusting habits, no one would suggest he set a good example. He inhaled and his vision swam. If he hadn't been sitting down he'd have fallen over. Jordan's yelling heralded his entry into the room.

Zillah came after him. 'Why are you smoking?'

'Because I like it,' said Jims. 'Put that child to bed.'

'There's no need to talk like that. He hasn't done you any harm.'

'No, his mother has.' He got up and switched on the television. A cartoon happened to be on and for five minutes Jordan was quiet.

'Give me a cigarette, please.'

'Buy your own. God knows, I give you enough money.' Jims drew showily on his cigarette, blowing smoke into Zillah's face. 'I don't expect you to be out of here until Friday,' he said. 'I am, in fact, giving you a week's notice.'

'Now, wait a minute. You can't do that. If anyone goes, you do. You're married to me, remember? I'm your legal wife. I've got children and therefore a right to your home.'

'You didn't really believe in that marriage ceremony, did you, my dear? I wouldn't have credited that the wool could so easily be pulled over your eyes. You believed Kate Carew was a registrar? You actually swallowed Kevin Jebb as a witness? You and I haven't even been cohabiting. Neither of our so-called marriages was consummated. You're just a friend I've taken in when you hadn't a roof over your head. Out of the goodness of my heart.'

Zillah stared at him. She couldn't speak.

'But I grant you've grounds for expecting some sort of maintenance from me. So I spent the morning negotiating a purchase with an estate agent. I've also had a pleasant chat with the owner. That's why I was so late back. And I'm glad to say the sale's been agreed. I've bought Willow Cottage for you. Aren't you pleased?'

As Zillah began to scream, Eugenie looked up from the floor and said, 'Mummy, do you mind? I can't hear the TV.'

Chapter 28

A boy delivering papers found Eileen Dring's body at six forty-five on Sunday morning. He was just sixteen and it gave him a bad shock. The body was still on the seat where Eileen Dring had settled for the night. But for the blood which had soaked through her clothes and the blanket with which she had covered herself, she would have seemed asleep. Perhaps she had been stabbed in her sleep and had known nothing about it.

The police knew her. There were no problems of identification. For several years she had had a room in Jakarta Road off Mill Lane in West Hampstead, paid for by Camden Council, but she had seldom lived in it, preferring to wander the streets and sleep out of doors, at least in summer. Kilburn and Maida Vale and Paddington Recreation Ground were among her haunts. They had never known her to come as far west as this. But Eileen was known to love flowers and had once been observed sleeping in the doorway of an empty building that had formerly been a bank, on the corner of Maida Vale and Clifton Road. It happened to be very close to where the flower and plant seller would pitch his stall in the morning, and perhaps she'd chosen it in anticipation of waking up to the scent of carnations and roses in the morning. The site of her death, the seat on which she was lying, was just in front of a crescent-shaped flowerbed, at present red, white and pink with geraniums, among which lay the detritus of meals and drinks consumed on the street.

It took only a short time to establish that the knife used to stab her was very similar to the one which killed Jeffrey Leach. Similar but not identical. Possibly one of a pair bought at the same time. So advanced are forensics by now that investigators can tell precisely the shape and size of a weapon used in these circumstances, the nicks, if any, on its blade, any minuscule unevenness in that blade's surface, for the knife itself is unique. So they knew it wasn't *the* knife but its twin.

The motive for the killing of Jeffrey Leach remained obscure but the motive for this one at first seemed transparent. The holdall Eileen carried with her and which lay under her head, usually held a blanket and a cardigan and scarf, a can of fizzy drink – she was strictly teetotal – a sandwich or two as well as her pension book. It was empty. There should also have been money, for Eileen had drawn two weeks' pension the day before and had spent only a little of it on the food and drink. Does anyone do murder for a hundred and forty pounds? Violent Crimes know it's done for half that, for a quarter; it's done for the price of ten grammes of cannabis.

On the other hand, they were sure Eileen was the victim of Jeffrey Leach's killer and the question of financial profit hadn't entered into that. So were there any links between the two victims apart from the close similarity of the weapons used? How about West Hampstead?

Leach had been living there for the six months prior to his death. Jakarta Road was two streets away from Holmdale Road, running parallel to it but linked by a cross street, Athena Road. Although they were yet to discover whether Eileen had ever frequented Holmdale, West Hampstead police – the police station was in Fortune Green Road – knew Athena Road to be a favourite pitch of hers. Twice they'd moved her on when she'd been found sleeping on someone's front lawn between the flower borders. Had she tried the same experiment in camping in the gardens of Holmdale Road?

Sunday had passed without Jims addressing a word to her. He stayed at home, but in silence. It was as if he'd lost the use of his tongue. Zillah wouldn't have believed until she experienced it that anyone could behave like that, not simply not speaking, but acting as if he were alone in the place. The children and she might have been inanimate objects or pieces of furniture for all the notice he took of them. It was as if they had become inaudible and invisible, and she'd hardly have been surprised if, seeking a chair to settle himself into, he'd sat on one of them or on her.

This policy of ignoring them made her, against her will and determination, conciliatory towards him. She prepared quite a nice lunch of scrambled eggs and smoked salmon with a salad, offered him the dishes, poured him a glass of wine. He took no notice of any of it but went to the kitchen, returning with a sandwich he'd made himself and beer which he drank out of the can. She found herself looking wistfully at him and forced her head to turn away. The afternoon he spent at his desk, apparently writing letters. She couldn't help thinking that if only he'd been of a different sexual orientation she could have won him over, seduced him, charmed him, but if he'd been different she knew very well she wouldn't have been with him in the first place.

At about five Moon and Stars Television rang. Eugenie answered and gave the response she always did if Zillah failed to get to the phone first.

'She's not available.'

348

Zillah snatched the receiver from her. The woman at the other end wanted to say that they were afraid they couldn't send a car in the morning after all. Of course she could still come under her own steam if she liked. Zillah, sensing she was no longer the attraction she once had been, thought she did like, though she was no longer quite sure. At any rate, she agreed. It would mean getting up at five thirty in the morning but it would be worth it. She could charm them, she could bewitch her audience. The phone rang again almost immediately. It was the cleaner from number nine to say she couldn't manage babysitting in the morning after all.

Zillah looked at Jims. He appeared to be signing his letters. She was afraid to ask him. She'd just leave the children in the flat. After all, he'd be there, and with luck no one would wake up until she was back home again. Eugenie wouldn't leave her brother to scream, would she?

Jims turned on the television news at five-thirty-five, sat inscrutably through items about floods in Gujarat, ongoing strife in Zimbabwe and the murder of an old woman in Kensal Green, before seeing himself scarlet-faced, then sheltering his flush behind his briefcase, as he emerged from the front door of Fredington Crucis House. The children watched it and so did Zillah, occasionally turning her eyes to cast fearful glances in Jims's direction. He wasn't blushing now but had become even whiter. The pictures weren't new, they'd previously appeared the evening before, but now they were followed by comments from all sorts of Party dignitaries including the Chairman of the South Wessex Conservatives who said stoutly that he had complete confidence in Mr Melcombe-Smith and in his shortly being able to give clear replies to all the questions that still remained unanswered.

'Why is my stepfather on the TV?' asked Eugenie.

No one answered her. The phone rang, Jims answered it, put the receiver back without a word and pulled out the plug. Unnerved, Zillah went into her bedroom, taking the children with her. Jordan had begun to whimper.

She dressed with great care. If real work came out of this interview, if it led to celebrity and getting her own television show, she wouldn't have to leave London and go back to Willow Cottage. Jims had said, in a nasty sarcastic tone – on Saturday night, when he'd still had a tongue – that she'd like the cottage very much now, the new decorations made all the difference. 'Especially the lovely contemporary fitted kitchen,' he'd added, as if that kind of language were habitual with her. But she wouldn't like it and wild horses would have to drag her there.

She put on her favourite white suit with a coral-red shirt because she'd heard that bright colours do best on television. Would they make her up or expect her to have done it herself? Zillah couldn't contemplate going out into the street in *London* without make-up on. Long Fredington was another matter and the very thought of it made her shiver. Once she was back from Channel Four and had taken Jordan to the child psychiatrist, she'd find herself a solicitor and see what could be done to force Jims out of the flat. Something must be possible.

It was pouring with rain. She'd left the flat on tiptoe, putting her key in the lock to close the door silently. She couldn't go back for a raincoat or an umbrella. Fearing for her hair and her flimsy shoes, she tried to shelter under an overhanging portico while hailing a taxi but the result of this was that other people got there before her. She had to come out and get wet. The cab driver who finally stopped grinned at her rats'-tail hair.

But Zillah soon discovered that she need not have worried. Another woman going on the programme looked, in her tracksuit and unmade-up state, as if she'd just got out of bed. The make-up department dealt with all that, dried Zillah's hair, cleaned her shoes, redid her face. The other woman told her confidingly that she'd been appearing on shows of this kind for years. She'd go along wearing laddered tights, knowing they'd give her a new pair. Zillah was shocked but delighted to learn these tricks of the trade. She'd begun to feel a lot better.

But when the programme began and she was able to watch it, sitting with the other interviewees-to-be in a waiting room, she realised something she must have been told but which hadn't sunk in. It was live. There would be no rehearsal, no preparation and no chance to say she hadn't meant that, cut that, please, or can we go back? The questions were very searching and even the inexperienced could tell they weren't kind. A young man, who looked very young, put his head round the door and beckoned to the tights woman. She would be the next – Zillah found herself using the word 'victim'.

It was a strange feeling watching the screen and seeing her walk on to the set. Zillah suddenly felt naïve and rather helpless. The woman, whom she hadn't recognised, turned out to be a pop singer of the seventies trying to make a comeback. The presenter, an ugly man with a beard and the rasping voice that had made him famous, asked her if she didn't think she was 'a bit over the hill' for what she had in mind. She wasn't exactly Posh Spice, was she? Maybe she'd like to sing for them now. They'd an accompanist on hand. The singer answered the questions bravely and sang not very well. While she

351

was singing the young man came back and beckoned to the teenage boy who was there because he'd got into Oxford at the age of fifteen. Zillah would be the last.

'They always save the best till last,' said a girl who'd come in to see if she wanted more coffee or orange juice.

After the singer came a woman reading the news, then a weather forecast, then advertising of the programmes for the day ahead. She thought the singer might come back but she didn't. The boy came on and was interviewed by a kindly woman presenter who treated him as if he'd won the Nobel Prize. Zillah had been told the man with the rasping voice would be talking to her but she found herself hoping that plans had changed and she might get this woman who was now telling the boy that his family must be enormously proud of him. And he wasn't even very good, but shy and tongue-tied.

Zillah was called. The girl who'd enquired about coffee and orange juice led her along one passage and then another and on to the edge of what seemed like theatre-in-the-round, a circular platform, partly screened and curtained, thick with cameramen and soundmen and electricians. The brightly lit area she'd seen on the screen could just be seen in the centre.

'When I give you a sign, I'll lift my finger like this,' whispered the girl, 'you walk on from here and sit in that chair opposite Sebastian. OK?'

'Yes, that's fine,' said Zillah loudly.

Everyone in her vicinity turned and shushed her, fingers on lips. Such confidence as she had left began to ebb. Her heels were too high, she knew that now. Suppose she tripped? The boy genius came off and so did the kindly woman interviewer. The man called Sebastian told viewers they were now to expect the guest of the day, Zillah Melcombe-Smith, bigamist, wife – or was she? – of the disgraced MP James Melcombe-Smith, and widow – or was she? – of the 'Cinema Slayer's' victim. Zillah suddenly felt very cold. That kind of introduction wasn't at all what she'd expected. But the girl who'd brought her here was holding up one finger, so she had no option but to set off on what seemed like the longest and slowest walk of her life to the chair opposite Sebastian.

He stared at her as if she were something peculiar in a zoo, an okapi or echidna. 'Welcome to *A Bite of Breakfast*, Zillah,' he said. 'Tell us what it feels like to be a widow, a wife and a bigamist all at once. It can't happen to many women, d'you think?'

Zillah said, 'No,' and, 'No, it can't,' but could think of nothing else.

'Well, let's start with the bigamy, shall we? Maybe you're one of those people who don't approve of divorce. A Catholic, are you?'

Her voice came out thin and hoarse. 'I'm not.' Suppose her mother was watching! She'd only just thought of that. 'My husband – my first husband – said we were divorced. And my husband – my present husband, I mean – he said I was.' Whatever she didn't do, she had to stick to that. 'I thought I was divorced.'

'But when you married James in the House of Commons Chapel' – the way he said it made it sound like St Peter's in Rome – 'you told the vicar you were single. A single girl and fancy free, that was about it, wasn't it?'

Why had no one picked on that till now? Her tone trembled: 'James – James thought it best. James said – I didn't know I was doing wrong. I thought I – I –'

'Well, never mind. It all came right for a while with your first husband's tragic death in the cinema.

A terrible thing, of course, but in some ways it happened at just the right time. What was your reaction?'

Her reaction in the here and now was to burst into tears. She couldn't help it. She felt driven into a corner from which the only escape was to be led away to prison. Falling forward, anything to stop looking into his awful bearded face, she put her head on her knees and sobbed. What he was doing, saying, what all those cameramen and soundmen were doing she didn't know. She felt a touch on her shoulder, jerked up, put her head back and howled. The kindly woman presenter took her arm, helped her up. She couldn't really tell because of the beard, but Sebastian seemed to be smiling. Behind her, she heard him say something for the benefit of viewers about her being overcome with grief. Still on camera, she did what she'd feared to do, tripped and nearly fell over. As she left the set, crying and limping, a cameraman whispered, 'Great television. It's what presenters dream of.'

That programme was really the end of the battle for Zillah. She went back to Abbey Gardens Mansions in a cab. It was still only nine o'clock. The children were watching television and she recognised the same channel as that on which she'd just appeared.

'Did you do that on purpose?' asked Eugenie. 'That crying and falling over?'

'Of course I didn't. I was upset.'

'When he said about your first husband's tragic death, what did he mean?'

Zillah had never thought about that, about the children watching the programme and in this way, this terrible way, learning about their father's death. Looking into Eugenie's beautiful, troubled, reproachful face, she could tell that the child knew, but still she couldn't answer her. Not *now*, not in the midst of all she was going through.

'That's why we never see him,' said Eugenie.

'I'll tell you later, I promise I will.'

'Your mascara has run all down your face.'

Zillah said she was going to wash. 'Where's Jims?'

'In bed. He didn't go out and leave us alone, if that's what you think.'

She wanted to tell the child not to speak to her like that but she was afraid. It was a dreadful admission to make, that she was afraid of her own seven-year-old daughter. Nevertheless, it was true. How would it be when Eugenie was a teenager? She would be able to do exactly as she liked with her mother, she would rule the place. Willow Cottage, Long Fredington, Dorset. Zillah realised she was resigned to returning there. Consulting lawyers was no longer feasible. Jordan was crying again. He'd probably been crying since before she came in and while she was talking to Eugenie, but she hadn't even noticed, she was so used to it by now. They were due at the child psychiatrist's in an hour's time.

'We've never even seen her,' Michelle said indignantly. 'We don't know who you mean. We've never had an old homeless woman sleeping in our front garden.'

'Not homeless, Michelle,' said Violent Crimes. 'She had a home. That's the point. Her home was in Jakarta Road. What about you, Matthew? Do you remember her?'

Matthew had been writing his column when they came. They hadn't phoned first. The thought was inescapable that they had hoped to catch the Jarveys unawares. Plotting their next crime perhaps or disposing of the weapon. 'I am old-fashioned,' he said, 'but I would prefer you not to call my wife and me by our Christian names. You didn't when you first spoke to us, so I can only think that since then, for some reason, we've forfeited your respect.'

Violent Crimes stared. 'Well, if you feel like that, of course. Most clients say it establishes a friendlier relationship.'

'But we're not clients, are we? We're suspects. In answer to your question, I don't remember Mrs Dring. To my knowledge, I've never seen her. Now will that do?'

'We'd like to search this house.'

Michelle shouted, 'No!' almost before she knew what she was saying.

'We can get a warrant, Mrs Jarvey. All your refusal does is delay things.'

'If my wife will agree,' said Matthew wearily, 'I will.'

Michelle shrugged, then nodded. From believing, a week ago, that no one could suppose a couple like themselves guilty of violence, she had come to understand, only too easily, how Violent Crimes must see her and Matthew. Already she could imagine their photographs, their rogues' gallery death-row portraits, in some true crimes collection of the future. A sinister pair, he cadaverously thin with the skull-like face of an Eichmann or a Christie, a man who purposely starved himself and made a living out of writing about anorexics, she a waddling tub of lard with a deceptively pretty face sunk in pillows of fat. It made no difference to this picture Michelle had of herself, and the husband she adored, that since he embarked on his television programme he'd been steadily eating a little more every day and that she had done no more than nibble at a piece of fruit or a slice of chicken since the investigation began. She still saw them as grotesque.

The searching began. Four officers worked over

the house. They didn't say what they were looking for and neither of the Jarveys would condescend to ask. After the early rain the day had become warm and sunny. They went out into their garden, which, front and back, was no more than a lawn surrounded by flowerless shrubs, sat on the swing seat, silent but holding hands. Both were thinking of Fiona.

Their neighbour had gone off to work at eight thirty as usual. Carefree was how Michelle saw her, for though she and Matthew had fallen in love at first sight, she found it hard to believe in the passion Fiona claimed to have had for a man she'd known for such a short time. And such a man! She'd gone off to work, no doubt making money hand over fist for herself and her clients, with never a thought for the people she professed to be her friends but whom she'd made the police suspect. She must have more money than she knew what to do with if she was talking, as she had last time they saw her, of compensating two of those women of Jeffrey Leach's for what they'd lost through him. Michelle no longer believed she was sorry for what she'd done. She wouldn't have put it past Fiona, once she'd seen of the murder of Eileen Dring on television last night, to have phoned the police and told them the Jarveys had known the dead woman. Wasn't it rather too much of a coincidence that they'd known both murder victims?

They went indoors again after the search was over. Of course, nothing incriminating had been found. But, 'We shall be in touch,' Violent Crimes said. 'We shall want to talk to you again.'

Michelle felt as some people do after their homes have been burgled. Not just an intrusion but a violation, a desecration. She imagined the officers going through her underwear drawers, sniggering at the size of her bras and knickers. Finding those Xrays of Matthew's spine and pelvis, which had been taken when a specialist suspected his bones were becoming brittle. Marvelling and exchanging amused glances over their wedding photograph album. She'd never feel the same about her house again. She and Matthew had begun their married life there in such an ecstasy of joy and hope. In the kitchen she began to prepare his lunch. For herself, she felt less like eating than ever.

He came out to her. 'I love you.'

'I love you too, darling,' she said. 'Nothing makes any difference to that.'

'Thanks,' said Jims, 'that's very kind of you.'

He'd been astonished when Eugenie brought him a cup of coffee in bed. It wasn't very good, being made from less than boiling water, instant coffee and dried milk. Nevertheless he was touched and vague thoughts fluttered through his mind of how, had things turned out differently, he and his stepdaughter might one day have become friends. At least, unlike her mother, she had a brain.

'She's gone to do some interview,' said Eugenie.

'So what's new?'

Eugenie laughed and then, to his surprise, so did he. And there he'd been thinking he'd never smile again. So Zillah had gone out – no doubt to bad-mouth him – leaving him to look after her kids without first asking him. And he'd do it. He hadn't much choice. It would be the last time.

He heard her come back. Because he'd known her so long, he could tell from the way she shut the front door and walked across the hall what kind of a mood she was in. A desperate one, by the sound of it. He lay in bed for a further half-hour, then got up and had a bath, a long, hot soak. Where she was going with the kids this time he neither knew nor cared, but he waited until the door had closed and he heard the lift move before emerging into the living room. He had dressed with care, but then he always did. What sort of a mess had he got himself into that he was being driven out of his own home by that woman?

He walked for a while. It was a beautiful day now, the rain clouds swept away by a high wind, which had since dropped and the sun had come out. He found himself in South Kensington outside the Launceston Place restaurant where they were happy to let him lunch, though he hadn't booked. His thoughts drifted from Zillah to Sir Ronald Grasmere and the terms they had agreed on for Willow Cottage, then to Leonardo. Jims hoped he'd been unable to get a taxi and been forced to walk to Casterbridge, that the train had been cancelled or that weekend works on the line had necessitated part of the journey being made by bus.

A cab took him back and Big Ben showed twenty minutes past two as he went into the Commons by way of Westminster Hall.

Two messages awaited him. The one from the Leader of the Opposition was peremptory and cold. No messing, thought Jims. He'd see him at three sharp. It was a command. The Chief Whip's message was couched in rather more wistful terms. Would Jims like to come and 'meet with him' – why did even his own party use this awful language? – in his office for a pre-dinner drink and review of 'the situation'? Jims threw both into a waste-paper bin and, drawing in his breath, remembering how he'd confronted the press on Saturday morning, he strolled into the Commons Chamber.

All eyes were immediately on him. He had known it would be so and was careful to meet no one's gaze. Two members sat near where he always sat, on the second from the back of the back benches. With assumed nonchalance, though his heart was pounding, he moved to sit between them. One ignored him. The other, whom Jims of course knew but whom he'd never thought of with anything like friendship, leant across and gave him a small fatherly pat on the knee. It was so unexpected and so bloody *kind* that Jims, grinning at him and saying, 'Thanks,' felt something happen that hadn't occurred for twenty years. Tears came into his eyes.

They never fell. Jims didn't give them the chance. He remained in the Chamber for twenty minutes, apparently listening but in fact hearing nothing, and then he rose to his feet, looked one by one at such members as were present, then at the Speaker ('We who are about to die salute you') and walked towards the door. There he paused and looked back. He would never see this sight again. It was already receding into his past, like the fading memory of a dream.

The Central Lobby was almost empty. Yesterday he had sent his resignation to the Chairman of the Parliamentary Conservative Party and his relinquishment of the whip to the Chief Whip. There was nothing to stay for except one small consultation. A Member who'd been in here for forty years and who knew all about procedure was expecting him in his office with helpful hints on ceasing to be a member. It couldn't be done as easily as leaving the Party.

'The Chiltern Hundreds,' said Jims.

'Pity about that, old man, but it's taken. You remember – well, a little contretemps in the matter of the former Member for . . .'

'Oh, yes,' Jims cut in. 'Paederasty, wasn't it?'

'Possibly. I try to put a distance between myself and that kind of thing.'

'There must be other offices of profit under the

crown. What about the Lord Warden of the Cinque Ports?'

'I'm afraid His Royal Highness the Prince of Wales has that.'

'Of course.'

A ledger was consulted. 'There's the Stewardship of the Tolpuddle Marshes. It carries a nominal annual stipend of fifty-two pence and acceptance of it would of course disqualify you from membership of the House of Commons.'

'Sounds perfect,' said Jims. 'I've always wanted to have my say in the fate of the Tolpuddle Marshes. Where exactly are they? Wales, isn't it?'

'No, actually it's Dorset.'

The aged Member afterwards remarked to a crony of his that Melcombe-Smith had laughed so much he was quite concerned, supposing that the shock of the wretched man's recent experiences was bringing on some kind of breakdown.

Jims wasn't going to hang around for any scoldings, reproaches or impertinent enquiries. He walked out into New Palace Yard as Big Ben struck twice for three thirty, an awesome sound to which, for the first time in years, he gave his full attention. The afternoon was beautiful, sunny and hot. What should he do now?

The child psychiatrist told Zillah he was also a doctor of medicine. She didn't know why he bothered, she hadn't brought Jordan all the way to Wimpole Street because he had a sore throat. Jordan hadn't stopped crying since they got into the taxi. Just before they left he'd been sick. It wasn't surprising, she thought and told the psychiatrist, that a child who was always crying should also be frequently vomiting. Eugenie, who had to come because there was no one to look after her at home, sat on a chair in the consulting room, wearing the wry and cynical expression of a disillusioned woman six times her age.

When he'd talked to Jordan, or tried to, the psychiatrist said he'd like to give him a perfunctory physical examination. Zillah, who was nothing if not a child of her times and was in a nervous state anyway, immediately envisaged sexual abuse, but she nodded miserably. Jordan was stripped and examined.

It took two minutes for the psychiatrist to sit him up, give him a pat on the shoulder, and covering him with a blanket, say to Zillah, 'This child has a hernia. Of course you must have a second opinion but I'd be very surprised if that's not what's wrong with him. And another may be forming on the other side.' He gave her what she interpreted as a nasty look. 'If he's been crying and vomiting he's had it for a long time. Pain doesn't start until the hernia's reached a critical stage. It may even be strangulated.'

In newspapers a tremendous story is always followed by a period of anticlimax. The tension cannot be sustained. Some cataclysmic revelation has burst upon the world and there can be follow-ups, but sometimes these are unusable, due to the principal being dead or due to appear in court or missing. But something must be found to fill the gap between the shock and triumph and the next amazing journalistic coup. Natalie had 'outed' Jims and ruptured his discretion, but was chary of writing much more about him while he seemed to be suspected of Jeff Leach's murder. The time had come to produce a history of Jeff's life, a catalogue of his women. So far only his wife and the woman he was living with had been publicly named. A stunning move might be to acknowledge that she herself had been among his lovers. She had no inhibitions at all about doing this and her boyfriend was as hard-headed about things as she. But who else should feature in her story?

She had often thought of 'the funny little thing' he had mentioned at lunch the last time they'd met, a woman with a peculiar name. He'd called her Polo and she lived near Kensal Green Cemetery. It might be a good idea to hunt this woman down. An interview with Fiona Harrington was a must and maybe another with Natalie's own predecessor. She knew very well that hadn't been Jeff's ex-wife but a woman called – she tried for a while to remember her name. It would come back to her. Jeff had talked of her frequently enough, and mostly with bitterness, while he and she were together.

A restaurateur? A doctor? The chief executive of some agency or charity? She'd let her memories of Jeff's references to this woman and the few sentences he'd spoken about 'Polo' lie at the back of her mind. There was no hurry. One day soon she'd delve down into the jumble in there and maybe some interesting things would come to the surface.

Chapter 29

House-to-house enquiries were conducted in the neighbourhood surrounding the spot where Eileen Dring had died. Officers called at the Wilsons but left as soon as they discovered who Laf was. He'd already told them of his trip to the theatre on Saturday night with his wife and their friend from next door, had sent in his report by Sunday evening, as soon as he heard about Eileen's death on the radio. In it he described how he and Sonovia and Minty had seen the old woman alive, well and awake at five minutes to one on Sunday morning. He talked in more detail to the superintendent in charge of the case, but he said nothing about Minty's curious behaviour in the tube on the way home, her hallucinations and talking to herself. After all, as he said to Sonovia later, she was a *friend* and you didn't say things about a friend behind her back. You didn't, for instance, say she'd had too much to drink.

Minty was at work the first time they called. Sonovia had told them over and over that she would be, but they still called. Getting no answer, they went to the next house, and Gertrude Pierce came to the door. As soon as they told her who they were and what they wanted she called her brother. 'Dickie, there's a woman been murdered at the end of the street.'

Mr Kroot appeared, hobbling on two sticks. His already pale face drained of colour. He had to sit down. Gertrude Pierce gave him something to inhale and something else to swallow for his angina and the police officers wondered if he was going to drop dead in front of them. But after a minute or two he rallied. 'You want to put that woman next door through the third degree,' he said in his wavering old voice. 'She's a funny one. Her and her auntie, they've not spoken a word to me for twenty years.'

'That's right, Dickie,' said his sister. 'I wouldn't have been surprised if she'd murdered *me*.'

Jims had taken a taxi up to Park Lane. There he sought out a prestigious West End estate agent, handed them the keys to the Abbey Gardens Mansions flat and those to Fredington Crucis House and requested them to sell both properties. His agent would handle everything. He was going abroad for an indefinite time.

This idea for his future had come into his head on the spur of the moment. In fact, he had no plans and could hardly see beyond the present. He strolled down to Hyde Park Corner and decided to return to Westminster, as he had read MPs living in north London used to do, by walking on grass. Once you could have come all the way from Bayswater through Hyde Park, Green Park and St James's Park, and barely set foot on stone or tarmac. This was no longer quite possible but still he managed to walk on turf and under trees as far as the Palace and, having crossed a couple of wide thoroughfares, was once again in a cool and leafy paradise. No one recognised him, no one stared. He thought about never having to set eyes on Zillah again. He thought about the very large sums of money that would accrue to him through the sale of his houses, something in the region of three million. Jims wasn't in need of the money, he had plenty, but it was nice to know it was there and more of it coming in.

After a while he set foot on the bridge that spans the lake and, pausing in the middle, looked from Buckingham Palace on his right to Whitehall, Horse Guards and the Foreign Office on his left. It hadn't changed much in a hundred and fifty years, apart from the addition of the London Eye, the great wheel that rolled across the sky behind Downing Street, silver and shining, all spokes and capsules like big glass beads. The sunlight glittered on the water, the weeping trees made deep shadows, swans glided under the bridge and the pelicans gathered on their island. But the idea of leaving had begun to take hold. He *would* go abroad. It might be years before he returned. How long before he saw that view again?

On the move once more, he recalled a story he'd heard about a chamberlain at some oriental court who, inadvertently breaking wind in the presence of the potentate, was so stricken with shame that he fled immediately and wandered the earth for seven years. Jims, however, felt not in the least ashamed, he simply wanted to avoid the argument, recriminations, inquests, speculation and need to defend himself. 'Must', said the first Queen Elizabeth, 'is not a word to use to princes.' Well, 'why' and 'explain' and 'justify' were not words to be used to him. He'd go tonight. The car, of course, must be left for his agent to garage somewhere or sell. He didn't want to be encumbered by it. The same applied to his clothes. It occurred to him that if he ever wore a suit again it would be purely for the pleasure of admiring the look of himself in the mirror. But really he preferred his appearance to be admired by someone else.

Morocco, he thought, he'd always wanted to go there and for some reason never had. New Orleans, Santiago, Oslo, Apia – all places he hadn't yet been to. Politics had enslaved him, kept him to the grindstone, stolen all his time. It was over now. As he entered Great College Street from the northern end Big Ben was striking five. He had never before noticed how sonorous and deep-throated were its chimes and how forbidding. The porter who had done their shopping was standing behind the desk.

'Is Mrs Melcombe-Smith back yet?' He thought this a cunning way of phrasing it.

The porter said she'd just gone out again. To take 'Master Jordan' to an appointment in Harley Street, he thought. Relieved, Jims thanked him. Was there anywhere else in the world where a child of three would still be referred to in these terms except this tiny spot of England, London, Westminster, the environs of Parliament? Pity, really. He liked feudal ways and would soon be leaving even their vestiges behind.

Not quite convinced, he entered the flat cautiously and, finding it as empty as he'd hoped, threw essentials into an overnight bag along with his passport. The estate agent had promised a valuation of the place by the following afternoon. His garage, which had his car keys, would pick up the car at much the same time. They could get on with it, he wouldn't be here. Quietly, he went down by the stairs and out into the street by the car park. There he hailed a taxi and asked the delighted driver to take him to Heathrow. The first flight going somewhere he'd never been he would take.

As he sat back in the cab, all his worries, his real anguish at hopes blighted and ambition wrecked, vanished like smoke in the wind. At first he couldn't define the source of his sudden surge of happiness and then, all at once, he could. It was called freedom.

Minty had just got out of the bath at six fifteen when

the police came back. The police are nearly as likely to be favourably impressed by cleanliness, neatness and respectability as anyone else. In almost everyone's mind, crime is associated with dirt and squalor, with late rising and late retiring, a routineless existence, head lice, drugs of all sorts, blocked drains and unidentifiable smells – and with bizarre dressing, too, punk hairstyles, body piercing, an excess of leather, boots and fingernails painted anything but red or pink.

Minty smelt of soap and lavender shampoo. Her fine soft hair, the colour of dandelion down and freshly washed, looked windblown. The bath hadn't cleaned make-up off her face because she had never worn it. She was dressed in pale-blue cotton trousers and a pale-blue and white striped T-shirt. The house was no less clean than its owner and french windows were open on to a neat if sterile garden.

The police, who were the same pair that had called next door, remained uninfluenced by the ramblings of a paranoid old man. They found Minty transparent and saw that answering the questions put to her gave her no problems. She seemed conspicuously innocent and she was, for the only old women in the neighbourhood she'd been interested in were Auntie and Mrs Lewis. One of them had apparently disappeared and the other she had herself got rid of. The name Eileen Dring meant nothing to her, but when they asked if she remembered seeing her on the seat by the flowerbed just before one on Sunday morning, she nodded and said yes, because Laf had told her yesterday he and Sonovia were going to say yes, they'd seen her, and she, Minty, had been with them. As it happened, she couldn't remember at all well just what she had seen at that point, she'd been so angry and at the same time so determined, now that at last she had Mrs Lewis in her grasp. But if Laf said this Eileen Something had been there, no doubt she had been.

'And then you said goodnight to your friends, went home and maybe straight to bed?'

'That's right. I locked up and went to bed.' She wasn't telling them how she'd gone straight out again and found Mrs Lewis and dealt with her once and for all.

'Did you look out of your bedroom window at all?'

'I expect I did. I usually do.'

'And did you see anyone in the street?'

'Not in the street, I didn't. Her from Iran opposite, the one who wears the black thing covering her up, all her lights were still on. That lot never go to bed.'

'Thank you, Ms Knox. I think that's all. Unless you can think of anything we ought to know.'

She couldn't, but still she added a word or two about how wicked murder was and people who committed it ought to be put to death. She was all for bringing back hanging, she said. And that was all. There was no point in telling them about Mrs Lewis, they wouldn't believe her, they'd be like Laf and Sonovia. Apparently they were satisfied because they soon went away.

After she'd come back that night, the first thing she'd done had been to wash the knife and her own hands at the same time. Of course she'd had a bath afterwards, but she'd have done that whatever time she'd got in. The knife still worried her. It was back in the knife drawer but she couldn't get it out of her mind, she'd been thinking about it on and off all day while she was ironing those shirts. She pictured it contaminating all the other knives in the drawer. That she'd scrubbed it in detergent and disinfectant, the whole place smelt of TCP she'd used so much – made no difference. She'd have to get it out of the house. The bins in the Harrow Road were full again, she'd noticed on her way home, and the idea of carrying it up Western Avenue or all the way down Ladbroke Grove made her feel nauseous. She remembered how it had been last time, having to *wear* that dirty knife next to her skin. In fact, the way she thought of it now, she not only didn't want it near her, she didn't want it anywhere near her own property, let alone in her clean knife drawer. She wanted it miles away. But could she bear to carry it for miles?

She'd have to. As Auntie always said, the world was a difficult place to live in but it was all you'd got. In some ways she was rather sorry Auntie had gone away. Without Mrs Lewis, Auntie was OK to have around. She was company. Maybe she'd come back one day. Minty opened the knife drawer and took out the fateful one. She'd thought so much about it and it now loomed so large and important in her consciousness that, like Macbeth, she fancied she saw 'gouts of blood' on its blade and dried blood in the crevices where blade joined handle. Ghost juice, that was, not real blood. It couldn't be so, she'd scrubbed it too thoroughly, but it was as if her eyes knew nothing of what her hands had done. With a little cry of disgust she dropped it on the floor. This only made things worse, for she had to pick it up again and then scrub the floor where for a few seconds it had lain. Everything in that drawer would have to be rewashed and the drawer itself washed, of course. There seemed no end to it and she was already weary.

She wrapped the knife in newspaper, inserted it into a plastic bag and strapped it against her leg. With no idea of where she was going, she left the house and walked up the street to the Harrow Road. It was a fine, sunny evening and a lot of people were about. But not in the vicinity of the seat by the flowerbed which was cordoned off with blue and white crime tape. Minty, who had never seen this sort of thing before, supposed it was something to do with the council clearing up the flowerbed, getting rid of all that filthy greasy paper and the fried fish skins and chocolate bar wrappers. It was time it was done. People lived like pigs.

An 18 bus came and she got on it. At the Edgware Road crossing she got off and changed on to a 6 which took her to Marble Arch, and a number 12. At Westminster, though she had no idea where she was, she could see the sparkle of sun on the river. She walked towards it. The traffic was heavy and the crowds huge. Most of the people were young, a lot younger than herself. They surged, but sluggishly, along the pavements, taking photographs of the tall buildings, stopping to stare over the parapet of the bridge. She'd thought, when first she saw that flash of water, that she could drop the knife into the river, but now she was near it she saw how difficult that would be. And it might be against the law. Minty was always threatened by two disasters when she thought of breaking the law. One was the loss of her job and the other that it would cost her money. Also, lately, she'd been very conscious of people thinking there was something odd about her. Looking at her as if she weren't normal. Laf and Sonovia had looked at her that way when she'd talked to Mrs Lewis in the Underground. Of course they couldn't see Mrs Lewis, she'd known that. They hadn't been able to see Jock. It was a well-known fact that some people couldn't see ghosts. But that was no reason to treat a person as if she were mad. If she went on to that bridge and dropped a long, funny-shaped parcel over and into the water, that was what onlookers would think, that she was odd, crazy, mad.

She wandered along in a westerly direction where the crowd had thinned to not more than a couple of people going into the Atrium and a couple more waiting on the steps of Millbank Tower. It wouldn't do to get lost. She must stick close to a bus route. At Lambeth Bridge she turned up the Horseferry Road. Traffic was dense but the pavements were deserted. Finding herself quite alone and unwatched beside a litter bin, Minty dropped the knife into it and walked quickly away towards the bus stop.

That evening, while Minty was roving Westminster, the police in Kensal Green caught two boys climbing through a window into an abandoned shop. Once it had sold crystals and flower remedies and substances used in ayurvedic massage, but custom had never been good and it had closed for ever more than a year ago. The windows at the front had been boarded up and so had the door at the back. This led to a little yard enclosed by a high wall, the rear of the house in the street behind and a temporary structure of chipboard, corrugated iron and two doors from a demolished house. Although the only access to this yard was by way of a narrow alley blocked by a locked gate, it was full of rubbish, cans and broken bottles, newspapers and crisp bags. Across the back doorway itself a board had been nailed diagonally with another pinned across it but a small window had been left unboarded and had long since been smashed. The only law-abiding tenant among twelve in the house behind had seen the boys climb in through this window and had phoned the police.

They were children, both under ten. When the two officers found them they were upstairs in a dark little hole of a room where they had lit a candle and spread a brightly coloured crocheted shawl on the floor. This served both as something to sit on and keep them off the rough and splintery wood floor, and as a tablecloth. Laid out on it, as for a picnic, were a can of Fanta, two cans of coke, two cheeseburgers, two packs of cigarettes, two apples and a box of Belgian chocolates. Although still warm outside, it was cold in here, and the younger of the boys had wrapped a woolly scarf round his neck. Neither officer recognised it but one of them remembered that a long red scarf was missing from the holdall found beside the dead woman. It had been such a feature of Eileen Dring's habitual winter dressing that a lot of people identified her by it. They took the boys out of the house and back to their homes.

At first neither would say where he lived. A difficulty was that the police are not permitted to question children below the age of sixteen except in the presence of a parent or guardian. Eventually, after a lot of nudging and kicking from his friend, one of them gave his name and address and then, rather defiantly, the name and address of the other. Home for Kieran Goodall was half a housing association house in College Park and for Dillon Bennett a flat in a block on a council estate on the banks of the Grand Union Canal. No one was at home when they reached the street at the intersection of Scrubbs Lane with the Harrow Road, but Kieran, aged nearly nine, had a key. The place was dirty, untidy and furnished with grocer's boxes, two ancient leather armchairs and a card table. It smelt of marijuana and the centimetre-long stubs of two joints, still transfixed by pins, lay in a saucer. The woman officer stayed with Kieran while the man phoned for assistance and then drove Dillon home.

Two more officers from Violent Crimes were waiting for him when he got to Kensal Road. Dillon's mother was in and with her were her teenage boyfriend, her fourteen-year-old daughter, two other men in their twenties and a child of perhaps eighteen months. Everyone but the baby was drinking gin with beer chasers and the men were playing cards. Ms Bennett was rather the worse for drink but she agreed to accompany Dillon and the officers into the bedroom he shared – when he slept there – with his sister, the baby and a brother, aged thirteen, who was out.

Dillon, who hadn't said a word in the car and had left what talking there was to Kieran, answered the first questions that were put to him with 'Don't know' and 'Don't remember'. But when asked what he and Kieran had done with the knife he shouted loudly enough to make everyone jump that they'd dropped it down a drain.

Back in College Park reinforcements had turned up. They and the woman officer and Kieran waited. They were unable to talk to him and he said nothing to them. In silence they wondered. Was it possible that these two children had killed Eileen Dring for a shawl, a scarf, a can of drink and £140?

It was Laf's birthday and the whole family were gathered in Syringa Road. Julianna was there, her university term having just ended, and Corinne had come over with her new boyfriend. Daniel and Lauren had brought their daughter Sorrel and brought, too, the welcome news that Lauren was pregnant. The Wilsons' youngest child, Florian the musician, would look in some time after supper.

A question of some importance to them was whether or not Minty should be invited. For the sake of everyone's working hours, the party had to be in the evening. Minty would be at home.

'I thought it was supposed to be just family,' Sonovia had said.

'I think of Minty as family.'

374

'If I didn't know you inside out, Lafcadio Wilson, I'd sometimes think you fancied Minty.'

Laf was shocked. A man with a rigid moral code, he was horrified by even the fringes of adultery. His biggest nightmare (after untimely death) was that one of his children should be divorced. A bit premature, as Sonovia always said, since so far only one of them was married. 'Don't you be disgusting,' he said severely. 'You know how I hate that kind of talk.'

Sonovia always realised when she'd gone too far. She said rather huffily, 'It's your birthday. You do as you like. Maybe you'd like to ask Gertrude Pierce as well.'

Not deigning to reply, Laf went next door with the paper and invited Minty to his party.

She responded in her usual way, without enthusiasm, without saying thank you: 'All right.'

'It'll be just the family but we think of you as family, Minty.'

She nodded. It was as if, he thought, she accepted these things as her right. But she offered him a cup of tea and the kind of biscuit that brought the adjective "clean" into his mind, it was so pale, thin and dry. Rather like Minty herself, in fact. It had worried him in the past that she seemed to see things that weren't there and to talk to unseen people. Now she was calm, like an ordinary person. And when she arrived at the party she was the same, saying a cheerful 'hello' to everyone, helping herself, if cautiously, to food from Sonovia's lavish buffet, and when Florian turned up an hour earlier than anyone expected, greeting him with 'You are a stranger. Haven't seen you for a long time.'

The conversation turned to the murder of Eileen Dring. Laf had known it would and hoped it wouldn't. He refused to take part in it and thought his children ought to have known better than to speculate about one rumour that the chief suspects were a married couple in West Hampstead, and another that two young kids were responsible. He deflected Daniel away from it by reverting to the problem he'd first raised with Sonovia weeks before. Ever since then he'd been thinking of it on and off without coming to any conclusion. 'Suppose you killed someone without knowing it was wrong? I mean, suppose you had a sort of delusion that someone wasn't what they are but was - well, Hitler or Pol Pot, someone like that, and you killed them. Would that be wrong or wouldn't it?'

'What's brought this on, Dad?'

Why did one's children, better-educated than oneself, always ask that question if one ever dared say something out of the ordinary? Why did they always expect their parents to be mindless idiots? 'I don't know,' he said. 'I've been thinking a lot about it lately.'

' Did he know what he was doing,' asked Corinne, 'and if he did, did he know it was wrong?'

'Eh?' Laf said.

'It's a sort of test applied to defendants.'

'But is it wrong?'

'These days a psychiatrist would be called to examine him. And if he hadn't known what he was doing they'd put him away somewhere in a hospital for the criminally insane. I'd have thought you knew that, Dad. You're a police officer.'

Exasperated, Laf said, 'I do know it. I'm not asking if he'd have committed a crime. I know about crime. I'm asking if what he did would be *wrong*. What they used to call a sin. Morally wrong.'

His younger daughter, attracted by something more interesting than the conversation her mother had been having with Minty on the subject of spray starches, had been listening. He turned to her. 'You're doing philosophy at university, Julianna. You ought to know the answer. Would it be wrong?'

'That's not philosophy, Dad. That's ethics.'

'OK, but would it be wrong? Would it be a sin?'

Julianna looked as if the word embarrassed her. 'I don't know about sin. You'd have to know you were doing something against your moral code for it to be wrong. I mean, an Aztec who sacrificed a child to please his god would think he was doing right because it would be in accordance with his moral code, but the Catholic conquistador would know it was wrong because it was against his.'

'So there's no such thing as absolute wrong? It just depends on when and where you live?'

'Well, and on whether or not you're schizophrenic, I should think,' said Daniel.

It was to everyone's surprise that Minty spoke. 'Murder's wrong,' she said loudly. 'It's always wrong. It's taking away someone's life. You can't get round that.'

'If there was ever a gloomy subject for a birthday party', said Sonovia, 'this crowns it all. Open another bottle of wine, for goodness' sake, Laf.' She was at the window, where she'd moved when everyone converged on Laf and his problem in ethics. 'Minty,' she exclaimed. 'Look at this. There's an ambulance next door. It must be for Mr Kroot.'

Though midsummer, it was quite dark by now and raining, but they all crowded to the window to see the paramedics come out, not with a stretcher, but a wheelchair in which the old man sat, a blanket over his knees and another over his head.

'Heart attack or stroke,' said Sonovia. 'Take your pick. It could be either.'

Julianna was coming round with freshly filled wineglasses when the doorbell rang. The paramedic on the doorstep handed Sonovia a key and said, 'He says, will you feed his cat? There's tins in the cupboard.'

'What's he got wrong with him?'

'I couldn't say. There'll have to be tests.'

Kieran Goodall's mother Lianne finally came home at midnight. Though not verbally reproached for her absence from the house, she obviously believed that the best form of defence was attack. First she told the police officers that she wasn't Kieran's mother but his stepmother, so couldn't be held responsible for his behaviour. His mother had disappeared years ago and having married Lianne, his father also had gone. He and she, without claim on one another, had lived here for the past five years. Maybe she was his guardian, no one had made her so, it had just happened. Having asked, 'What's he done?' she hadn't waited for an answer but had launched into a tirade against the Social Services who, she said, had been only too pleased to 'dump' him on her and hadn't even tried to find his natural parents. Told about the money missing from Eileen Dring's holdall and the money found on Kieran and Dillon, she said that crazy old people ought to be stopped from carrying large sums about with them. It was a temptation to young kids. Kieran was asked about the knife. He'd put it in a litter bin, he said, and began shrieking with laughter.

'If you've had one of my knives, Kieran,' said his stepmother, 'I'll knock the living daylights out of you.'

Half a mile away in Kensal Road, Dillon Bennett had withdrawn his remark about putting the knife down a drain. He'd never seen a knife. By now, sitting in one of the battered leather armchairs squeezed up against his sister who had one arm round him, he told his questioners Eileen Dring had been dead when he and Kieran came upon her.

'How did you know she was dead, Dillon?'

'She was all over blood. Buckets of it. She had to be dead.'

His head drooped and he fell asleep.

Chapter 30

It seemed to Michelle in vain that she told Violent Crimes she and Matthew scarcely knew where the site of the murder was. This part of London was unknown territory. Like all Londoners, they had heard of the cemetery, but that was all.

' "Before we go to paradise," ' quoted Matthew, ' "by way of Kensal Green." '

They gave him uneasy smiles but Michelle thought they didn't believe her. An alibi? They no more had one for this killing than for the one in the cinema. As always, they could only alibi each other and what was the use of that? They'd been in bed, asleep.

When they'd arrived this time, Matthew had just come back from the studios where he'd been making the first in the next series of his programme and she'd been in the kitchen chopping mint for sauce. Matthew had progressed with such leaps and bounds that though he wouldn't, of course, eat lamb, which mint sauce naturally accompanied, he was growing quite fond of having it on potatoes and last week had even eaten a miniature Yorkshire pudding. Violent Crimes fixed his eyes on the knife in her hand, a big thing like a butcher's cleaver that could only be used to kill someone if you chopped their head off. But she had put it down and covered it and the mint with a sheet of kitchen roll as if she were guilty of the crime they seemed to suspect her of committing.

As usual these days she'd only been able to pick at the meal she'd prepared. But Matthew, by his standards, had eaten heartily of the potatoes and mint sauce, several slices of chicken, with caramel custard to follow. Six months ago he'd have thrown up at the sight of caramel custard. He talked about the programme, that this first one concentrated on how taking on a new interest in life, earning money and meeting new people could have a beneficent effect on the anorexic and citing himself as an example. Michelle always saw him with the eyes she'd seen the thin young man she'd fallen in love with, but even she, once she'd struggled to look at him as a stranger might, could make herself aware that he was very different in appearance from what he'd been the year before. This question of the images a woman might create of others and of herself interested her. She knew now that she'd always seen herself as fat, as a child, as a teenager, all through the years when she was normal sized, and she did so now after all the weight she had lost. Did Matthew always see himself as emaciated?

She went upstairs and mounted the scales. They registered a weight loss so dramatic that it would have been frightening in anyone who didn't know the reason for it. Stepping off, she looked at herself in the mirror and tried to apply that 'stranger's eyes' test. Up to a point she succeeded and for a moment or two the woman of twenty years ago looked back at her, a woman with just one chin, with a waist and a stomach which, though hardly flat, no longer made her appear in the seventh month of pregnancy. Once she'd turned away the fat lady was back. But what did it matter? What did any of it matter compared with their situation as suspects in two murder cases?

Matthew was washing the dishes. Or, rather, he had reached the stage of drying them. The mirrored woman, though not truly believed in when her reflection was gone, had just the same given Michelle the kind of self-esteem she hadn't known for a long time. She physically trembled when she realised what it was: sexual confidence. She put her arms round Matthew from behind and laid her cheek against his back. He turned round, smiling. It was years since she'd seen that particular look on his face. He put his arms round her and kissed her the way he'd kissed her the second time they'd met, and with a tremor of joy and pain she understood that after the years of terror he was courting her all over again.

Jims had arranged everything, from his solicitor's letter requesting Zillah to quit Abbey Gardens Mansions by the end of the week to the removal van which arrived at eight sharp on Friday morning. Another letter, this time from Jims himself and couched in the coolest terms, informed her she could keep her car. He would pay for Jordan's operation to be carried out privately in a Shaston nursing home. Sir Ronald Grasmere, for old friendship's sake, would permit her to move into Willow Cottage before completion of the purchase. He had already signed the contract.

A man who called himself Jims's agent (he seemed to have so many) came in and labelled every piece of furniture in the flat either 'for store' or 'for Long Fredington'. Even Zillah had to admit Jims had treated her handsomely. By now she was resigned to the end of those dreams of TV stardom or fashionable life, Buckingham Palace garden parties, the Royal Enclosure at Ascot and cruises on a peer's yacht. It was over and the crunch had come. But this time things would be very different. Her native optimism reasserted itself. She had the car. She had a vast wardrobe of new clothes. Willow Cottage was no longer rented from the wicked squire, it was *hers*.

Letting herself and the children in, she found the place even better than she'd been led to believe. The whole house carpeted and curtained, everything new in the bathroom and kitchen, gold taps and marble counter tops, built-in cupboards in all the rooms, a huge television and video. Almost with enthusiasm she arranged the furniture and made up the beds. She picked up the new phone and called her mother.

Eugenie surveyed the place without fervour. 'I liked it better the way it was.'

'Well, I didn't,' said Zillah.

'Want to see Titus.' On painkillers, Jordan was bemused but he'd stopped crying. 'Want Titus and Rosalba and Daddy.'

Zillah's eyes and Eugenie's met, as if they were the same age. 'Perhaps Annie will bring Titus and Rosalba round later.'

Annie didn't come round later but someone else did. He tapped on the back door at eight o'clock, just after Zillah had put Jordan to bed. Zillah had no idea who this very tall, rather good-looking man in his fifties might be and she stared at him, smiling uneasily.

'Ronald Grasmere. I live up at the big house, pal of old Jims.'

Zillah introduced herself by her Christian name alone. She was vague about what her surname might actually be these days. 'Sir Ronald, please come in.'

'Call me Ronnie. Everyone does. I've brought you a few strawberries from the kitchen garden and the last of the asparagus. It's not what it was a month ago but I think it's still worth eating.'

So this was her bogeyman, the slum landlord, the grinder of the faces of the poor, the fascist beast, as Jerry used to call people of his kind in their student days. The strawberries he'd brought were crimson, glowing, dewy and firm, rather different from what was on sale in Westminster shops. Eugenie appeared in her dressing gown.

'There's nothing to drink,' Zillah said. 'You could have a cup of tea.'

Sir Ronald laughed. 'I think you're wrong there, my dear. Just take a look inside that cupboard.'

Gin, whisky, vodka, sherry, several bottles of wine. Zillah gasped.

'Don't look at me. Nothing to do with me. That chap of old Jims saw to it when he came in the other day. Now what do you think of this little place? Not bad, is it, though I say it myself.'

The begging letter that came through Fiona's letter box, along with a flyer for a restaurant in West End Lane and her American Express monthly account, was from a woman she'd never heard of, someone called Linda Davies. As soon as she realised what it was she recoiled from it, screwed it up and was on the point of throwing it away. Then she remembered a resolve she'd made when first she'd read in the newspaper about Jeff's past. Slowly and with a certain amount of distaste, she retrieved it, smoothed out the creases in it and read to the end.

Linda was one of the women Jeff had lived with and used. 'Preyed on' was the expression she employed. She wrote that she had taken out a mortgage on her Muswell Hill flat so that he and she could start a business together. Soon after she handed him the money he'd disappeared. Then followed a tale of disaster piled on disaster: Linda Davies's loss of her job, her struggles to pay her now huge mortgage, her succumbing to Chronic Fatigue Syndrome. She'd read about Fiona in the newspaper, that she'd been living with Jeff when he died, was well-off and successful. All she was asking was for a thousand pounds to pay off her debts and enable her to make a new start.

Fiona felt physically ill when she read it. There seemed no end to Jeff's perfidy. How many other women had he wronged? Did the police know? One of them might be guilty of his murder. Throughout the investigation she had never really thought about who might have killed Jeff. She had given the police the names of a few possible enemies but not with much conviction. It didn't matter to her. If she had considered it at all it was some semi-underworld character that she'd vaguely settled on. Now she thought it might have been one of these women.

But when there was a second death, an old woman murdered by the same means, she revised her view. The perpetrator must be someone who knew both victims. And who fitted that description better than a woman from his past? Who better than herself? She phoned Violent Crimes as soon as she thought of this and before he had a chance to fasten on to her. But she didn't mention Linda Davies.

By now the police had dismissed the idea of Kieran Goodall and Dillon Bennett as Eileen Dring's killers. But they were useful witnesses. If their fantasies of how they disposed of the knife had varied and changed from hour to hour, their separate stories of the time they arrived at the murder site and what they saw when they got there tallied in every detail. They had arrived on the scene at one thirty on Sunday morning, a fact both knew because Dillon was wearing his new watch. This watch was another cause of speculation, dismissed for the time being on the grounds of there being more important things to attend to. It was stolen, that went without saying, though Dillon's stepmother swore she'd given it to him for his birthday the previous month. Wherever it came from, it showed exactly one thirty. Both boys had looked at it. Watching videos had taught them the significance of noting the time at crime scenes, for they knew this was a crime, though they weren't frightened. Another interesting – and appalling – factor was that neither saw anything out of the way in being out in the streets in the middle of the night. Nocturnal wanderings were what they did. They slept half the day and mostly missed school.

Kieran and Dillon had lifted Eileen Dring's head, remarking that it had felt warm to the touch and not stiff, pulled out the bag, emptied it on to the pavement and helped themselves to its contents. The money was an unexpected windfall. They took everything but Eileen's cardigan for which they had no use, and carried off their haul to the abandoned shop where they had a sanctuary they called their 'camp'. If they'd seen anyone on the streets in those small hours they hadn't noticed or weren't telling. The police were done with them. It was now a case for the Social Services.

The two police officers sat in Fiona's living room, listening to the history of her encounters with Eileen Dring through the years. Too late, Fiona understood what she'd done in volunteering information that might have remained undiscovered. Gradually it seemed to dawn on these two officers that here was a prime suspect, a woman who'd been living with one victim and been friend and benefactor to the other.

'You mean she sometimes slept in your garden?'

'No, but I offered her the use of my shed. Only I felt awful about it. I thought I should have said to come inside and sleep in the house and I said that to her. But she told me she'd got a room of her own if that was what she wanted. Sleeping indoors didn't suit her and she wouldn't have my shed either.'

'Why did you make these offers, Miss Harrington?'

'I suppose I was sorry for her.'

'Did you ever give her money?'

'She wasn't a beggar.'

'Maybe not but did she ever try to get money from you?'

Were they implying Eileen had blackmailed her? Fiona felt herself trapped in a snare of her own devising. She remembered various occasions of quixotry, a handful of change here, a five-pound note there, and Jeff's indignation.

'Jeff told me not to give her anything, but I did sometimes. I tried not to do it near here. I'd give her money if I came upon her somewhere else – near a flower shop, I mean. She told me a lot about herself. Her children had died in a fire. They got her out but hadn't been able to save the children. That turned her brain, I think. She'd been strange ever since.'

She could tell by their faces that these facts were already known to them. They asked her if she could account for her movements on Saturday night but she could only say she'd been in bed asleep. With Jeff's death, she said, staying up late, going out in the evenings, had come to an end for her. They told her to phone the bank and say she wouldn't be in and they asked her to accompany them to the police station. She was too horrified to argue, too aghast even to ask for an explanation. There she sat on a hard chair in an interview room for several hours, answering a string of questions but turning over in her mind how she could prove she'd been at home on Saturday night.

Then the answer – or an answer – came to her. She hadn't slept well. She never had since Jeff died and her dependency on sleeping pills troubled her. Night after night she tried to sleep without taking one and almost always she succumbed. So it had been on Saturday. Some time after midnight, nearly an hour after, she thought, she had got up and gone to the window, hearing as she crossed the floor a door closed in the house next door. That was all you ever heard, the shutting of a door or a light being turned on or off. And when she drew back a curtain she saw the light from Michelle's and Matthew's bedroom window go out. It had shed a bright rectangle on to their front lawn, a light that was abruptly withdrawn, she told Violent Crimes.

And she saw at once that they doubted her. 'We'll see if we can get some other neighbour to corroborate that.' It would let you and those Jarveys off the hook, she could tell they were thinking. She clasped her hands together, almost praying. If she could undo the harm she'd done to Michelle and Matthew she'd be as happy as if she'd exonerated herself.

Calling next door when they'd let her go brought fresh unjustified guilt. She felt the police must be watching her. Who, for instance, was that boy on the other side of the street? He looked no more than eighteen but he was probably twenty-five. He was sitting on a garden wall, apparently reading the *Standard*. Fiona thought he could be a policeman who had been sent to follow her home and see what she did. She was looking over her shoulder at him when Michelle opened the door. He'd think she and the Jarveys were in some sort of conspiracy together.

When Michelle heard Fiona's story of her day, she couldn't help feeling a flash of exultation that her neighbour, who had brought all this trouble on Matthew and her, was now in the same jeopardy as themselves. And even as she thought this she reproached herself for her mean-spiritedness. It was such a far cry from the way she'd felt about Fiona a month ago. Michelle took Fiona's hand and kissed her cheek to make things better but still they weren't better. Matthew opened a bottle of wine and Fiona drank hers greedily.

'I'm sure he's a policeman on surveillance.'

Michelle went to the window, noticing as she did so how easy it was now for her to get up out of soft cushions and how lightly she walked. 'It's not a policeman,' she said. 'He's the nephew of the woman who lives there. He hasn't a key and he's waiting for her to come home.'

'You don't think I'd have harmed Jeff or Eileen, do you?'

Michelle didn't answer. It was Matthew, always brave and always one to speak his mind, who said, 'You thought *we* had.'

Fiona said nothing. She walked to the window, stood by Michelle and gazed out into the street. Suddenly she wheeled round and said, 'I've had a begging letter. From a woman Jeff – got money out of.' Michelle laid a hand softly on her shoulder. 'Oh, I know what he was. I've learnt a lot since he died. She wants a thousand pounds.'

'You're not going to give it to her, I hope,' said Matthew. 'She's hardly your responsibility.'

'I *am* going to. I've just decided, just this minute. I can afford it. I won't even notice the difference.'

Chapter 31

Mill Lane was a very different place in July from what it had been in December. Or perhaps it was that Zillah was a different woman, for the weather was cold for the time of year and this was the kind of day when an anticyclone would as likely create a misty chill as warm sunshine. She was coming back from the Old Mill House where she'd left Eugenie and Jordan playing on Titus's new climbing frame, while she drove to the supermarket. Jordan was due to go into hospital for his operation in four days' time but these days only cried when he fell over. Zillah was dressed in the new natural-coloured linen trouser suit she'd bought in a boutique in Toneborough and, though she wasn't quite warm enough, she knew you had to suffer to be beautiful.

Treading carefully, watching her feet on the flat stones of the ford so as not to wet her narrow-strap sandals, she looked up to see Ronnie Grasmere approaching down the lane, accompanied by an enormous dog like an animated black hearthrug. For a moment she thought the dog was going to leap on her and, more to the point, on her suit. Ronnie, who was carrying a gun, said a quiet but commanding, 'Sit,' and the animal immediately did so, its forepaws straight, head held high. Zillah was impressed and said so.

'No point in having a dog if he's your master.'

Zillah nodded. Never before had she known a

voice to be so plummy and old Etonian. 'And where are you off to, my pretty maid?'

Resisting an impulse to say she was going a-milking, Zillah told him.

'I say, d'you have to do your own shopping? What a shame.'

'Most people do, don't they?'

His answer was hearty laughter. 'Shoot, do you?'

She was more than ever aware of the gun sort of folded over his arm. Broken, did they call it? 'I never have.' Sensing it was the kind of thing he'd like a woman to say, she added, 'I'd be scared.'

'Not you. I'll teach you.'

'Would you really?'

'Look, I have to take this great beast walkies, so alas I must leave you. But why don't you have dinner with me one night? Tonight?'

'I couldn't tonight.' She could have but playing hard to get was never wrong.

'Tomorrow, then?'

'That would be nice.' It would be her twenty-eighth birthday.

Ronnie said he'd pick her up at seven. They'd go to a pleasant little unpretentious place outside Southerton called Peverel Grange. Zillah knew its reputation as the best restaurant in South Wessex. She walked back to Willow Cottage feeling better than she had for months. Annie would probably babysit for her or she'd know someone who would.

None of the neighbours in Holmdale Road had been able to confirm Fiona's story. They were Londoners and took very little notice of what the people next door or the people opposite did. Their requirement in the neighbours was that they should keep from playing music at night, control their children and keep their dogs in. Only one couple had even known the Jarveys' name. All of them knew more about Fiona, whose notoriety came from her having been the murdered man's partner. But where she had been that Saturday night, home or away, no one could tell. On the subject of cars they were more vociferous. Violent Crimes and Miss Demeanour had nothing to do with motor vehicles, except the ones they drove themselves, and were uninterested in the conduct of users of the two train stations who clogged West Hampstead streets with their parked cars. When would Camden Council introduce residents' parking was the question four out of five householders asked. Violent Crimes neither knew nor cared. They were no nearer having a clue where the Jarveys and Fiona Harrington had been that night than when they started.

Newspapers had begun asking when the Cinema Slayer would strike again. It would have been easier for them if the two victims hadn't been such disparate characters, if they'd been, for instance, young women. Then the stories they carried might have included warnings that no girl was safe on London's streets. But what had a young, good-looking, comfortably situated man in common with an elderly female vagrant, except that neither had any money or owned property? All they knew was that there was nothing rational about this killer, no plan of action and apparently no particular category of victims he or she targeted. Not politicians or vivisectionists, prostitutes or rich old women, capitalists or anarchists. What did the killer get out of it? No financial benefit, no sexual satisfaction, restored security or freedom from menaces. Newspapers started calling the murderer the 'mindless' or 'aimless' killer.

The neighbours in Holmdale Road had known Michelle and Matthew only well enough to say

'Good morning' or 'Hi' (according to age) and Fiona only as the woman who had lost her fiancé in a very dreadful way. Being questioned as to these people's movements on the night Eileen Dring was killed changed their attitude to this no longer harmless couple and this no longer blameless young woman.

There was no concerted campaign of ostracism and no dramatic shunning. But the woman whose nephew Fiona had suspected might be a detective began looking the other way when she passed her and the man next door to her, who'd always looked up from his weeding to comment on the weather, now kept his head down. The red graffiti that appeared on Fiona's gateposts might have nothing to do with the murders, it might be coincidence, but, if it was, the aptness of the graffitist spraying *Kill, Kill* on the stucco wasn't lost on her.

Fiona thought it was the police back again when the doorbell rang on a Saturday morning at about ten. She felt like telling them to arrest her and have done with it. A point had been reached when she was beginning to understand how people made false confessions of murder so that they would be left alone and have a little peace. She opened the door to a woman about her own age. It wasn't Miss Demeanour but someone of similar build, age and dress. Another police officer?

'Good morning,' the woman said. 'My name is Natalie Reckman. I'm a freelance journalist?'

Fiona said, rudely for her, 'What do you want?'

'They've made a real mess of your gateposts, haven't they?'

'They're brainless morons. I don't suppose it's personal.'

'No? May I come in? I don't want to talk about Jeff's murder or who did what to whom. I was once his girlfriend too.'

'When?' Fiona's mouth had dried. She felt a frisson of terror.

'Oh, long before you. Don't worry. A woman from Kensal Green came between me and you.'

Fiona had to know. She couldn't resist it. 'Come in.'

Though the feature on the women in Jeff Leach's life had been shelved, Natalie hadn't been able to put it into the back of her mind as she had hoped. It kept surfacing. And one morning, when she woke after a dream in which she was hunting for the missing Jims Melcombe-Smith in Guatemala, the name of her predecessor came back to her. There it was, absolutely clear as if her memory had never mislaid it: Nell Johnson-Fleet and she'd worked for a charity called Victims of Crime International or VOCI. Of course, Johnson-Fleets are not exactly thick on the ground, and Natalie soon found her address and phone number in the phone book.

Perhaps something was telling her the time had come to concentrate on this story. She made herself recall that last conversation she'd ever had with Jeff. In Christopher's in Covent Garden it had been and when she'd asked who came after her he'd said, 'A funny little thing who lived opposite Kensal Green Cemetery. I don't think I'll tell you her name. I called her Polo . . . ' Knowing Jeff as she did and in possession of this limited information, had she a chance of finding this woman? For a start, he probably hadn't meant she lived precisely opposite the cemetery but on the other side of the Harrow Road in one of the streets that lay behind it. Natalie got out her London atlas and turned to page 56. There was a positive web of little streets in that hinterland. Instead of making a list of them, she photocopied the atlas page. At a cost of £200 you could buy a CD to put on the Internet which would give you the names, addresses and a dossier of every single citizen of the United Kingdom. Or so she'd read in some cyberspace magazine. But would it help? She thought she still preferred the old-fashioned electoral register.

Why would he have called the woman Polo? He had that peculiar addiction to Polo mints, chewed up a tube of them every couple of days, so this woman must have had something in common with them. Incongruously, she remembered Jeff's funeral and the wreath of white rosebuds his father and the person called Beryl had sent. It had looked just like a mammoth version of a mint with a hole in it. Mint, she thought, mint, hold on to that, as she consulted the voters' list for the London Borough of Brent.

A woman called Minton was perhaps what she was looking for. Could you be called 'Peppermint'? She turned page after page. Those eligible to vote are listed in the electoral register according to street, not name. If she was very young or a lunatic or a peer she wouldn't be listed, but she couldn't be under eighteen, could she? Jeff had surely never gone for very young girls. If she wasn't a British citizen she wouldn't be there either. Natalie thought that a distinct possibility as she ran her finger down the side of the pages. A lot of immigrants settled in this area, many of them waiting for naturalisation. Surely, when he'd briefly talked of 'Polo', said where she lived and that he owed her money, he'd have mentioned that she was Asian or African or from Eastern Europe.

She'd started a long way back, almost as far as the North Circular Road, the borough limit, and now she'd come close in her search to the Harrow Road and the cemetery. Only Lilac Road remained after Syringa and then she'd have to acknowledge that this line of investigation had failed. Her finger on the left-hand margin stopped. Here, at number 39, was something. *Knox, Araminta K.* No one else in the house, apparently. Just this one single woman.

'Minta', she probably called herself. That would be a gift to Jeff who would immediately have thought of his Polos. She could hear him saying it. 'I shall call you Polo.' Polo, Polo, the rick stick Stolo, round tail, bobtail, well done, Polo. She lived alone, so very likely owned her house. Natalie remembered Jeff trying to make her take out a second mortgage on her flat to start some business he enthused about. By then she knew him well enough to be quite sure he'd do no such thing, but spend the money on horses and other women. Was that how he came to owe this Polo a thousand pounds? Because he'd got her to mortgage her house?

It was a bit far-fetched, perhaps. Certainly a woman living in that neighbourhood, in Syringa Road, wouldn't be well-off; she wouldn't be able to afford to lose such a sum.

'I don't want to hear this,' Fiona said, wishing she'd never asked this Reckman woman in and determined not to mention Linda Davies.

'Well, no, it's not very pleasant for me either. I was fond of Jeff myself. But I knew what he was.'

Like a child being told frightening things, Fiona covered her ears. Not usually timid or shy, she found this woman overwhelming. The trouble was that even with her hands over her ears she could still hear.

'It was a thousand pounds. He told me himself. As I'm sure you know, he had lunch with me on the day he was killed. I'm certain this Araminta Knox couldn't afford to lose that amount. Not living in a little backstreet in what's practically Harlesden. Did he have money off you?'

'We were going to be married!'

'Well, hardly, my dear. He was married to Zillah Melcombe-Smith, aka Watling, aka Leach. I'll tell you frankly that while he was with me I paid all the bills and let him have the use of my car. *And* gave him pocket money. He called it loans but I was never under any illusions of that sort. I suppose it was the same thing with you. When did you think your wedding was going to be, may I ask?'

'August,' said Fiona, 'and no, you may not. I'd like you to go now, please.'

Natalie was quite willing to comply. She'd got a great deal: the furnishings of the house, the carpets and paintings, Fiona's clothes and her general appearance, as well as a lot of admissions as to her feelings for Jeff. 'You really ought to be gratified,' she said as a parting shot. 'He must have left this Araminta for you, you know.'

'For my money,' said Fiona bitterly and then wished she hadn't.

Once Natalie had gone, she began to cry. Ever since Jeff's death her illusions, as that woman called them, had gradually been stripped away. She would soon be left with nothing but her bare love, bruised and scarred as it was. After a while she dried her eyes, washed her face and looked for Araminta Knox in the phone book. There she or someone called Knox was, at 39 Syringa Road, NW10. Why are we such inquisitive beings that even in great despair and sorrow curiosity impels us to seek answers that probe into old wounds?

She went next door, passing, of course, the offending gateposts on her way out. The informality of using the back door was gone, she was sure, for ever and she was back to ringing the bell. They still kissed, she and Michelle, lips not quite touching cheeks. 'I really came to ask you both to come in and have a drink with me. There's something I have to tell you. Do come.'

They hadn't done so for a long time. Not since, like a crass fool, she'd said that stupid thing to the police about their disliking Jeff. Michelle hesitated. Perhaps there was something in Fiona's face, a look of beseeching, of tears hardly dried, that made her say, 'All right. Just for half an hour.'

The first thing Michelle noticed when she came into Fiona's living room was that there was something different about the mantelpiece. An expensive-looking alabaster and silver urn had joined the clock and the candlesticks. She said nothing. Fiona had put champagne on ice. 'Is there something to celebrate?' Michelle asked.

'Nothing. When you're feeling really down, you put out more flags, don't you?'

Matthew extracted the cork skilfully, without spilling a drop. Raising her glass, Fiona said, 'I want to ask your advice.' She told them what she knew of Araminta Knox.

'Have you told the police about her? Have you told them about the one who wrote you the begging letter?'

Fiona looked at Matthew in surprise. 'Why would I do that?'

'It's another suspect, isn't it? Someone else for them to persecute instead of us.'

'I did what I told you I'd do about Linda Davies. I sent her the money. And it made me feel better, a bit better.'

Looking down at the glass in her hand, watching the bubbles rise, Michelle said, trying to keep her tone equable, 'You sent her a thousand pounds? You sent her a cheque?'

'I thought she might not have a bank account so I sent notes, fifty-pound notes, packed into a padded bag. And I felt I was – well, righting the wrongs Jeff did. I'd begun to do that. I know what he was now, you see. I know he preyed on women' – she used Linda Davies's expression, her voice rising – 'and had no compunction about it. Rich women and poor women, it didn't much matter to him so long as they kept him and put a roof of their own over his head. His death was a lucky escape for me, wasn't it?'

'Oh, Fiona, I'm so sorry . . .'

'Perhaps that was my motive for murdering him. What do you think? A means of escape I hadn't the courage to take any other way. The trouble is I still love him, just as much as I did when I thought he was honest and decent.'

After they had gone Fiona sat for a long while staring at the urn on the mantelpiece. She had thought of scattering Jeff's ashes somewhere nearby, perhaps on Fortune Green, but these latest revelations about his life had changed her mind. The urn had cost her a small fortune, which was quite funny, really, if you were in the mood to be amused. She took it off the mantelpiece and, crawling on all fours, put it at the back of the dark cupboard under the stairs.

Chapter 32

With Jock gone and his mother gone, Minty grew more confident. Coming into the house gradually ceased to be an ordeal. When she went upstairs to bed or to have her bath, she no longer feared seeing Auntie and Mrs Lewis in a bedroom doorway. Auntie's absence had by now been of long duration. She hadn't seen her since June – or was it May?

Like a member of a tribe placating the god, she faithfully put flowers on Auntie's grave, though since confusing the original one with another, she had become much freer about where her offerings went. Any grave with an angel playing a musical instrument would do. The dead were everywhere, could go anywhere and, now Auntie had left the house, Minty had no doubt she ranged the cemetery from resting place to resting place. She was always careful, though, to choose a woman's. Auntie, who had so much disliked marriage, would never lay herself down in the neighbourhood of a man's bones.

While she kept up the practice of bringing flowers every week, ranunculus and zinnias, carnations and by now chrysanthemums, she knew Auntie would be pacified. It was with a little shiver that Minty sometimes remembered how indignant she'd been at past failures in this particular regard. Never again. A life free of ghosts would be a life of peace.

The weather had become hot and sultry. Sometimes a thick mist of fumes and emissions hung over the Harrow Road. Everything seemed dirtier and smellier than in winter and taking two baths a day was a regular thing for Minty. Fourteen months had passed since first she met Jock and nine since his death. Having barely thought of him for a long time, she was aware that he had re-entered her mind so that she wondered how it would have been if he'd lived. Would she have been happy? Would she have got pregnant like Josephine? It gave her something of a shock when she realised she'd have been Mrs Lewis too. All the baths she took reminded her how he'd taken her savings and when he died, let his mother inherit them. What had become of that money now? She was as far off getting a shower installed as ever and now she began to wish she'd used the money for that purpose so that there had been nothing to give Jock.

Then, one warm morning that promised another hot day, when she'd had her bath and was dressing to go to work, she heard his voice. She heard him singing at her out of her bedroom wall. Not 'Walk On By' this time but 'Tea for Two'.

'Tea for two and two for tea . . .'

She was too frightened to make a sound. Then, as the phrase was repeated, followed by the next line, and he broke off to laugh, she managed to whisper, 'Go away, go away.'

He seemed to take notice of what she said, for instead of addressing her again, he began talking to other, equally invisible, people: a group of nameless friends, with voices she'd never heard before and which mingled, indistinguishable from each other and uttering a rattle of meaningless words. Then Jock intervened, offering them a mint or making one of his strange jokes, the like of which Minty had never heard elsewhere. If she were to see him she thought it would be the death of her but she didn't see him.

She saw none of them and what made her more terrified than she'd ever been was a sudden easily identifiable voice replying to him. His mother's.

Like her son, she'd been banished only for a while. Minty shivered, touching wood, doing more than that, clutching it, holding hard on to the edge of a table, the frame of a door. She ought to have known you can't get rid of ghosts so easily, you can't stab them and kill them like those gangs killed real people. It wasn't the way. Were they with her for life, these men and women she didn't know? Jock's family? That ex-wife of his, his relatives?

The post coming, the rattle of the letter box, the thump of something falling on the doormat and the crash of the lid closing again, distracted her. A welcome interruption that sent her downstairs, still combing her wet hair. She never got much post. What came was mostly services bills and advertisements from estate agents wanting to sell her houses in St John's Wood. Like Auntie, when an unfamiliar envelope arrived she spent a long time scrutinising it, studying the postmark, deciphering the handwriting or frowning over the printing, before putting her thumb under the flap and opening it. Here was the usual junk mail and with it a mysterious package. It was a thick, padded brown envelope, the like of which she'd never received before, and her name and address were written on a white label. It had cost more to send than ordinary first-class mail. Carefully, she slit the flap and opened it.

Inside was money. Twenty fifty-pound notes, held together with an elastic band. No letter, no card, nothing else. But she knew who it was from: Mrs Lewis. She was dead but there must be someone still on earth she could get to do this for her, someone else she'd haunted and spoken to. Maybe Jock had had a brother or sister; he'd never said he hadn't.

Minty decided that was who it was, a brother who'd inherited the money Mrs Lewis left. She'd not ignored the things Minty had said about giving back her money, they'd gone home and when she appeared to her son she'd asked him what she ought to do.

Maybe that's what they'd been talking about, that crowd whose anonymous voices had jabbered and whispered in the bedroom. Give her back the money, Mother, they'd been saying, and though she'd argued and perhaps Jock had argued too, the brother and his wife had told her it was only right to return the money. It was the only explanation. Not all Jock owed, though, only a thousand. Minty could hear – in her mind's ear, not ghosts talking – that mean old Mrs Lewis insisting on the smaller sum and winning her son over.

Mr Kroot's old cat was asleep in one of Sonovia's armchairs. As usual, because it never sat sphynx-like as most cats do, but lay stretched out and slack, it looked dead. You had to examine it closely to discern the minuscule rise and fall of its thin side.

'It's moved in, my deah.' Sonovia contemplated the cat with detachment. 'It turned up on the doorstep and that was that. I must say, it's easier giving it its food in here than going round to that dirty place. Ooh, the smell in that kitchen, you wouldn't believe it. What Gertrude Pierce did with herself all the time she was here I never will know. Laf went in to see the old man, you know. Went into the hospital, I mean. I said not to. What have they ever done for us, I said. But he would do it.'

'Let bygones be bygones,' said Laf, the peacemaker. 'I mean, I don't know for a fact if he said that about going back to the jungle. It was repeated third-hand to me. It might have got sort of distorted on the way. He's in a bad way, Minty. I took him a half-bottle of Scotch, he's not supposed to have it in there, but you should have seen him. His whole face lit up. It's a terrible thing to be old and alone.'

'I'm alone.' As she spoke Minty heard the voices returning, at first like the murmur of a crowd a long way off, then jostling each other and interrupting and sometimes laughing so that she couldn't make out a single word. As if Laf and Sonovia weren't there or didn't matter, she said, 'Well, I suppose I've always got people with me. Wish I didn't. You can have too much of that.'

The Wilsons exchanged glances and Laf went to get the drinks. Sonovia and Minty went into the garden and sat down in the patio chairs, and Minty admired her neighbours' hanging baskets. The garden was all dahlias and hollyhocks now, the lawn yellowing from the drought. Not a breath of wind stirred the boughs of the cherry tree. The sky was colourless, a sheet of unbroken whitish cloud in which the sun showed like a pool of dull yellow. Laf came out with a tray on which were tall glasses filled with amber liquid surfaced by maraschino cherries and chunks of apple and cucumber. Pimms was his summer craze. He offered the drinks proudly and handed round a dish of macadamia nuts.

'Not cold, are you, my deah?' Sonovia said to Minty who had shivered. She'd just heard Jock's voice say, 'I can tell you're an old-fashioned girl, Polo. There aren't many around like you.'

'Something walked on my grave.' Minty was afraid to say it. She made herself, as if it were a way of forcing the ghost voice to go away. 'Or maybe on Auntie's, over in the cemetery.' She saw Sonovia and Laf exchange glances again but she pretended she hadn't. It couldn't have been Jock's voice; she'd banished him and he'd gone. She'd imagined it or the drink had brought it on. She shivered again and remembered what she'd come for in the first place. 'You had the builders in last spring, doing something in the kitchen.'

'That's right, Minty.' Laf was always relieved when she said normal, ordinary things, when she talked your language. He smiled encouragingly. 'It was when we had the new units put in.'

'Will you do me a favour?'

'That depends on what it is,' said Sonovia, but Laf said, 'Of course we will. That goes without saying.'

'Well, then, will you tell them to come next door and look at my bathroom and work out what putting a shower in would cost?'

'Nothing easier. And when he comes Sonny will let him in and keep an eye on him while he's there.'

When she'd first seen him – that is, seen his ghost – he hadn't spoken. He'd been silent and somehow menacing, so that he'd frightened her the way he never had done when he was alive. She remembered very clearly how she'd come home from work and seen him sitting in that chair with his back to her, his hair dark-brown, his neck brown and his leather jacket black. His feet had shuffled back as if he'd meant to get up and that was when she'd shut her eyes because she was afraid to see his face. When she opened them again the ghost was gone but she knew he'd been there because when she felt the seat of the chair it was warm. She thought he might follow her upstairs but he hadn't, he hadn't been upstairs, not that time. Later on she saw him in that room again and in the hall and in her bedroom. She saw him in the shop. He'd never spoken.

Most people would say it was worse to see a ghost than to hear one. She wasn't so sure. Auntie and Mrs Lewis had chattered away and been very clearly visible. When Jock spoke to her it was against a background of voices muttering and whispering but only his words were understandable. The rest of it was like a twittering in a foreign language, it was like those Iranian people talked when they came out of the house opposite in a crowd. She'd rid herself of Jock's ghost and his mother's ghost by stabbing them with those long knives. But you couldn't be free of sounds that way. You'd somehow have to block your ears.

Like the ghosts she could see, the ghosts she could hear weren't there all the time. At night there was peace. Then she had silence in which to think. Stabbing the ghosts had maybe only got rid of the sight of them but she now knew it wasn't permanent. It worked for a while but only a while, and when the ghosts came back they let their voices come first to warn her that soon she'd see them. Putting flowers on Auntie's grave had been even more effective than the stabbings, for she'd never seen or heard Auntie again. Jock must have a grave somewhere, his mother must have a grave. If she could find out where those graves were she could put flowers on them as well.

When the voices had been with her for a week and Jock had said all the things to her that he used to say – Adam and Eve and Pinch Me, you're an old-fashioned girl, Polo, it's only April Fools' Day till twelve and after that it's Tailpike Day, only two thousand, Minty, it's our future that's at stake – she went into the cemetery by her usual gate, stopping on the way to buy flowers from the man with the stall. It was a Saturday but there was hardly anyone about. This time she'd brought a bottle of water, cold from the kitchen tap, to refill the vase. She bought pale-yellow chrysanthemums, the kind that have short petals in their centres and long thin ones on

406

their rims, and white gypsophila like snowflakes and alstro-somethings that she couldn't pronounce.

Maisie Julia Chepstow, beloved wife of John Chepstow, who departed this life on December 15th, 1897, aged 53. Asleep in the arms of Jesus. Auntie's grandmother. Minty had told herself this so often that now she believed it. She pulled out the dead flowers and poured away the smelly green water that had petals and a dead snail floating in it. There was enough fresh water to rinse the vase out before filling it. When the yellow and white and peach-coloured flowers were arranged, she knelt down on Maisie Chepstow's grave and did something she hadn't done for a long time. She prayed to Auntie to take away Jock's voice and the voices of the crowd that accompanied him wherever he was.

A bath when she got home. Laf didn't come in with the paper until quite late in the afternoon. She hadn't heard the voices since she offered up that prayer but she was still going to ask. 'How can you find out where someone's grave is?'

'You'd have to know where they died. Maybe you could get the death certificate. People don't have graves much these days, Minty. They get cremated so they'd be ashes. Why do you want to know?'

That business about the death certificate confused her. She knew she'd never be able to do those things, go to the right place, talk to the right people. Perhaps Laf would do it for her. 'It's Jock's grave I want to find.' She wasn't going to mention his mother. Not yet, anyway.

'Oh, right.' Laf was embarrassed.

'D'you think you could?'

'I'll see,' he said. 'It might not be possible.' He was moved by pity for her. 'Minty, wouldn't it be a good idea to – well – put the past behind you? Try and

407

forget him? You're young, you've got your whole future before you. Can't you forget the past?'

She shook her head. 'I can't,' she said and, in a burst of frankness, 'I keep hearing his voice talking to me.'

Saying he'd see what he could do, Laf went home. Daniel was there. He'd been visiting a bed-bound patient in First Avenue and had called in for tea.

'I suppose it's time someone told her the truth,' Sonovia said.

'I don't think so, Mum. I wouldn't.'

'She could go right over the edge.' Laf cut himself a slice of a very sticky banoffee pie. 'I mean, what's best? To believe your boyfriend loved you and met his death in a train crash? Or that he deceived you rotten and is still alive and kicking somewhere, living off some other woman?'

'You checked up, did you, Dad?'

'I was always more or less certain. That letter she had was an obvious con. Then I checked when the inquiry into the crash was on back in May. Thirty-one people died. They thought at first it was hundreds but it was only thirty-one. I say "only", that was bad enough, my goodness.'

'And there was no Jock Lewis among them?'

'You should think of your heart before you eat that stuff, Lafcadio Wilson.'

'Who put it on the table, I'd like to know?'

'It was meant for me, Dad. No Jock Lewis?'

'No Jock or John Lewis. And what's more, no man not accounted for. Every man on that list had a name and an address and age and dependants or whatever, and not one of them could have fitted him. And now she wants me to find his grave.'

'Just say you can't, Laf. Pass it off. She'll soon forget about it.'

'What does she want his grave *for*?'

'What d'you think, Dan? To put flowers on like she does on her auntie's faithfully every week.'

Mrs Lewis had only sent her half what she owed her. Or Jock's brother had. If she'd had his address she'd have written to him and asked for the rest. Still, she'd got enough for what she really wanted, the only thing she wanted when you came to think of it. The man hadn't come yet but Laf said she'd easily have it done for a thousand pounds and he'd picked up some brochures for her from a builder's merchant in Ladbroke Grove. Looking at the pictures, she could see she'd never afford a separate shower cabinet, the kind you walked into. Laf had been wrong there. Still, having one put in over the bath and a glass wall with hinges built to keep the water off the floor, that would be just as good. Better, really, because a cabinet meant one more thing to clean every day. So long as there wasn't a messy shower curtain that would get splashes of dried soap all over it.

The voices crowded in on her while she was studying the one she'd have installed. Jock and Mrs Lewis and another that must be Jock's dad. It couldn't be his brother. His brother was still alive. He must have been to send her the money. Maybe the ex-wife was dead too and the brother's wife. Were they all there because she'd never visited Jock's grave?

They never answered but she asked just the same. 'Where's he buried? Where have they put Jock?'

Silence. It wasn't a reply, more a piece of knowledge that suddenly appeared inside her head. No one said it, for the voices had once more gone away. The thought, the fact, came in and she knew absolutely that it was true. He's in the one by

Chelsea football ground. As if she hadn't understood, it came again. The one by Chelsea football ground.

Edna had lived down there. When she was a little girl and Edna was still alive, had another ten years to live, Auntie used to take her over there to Edna's for tea. She had a little grey house, one of a long, flat-fronted row, with a front door opening on to the pavement. Minty went over there in the evening after work and she took a knife with her. One of the smaller ones from the drawer. She went by bus, or rather a series of buses, ending up on the 11, which took her to Fulham Broadway.

It was years since she'd been there, twenty-five years. Even then, the football hooligans used to break the place up if their team got beaten by Chelsea. Auntie had pointed out smashed shop fronts to her and turned the demonstration into a lesson on the wickedness of destroying property. No smashed windows now, none of the old shops. The place had been smartened up. She went to look at Edna's house. It was as bright and fresh now as the Wilsons', with a red front door and carriage lamps, frilly curtains inside the windows and window boxes full of flowers outside them. All the houses were like that, only the flowers were of different kinds and the doors blue or yellow. Edna always wore a crossover overall and slippers, and a turban like she had on the production line during the war. Most of the time Uncle Wilfred was in his darkroom developing his photographs. He wanted Minty to go in there with him but Auntie wouldn't let her, not unless the door was left open, which it obviously couldn't be in a darkroom. She didn't know why it was forbidden, hadn't then and didn't now, though she could still remember the meaningful glances Auntie and Edna

410

exchanged when Uncle Wilfred shrugged and turned away.

She entered the cemetery from the Old Brompton Road end. Although she had often gazed at it from Edna's windows – there was little else to do – she'd never been in before. And she found it frightening in a way Kensal Green never was. This had something to do with the eight-sided chapel and curving colonnades you had to pass by or between, something perhaps with the gloom of the evening, a typical London summer evening of heavy cloud and excluded sun and windless thick air, though it was still a long way off twilight. There was a tomb with a lion on it like the lions in Trafalgar Square and another piled with black cannonballs. As she walked she was sure she would meet her ghosts, or some of them, or one. Jock himself frightened her more than the others. With old women, even with their shades, she could cope. But she sensed in Jock a violence she had never known from him in life. It was as if, in death, he was slowly realising his full potential of savagery and malice.

As she looked to the right and left of her for his grave, for a new grave, perhaps only a mound with as yet no memorial stone, she tried to comfort herself with the thought of the new shower that was coming, that Jock's brother or sister-in-law had been considerate enough to pay for. But the distraction barely worked. She knew by this time that there were no recent burials in this dark, forlorn cemetery, which had an atmosphere about it of having been forgotten and abandoned. For the first time she noticed there were no people about, no visitors apart from herself. This made it seem as if the place were not really there at all but belonged in another world, empty of anything, men and women, animals, even ghosts. And somehow this was more frightening than the ghosts themselves, for she might be trapped in it, caught up in a timeless deserted waste for ever. She looked at the ground, at blades of grass, at the grey, still air, and saw not even a bird, not even an insect. Then she started to run, away from the colonnades, the immovable, eternal grey stone pillars, down, down, down to the gate and the street and houses and people . . .

Chapter 33

In the course of her work Natalie had often thought of how she would handle the press should a journalist contact her. The advice she gave herself was much the same as that offered by a lawyer to his or her client in confrontations with the police. Say nothing, or, if you must speak, use monosyllables. Like most reporters and most policemen, she seldom encountered members of the public who took this advice. Nell Johnson-Fleet was the exception.

Opening the door of her Kentish Town flat, she looked straight into Natalie's face but said nothing. Natalie, who was looking straight into hers, said who she was and might she have a word.

'No,' said Nell Johnson-Fleet

Like all Jeff's women – Zillah had been the odd one out – she was a tallish, thin blonde and dressed as he liked them to be, in trousers and a sweater. Natalie well remembered his preferences. 'I was one of his girlfriends too. Victims, if you like. It might be a help to talk about it, don't you think?'

'No.'

'Perhaps you prefer to put it all behind you? Try to do the impossible and forget it ever happened.'

Gently, Nell Johnson-Fleet closed the door. Natalie wasn't one to give up as easily as that. She rang the bell again and, getting no answer, went round the corner of the street where she sat down on a wall and dialled the woman's number on her mobile. The call was answered with a curt, 'Yes?'

This, at least, was different. 'It's Natalie Reckman, Nell. I hope you're going to let me in for just five minutes.'

'No,' and the phone went down.

You had to admire it, Natalie thought, returning to her car just as the traffic warden was approaching. It was a wonderful technique. A good thing most of the public weren't like that. On the other hand people went through moods, they had good days and bad days, and this might be a bad one. Nell Johnson-Fleet might have had a row with her boyfriend or seen him with another woman; the way she happened to be this evening was no guide to her normal behaviour. She'd try again tomorrow, give her a chance to regret passing up her opportunity. Now for Kensal Green.

The police had left them alone for nearly two weeks. They had threatened to come back but they never had. Michelle had begun eating again, not much and sensible food, but she no longer felt as if every mouthful would choke her. Her weight had gone down to what it had been ten years ago. And while she was quite content with a salad and single slice of bread for lunch, Matthew was regularly eating a two-egg omelette. He'd begun to drive the car again, uncertainly at first, like someone who has just passed his test, but with increasing confidence. When they hadn't seen or heard from the police for long enough to feel safe, they did something they hadn't done since they were first married. They went away together for the weekend.

For the first time since she'd known her, Michelle fancied she saw envy of her in Fiona's eyes. This didn't please her, it was the last thing she wanted to

414

excite in anyone, but she noted it because it was so unusual.

Fiona envied her for having a husband who loved her and wanted to be alone with her in an hotel in the countryside. 'I hope you'll have a lovely time,' she said. 'You deserve it.'

They did. But the lovely time was very different from what Fiona (and anyone else who saw them and thought about it) envisaged, imagining gentle walks, quiet drinks in little pubs, a visit to a beauty spot and perhaps some candlelit dining. It was much more like a honeymoon. In Matthew's arms, having a late lie-in, Michelle went back in time to their early days and felt no older than she had seventeen years before in the first bliss of their passion.

The Kentish Town block of flats had been grim in Natalie's estimation, but was nothing on Syringa Road, Kensal Green. That, she decided, parking her car without difficulty in this non-restricted zone, must be the seat on which Eileen Dring had been killed. Or a replacement seat, surely. It looked new. The flowerbed behind it had been dug up and now showed a healthy growth of young weeds. Something of a coincidence, she thought, that one of the murder victims had died within a stone's throw of where the other victim's girlfriend – or one of them – lived.

Two rows of squat Victorian houses, with mostly neglected and very small front gardens, some of them packed full of bicycles, pushchairs, the occasional motorbike, rolls of wire netting and pieces of broken furniture. Disproportionately large bay windows jutted out downstairs, dusty plaques under their eaves were engraved with names such as Theobald Villa and Salisbury Terrace. One house only had been smartened up and to an extent which offended Natalie's taste. This was number 37, whose front had been refaced with blocks of (probably fake) grey granite, whose paintwork was white and front door a deep rose pink. Multicoloured dahlias and dark-blue Michaelmas daisies filled the garden. Next door, Natalie's goal, was neat but dowdy, the garden paved over, the paintwork worn though clean. Jeff must have been on his uppers to come looking for succour down here, she thought. And then she recalled the leaps-and-bounds increases in London house prices, that this place was not so very far from fashionable Notting Hill and a tube stop on the Bakerloo Line was just a little way down the Harrow Road. If he could have got his hands on a house here . . .

She rang the bell. A woman came to the door and stared at her. It wasn't a stare like Nell Johnson-Fleet's and she wasn't at all like Nell Johnson-Fleet, not Jeff's type except insofar as she was fair and thin. A little wispy woman, very white-skinned with pale, no-colour eyes, thin lips, hair like a baby's. But what startled Natalie, what almost *frightened* her, was that she looked mad. Natalie would never have used this politically incorrect word except to herself, in her own thoughts. No other really described Araminta Knox's wide stare, her large pupils, the tiny smile that came and went.

'Ms Knox?'

A nod and the smile flickering.

'I'm called Natalie Reckman and I'm a freelance journalist. I wonder if I might talk to you about Jeff Leach.'

'Who?'

She plainly didn't know what Natalie meant. There had been not the faintest flicker of alarm or memory or pain or anger in those glassy eyes. And there would have been, for this was the sort of woman unable to conceal what she felt, unaware, showing every nuance of emotion in her expression. She'd either come to the wrong place, got the wrong woman, or Jeff had used one of his not very subtle aliases. 'Jerry perhaps? Jed? Jake?'

'I don't know what you're talking about.'

'You didn't have a boyfriend who was murdered in a cinema?' Natalie never minded what she said to anyone. She couldn't, not in her job. 'Jeff Leach or Leigh?'

'My fiancé died in the Paddington train crash,' said Minty and shut the door much more sharply than Nell Johnson-Fleet had.

It was possible she was on the wrong track. Natalie remembered that she'd assumed this was the right woman only because Jeff had said she lived near Kensal Green Cemetery and had called her Polo. Polo was a mint and the one person in the whole area with the right kind of name was Araminta Knox. But he might have called her Polo for any number of other reasons. Because she liked those mints he ate, for instance, or even *played* polo. Just the same, she rang the bell of the gaudy house with the pink front door.

The occupant was a big, handsome woman in a tight black skirt and scarlet shirt, technically black but in fact almond-coloured with a Roman nose and full lips. Natalie said who she was and what she wanted.

'Would you mind telling me your name?'

'Sonovia Wilson. You can call me Mrs Wilson.'

'Have you ever heard of a Jeffrey or Jeff or Jerry Leach or Leigh?'

'No. Who is he?'

'Well, I thought he'd been your neighbour's boy-friend.'

'She's only had one and he was called Jock Lewis.

417

Or so he said. He *said*, or someone did, that he died in that train crash, but he never did and I know that for a fact. What d'you want him for?'

'I don't want him, Mrs Wilson. It wouldn't be much use if I did, seeing he's most likely the Jeffrey Leach who was murdered in the Marble Arch Odeon. J. L., you see, it was always J-something and L-something with him. May I come in?'

'You'd better talk to my husband. He's in the force.'

In a quandary, Laf didn't know what to do next. What to do at all, come to that. He and Sonovia watched Natalie Reckman cross the road and get into her car.

'It's only what she *thinks*,' Laf said. 'We've known since the beginning Jock Lewis wasn't killed in that train crash. The only evidence she's got for thinking Minty's friend was this Jeffrey Leach is that they've got the same initials.'

'Well, not really, Laf. She seems to know Leach had a girlfriend who lived round here that he called Polo.'

'Jock Lewis never called Minty Polo, so far as I know.'

'We could ask her,' said Sonovia. 'I mean, I could. I could say something casual, like "Didn't you tell me Jock was fond of Polo mints?" or get the conversation on to pet names and ask if he had one for her. And then, if she came out with it, I'd tell her. I mean, she ought to know, Laf, you've got to admit it.'

Laf turned away from the window, sat down in an armchair and motioned Sonovia to another, with the masterful gesture and wearing the steady frown he used only on the very rare occasions when he thought his wife had worn the trousers long enough. 'No, I've not got to admit it, Sonovia.' He called her by her full name only in his severer moments. 'You're not to say a word to Minty. Is that understood? This is one of those times when we've got to heed Daniel. You remember what he said? It was the last time you asked if she should be told about Jock. "I wouldn't," he said. "I wouldn't." You told me yourself what he said. Now when our son became a doctor of medicine I made up my mind I'd take his word on medical matters like I take Holy Writ. And you've got to do the same, right?'

Meekly, Sonovia said, 'Right, Laf.'

Dressing to go out on her fifth date with Ronnie Grasmere, Zillah thought it was the babysitter when the doorbell rang. She zipped up her new black dress – tight but not too tight, low-cut, flattering – slipped her feet into her Jimmy Choo shoes and ran downstairs. Two men were on the doorstep. Even if one of them hadn't been in uniform she'd have known they were police officers – she could detect them from a distance now. Immediately, with a lurch in her lycra-controlled stomach, she concluded they were here to arrest her for bigamy.

'Mrs Melcombe-Smith?'

One thing that phoney marriage had done for her: everyone assumed it had been genuine. 'What is it?'

'South Wessex Police. May we come in?'

They'd found Jerry's car. The boneshaker. The twenty-year-old Ford Anglia. That was all it was about, his old banger. In Harold Hill.

'Where?' said Zillah.

'It's a place in Essex near Romford. The car was parked by the side of a road in a residential area where there are no parking restrictions. A resident called us to complain about it. He said it was an eyesore.'

Zillah laughed. 'What am I supposed to do about it?'

'Well, Mrs Melcombe-Smith, we thought you might know how it came to be put there.'

'I don't know but if you want my opinion, Jerry – I mean, Jeffrey – dumped it there because at last he'd found a woman with a nice car who'd let him have unlimited use of it. For the first time in his life probably.'

They exchanged glances. 'He didn't have any particular associations with Harold Hill?'

Eugenie had come into the room. 'Who's Harold Hill, Mummy?'

'It's a place, not a person.' Zillah said to the policeman who'd asked, 'He never mentioned it to me. I should think he just used it as a rubbish dump. He was like that.'

'Who was like that?' Eugenie asked after they'd gone and the babysitter had come. 'Who used a place as a rubbish dump?'

'Just a man,' said Zillah.

Neither child had once referred to their father after Eugenie first asked and got no reply. Accomplished at putting off unpleasant things until tomorrow or next week, Zillah sometimes wondered if she would ever need to tell them any more. Or did Eugenie already know from the newspapers, from gossip, from words overheard? If she did, had she told Jordan? Zillah certainly wasn't going to say anything in front of the babysitter, a woman who hadn't yet got above herself as Mrs Peacock had. This time, when the doorbell rang, it was Ronnie Grasmere.

'I don't like him very much,' said Eugenie as Zillah got up to let him in. 'You're not going to marry him as well, are you?'

Minty didn't think much about the woman who'd

called once she was gone. Maybe she'd been from the police and knew Minty went to the cinema a lot. She hadn't noticed that the woman had gone next door and she went to call on Laf and Sonovia herself to ask about the shower man. Although they'd been out in the garden, having a glass of wine and a late snack, they'd heard the bell. Laf plied her with Chilean Chardonnay and Duchy Original ginger biscuits, and seated her in one of their white patio chairs – the fourth one was occupied by Mr Kroot's old cat – but she thought they'd given her funny looks. She asked Sonovia about the shower man and Sonovia said he'd promised her to come at the beginning of next week.

'When it's builders,' said Laf, 'the beginning of the week is Thursday morning and the end of the week is next Monday.'

Sonovia laughed but Minty didn't like it much. Jock had been a builder and Laf ought to have remembered. Still, she told them about her search for his grave. They might have some advice.

'What makes you think he's in Brompton?' Sonovia asked in the kind of smiley way she talked to her four-year-old granddaughter.

'I had a feeling. Not voices telling me, it wasn't that. I just *knew*.'

'But you didn't know, my deah. You just thought. I don't trust these feelings. It's the same with premonitions. Nine times out of ten what you've felt isn't true at all.' Laf gave Sonovia a warning cough but she went on just the same. 'You have to find out these things for sure. With certificates and – and things.'

Minty looked helplessly at Laf. 'Will you do it for me?'

He sighed but he said in a hearty voice, 'Of course I will, you leave it to me.'

421

'What does she mean, "not voices telling me"?' Sonovia said when Laf had seen Minty out. 'She really is going crazy, she's worse than ever.'

Unhappily, Laf shook his head, then nodded. 'It'll be easy finding out where Jeffrey Leach is buried, it's done in five minutes, but do I want to, Sonn? I mean, what am I going to tell her? "Oh, yes, he's up in Highgate or whatever but he wasn't really Jock, he was the one murdered in the cinema and his name was Leach"? As I've said, that I won't do.'

'You'll just have to pass it off.'

'That's what you always say but it's not so easy. She'll ask me again, won't she?' And then, he thought, but didn't say aloud, *am I going to say anything to the DI*? I mean, the guy was stabbed, murdered, and she'd been his girlfriend, she'd been or thought she'd been, engaged to him. But she's my neighbour, she's my friend, I can't do that to her. She's not right in the head but as for murder, well, she'd no more do murder than I would. He shivered.

'Not cold, are you?'

'I'm getting that way. And the mosquitoes are coming out.'

Sonovia gathered the sleeping cat up in her arms. 'Dear God, I've forgotten to tell you. Mr Kroot's dead. He passed over this morning. It went straight out of my head. Picking up the cat reminded me.'

'Poor old boy,' Charitable Laf looked doleful. 'I dare say he's better off where he is. Keep Blackie, shall we?'

'I wouldn't leave him to the tender mercies of Gertrude Pierce.'

When Minty had let herself into it, her own house had a ghostly feel. Perhaps any empty house is like that at dusk, until the lights are on, until the curtains are closed or laughter breaks through. No laughter but such silence, such stillness, such a sense of waiting for things to happen. The house is holding its breath, bracing itself for what will come in.

Instead of switching the hall light on, any light on, Minty walked slowly about, challenging the house to show its ghosts. She was a little afraid to turn round but she did, walking back the way she had come, going round and round. At the foot of the stairs she looked up them, as up a well by night, for there was no light at the top. Out of the deep shade Jock came down. He was just the same ghost as he'd been when she first saw him. It was as if she'd never got rid of him. It only worked for a little while. For three or four months, she thought, as she met his pale, stony eyes.

She closed her own eyes and slowly turned round so that her back was towards him. There was absolute silence. If he touched her, his hand on her neck or his breath cold against her cheek, she thought she would die. Nothing happened and she turned round again, forcing her eyes open as if strength were needed to push the eyelids up. No one was there, he had gone. From outside came the sound of a car moving along the street, its windows open and rock music thudding out. She thought, *he comes back because I can't find his grave, because I can't put flowers on it like I do on Auntie's.*

'Now listen, Minty,' Laf said when he'd brought round the papers. 'I've done that bit of detective work you wanted. Your Jock wasn't buried. He was cremated and his ashes scattered.' Up to a point, this was true. Laf always tried very hard not to tell lies, only straying from the straight and narrow path when the truth was too cruel. For instance, Jeffrey Leach had indeed been cremated but his ashes had been collected from the undertakers by Fiona Harrington who had told a police officer acquaintance of

Laf's what she intended to do with them. 'Somewhere in West Hampstead,' he said, and was disappointed to see Minty's face fall.

'Where could I put my flowers?'

Laf had a picture of a cellophane-wrapped bunch of chrysanthemums lying isolated and forlorn on the pavement in West End Lane. It would be as if someone had died there. Though he wasn't usually so cynical on the subject of human nature, he wondered how long it would be before a dozen other similarly wrapped bouquets joined it, the 'mourners' having no idea to whom they were paying homage.

'Well, Fortune Green was what she said.'

A sort of green triangle with trees, he thought vaguely. He expected more requests or even demands from Minty but when one came it was very different from what he anticipated.

'Will you get Sonovia to phone the builders again?'

'Give them time, Minty,' he said, rather taken aback.

She seemed to be listening for something as she stared into a corner. Then she shook herself like someone coming out of a daze. 'You said the beginning of the week is Thursday and the end of the week next Monday but Monday's gone and they haven't come. I'm never going to get my shower at this rate.'

Chapter 34

One of the last sightings of Jims was in Le Tobsil restaurant in Marrakesh. A Liberal Democrat MP, visiting that city with his wife as part of a Moroccan tour, saw him through the window. He couldn't have afforded to eat there himself. The MP wouldn't have been surprised to have found him with a young and handsome male companion, but Jims was alone. He mentioned this interesting glimpse to a friend in an e-mail and the friend told a newspaper. That was the beginning of the ongoing and endlessly fascinating 'Disappearance of Gay MP' story.

In late August a journalist claimed to have encountered him in Seoul, where Jims granted him an interview. But everyone who knew Jims was highly sceptical about this as none of them could imagine him setting foot in Korea, while the text itself with its admissions of shame, regret and contrition sounded very unlike him. Neither his agent nor, naturally, his bank was prepared to divulge anything of his whereabouts, though presumably they had some idea. Attempts were made to get the truth out of Zillah, though it took a while to find her as by this time she had let Willow Cottage on a year's lease to an American novelist and moved into Long Fredington Manor with Sir Ronald Grasmere.

'I've always wanted to come back here,' said Eugenie, 'and now we're moving out again.'

But no one took any notice, as usual.

Zillah had no idea where Jims was and cared less. From now onwards all her efforts were to make Ronnie happy and convince him he was mistaken when he said that, following his recent divorce, he was done with marriage for ever.

From time to time Violent Crimes or Miss Demeanour appeared on television – the only slot they got was two minutes at the end of *Newsroom Southeast* – to tell an apathetic public that they would never give up the hunt for the Cinema Slayer and killer of Eileen Dring. An arrest would be made in the not-too-far-distant future. They had many leads on which their team was working day and night. Fiona and Matthew and Michelle sometimes watched these programmes but without much anxiety or sense of involvement. Their ordeals were over. The police had shown no interest in any of them for weeks now. Their neighbours once more passed the time of day with them, no one crossed the street when they approached and Fiona had had the graffiti on her gateposts removed and painted over.

Gradually, she was recovering. She no longer expected it to be Jeff when the doorbell rang or to find him waiting for her when she came home. The time was past when she woke from her sedative-induced sleep to wonder why he wasn't lying there beside her. These days she could agree with friends she had thought unkind that after all, she'd only known him for eight months. It wasn't really long enough to be sure of one's feelings. Knowing what she now knew of him, she'd never have been able to trust him, he'd deceived her so often and told so many lies. Sometimes she asked Michelle if she was forgiven for categorising her and Matthew as among Jeff's enemies, and although Michelle always said yes, of course, and to forget all about it, Fiona went on asking her as if she doubted the sincerity of her replies.

Michelle had lately been rather quiet and thoughtful so that Matthew often asked her if anything was wrong. She smiled and said, 'Far from it. Everything is fine,' and with that he had to be satisfied. He wanted to repeat their weekend away, perhaps abroad this time, and Michelle said she'd love to, but could they postpone it for a few weeks? He'd met quite a lot of new people through his television programme and they'd done an unheard-of thing and had a dinner party for eight, a number which included Fiona and a personable man in his thirties Michelle thought might do as Jeff's replacement. Matthew said not to matchmake, it never worked, and Michelle promised she'd do no more.

One evening, when they and their next-door neighbour had met for drinks, Michelle made something very close to a little speech of thanks to Fiona: 'It was your food ideas which really started Matthew eating properly. It came out of your inventive mind. And it was poor Jeff' – she could call him that now - 'who taught me to lose weight. He didn't know that's what he was doing but he was. Those taunts of his didn't make me do what those stupid police seemed to think I'd done, they changed me from a great, gross, fat woman into a – well, a reasonable size sixteen.'

'You were always beautiful to me,' said Matthew.

She smiled at him and squeezed his hand. 'It did make me hate him for a bit. I can admit it now I don't think anyone will mind.' But although she saw as much of Fiona as she had ever done, though she kissed her affectionately and constantly reassured her, she remembered what she had said to Matthew at the time of the betrayal: 'I can never feel the same about her again, never.' It was still true, though she hid it and would always hide it, even from him.

She was healthier than she'd been for more than ten years or she *looked* healthier, so Matthew was concerned when she said at eight in the morning that she was off to their GP's morning surgery. She'd made an appointment and told him she wouldn't be long.

He felt a sudden surge of terror. 'What's the matter with you, darling?'

'I won't know till I've seen the doctor, will I?'

It was then that he thought he saw bewilderment in her face and some apprehension of misfortune. She decided against telling him her symptoms, said only that she wouldn't be long and he mustn't worry.

The story Natalie concocted out of her hopeless encounter with Nell Johnson-Fleet and her second abortive attempt on her, the troubling meeting with Linda Davies, her sad interview with Fiona Harrington and her incomprehensible confrontation with Araminta Knox were, she had to admit, something of a failure. None of the newspaper editors to whom she offered it was interested. Other stories had replaced the Cinema Slayer and the Old Bag Lady in the public consciousness. It might be another matter if all that talk of clues and leads on the television last night led to an arrest, but otherwise . . .

Natalie had done her best with it. She had even had one more go at the voters' list, widening her search, just in case another woman with something that might be construed as 'mint' in her name turned up. She even went back to Laf and Sonovia, and tried to dig deep into their memories but all they said was that they couldn't describe a man they'd never seen. After that she followed the modern procedure that used to be known as 'spiking' the story and kept it on a floppy disc for what she thought of as the unlikely event of the murderer being found.

The Wilsons had been dismayed by this further visit. Laf saw it as an attempt to implicate Minty in something she couldn't possibly know anything about. It never crossed his mind that she might be the killer, not gentle, quiet Minty with her strong moral sense and horror of violence. How many times, for instance, had he and Sonovia heard her say she was in favour of a return to capital punishment? But it was strange about Jock Lewis. No evidence that he could find had linked him with Jeffrey Leach until the police found the 'boneshaker' in Harold Hill. Nothing had been in the newspapers about that, it was hardly a newsworthy item, but Laf, of course, knew it. Without saying a word to Sonovia or his children, without telling any of his fellow officers why, he managed to get a look at the car himself. The trouble was he simply couldn't remember. Several times he'd seen the 'boneshaker' outside Minty's house but he'd never taken much notice of it beyond remarking to Sonovia that since the MOT test came in you saw far fewer old bangers about on the roads. He couldn't even remember whether it was dark blue or dark green or black. The Harold Hill car was dark blue but so dirty, so encrusted with dead leaves, smoke deposit and squashed insects, that it would have been hard to say if it was *the* car or not, even if he'd remembered more about it.

'I wish I'd seen him from the window,' Sonovia moaned. 'I can't understand why I didn't persist. It's not like me.'

It was coincidence that Jeffrey Leach and Jock Lewis both had twenty-year-old cars, shared a pair of initials, had both once lived in Queen's Park, but no more than coincidence. Jock had disappeared out of Minty's life a year ago while Jeffrey Leach wasn't killed till April. He wasn't going to mention it to the DI, who'd only think he was getting above himself. Besides, Minty was a *friend*.

But she was getting more and more peculiar. It was only the other day Sonovia had said to him that if you didn't know she was on her own you'd think she was surrounded by crowds of people all the time. Invisible people, that is. You could never hear much through the walls, these old houses were well-built, whatever they said about the neighbourhood, but she'd heard Minty shouting to go away and leave her alone and only the other day she'd been sitting in the garden when Minty had come out to hang up washing and was talking nineteen to the dozen to some old woman and a man she called Wilfred, and Winnie Knox who'd been dead three years. It made Sonovia's blood run cold to hear her.

The police couldn't make up their minds whether Leach had dumped the car himself when Fiona told him to use hers or whether his killer had done so. Only his fingerprints were on the inside of it, his and those of an unknown woman.

Six weeks had passed since Sonovia first asked the builder for an estimate for Minty's shower. When he didn't come she complained and he said he'd been ill with 'summer flu'. Sonovia wondered if it was a good idea for him to come at all, if any stranger should be allowed at number 39 when Minty was so odd, talking to people who weren't there, always looking over her shoulder and shivering.

'She's harmless,' Laf said, on his way next door with the Sunday paper.

'I know that, my deah. It's not him I'm thinking about, it's her. I mean, people getting the wrong impression. It's enough to get the whole street a bad name.'

'You get that shower done for her. It'll be a tonic. Lift her out of her depression.'

Laf went next door. Minty still had her latex gloves on, she'd been scrubbing the kitchen floor. On an impulse, Laf asked her if she'd come to the cinema with him and Sonovia next day. In her characteristic way she said she didn't mind and could she make him a cup of tea? Not once while he was in there did she seem to hear voices or talk to invisible people or look over her shoulder.

They'd gone. It was because she'd done it. She'd been up to Fortune Green that morning with a bunch of flowers, a nice clean bowl that Auntie'd once used for her Christmas puddings and water in a fruit juice bottle with a plastic screw top. The bottle had been washed out when she'd drunk the juice and put in Dettol with the hot water to make sure it was really clean. It was easy getting to West Hampstead on the tube from Kensal Rise. She'd bought the flowers from outside the cemetery in Fortune Green Road.

Why hadn't his brother put Jock's ashes in there? Come to that, why West Hampstead at all? So far as she knew, Jock had never lived there, never even been there. The answer must be that the brother did. The flowers she'd bought were Michaelmas daisies and golden rod, there wasn't so much of a selection at this time of the year. It wouldn't be long before the leaves began to fall. She could feel a nip in the air. On the green she stood under a tree and looked about her, wondering where the ashes had fallen. She squatted down and examined the ground, not actually touching it because that would have dirtied her hands, but just peering about her, searching. A woman passing with a dog stopped and asked her if she'd lost something. Minty shook her head fiercely, though it was true, she had lost something, or *someone*, and she was looking for what was left of him.

Her scrutiny eventually rewarded her with the sight of something pale sprinkled over a patch of bare earth where for some reason the grass didn't grow. A cigarette had been stubbed out close by. This she kicked out of the way with the toe of her shoe. She put the bowl precisely where the greyish powder lay most thickly, poured in the water and arranged the flowers. They looked very nice. She could almost fancy she heard his voice say, 'Thanks, Polo. You're a good girl.' It was only her imagination, the result of her thinking what he might say, not his actual voice speaking. She put the bottle along with the wrapping from the flowers into a litter bin and walked back down the hill to West Hampstead station.

Matthew was opening his letters. His post increased almost daily. Fifteen had come that morning, some sent on by BBC Television, others from the agent he'd been obliged to engage. A lot of them were straightforward fan letters, some included questions about health and eating habits their writers expected him to answer, some – a very few – were abusive, asking him who he thought cared about a man too stupid to eat wholesome food when half the world was starving or wanting to know where he found 'the obscene freaks' who appeared on his programme. There was an invitation from the Eating Disorders Association asking him to become one of their patrons. He answered all his letters except the abusive ones and these he threw away quickly lest their contents prey on his mind.

Today there were no nasty letters. He almost wished there had been, for a few insults might have temporarily taken his mind off Michelle's health or its reverse. Twice he typed in her name instead of that of the recipient and once, instead of 'cancel' – this to a man wanting to know if he should keep going his subscription to a slimmer's magazine – he wrote 'cancer'. Before pressing the back space, he looked at the word and shuddered. Using the euphemism he despised when others uttered it, he asked himself what he'd do 'if anything happened' to her. The bald term he couldn't use, not even in his thoughts. And as he excised the letter which made all the difference, the 'r' that changed an innocuous word into one of foreboding and dread, he spoke her name in a whisper and then more loudly. 'Michelle,' he said. 'Michelle.'

She answered him. She'd just that moment let herself in by the front door. 'I'm here, darling.'

Her face was flushed and she looked excited. 'I've something to tell you. It's good news – can't you tell? Well, I think you'll say it's good. I did the test at home, I did it a month ago but I still didn't believe. I thought my hormones were all confused, I thought maybe it didn't work on someone of my age, but the doctor says yes and I'm fine. I should be fine, there's no reason why not . . .'

He'd gone as white as in the worst days of his starvation. 'What are you saying?'

She stood in front of him and he got to his feet. He put out his arms and she moved slowly into them. 'Matthew, he or she will be born in March. You are pleased, aren't you? You *are* glad?'

He held her and kissed her. 'When I can truly believe it, this will be the happiest day of my life.'

Chapter 35

The crowd of people were invisible but they were there in force. They thronged through her head, their voices audible as soon as she was alone and sometimes when she wasn't. Jock wasn't there. Minty hadn't heard him since she put those flowers on his ashes. The last time was when he came walking down the stairs, but she heard his voice, clearer and louder than the others. These were people she knew and people she had never met or even heard of. Not Auntie, never her, and not Mrs Lewis any more, but Bert who'd married Auntie and Jock's brother's wife, Auntie's sisters Edna and Kathleen and their husbands, and more whose names she didn't know. Yet.

She hadn't known Jock's sister-in-law's name until Bert told Kathleen. 'This is Jock's sister-in-law, Mary, Kathleen,' he'd said and Auntie's sister said she was pleased to meet her.

Then it was Edna's turn to meet this Mary. At least Auntie's voice wasn't among theirs and Minty knew this was because of the praying and the flowers on her grave. Jock's wasn't, for the same reason. She couldn't do those things for the others, she couldn't spend her life hunting for graves of dead people, which might be anywhere in the country, anywhere in the world. Their invisibility was only temporary. After a while they began to take shape and form, Bert first, thin and insubstantial, not much more than a darkness that shouldn't have been there. How did she know it was Bert? She'd never seen him, never heard his voice, she wasn't even born when he came into Auntie's life and went out of it, but she knew.

Kathleen and Edna were weak and transparent, and sometimes she saw them as shadows only. Mary too, another inhabitant of her life she'd never seen and one she'd never even heard mentioned. The daughter-in-law Mrs Lewis loved and welcomed when she came to join her. Sunlight had penetrated the gap between the half-closed curtains and on to its brightness their three shadows fell, but without bodies to cast them.

The evening she went to the cinema with Laf and Sonovia – their first visit for a long time – all the ghost voices stayed at home or went away to wherever they lived when they weren't bothering her and all the ghost shapes were swallowed up by the night and the bright lights. It might be because she was with real living people that they left her alone. On the other hand she'd seen Kathleen several times while she was with the Wilsons and there was the time when Jock had actually followed her into Sonovia's bedroom when she'd tried on the blue dress. It was hard to know. Most of the time she was confused and bewildered.

She had other worries to plague her. Josephine had started talking about giving up the shop and being a full-time housewife and mother, though there was no sign as yet of motherhood. Ken had been offered a partnership in the Lotus Dragon and had accepted it. There was no real need for her to work. Minty wasn't to trouble her head about it. Whoever took over would be bound to keep her on. 'No one can iron shirts the way you do, Minty,' said Josephine. 'They'd be mad to let you go.'

That word 'mad' always made Minty nervous. Someone had said it to her on the bus when she'd told the voice that was hissing and whispering at her to go away. 'I don't know,' she said, trying to ignore Mary Lewis who had her ghost lips to her ear and was saying she'd have to have computer skills and business qualifications for them to keep her on. Being skilled at ironing wasn't enough these days. 'I don't know. Suppose they give up the shirt service? Suppose they just do dry-cleaning.'

'They'd have to be mad.' Josephine was very keen on that word. 'Don't worry. I may decide to stick it out a few more years. Till I fall for a baby, anyway.'

Minty ran her hand down the length of the new knife she still wore strapped to her right leg. She'd have felt half-dressed without it now, though she sometimes wondered what she was going to use it for. Mary would have been a good candidate, only Minty had only seen her shadow, a thin woman with long hair and long legs. But she no more appeared in the shape of a real human being than the aunts did or the uncles. They just chattered away among themselves, the best of friends, when they weren't talking to her. Except for Mary who was always rowing with Kathleen.

She didn't know which was better, seeing them *and* hearing them or just hearing them. She tried to find things to do that they'd hate, walking the streets, getting in a jam-packed tube train, going down to Oxford Street where there was always such a dense crowd strolling aimlessly along the pavements that you could lose yourself among the people. For a while their voices would go away but they always came back to persecute her. The evening she went out with Sonovia and Laf the cinema was full of people; it was a good job Laf had booked, there wasn't an empty seat that she could see. The ghost voices who talked to her when she went alone to the pictures in the afternoon had disappeared. Every time this happened she couldn't cure herself of hoping they were gone for ever. She sat listening for them, savouring the quiet, oblivious to what was coming out of the screen, until Sonovia asked her in a whispered hiss if she was in a trance.

When Josephine was in the shop and when Ken dropped in, when one customer after another came in, her head was mostly silent. That was why she'd stopped going home at lunchtime. She knew they'd be there and it would be like walking in among a mass of chattering people, all expectant, all waiting for something, like the theatre audience before the curtain went up on *An Inspector Calls*. She didn't want to be their play, their show, but over that she had no control.

Food was the reason she went home that Thursday lunchtime. She'd forgotten her sandwiches, though she'd made them, chicken and lettuce and tomato on white bread, wrapped them in greaseproof paper and polythene, and put them in the fridge. *Left* them in the fridge. It was something she'd never have done normally but that morning she'd rushed out of the house to escape Mary's voice and Uncle Wilfred's. She walked, though she'd gone to Immacue on the 18 bus. It was a nice, sunny day, autumnal though and with a nip in the air. A year ago she'd have been looking forward to going out with Jock in the evening, not dreaming that the train he was coming on from Gloucester would crash and kill him. He'd be saying his funny things to her. I went into the garden to fetch a cabbage leaf to make an apple pie and there I met a great she-bear who said, What, no soap? And promptly married the barber. There, she'd remembered it word for word.

It was a long walk and being used to it made it no shorter. Past the Flora pub and the Church of the Redeemer of God, past the eastern entrance to the cemetery, Kensal Green tube station, the garage, the boarded-up shops, the seat and flowerbed where she'd got rid of Mrs Lewis. She turned off the Harrow Road before the western gate of the cemetery was reached and into Syringa Road. Her key went into the lock and she turned it, knowing what she'd find inside, voices and the sounds as of a crowd jostling each other.

The hall was still and, for a moment, she thought the whole place was silent. She closed her eyes, enjoying the peace. Then the voices began as whispers, Mary and Edna arguing, as they always did, Kathleen muttering about Jock's ashes being in Brompton Cemetery. Just because Laf told her that story about Fortune Green didn't mean they weren't in Brompton. They were up in the far north-east corner and she could see the gravestone, Kathleen said, she could see his name on it and the dates of his birth and death. Edna broke in and said it was morbid living by a cemetery, she knew the effect it had had on her. If she had her time over again she'd move somewhere else.

Minty took a few steps towards the kitchen. Then she stopped, listening. A terrible thing had happened, the thing she knew couldn't happen. From upstairs, she heard Jock singing.

'Just walk on by
Wait on the corner . . .'

His voice had lightened and risen a little. Perhaps that was what happened when ghosts sang. Their voices thinned and blurred as their bodies did. This time, she was sure, she'd see him. Maybe he'd come walking down the stairs, the way he had before. It hadn't worked, the giving him flowers, he hadn't liked them or it was the wrong place. She'd chosen the wrong place, armfuls of flowers should have been scattered everywhere on the grass, on the earth, on the paths, it wasn't like a grave. She began touching wood, the banisters, the doors, the door frames, white wood and pink wood and brown wood. Her hands were shaking and she sobbed.

The singing stopped. He called out, 'Are you there?'

His voice had changed. It was lighter and quicker, not chocolate mousse any more, but it was his voice. And at last he was talking to her. While he was alive she thought she'd never want him to stop talking, she couldn't get enough of his voice, but now she could. Not for the world, not for rest from all the other voices, could she have brought herself to answer him. How could you love someone so much and then hate him if it was the same person? She'd die if she answered him or the house would fall down or the world end. Perhaps this was the beginning of his moving back with her, speaking to her, taking shape when he chose or being a shadow on the wall when the sun shone.

She held on to brown woodwork with both hands. The flowers hadn't worked, only one thing really worked, at least for a time. Slowly she took her hands away, they were icy cold against the bare skin of her waist. She lifted up her T-shirt, undid the waistband of her trousers and withdrew the knife from its wrappings, holding it dagger-wise. Her whole body was trembling now.

Perhaps because she hadn't answered him, he called again. The same words: 'Are you there?'

She turned round and stepped back to stand at the foot of the stairs, holding the knife behind her. This time she'd do the job properly, even if she had to do it every few months . . . When he appeared at the top, the shock, though she expected it, was almost too much for her. Her vision blurred and she stared upwards into a dark fog through which he came walking down the stairs. And then, with a shaking hand, she stabbed haphazardly at his body, again and again, wild thrusts and glancing blows. At his first scream the doorbell rang, a long, imperious, shattering ring.

Minty dropped the knife and gave a whimpering cry. Very quickly it came to her what she'd done. The man was real. He wore jeans and a black leather jacket but he wasn't Jock. Real blood was coming from his body, seeping bright scarlet through his blue shirt. He lay half on the floor, half on the two lowest stairs, groaning and holding with a cut hand a wound just below his waist and exposing another on his upper arm. She'd tried to kill a real man. No voice had told her to do it, she'd told herself.

The bell rang and rang, and someone was kicking at the door panels. If Minty waited a moment before opening the door it was because she couldn't move, she couldn't walk. But she did walk, she staggered and fell against it, she fumbled at the doorknob and at last it came open.

'What's happening here? What's going on?'

And then Sonovia saw the wounded man and the knife which had fallen across his thighs. She let out a series of short sharp screams, her hands up as if warding off blows. Laf came running out from next door. Minty was too afraid to think of anything but escape. Her strength came back, running through her like some fiery drink, she jumped over the little low fence between her garden and the Wilsons', and ran down the road just as Laf had turned in through her gate.

He called for help. He phoned 999 and his own DI. It was a piece of luck for the man on the floor that Laf was at home, on a day off, for Sonovia, usually so calm and practical, was in the throes of full-blown, old-fashioned hysterics. What was needed now, more than the police, was an ambulance. It arrived within four minutes and the man who had come to give Minty an estimate for her shower was carried out on a stretcher. This was a routine, not a necessary, measure. Shock, more than his superficial wounds, had laid him low.

But the police knew now, Laf knew, who was responsible for the cinema death and that of Eileen Dring.

'You couldn't really call them murders,' Laf said to Sonovia later that day, when she'd calmed down and they were having a shock-remedy drink. 'Not really. She didn't mean to harm real people. She didn't *know.*'

'I just hope the doctors realise that. Thank the Lord, poor Pete's going to be OK.'

'What made you ring her doorbell, Sonny? Some sixth sense?'

'Not at all, my deah. I couldn't claim to have *that.* I was at the window and I saw her come home, which was most unexpected, and I thought I'll just pop in and tell her Pete's there in case it gives her a shock.'

'What did she come home for?'

'It breaks your heart, it really does. After the ambulance had been and gone I was dying for a drink of cold water and that stuff that comes out of the tap – well, you don't know what it's been through, do you? I looked in her fridge and there were her sandwiches, all nicely wrapped up and waiting for her to fetch them. It brought the tears to my eyes, Laf.' And Sonovia began to cry, sobbing against Laf's shoulder.

'She'll be all right,' he said. 'It'll be best for her this way,' though he was by no means sure of this, any

441

more than he had been when they found Minty three hours before.

It was Sonovia who'd said where she might be found.

'Her auntie's grave is in there.' It couldn't be, but what was the point of showing the poor thing up as a liar now?

Daniel and his wife and child had come over by then, to be with Sonovia and comfort her. So Laf had gone out with the DI and a detective sergeant and two women officers to search for Minty. The afternoon had grown very warm, sultry and amber-coloured, the air heavy and dusted with gold, as it sometimes is in September. They went into the cemetery by the western gate half an hour before it was due to close. The man selling flowers said he'd seen Minty hours ago, she'd come running, out of breath and shivering, but she'd bought more from him than ever before, and she was a regular customer. Chrysanthemums she'd had and Michaelmas daisies, pink and purple asters, and the most expensive things he had, white lilies and pink ones. He'd never have believed she could afford them . . .

It took only about ten minutes to find her. When they did she was fast asleep. She was lying curled up like a child amid bunches and bunches of fast-withering flowers, on the grave of someone called Maisie Julia Chepstow who'd died a hundred years before. No one knew why she'd picked that one. The only man who knew and could have told them was dead, his ashes in an alabaster urn, forgotten at the back of a dark cupboard.